Joy
I hope you enjoy my first
mystery.   *Lee E. Meadows*
      11-15-97

SILENT CONSPIRACY

Lee E. Meadows

Proctor Publications of Ann Arbor • Michigan • USA

Copyright © 1996 by Lee E. Meadows

Library of Congress Catalog Number: 96-72290

Cataloging In Publication Data
(Prepared by Quality Books, Inc.)

Meadows, Lee E.
   The silent conspiracy / Lee Meadows.
   p. cm.
   ISBN: 1-882792-38-6

1. Afro-Americans--Michigan--Detroit--Fiction. 2. Detroit (Mich.)--Fiction. 3. Detective and mystery stories.   I. Title

PS3563.E346S45 1997   **813'.54**
                                                            QBI96-40852

This novel is a product of the imagination of the author. All the characters portrayed are fictitious. None of the events described occurred. Though many of the settings, buildings and businesses exist, liberties have been taken in several instances as to their actual locations and descriptions. The story has no purpose other than to entertain the reader.

Acknowledgments

The realization of a dream is rarely accomplished through idle contemplation or isolation. It requires the commitment, support, belief and assistance of dream makers. And it takes a special kind of person to recognize that the success of their own dream is intricately woven into the success of other dreamers. This project is a reflection of a line of dreamers and doers. And all of them have my heartfelt thanks.

Among them is the staff at Lansing Community College's Criminal Justice Center. They have always been a valuable resource for professional growth and a sounding board for discussing the realities of investigative work. Any technical errors in this book are a result of my notetaking.

Also, Walt Conyers, Paula Cunningham and Dr. Ernest Betts have been the kind of supportive friends that any writer would need. A large part of getting this book finished can be attributed to their constant harassment. It was just their way of saying, "get it done."

I also had the good fortune to be born into a large family and then married into another, so it would take several pages of thank you's in order to cover brothers, sisters, in-laws, aunts, uncles, cousins, nieces, nephews and the various assortment of extended family who've all given support in their own way. Thanks family. You all know who you are.

I'd like to thank the staff of Proctor Publications as well for their ability to move this book from its raw beginnings to its polished end with professionalism and dedication. Through my work with them I have come to observe that commitment, perseverance and an unwavering belief in one's talents are the hallmark values that define Proctor Publications. It's a place where dreamers have an audience.

But above all, none of this would be possible without the unconditional support of my wife, Phyllis. She, more so than anyone, has had to live with my need to tell this story. She's clearly Number One among the dream makers. Thanks honey!

SILENT CONSPIRACY

Chapter 1

Erotica wasn't a common name, but then she was far from a common woman. That would prove to be one of my better insights.

I'd almost made it to the final dregs of self abuse when, like a Dickens apparition, she materialized through the gray hanging smoke that floated about the boisterous crowd at Artie's Bar & Grill. I, along with every other healthy male among the early evening crowd took immediate notice of her as she moved fluidly and with purpose, headed in the direction of my booth. I was sitting there playing a drinker's concerto with a gin and tonic and had just crushed my third toothpick into the chipped marble ashtray when she granted me a most pleasant surprise by sliding gracefully up to my table and stopping next to the leatherback seat across from mine. There were many things about her worth a second look. And by the time she was standing next to my booth, I was working on my fifth or sixth. Her body was a marriage of strength and beauty. Sometime during this delightful visual overload I took note of the word 'Erotica'. It was an exquisite piece of jewelry, formatted in diamonds and shaped like Catholic trained handwriting. She was wearing it on a silver boy-link chain where it came to rest just inches shy of her equally exquisite cleavage. A slow pan up to her copper toned eyes pierced the carnal layer of my soul.

I'm a private eye. I'm supposed to notice those things. She hadn't said a word yet, but trouble often accompanies the unspoken. In a situation where curiosity and lust fought for equal observation time of this tall slim desire, I knew that somewhere beyond the physical world, someone anxiously chiseled out an eleventh commandment.

Up until this moment a good part of the month had been spent looking into things only tabloid journalists, gossip columnists and talk show hosts would find orgasmic. Plenty of activity. Endless hours staking out a motel, pictures of rendezvous, illegally recorded conversations and peeping through keyholes for that one conclusive fact. I don't complain. Most of what I do sends me down the darker, seduced side of the human experience. But, hell – it's all billable. Lately I had the evidence on two philandering husbands, an abusive mother and a promiscuous wife who needed satisfaction from two partners...at once. I didn't see hanging out in the slimiest gutters of individual preferences as the next step on my career ladder, but for an ex-Oakland Raiders defensive back turned PI, it kept me doing what I do best...hiding in the shadows waiting to make a hit.

I had spent the latter hours of that muggy afternoon in my office pulling together the final pieces of my discoveries while drinking the cool water from the ice cubes melting like rivulets of sweat into my silver and black water mug. The uncirculating dead air in my back office was as thick as an Irish brogue. My small bladed fan was a poor substitute for air conditioning, but then I valued simplicity. Wet circles formed under my arms, adding another ring to the already stained surroundings. Outside, traffic began its congestive ritual of hurry home before the natives came out. Bumper to bumper, like preschool children tied together so they won't get lost, they moved slowly through the late summer heat to the sanctity of their manicured lawns and strip malls.

I made the last call of the day and left another message on another answering machine. I crumbled my last set of scribbled notes and double banked it off the wall into the half full trash basket in the corner. I swiveled away from the desk and caught sight of the four framed pictures occupying space on the wall behind me; my BA in Criminal Justice from Prairie State, a small black college in Texas, a picture of me and my brothers taken during the last known time the four of us were sitting in the same spot, a certificate of appreciation from the City of Oakland, California Police Department where I worked for twelve years and a picture of me with the entire roster of the 1980 Oakland Raiders. I'm the smiling defensive back in the left corner of the front row: Lincoln Keller, Number 44.

"It's been a long run back from the Oakland Alameda County Coliseum number 44, but you could've been doing something useful...like dog grooming." That prevailing mood dogged my view of people and things well into the early evening when I decided to nurse my thirst here at Artie's. I figured it was a better way to write off the day and the people in it.

Artie's is the last of the great dumps. An unwavering parthenon of vice and virtue. The final testament to civilization pulled inside out. A timeless work of nostalgia, complete with a double U-shaped bar, red vinyl barstools, a stained green carpet that looked like the work of a 19th century expressionist and an eclectic blend of foxes, wolves, crows, dogs, peacocks and other lesser known members of the animal kingdom...birdbrains notwithstanding. Detroit's east side has its share of legends and legendary acts, many of which can trace their roots to Artie's.

I love the place.

But not everyone in it. When I got here I eased past the many faces that have long become familiar, trying to keep myself oblivious to their scattered, self-proclaimed, inflated reputations in need of an audience. Rather than offer them solace in my customary booth, I decided to sit alone and ordered my usual thick, well-done burger on a wheat bun with fries...chased down with a gin and tonic. A cholesterol diet only a hardened artery could love. It was too early for the regular four-piece jazz band so the musical interlude was filled by a raspy voiced songstress who strained through 'Night And Day' with a voice that was Dead and Gone...and whose long sweat tipped red hair had seen better days. She was accompanied by a bandy legged porker masquerading as a piano player. Ada, the gap toothed, gum cracking thirtyish waitress with dyed brown hair and an equally colorful disposition, didn't bother to write down the order.

"If you fuck the same way you order, you can't be getting very much," she said. Her contemptuous smile highlighted a face that had too much eye shadow. She was a top heavy, bottom up sausage with too much sexual need and not enough tact.

I was hungry for Artie's food, not Ada's sociological observations. I let it go. She humphed and parted the unmoving patrons. That's when Erotica materialized and brought new meaning to lust-at-first-sight.

"Mr. Keller?" she asked, apparently already confident of the answer.

"My father owns the 'Mister'. I'm Lincoln."

"Lincoln. Like the President?"

"No. Like the Towncar," I answered as I nodded for her to please sit down.

She unhooked the frog closures of her black side split tunic, revealing her bare shoulders. Her aerobically carved figure and peaked breasts were covered by a black form-fitting strapless evening dress that revealed just enough of her chestnut flesh to invite speculative inquiry. Her unruffled skin could have easily disguised her true age...which I guessed to be early thirties. She had the kind of features that male fantasies enhance and embellish over strong drinks and weak conversation. Carved from thousands of years of African mythology, she could have commanded a nation of warriors to die a thousand times for one more chance to see her smile. She had almond shaped eyes with deep arched eyebrows. A small rounded nose complemented a high cheekboned face and jet black hair trimmed neatly just above her shoulders.

She was a curvaceous cathedral where every brickhouse came to take notes.

As she completed her slow descent into the booth I assessed her height at about five seven with full lips that should grace magazine covers.

The dress served as a background to the blue, green and pink stripe that began at the top corner of her left breast and did a diagonal wrap around her body and ended at the split that exposed her tightly muscled right leg. In a place where truth is shielded by darkness and lies brighten the boredom, she was all class and style. So what was she doing meeting with me in a dump like Artie's? I decided not to ask how she knew to find me here. I had a feeling she wasn't going to tell me.

Instead, I pointed with my eyes at her necklace. "Erotica? That an introduction or a warning?"

There was just the slightest moment of hesitation as she unconsciously touched her necklace, suddenly realizing how I'd performed my marvelous feat of recognition.

She smiled. "An introductory warning. For a moment I thought we'd met before, but you were just reading the merchandise." Her voice had that suggestive tone. Subtle and daring in its invitation.

"Only the fine print. We've never met."

It was the truth stretched sideways. We had met before, not that she would remember or know. Somewhere in the farthest corner of my mind, in the deepest crevice where secrets are hidden, 'Erotica' was a distant memory, fantasized out of the centerfolds, advertisements and adolescent lusts that shaped my perceptions of the woman I'd most like to ravage. She was a statement to the ultimate physical ideal only discussed by the voices of the conscious and subconscious, locked away for hours of imaginative amorous consumption. Chocolate decadence with a saucy smile and a body that would have qualified as the eighth wonder of the world...or the eighth deadly sin. Made no difference to me at the time.

"Rumor has it that you're a pretty good detective," she said as she removed a Virginia Slim from the packet in her black velvet purse.

"Rumors tend to understate or exaggerate," I remarked. I flipped open the water stained match book cover and ignited the flame on the first strike. She leaned forward and drew softly through the filter until the tobacco tip crackled. She exhaled the first line of smoke toward the already smoke plagued ceiling. "You here to check out the rumor?"

"I'm here to hire a detective. Someone I know says you're pretty good. True or not?"

"If I was only pretty good I couldn't stay employed. Actually, I'm very good...when motivated."

She blew another line of smoke in the air, leaned back against the booth, creaking the overused leather, and gave me a half smile. "Then I'd like to hire you."

"Why?"

"It concerns my husband."

"Usually does most husbands."

"Most husbands don't concern me. Just the one I'm married to."

"Then shouldn't he be here doing the hiring?"

"Male pride prevents him from asking for help." She blinked. Not long enough to be considered a short nap, not short enough to be considered a long irritation eyelash. It was hesitant. Something behind the statement.

Our banter was interrupted by Ada. "Another for you and your..." she eyed Erotica with suspicious contempt, "...date, Linc?"

I nodded. Erotica ordered a perfect manhattan. Ada hummed in monotone agreement and sauntered back through the noisy crowd.

"Have I unknowingly wandered onto sacred territory?"

"Ada tries to lay claim to anything breathing. What she can't have she wants."

"I see." She was only slightly amused. And then getting down to business, she asked, "Ever hear of The Sentiments?"

I shrugged the truth. No, it didn't ring a bell.

"Here, let me show you something." She opened her black velvet purse, took out a medium sized manila envelope and slid it across the table. "Have a look. These are from about forty years ago. This is all I have of them."

I opened the envelope and removed its contents. The first thing I noticed was a black and white picture of five very twentyish looking men dressed in similar one-button suits, ruffle lapel shirts and wavy hair styles that we used to refer to as 'heavily conked'. They were posed according to height so that the group would V up from the center. In the center of the group was the shortest facing straight into the camera with his arms folded and one leg crossing the other. He looked familiar...like someone I'd seen but hadn't noticed. The four other members of the group were divided two on one side and two on the other with the two tallest on the ends. They posed like bookends. The picture was taken in a room with only a large curtain serving as a backdrop. The caption underneath was written in bold letters: **The Sentiments**. There were also included in the envelope several flyers and small posters written specifically about the group. The references included the dates and locations of where they were performing. I recognized the names of some of the various night clubs and lounges, many of which were famous during my parents' youthful heydays. There was a noticeable consistency among the different performing dates.

"Five guys from the 1950s who sing. There's a nostalgia craze right now. They shouldn't have trouble finding an agent," I mentioned as I took the last swallow of my drink, hoping to have it empty by the time Ada comes back. "And how does this concern your husband?"

Her eyes widened for just a moment. "About forty years ago this group just disappeared. Individually...as a group. All of them, just vanished. I don't know how else to put it. And I don't know that much about them myself except for what I've just given you. And this is what I got from my husband. I haven't been able to find anything they've done in any of the record stores. But it's very important for my husband to know whatever happened to them."

"Why?"

She hesitated, and then said, "Mr. Keller, my name is Erotica Tremaine."

She said it as if that explained everything. Tremaine. I knew that name. And all the silly rhymes that came with it from low budget, home made television commercials. You know the name, so call Tremaine. If it ain't Tremaine, it ain't the same. Tremaine Home Improvement. One of the more successful black-owned businesses in the lucrative and fiercely competitive home improvement business in southeast Michigan. His commercials were just bad enough to be good for a grin. You couldn't have grown up in Detroit during the late Fifties or early Sixties and not have seen his commercials for home remodeling, carpeting, kitchen installations and lawn care. He was endearingly known as Mr. 'ReModel'. He consistently made Detroit's branch of the NAACP list of successful African-American men.

He was also sixty-plus years. Had to be. But what better opiate than money to draw the fountain of youth to your living room...or bed?

Off in one of the various corners of Artie's I heard the usual taunts that follow when someone has run the pool table. A lot of hand slapping and dissing. Despite the loud laughter, verbal jaunts and background noises that customarily echo throughout most dumps, Erotica's voice seemed to skip across the surface of those interruptions on an effortless path to where I sat coolly attentive.

Ada returned with our drinks, setting each down with skilled indifference. "Still running your tab?" She knew the answer was yes before she asked the question. I thanked her and let the moment of silence direct her toward another table. Erotica's bright red nail polish seemed to sparkle as she clasped her fingers around the glass.

"And I'm going to have to ask you to please take my word for it," she continued. "It's something that has bothered my husband for so long. I was told you're good at finding truths and keeping those truths secret. I'm here because I need your help." She wasn't pleading, but that's where it was headed.

While she took a slow sip of her drink I used the moment to stick another toothpick in the corner of my mouth. Given the strength of her allure, it seemed an unsatisfying substitute for oral gratification. My former psych prof would have been pleased.

"You've tried contacting relatives, friends and such?"

She nodded. "I've tried. I've talked to a lot of them. I keep running into dead ends. That's why I'm talking to you."

"I don't come cheap."

"I look like I'm on welfare?" She opened her purse and took out a black leather covered checkbook. She wrote out a check and slid it across the table. "I trust that's enough to get you started."

A thousand dollars was a good retainer. The check was from her own personal account. Her husband's name wasn't on it. "There's some background things I'll need to know. Plus, I'll need you to sign a standard contract for services. I don't have one on me right now."

She sighed. There was a hint of relief in her voice. "So, we can start right now?"

"Yes, Mrs. Tremaine, but on one condition."

"And that is...?"

"The name is Lincoln...or Linc."

"I know," she sighed. "Like the Towncar."

"No. Like in Mod Squad."

"In what?"

I shook my head to say never mind for now. "Just remember to call me Linc."

She smiled her okay.

Chapter 2

I folded the check and dropped it in my shirt pocket. "Good, because the meter's just started."

Thanks to two more rounds of drinks and a cigarette, hers, most of what she told me seemed to make sense. Why wouldn't it? I asked several questions, most of which she couldn't answer. The one she wouldn't answer was exactly what was Leonard Tremaine's interest in the disappearance of The Sentiments. But I knew when the customer is right.

I also knew when the customer wasn't going to tell me any more than she already has. Yet. I took out one of my business cards. "My office number. There's an answering machine if I'm not around...just in case you should think of anything else I need to know." She looked at the black card with silver lettering and gave me a curious smile. "How do you want to be contacted?" I added.

She wrote down her number on the back of one of her husband's business cards. Tremaine Enterprises. Just black on white with an office phone number. Quick and to the point.

"I guess he never played for the Raiders," I stated.

"You played for the Los Angeles Raiders?" she asked, as if someone had already told her that but she wanted to hear it from me.

"No. I played for the Oakland Raiders," I corrected.

"There's a difference?"

I leaned forward. "There's a big difference!"

She seemed to take my word for it and then stood up, a radiant light in the tunnel of darkness, and extended a slender, well manicured hand. "I can't thank you enough Mr. ...uh, Linc."

"...and don't start now. Let's wait and see what happens tomorrow."

"Until tomorrow then." She turned and disappeared among the wave of regulars, freezing their actions like a football replay. I waited for the blue trail from the telestrater to point out how she'd just run the play.

I felt a little juiced, so I finished off my gin and tonic, thanked Ada with a bigger tip than she deserved and heel and toed my way to that war ravaged area that Artie's used as a parking lot.

My 1987 Nova sat untouched, the steering wheel locked in place with the 'Club'...and the tires were still in place. Something one needs to look for around here.

I sat steady behind the steering wheel, removed the 'Club' and fired up the engine. After two hundred and fifty thousand miles she still ran like a small tank.

I eased out onto the busy boulevard as a black Buick slowed to let me in. I waved thanks and tuned the radio to WJAZ. The sounds of Wes

Montgomery's talented thumb on jazz guitar was all the background I needed to help me sequence my next steps.

The night was balmy and unusually still. The night patrons moved in a lethargic dance of drained energy and unrequited passion. Adrenaline replaced the alcohol in my blood stream and I knew sleep was hours away. I checked the digital clock; it was only a little past eight-thirty. I decided to begin my research digging up some additional info on The Sentiments. It was a fortunate coincidence that I had at my immediate, well, almost immediate, disposal one of the world's most accomplished masters of music history. He's also my older brother and the able heir of our father's priceless collection.

***

The city of Detroit, like most big cities I suppose, has its own share of odd enclaves that exist within the city borders and are somewhat of an enigma to its general surroundings.

Such was the case for LaSalle Boulevard.

Its houses are a fascinating display of architectural creativity and expression surrounded by the hard bitter reality of decaying neighborhoods and aggressive renewal. Like someone dropped the Garden of Eden in the middle of the Chisolm Trail.

I'd made the exit off the Lodge expressway onto Grand Boulevard and followed the three-laned artery past the red bricked monolith known as the Henry Ford Hospital and soon after past the famous two-story home that launched the birth of Motown Records, now a historical museum. I came upon LaSalle Boulevard.

The right turn onto the landmark street on Detroit's northwest side was a visual ascension from the solid one- and two-family structures along Grand Boulevard. The one-laned street held a beautiful collection of homes designed during a time when front columns, rotundas, large room extensions, long walkways and structures were built with a sense of permanence and caring that would make an historical preservationist salivate. The homes were common in their individuality. Preserved and maintained like works of art from a past millennium.

I parked in front of a two-story, gray bricked structure with extensions on both ends and four white columns stationed like centurions under the portico. It occupied a corner lot and reminded me of a home a university would designate for a president. The home had an air of majesty. If Detroit was the home of the United Nations, then LaSalle Boulevard would have been the area where the diplomats would reside.

I followed the long brick walkway up to the cement steps until I stood outside of a black wrought iron door that led through an archway.

I pushed the dimly lit button that marked the doorbell and waited a scant few seconds before the large oak door with the patterned glass design was opened by a woman of medium height, mocha skin, exotically brown eyes and a shortly coifed afro. She was wearing a pink halter top, cuffed beige shorts and brown sandals. I hadn't seen her smile for too long.

"Lincoln!" she yelled as she opened the primary door. "My God. Get in here." She gave me a tight hug around the neck. "Where have you been keeping yourself?"

"Mostly out of trouble, Rae. How are you?" I asked returning the hug.

"Getting grayer by the day. Most of it brought on by your worrisome brother."

"That ain't gray, sister-in-law...it's platinum. Just means the cost of keeping you is going up."

"Liar! Come on in." I stepped into a black tiled foyer with a long throw rug. "What brings you out at this time on a week night?"

"Blood bank was closed so I thought I'd try here. This a bad time?"

"No. I just finished loading the dishwasher and Rosie's downstairs reliving the golden years, so your timing's perfect."

Her genuine greeting and warmth reminded me of the mothers back in my old neighborhood on Russell Street. They always seemed to have time to give and you were never an imposition. She was a great sister-in-law.

"Can I offer you something cool to drink, Linc? Or perhaps some dessert? We have apple pie and ice cream."

"Apple pie a la mode?" I said, the entire inside of my mouth salivating like Pavlov's Atomic Dog.

"Heated so that the ice cream melts down the sides," she added temptingly.

"Please. I'm a weak man. Don't do this to me."

"Then you'll not insult me by turning down my offer?"

"What? And have the spirits of thousands of mothers descend upon me and whip upon me with a switch? I think not!"

I didn't hear my brother sneaking up behind me until he spoke. "A wise choice, Linc. My wife is a difficult person to refuse. That's why I married her."

My brother Roosevelt Keller is an inch or two shorter than my six foot, one inch height, with a dark complexion, thin mustache and a slow receding hairline. He wore a sleeveless white T-shirt with the letters W H I P emblazoned in a dark cloud with a bolt of lightning piercing through the middle. Underneath the letters it said 'We're here for you. Twenty four seven'. WHIP is the AM radio station where he works as both Station Manager and on-air personality.

He has a mildly built torso inside a pair of cut off jeans and Velcro laced Nike's.

"So, where the hell you been, man?" The lighthearted tone offset the unexpected headlock. "You taken up with some flygirl and forget your family?"

"Been busy. Lot of late nights and long days," I answered the best I could into the crook of his arm. "Too many people looking for what they can't find at home."

He shook his head, smiling impishly when it looked like his wife was going to do to him what he was doing to me if he didn't stop. "When are you and Jeff gonna' stop playing Spy Guys and get a real job?" he asked as he gave me my neck back. Jefferson is the eldest and the baddest. And my partner.

"We are working real jobs...it's you media types who get lost in the glamour and glitter of what's real."

"Hey, managing a radio station is honest work. It's creative and consistent employment. Everyday I'm making sure that talented young people have an outlet in which to express themselves. It's a good thing and pays the mortgage."

Roosevelt Keller, the second eldest of the Keller quartet, had achieved some degree of local fame as an on-the-air personality for the once fledging WHIP, 1420 on the AM dial. Their specialty is R & B Oldies from the Fifties and Sixties. Over the years he's managed to move the station from a ratings disaster to a strong competitor in the market. His duties of managing the station have moved him away from time in the studio to behind the scenes, helping to keep the station strong. He fills in when a disc jockey can't make the shift. His popularity has reached such heights that he has an unprecedented lock on invitations to the best restaurants, tickets to the best plays and concerts, as well as moles in every social structure that connects Detroit to its surrounding suburbs.

"So, Linc. What's up?"

"I just met with a new client. Interesting request. Thought you might be of some help." I gave Rosie the Headline News version of my interview with Erotica. "Group was known as The Sentiments. You ever hear of them?"

"No. But that doesn't mean anything," he replied dismissively. "Let's go check the database."

Rae returned with a tray carrying two gold laced plates. There was a rather large slice of apple pie on each plate with a crown of slowly melting vanilla ice cream dripping sensuously down the sides. The two tall glasses containing the milk had frost around the rim and just an inkling of condensation.

"Here you go. This should keep you two occupied while I cozy up to something."

Rosie grabbed the tray. "Yeah, well it better be a good book and not some baggy pants, untied shoestring, cyber-hormoned tackhead."

"You just described the reasons why I married you," Rae said as she waved us away.

Rosie balanced the dessert tray and I followed him through the foyer to an open door that led to a basement.

The basement was spacious. It also had a green and white decor which we all knew were the colors of the Michigan State Spartans. The wall-to-wall carpeting was done in large green and white squares with an MSU emblem embroidered in the middle.

The furniture was all Indonesian rattan frames and wrapped joints. The two and one seater Papasans and swivel chair had different colored cotton pads and were pointed towards a 36 inch Sony television that sat on a shelf that contained an assortment of books and magazines. The glass topped coffee and end tables were stained deep walnut with a lacquer coating. There were tubed black lights along the ceiling complementing the regular lighting from the lava lamps on the table.

Rosie was a serious Spartan.

I followed him to a large glass encased room that had curtains drawn all the way around making it impossible to look inside. He asked me to open the door.

I did.

"Some database, huh?" he said with excitement.

"That, my brother, is the proverbial understatement," I replied.

And it was.

I stared at what had to be the largest single collection of albums I'd ever seen. A collection begun by our father, but growing steadily under Rosie's watch. There were built-in hardwood shelves that were nine layers top to bottom and with albums neatly stacked tightly together. The shelving was built around the entire area, with just enough room for Rosie's high tech, high touch entertainment unit.

"I see you've added a couple of more shelves since I was last down here."

"Don't you know it! There's over seven thousand albums in this room. About one thousand 78s and close to three thousand 45s," he said pridefully.

"Dad would be proud. He left his collection in good hands. Have you finished getting this stuff filed?" I asked.

"I have a student, from Michigan State naturally, who's been coming in a couple times a week during the summer and entering the information on my computer." He pointed to a Gateway 2000 sitting on a computer desk in the corner.

He placed the dessert tray on the glass covered coffee table and sat down on the orange pillow chair. "This is my haven away from the madness," he said in a tone that was both therapeutic and recreational. "I retreat here as a way of staying in touch with...well, never mind. Let's see if we can find anything by The Sentiments."

"Wouldn't it be easier just to pull up the database on your computer?"

"The fun is in the search, Linc; to actually touch this music that connects our generations and speaks very passionately of our heritage. Computers can't do everything. To touch the album jackets and look at the pictures and think about the era that the music tries to capture. I would never go to a computer when I can touch all of this."

Rosie made a lot of sense and that bothered me. "So how should we proceed?"

With an impish grin he said, "Based on what you've said, they must have recorded at a time when neither one of us understood or cared about music, so they must have recorded when Dad was the collector." He pointed to three shelves located near the front of the room. "Start looking over there. Meantime, I'll put on music to conduct a search by."

I took a quick bite of my apple pie, wiped the edge of my mouth and strolled over to the shelves. I knelt down and began flipping through the albums, one by one.

His collection was impressive, just going by the first ten albums that I saw.

"I just recently managed to get my hands on a mint condition copy of Dinah Washington's 'September in the Rain' for only fifteen hundred from another collector." Rosie's back was turned and I'm not really sure if the statement was directed at me as much as it was a statement about himself.

I continued flipping through the albums. Gazing in awe at each album that predated my birth, but was a connecting point in music history.

"The first album I ever bought was 'Meet the Temptations'. I was so proud when I brought it home and put it on our stereophonic player." He was looking through other albums as he talked. "Hey, Linc, remember those large needles we had on our record players?"

"Umm-huh," I said with equal distraction.

"Man, we used to really wear those things out. Needles on vinyl. Sounds prehistoric compared to today's laser played CD's."

I could hear the soft slap of albums being placed against one another as he continued to search for our 'mood' music.

"You got a smile so bright, you know you could have been a candle...God that was good music. The Temps." Rosie was becoming more animated as he sang the lyrics from one of the first Temptation hits that we all grew up on and had committed to memory.

I found myself unconsciously humming along with his nostalgic romp.

I finished one stack and moved to a second shelf. As I pulled one album after another, I became humbled by how little I knew of the black recording artists of years gone by. There were names and faces that bore no recognition to me, but I'm sure would have delighted the heart and soul of my parents.

"Look at this," Rosie said with some laughter. "Sly and the Family Stone. 'Don't you Want to Get Higher.' It was one of Walt's favorite tunes. We used to pantomime on trash cans, closet shelves and broomsticks whenever we played this jam back in our glory days at Michigan State. Damn Sly Stone was an Emperor and fucked it up. Didn't matter. We'd all gather in our suite in Wilson Hall and party tough."

"Umm-huh."

"I'm serious, Linc. It was me, Walt, Cott, Hook, Strick, Pokey..."

" ...Pokey?"

"It's a long story. Carl, Tyme, Broadway Moe, Tex, Sticks, Booker, Frank, Otis, Easy Earl, Joe. Man, we would jam."

"All those brothers in one room. Sounds crowded...or questionable."

"Mind out the gutter, younger bro." As Rosie continued his rapid run down Nostalgia Road I was looking at an album cover that featured the blues music of Bessie Smith. She was someone I'd heard of in passing, but never really knew about...until now.

"Ah ha! Look at this; Blood Sweat and Tears," Rosie said with excitement. "David Clayton Thomas. Damn, that white boy could sing! And that band could play. I loved horn sections and they had a good one. Course then, Chicago had a good horn section, too. Toughest horn section I ever heard was Tower of Power. I saw them in concert in Sacramento. They had this sax player named Lenny Pickett. I think that boy was born with four lungs. He did a solo on 'Knock Yourself Out' that was beyond belief. It seemed like he blew for a half hour. They weren't your average white boys. Now, I don't take nothing away from Earth Wind and Fire's horn section. Shit, wouldn't you like to see those four horn sections in concert? I would. That would be a Tasmanian throw down."

I was thinking about the idea of a Tasmanian throw down when I pulled out an album and found what I was looking for. There they were; The Sentiments. On the front cover, dressed in button down suits and black laced shirts. This time they were posed in a line, short up front to tall in back. The album was entitled 'Sentimentally Yours'.

I suppose I held the album for several seconds without saying much. I wondered briefly how our father got a hold of it when none of today's computer literate record/tape/CD outlets could even know it existed. I could hear Rosie in the background praising the work of Thom Bell and Linda Creed in the days when they worked with, and produced, The Spinners, The Stylistics and Blue Magic. I was less attentive than before because now The Sentiments were very real to me. There were youthful faces on an album from 1955. In their eyes I could see belief in what was to come.

Finally, I said, "I found the album."

"All...right!" Rosie replied with genuine enthusiasm.

I strolled back to the couch, having flipped the album over to read the liner notes. Rosie stopped his search for mood music. On the back of the album was a review written by a former disc jockey who introduced the group, talked about their background and their talent. There wasn't anything new for information, but he saw the group as rising stars who would shine for years to come.

There were several more platitudes and supporting comments that prepared the listener for what he described as 'a musical dessert for which second helpings cannot come fast enough'.

Rosie stopped his search momentarily. "You want to hear it now?" he asked.

"Yes, indeed."

"I'll do you one better. I'll make you a tape of the music while we listen. That way you won't feel embarrassed to ask to borrow the album and I won't feel guilty when I tell you no."

I nodded in agreement.

"I stopped loaning out my albums after college. People wouldn't return them, or if they did it was weeks later and usually scratched with damn pizza stains on the vinyl."

"No argument from me. I'm primarily interested in two things...the group itself and the recording company." I removed the album...delicately...and read the inscriptions on the label; "Shadowcast Recordings...Detroit, Michigan?" I said somewhat surprised. "Never heard of that company."

"Me either," he said as he took the album over to his entertainment unit. He lifted the glass case and placed the album on the turntable. He took a blank cassette and placed it in the recorder. He delicately rubbed a finger across the touch-sensitive dial and the album began to play.

The first song, 'Sentimentally Yours' was an awakening for both of us. The harmonic interplay of their voices from lead to background was so subtle and smooth that you could hardly determine where one voice ended and the other voice began. Their five voices sounded like one symphony.

We both sat and listened, deeply and pleasantly impressed.

The next tune was an upbeat, cheek-to-cheek number entitled 'From My Heart to Yours' where the four background voices were primarily doing a harmonic do-wop while the lead singer endeared himself to any female listener.

Rosie and I said very little. We ate the melted parts of our desserts and saved our conversation for the few moments in between each tune.

I came to understand the reason for the praise. As we used to say back on the block, 'those boys were bad'.

I was content to sit and listen as Rosie stood up to turn the album over. He, in turn, went back to looking through his albums. I wasn't sure what he was looking for. I think he just needed the activity. He didn't say much. Just pulled out albums and smiled. From time to time he'd show me an album cover and we'd both grin. The covers brought back memories. Different memories, but memories anchored in some common experiences.

The last song on the album was entitled 'Our Road to Destiny' and was strangely ironic, if not prophetic, because they sang about how their futures were going to be the kind that others would marvel. It was a love song that had a cryptic insight.

The song ended. The album stopped and the cassette automatically clicked off. I was in a connecting mood of past and present. I wanted to know why The Sentiments hadn't made the jump to big time. Why? Anyone who heard their voices would have had to ask the same questions.

Rosie's loud, "Oh, no!" pulled me from my contemplative moment.

"What's up?" I asked.

He stood in front of me. Surprised and absorbed by the moment. "I was looking at the albums I have; some were double jacketed and I was thinking how popular they'd been when I removed this album." He slowly turned the album around and I saw the front cover. It was a black etched drawing of a rather overweight woman riding a hobby horse. "Rare Earth. 'MA'."

I said, "So what?"

"So this," he said back. He opened the double jacketed album and there, lying in the crease of the album, were five tightly rolled marijuana joints. I looked at the joints and looked at Rosie. He looked as if he'd just seen the burning bush. "It's Jamaican Red. Back in 1973, me, Walt, Tyme, Hook, and Cott bought one last twenty five cent pack two days before graduation. Rather than smoke the whole thing, we rolled one monster joint that we shared and then several joints apiece for all of us. We agreed to put the joints in a secret location and forget about them and at sometime in the future, when the time was right, take them out and smoke one in remembrance of the good old days."

"That was 1973?" I asked.

"Yeah. That was the year we all graduated from Michigan State."

"So that means those joints are..."

"...over twenty years old." His statement almost had a mystical quality to it. He stood in a trancelike state before speaking. "It's time. Linc, you will join me in this celebration, won't you?"

"Naw, bro. I don't indulge...anymore."

"Linc," Rosie said with building excitement. "I'm not talking about indulging. I'm talking about simple acknowledgment of success against the odds. I'm talking about Eldredge Cleaver meets Chaucer. Nikki Giovanni alters the poetic revolution with Emily Dickinson. Student demonstrations and an unfeeling bureaucracy. Institutional racism and Freedom Park."

"Rosie, I'm younger than you by a few years. I wasn't there with you."

"Yes you were. We all were in one way or another. Rice fields and riot gear. Flowers in a gun barrel and Kent State. Afros, bell bottoms, Pee-coats, black power wrist bands, tikis, love beads, hip huggers and hot pants. SDS and the UCLA Bruins."

"Rosie..."

"A gagged Bobby Seale and an ungagged Richard Nixon! Janis, Jimmi and Justice. Panthers in Oakland, Jackson State and the Chicago Seven. Soul on Ice and 'Do It'. Storm the Wilson Hall cafeteria and accept no compromises. You can't say 'no' when the souls of a thousand revolutionaries cry out to storm the Bastille one more time."

"I hadn't thought about it like that," I admitted, although I did have some privileged information about Oakland.

He became more animated. His gestures were sweeping. I think he was at the third level of obsession. "How best to cherish the memories of Michigan State and Walt, Cott, Tyme, Dirty Harry, Tex, Broadway Moe and the rest of the 'Soulful Wilsonaires'. This is about what we endured and preserved."

"Well, when you put it like that, what the hell," I said grinning slightly.

"Baby!" Rosie called out towards the stairs. "Come down here quick. The memories of a revolution are about to be relived."

I insisted on making one phone call before we called up the ghosts of the revolution.

Rosie took out War's 'The World is a Ghetto.' "Up against the wall!" he yelled. "Black Power gonna get your momma."

I raised my fist. "Power to the people."

Chapter 3

I maintained a deliberate, but fluid pace as I eased back down Interstate 96 in an attempt to reach my apartment. Rosie had always been a man of strong passion and conviction. His memories of those bygone years at Michigan State left me envious, not to mention somewhat hallucinogenic. Realizing that I may not have had the working capacity to make reasonable decisions on a timely basis, I popped the recorded cassette of The Sentiments' music into the cassette player. It didn't sound as nice coming out of my Nova's stereo speakers as it had in Rosie's music haven, but it was sure nice enough. These guys would have sounded good on an old Victrola. I began to hum along with a couple of the tunes that I particularly enjoyed. Despite the 1950's recording conditions, the music sounded error free and timeless.

Meanwhile, I was feeling hungry. The hamburger at Artie's and pie at Rae and Rosies' would not be enough for this case of the munchies. I knew that I desperately needed something to fill the empty refrigerator that took up valuable space in my apartment. My ride on I-96 wouldn't take me past any major food chain outlet so I'd have to settle for the neighborhood corner extortionists who sell various party goods and toiletries behind thick bullet proof glass panels and smile at the customer's stupidity. It works out, I guess, since I'm not the world's smartest shopper.

I stopped at the franchised convenience Stab-and-Grab outlet located two blocks from my upstairs apartment along Livernois Avenue. Its familiar green and white sign stood like a watchtower guiding me through the urban terrain to the safe port of its recently tarred and well lighted parking lot. The extra price I pay on items purchased contributed greatly to the franchise's recent aesthetic enhancements.

I rolled my Nova next to the only other car on the lot. It was a moody blue Jaguar, its silver trimming reflecting the brightly lit area. A man in his early twenties in a full length leather coat had his back partially turned to me as he listened nonchalantly to whoever spoke boringly to him through the receiver on the outside public phone. The leather coat would have looked good in the winter, but on a hot summer's night tonight it looked very non nice. I stepped out of my car, pushed down the door lock and as I turned toward the glass paneled door I happened to notice another late-teens young man moving slowly across the periphery of the parking lot. His motion seemingly stifled by a drug induced high or general confusion. Normal enough. Part of the urban landscape. A glance over to a darkened corner of the parking lot confirmed what my radar was signaling – it was a nondescript two door sedan. Looked to be a middle Eighties Chrysler model. I couldn't see the face behind the wheel, just his shadowy outline. It was the same set-up experienced by so many others who were less than attentive. The three would work as one. Their target was identified. Their timing would be precise.

Their presence brought me back quickly. I was back on red alert. I could have avoided the whole situation, but the late hour, my declining high, the munchies and my waning energy were reason enough for me to get in, spend a fortune on a few highly caloric items and retreat to the sanctity of my upstairs flat.

I entered and took in the familiar layout of the brightly lit, white tiled house of indigestion and searched for my usual beer, chips, dip, juice, cheese, meat, bread and the most recent issue of Ebony. I noted the man at the counter ahead of me; tall, thirtyish, with a light coconut tone and black wavy hair. He was what women from my adolescent days described as a 'pretty man'. Just light enough to attract moths but not enough to pass. He was dressed in a purple and white athletic outfit with matching running shoes and had brought more items to the counter than he had money to buy. He took longer than normal to decide on which ones to keep. Time seemed stretched now that I was in a hurry. He was a Ninetie's buppie. Lots of flash and low on cash. A credit card for every purchase and an excuse for every late payment.

The coffee toned, black haired man behind the bullet proof panel smiled patiently. His top front teeth gapped to take in extra oxygen.

It was during those long moments that I took another glance outside and confirmed what my mind had been putting together.

I wasn't being paranoid.

"Excuse me," I said to Pretty Man as he tried to decide between the cottage cheese and the onion dip. He was clean shaven. His look was contemptuous. Beginning bags under mahogany colored eyes. "Do you come in here often?"

"That any of your business, my man?" His tone was edgy. His voice cracked at the beginning and end of his question.

I shrugged. "No. Not really. But in the next few minutes, one of the three of us is going to be in trouble." I nodded toward the counter agent. "He's protected by the glass and the security cameras in the corner. I'm driving an '87 Nova and would be a waste of time. So that leaves you."

"Leaves me for what?" he asked, more curious and less arrogant.

"For the car jacking that's about to take place. That is your expensive Jaguar in the parking lot, isn't it?"

He nodded.

"There are two men in the parking lot and another sitting over in a car waiting for you to come out. You've obviously stopped in here a few times before or they wouldn't know you'd be here at this time."

"Are you sure they're waiting for me?" He paused. "How do I know you aren't part of their set up?"

"You don't. But I'm paying for my stuff and moving on. They already saw what I'm driving so they're not interested in what an '87 Nova will bring once it's been cut to pieces. You do what you think is right."

I motioned to have my groceries rang up while he stood there weighing what I said against what he believed.

I slipped the money under the paneled tray, grabbed my bagged groceries and turned to leave.

"Wait!" he yelled. "What should I do?"

"I don't know. It's none of my business." That stopped him for a moment. "Dial 9-1-1 and ask them to send a patrol car to this area. Tell them you suspect a car jacking. They'll come by soon enough. Meantime, stay in here and you and your car will be safe."

He nervously licked his lips. "Do you think they suspect anything?"

"They might if you keep staring out the window. Wander in the back or convince this guy to let you behind the counter until the cops arrive. Just don't go outside."

"What if they think..."

"Doesn't matter what they think. Only what you do," I said impatiently. "Just stay inside until the cops come and next time don't be so quick to show off your success by driving a Jaguar through this part of the jungle."

"But suppose...?" He stammered, his eyes darting from the parking lot to me to the guy behind the counter. "How about helping me? I'll pay you."

"With what? The cottage cheese or the dip?"

I didn't tell him I was armed. My .38 was holstered under my left shoulder. The successful flighty type can't believe someone would actually want to steal what they own. He'd want to shoot it out like some damn fool off a late night movie just to protect his property.

I wasn't into late night movies or successful airheads who drove Jaguars through blighted areas as a way of showing off.

I was tired and looking forward to spending the remaining night hours chewing the edge of my pillow and dreaming of a golden brown angel too top heavy to fly.

"Look, pretty boy. Don't leave a load in your shorts, okay? They'll make their move when you start towards the door. The one by the phone and the other walking across the lot will start toward you as soon as you step on the sidewalk. The guy sitting in the car will drive up quickly and park behind you making it impossible to back out. It's a very simple routine, but highly effective." I nodded toward the pay phone by the back exit.

"Make the call. Wait for the cops and like I said, learn to drive something expendable when you wander through this area."

I spun my plastic bag around a few times to tightly secure the over-priced edibles and stepped back outside to where my Chariot of Filth waited for me to beat a hasty exit.

I watched the movement in the parking lot and felt somewhat relieved when no one approached me from the back, front or side.

"Guess they'd lose money if you were hijacked, old girl," I said as I removed the key from the lock and opened the driver's side door. I placed the groceries on the passenger seat, fired up the engine and backed out of the parking lot and onto Livernois. I waved to the jail bound sociopath waiting in the darkened car. He ignored me. I expected that level of dis-courtesy from a future cellblock number.

Inside my Nova, WJAZ provided the soothing background jazz to prep me for a good night's sleep. The night lull was a misleading tranquilizer designed to minimize sensory penetration into the world behind the shad-ows. The night suits my nature. The day suits my needs.

It only took less than ten minutes of uninhibited driving before I reached the refurbished four-story apartment building where I rent a one-bedroom that has all the charm of a coffee house and the subtlety of falling timber.

I eased into the parking spot next to the apartment building where Jon, the security guard, patiently sleeps through the night. He appeared awake this time so I gave him the obligatory wave. I shook my head as one way to clear up the cobwebs. The incident at the convenience store had me a little more grounded or else I would have been giggling all night about my ini-tial inability to get the key in the door.

I walked up the dimly lit steps, taking out the keys and shifting the groceries in a delicate urban balancing act for which tickets were rarely sold.

A solid oak door and three locks provide all the protection I require for my restful retreat from the constant chaos of city living.

I dropped the bags on the all purpose octagonal shaped table inside my functionally adequate kitchen and then breezed through my apartment try-ing to get a fix on the lateness of the hour. According to the blue digital lettering on the microwave oven, it was just after midnight and I was drawn to my bed as metal is drawn to a magnet. I wandered into my bedroom and plopped down on the edge to allow my shoulders to slump without some parental comment.

I glanced at the answering machine. There was an orange colored 5 waiting for me to press the play button, but I refused.

The messages could wait.

Sitting on top of a stack of files was the remote for the television. My response was automatic. Pick up, click on, do a thirty second channel surf and park it on CNN Headline News until a late night movie grabs my interest. My fears were once again reinforced. Any belief that television would become a vast wasteland for mindless entertainment had long been confirmed. It was now a fact. It was now the perfect forum for talk shows that feature the socially repugnant. Unconsciously humorous people whose sole purpose is to remind us that our evolution has only been ten million years. Supported, rather seriously, by the late night infomercials. Only my sincere belief that we're only another ten million years from putting it all together keeps me from stepping in front of a bus.

I got up, walked out of the bedroom and plopped down on the pull out couch. I tore open a bag of chips, twisted the top off a beer and read through the file given to me by Erotica. Five guys known as The Sentiments mysteriously disappear during the 1950s and some forty years later, a woman not even born when they were last seen shows up and asks me to find them.

Interesting.

Assuming Erotica was unsuccessful with the regular avenues for finding missing people, I thought about a few tricks not generally known to the public.

I held up the black and white photograph taken at a time when their youth and potential were in abundance. I glanced at the accompanying newspaper clipping. The picture was somewhat faded and the paper had that parched brown look and a fragile feel. It was dated September 21, 1954. The clipping was taken from the *Michigan Chronicle* featuring a black and white photograph of five men dressed in double breasted dark suits facing the camera. Each flashed an infectious smile. The accompanying headline read: THE SENTIMENTS HEADLINE THE GRAYSTONE. I recognized the Graystone as one of Detroit's premier night clubs.

I quickly skimmed the article to get the gist of what was written. The Sentiments were described as vocal stylists headed to the big time. There was reference to their smooth blend of voices as well as their crispness of tone and delivery. I skimmed further and found out that they were five friends who grew up on Hastings Street. The papers were compiled according to the earliest documentation of The Sentiments up to the most recent news article. It was an historical record of lives thrown together at a time before I was born, brought to life by the persistent documentation of Erotica Tremaine.

It started with a faded, tattered small item from one of the black publications in Detroit. The year was 1948 and the place was a local community center on Detroit's north side called The Garvey Center. It gave a quick account of a group of five teenagers who called themselves The Sentiments and how they were the undisputed winners of a local talent contest. There were three other articles written to reflect other contests around Detroit that were won by this young group. All the articles were written during 1948 and 1949.

The first real picture of the group showed up in the 1949 Miller High School senior album. They were shown rehearsing by a piano in what appeared to be a classroom. It was also the first reference to the names of all five members. Starting from left to right was Lennix Williams, who was leaning on the piano. He was one of the tall ones. Next to him, smiling at something being said was the other taller one, Charles Treadwell, who was also holding a piece of sheet music and glancing at who I noticed was the shortest one in the other photos, Adam Carter. There was something about Adam that I couldn't put my finger on just yet. Standing behind the older male piano player was Michael Parker, and next to him was Henry Hill.

The caption underneath the picture read: Seen here rehearsing with music teacher Matthew Stewart, local singing group The Sentiments prepare for a bright future.

This was followed by a series of articles and flyers that featured their appearances around Detroit in a number of neighborhood night clubs. They were usually listed as the opening act for some other well known local and regional talent. The names read like a Who's Who of singers who preceded the Rhythm and Blues era.

The Sentiments appeared to be gaining a lot of local recognition from 1949 to the middle of 1950. They started appearing in places around Michigan like Flint, Lansing, Saginaw, Jackson and Kalamazoo. They were always featured in clubs that catered to an African-American clientele. They were usually the opening act and seemed to work pretty steady during the 1950s.

One reviewer for the *Michigan Chronicle* described their voices as "God's idea of an angelic chorus." In articles written by reviewers for the local black newspapers they were described as "a smooth blend of voices and talent", "Unchanneled enthusiasm mixed with a silk like quality", "They don't just sing, they engage". Apparently, The Sentiments had begun to build up something of a regional following.

More local reviews followed through the end of 1950. There was nothing to indicate that they'd performed in places like Chicago and New York. I'm sure it wasn't unusual, but given how their talent was described, something big should have happened by that time.

Since they were usually performing on weekends, I wondered what they did during the weekdays. Did they have jobs? If so, where? Did they have an agent? If so, who? I read through every article, letter or flyer that tracked their path to greater recognition and success.

In April of 1951, an article mentioned that the group was close to signing a record contract and recording their first album. There were a few other minor articles and the final article, September 16 of 1951, mentioned their successful appearance at the Graystone. After an hour of reading through the file, I rubbed my eyes, yawned and stood up to stretch. I walked around the desk, intrigued by what I thought was an interesting and puzzling question: why would The Sentiments, just as they were tasting success in Detroit, suddenly vanish?

I moved to my blue velour LA-Z-BOY rocker that sat by the casement bay windows. Below was a picturesque view of the constantly busy artery known as Livernois Avenue. It ran through the city like a two-laned beacon, guiding its denizens past one of the more renowned areas for black owned businesses. I liked the view. I liked the noise.

"Okay, guys. Let's see what rock has served shelter for the last forty years," I said trying to stifle a yawn.

It's the last comment I remember saying before drifting off.

Chapter 4

I was awakened by an alarm I hadn't set, but was as equally reliable in its intent. Ten minutes before the radio came on, I heard the sound of scraping outside my bedroom window. I recalled a gentle, sporadic noise which eventually became a constant crescendo of nails on glass. Highly effective in awakening the dead.

I must have moved from my LA-Z-BOY to my bed sometime after I fell in to the deepest of sleep. I swung out of my restful repose, stretching my limbs and suddenly mindful of the ten remaining minutes before my designated awakening. I tottered over to the window, opened the blinds and gazed into the light brown eyes of the neighborhood rodent terminator who had come to collect his earnings as per our contractual agreement. I opened the window and he slithered his tan body with its white undercoat through the slight opening and pounced on the floor, stopping momentarily to yawn and scratch the back of his ear.

"Where you been, Free Ride?" I asked as he stared up at me the way cats do when they want to make you feel stupid.

Free Ride was a cat of no particular origin. He was also big enough to eat Garfield. As far as I know he lives in the neighborhood as part of a community arrangement he devised where he gets food, shelter, petting and other forms of attention at his own discretion, and in return he keeps the area free of rodents. I wasn't available when he negotiated this arrangement, but I figured it wouldn't have mattered.

He wandered into the kitchen in anticipation of his usual rations. A bowl of milk, preferably 2 percent...he's concerned about his physique...and some Kibbles & Bits to add variety to his diet.

With my end of the bargain with Free Ride taken care of, I began my inquiry into the life and times of five men known collectively as The Sentiments. Having checked my messages, I showered, had coffee and toast, not feeling any more after effects of a few hits from a twenty year old joint. The view from my second floor bay window gave me a good sense of the outside temperatures. White clouds had begun to roll in during the early part of the morning, partially concealing the calm blue sky and adding a hint of soon-to-come autumn crispness to the late summer air. Thankfully, it won't be as hot as it was yesterday. I used the mild temperatures and the jazz from station WJAZ to lull me into a serene reflection of yesterday's activities that culminated with me being today in possession of a folder loaded with old articles about a singing group that predated The Temptations, The Dells, Little Anthony and The Imperials and possibly The Platters. I was going to try and determine why The Sentiments, just as they were starting to get some notice, would suddenly vanish.

I dressed in a pair of black casual Levi's, black cotton shirt, socks, tasseled loafers and a pair of gold wire rim blue tinted sunglasses. I slipped on my shoulder holster, checked my .38 and picked up my shoulder strapped, black leather carrying case.

I set the alarm to my apartment and eased downstairs to my Nova while giving Free Ride a free ride out the door and wishing him luck with the local rodent problem. The drive from my apartment to the office was made noticeably short by the absence of morning commuter traffic. I popped in the cassette tape of The Sentiments and let their voices pull me into the day.

Ten minutes later, I slid into the parking lot adjacent to the building where I shell out money to rent space for an office.

Keller Investigations is located on the top floor of a three-story gray brick building on Livernois Avenue, three blocks from the I-96 freeway. The building is home to several blossoming entrepreneurial businesses in need of a place to incubate. It's really a co-op minus the group sex. It's owned by Mr. Uhlander Means, Esq., a veteran defense lawyer who clerked under Thurgood Marshall and has been a general pain in the ass of the Detroit and Wayne County judicial system.

Scattered among the first and second floors are a Beauticians School, a business specializing in African Art, an Independent Insurance agent, a used mystery book store, a lawyer's office, a Beauty-Aid outlet, Madame Zachora's Psychic Readings and Numerology Paraphernalia, INFO-SEARCH and Keller Investigations. Businesses were always coming and going for whatever reason so there were usually two or three offices open.

I scaled the two flights of steps and opened the smoked glass door with Keller Investigations painted in bold black letters. The overhead light was on and I heard movement in the adjoining bathroom. Since I wasn't expecting company, I immediately went on the defensive. Sometimes resentful ex-husbands may like to drop in unannounced. I put my hand on my .38. "I'm assuming you're out of toilet paper which explains your presence in this office," I said to the closed door.

"Don't go for bad, bro. It might make me nervous," came the recognizable voice. I immediately relaxed.

I walked over to my government designed metal desk that I bought at an auction, and sat down in the ladder back swivel chair.

"Thought you'd be gone a few more days," I said as I looked through the pile of mail he'd dropped on my desk

The toilet flushed. I heard the water faucet turn on and off. Moments later, Jefferson Keller, my moody gravel voiced older brother stepped into the office, wearing a sleeveless blue denim shirt, jeans and blue and white Reeboks.

"The Terrell brothers didn't prove to be all that smart. They were predictable in a stupid sort of way," he said as he parked his angular, coffee toned frame behind his wooden desk and stroked his evenly trimmed mustache. A shimmer of light bounced off his very low and evenly cut pate. "I caught both of 'em shacked up with some red haired bomb crater at a trailer park just outside of Des Moines. She was charging a two-for-one. I just waited until they wore each other out from too much booze and boobs. Once they fell asleep, I picked the lock, handcuffed both of them and hauled ass. Our take on this is ten grand."

He opened a pack of Kool menthols and looked through the pile of mail left over from his not being around.

Being in business with one of my brothers has its advantages. I don't have to spend time getting to know the guy, since technically he was the first person I slept with. Besides, Jefferson Keller is a study in elusive understanding. As the bounty hunter half of Keller Investigations, he worked for the United States Marshal's Office, having retired almost two years ago. It was said that as long as a fugitive remained on the planet, Jefferson Keller could find and bring him in. I didn't know just how good he was until he approached me with the idea of being a partner in the business. Since I'd already had most of the basics in place, he felt that the transition time would be minimal. He invested a few dollars and said he'd only work with finding bail jumpers. He didn't want supervision, required no involvement from me and would meet his end of the business expenses. He was a loner by design. He didn't crave or want any help to do his work. If I agreed to those conditions, we'd be partners. I could continue with my private investigations, he'd bounty hunt.

"Linc," he said while making the final pitch for our partnership. "There are currently over six thousand fugitives from justice. That will keep us out of each other's hair and pay a lot of bills when I bring 'em all in."

Despite my initial reluctance, he convinced me that it was a good idea by pointing out the amount of money we'd save from not having to change the name on the door.

I gave in.

"You working on something or just wasting our hard earned money?"

I told him about the mystery surrounding The Sentiments. He listened, offering no insights or leads that might be helpful. I suspect it was all those years working for the government he learned to keep his thoughts off his sleeve.

"So I thought I'd follow up on a couple of other things in order to clear my head of this missing singing group."

"If you knew why, it would also tell you where. You have to find out why. Everything rests on the why."

I nodded. "I agree. No one seems to know why. It's part of the mystery."

"People hide for essentially two reasons. One, it's something they did or two, it's something someone thought they did."

I said, "Forty years is a long time to hide based on something someone thought you did."

"It's a short amount of time if you can't prove otherwise," Jefferson said as he picked up the phone and punched in a number. His remark would prove to be oh so prophetic.

I opened up my spiral case log book and chronicled the activities and people I'd met since Erotica first sauntered in and triggered my present journey into the past. I wrote down facts and impressions. The more I wrote, the more questions came to mind.

I finished about the same time Jefferson had made his last follow up call.

"You gonna be around the office a few days?" I asked.

He shrugged. "Depends." He dropped a pile of junk mail into the trash can, locked the drawer to his desk and stood up. "I got a couple of local pick ups. They both missed their court dates. Won't generate much income, but it's something. Why?"

"The nights get lonely."

"That's why they make rubber dolls. I'll call you later."

I used the available free minutes to pay a few bills, grabbed the folder and stepped across the hall to see Julie at INFO-SEARCH.

I tapped twice on the clear window and walked into the flat carpeted foyer where Mary Cooper, an early twentyish college student with chestnut skin and multi colored beaded dreadlocks greeted me with apple cider eyes and snapping gum.

"Hi, Mr. Keller. How goes the dick business?"

It's her favorite line that she says all the time and delivered with the same anticipated giggle that hopefully jollies her day until she makes it to class at night.

"Like always. Slow to start and Hard to stop." I always try a different retort to her statement so we'd always have something to look forward to. "Boss lady in?"

"Yeah." She glanced down at the unlit phone lines. "She's not busy. Go on in."

I eased passed her desk and through the open door where Julie Block sat staring at her Compaq computer screen, her fingers busily orchestrating the keyboard.

Her office is painted sky blue with white trimmings. The blue curtains match the thin unstained carpet. She has an L-shaped mahogany desk designed to provide ergonomic comfort for the more computer prone users. There's also a large black AM/FM cassette and CD player on the verandah under the window as well as two boxes for storing computer discs and a CD rack. A miniature grandfather clock sits on the left corner of her desk and next to it is a picture of her with her two daughters.

"Hey, Julie..."

She held up a halting finger. "One second, Linc. I just need to finish keying in this request."

Julie Block is a compact source of dynamic energy wired into a different universe than the one we currently occupy. We met two years ago when we both set up shop.

I'd moved back to Detroit from Oakland, California; she came back from Hell. She'd spent all of her twenties in a series of bad relationships, trying to support two daughters and the childish men who took out the anger of their insecurities on the most vulnerable and not the most capable. Somehow she weathered the storm, finally broke free and with her daughters in tow, moved into single parent housing on Wayne State University's campus, enrolled into a business curriculum and found she had a charismatic link with computer technology. What she never understood about men, she clearly understood about computers. No secret was safe as long as she had access to a software program and a modem. She started out as a research service for lazy undergraduate students, of which there were many scattered across Wayne State, University of Detroit, Lawrence Tech, Wayne County Community College and others. She later expanded her searches to include people, places and events. Armed with a business degree and info savvy, she opened the INFO-SEARCH firm and hasn't looked back.

Julie dresses to be seen and her bosomy, hourglass figure commands attention from the most evangelical of sinners. She wore a blue wool cutaway jacket and matching slim pants. A single diamond pendant hung from her neck. She has as many different color eye shadows as Imelda Marcos has shoes and doesn't hesitate to match the eye shades with the outfit and the shoes.

"There." She swung toward me, looking captured in her high back, black leather swivel chair. "What brings you beckoning to my door, Linc? Hopefully something billable." She raised one of her finely arched eyebrows and pierced me with coffee colored eyes.

"That's shooting me, Julie. Where would your business be if the Keller Boys weren't supportive clients?"

"Profitable. Not that you care. What am I doing that I'll have to write off as an expense?"

I opened the folder and talked her through what I had on The Sentiments. She listened, occasionally jotting down a few notes on the yellow legal pad she always kept nearby.

"There's a few things I can do, Linc. I can check with the phone lists I have on CD-ROM. I can also access some other databases that might be helpful. If I find any that match, I'll slide them under your door...with a bill, of course."

"Of course."

"If I had their social security numbers or old license numbers, it would be a lot easier."

"And that's why I don't have them. We don't want it too easy."

"It's your bill. Want me to check the Department of Corrections database?"

"Wouldn't hurt. It's an unfortunate reality, but I hope that you can eliminate it as a place to look and not the other way around."

"I'll cross reference where I can." She picked up the black and white picture of the five young stars to be. "You know, this picture might be helpful."

"Howso?"

"Well, once I upload a copy, I can do a number of enhancements, five, ten, fifteen years and so on and then see if those enhancements coincide with some of the pictorial databases I can access."

"You can do all that?"

"Not for free, but yeah. It's a simple process for pre-Twenty-First Century technology." She looked quickly through her notes. "How about this guy Matthew Stewart? Want him checked out as well?"

"Wouldn't hurt. When can I expect results?"

"When you write a check for two hundred as part of your intent to pay you bill."

"How about an expensive dinner at the restaurant of your choice?"

"Nice thought. But I've got a tray full of recipes I've downloaded that

I'm anxious to try on my girls. How about a check?"

"Whatever happened to trust?" I lamented.

"It was voted out of the last election."

I thanked her, told Mary I'd be right back with a check and placed two phone calls to other clients. I gathered my things, wrote out a check that I gave to Mary and strolled out to my car.

I knew Julie would do a competent job, but there were other things I needed to know before I hit the bricks looking for more bread crumbs on a forty year old trail.

I motored over to the Wayne State University campus to use their branch of the Detroit Public Library. As I rounded the corner to the crescent shaped driveway, I pulled in behind a red Pontiac Grand Am just as the driver drove away from a parking meter.

When you're hot, you're hot.

The number of quarters I dropped in the meter could have been used to buy a small island in the Caribbean. Instead it bought me two hours of parking time.

I entered the monolithic building through its brass trimmed rotating doors and followed the brown tiled floor past the architectural exhibits and up the steps to the circulation library. The brunette who greeted me was wearing horn rimmed glasses and a brown dress that revealed nothing about her figure. She was pleasant enough in her greeting and when I explained what I wanted, she eagerly found the appropriate microfiche and set me up at one of the view monitors. She even threaded the film through the machine and demonstrated how to fast forward, rewind, reset, enlarge and print. It was a bit more than I needed, but she seemed happy to assist. Happy people are real appealing to me.

I intended to research some of the significant events that took place in 1955. As the headlines from January 1st, 1955 appeared in the viewer, I was convinced that there was something in one of those headlines, bylines or easily missed articles in the corners that might shed some insight on what had happened to The Sentiments.

What I was learning about Detroit in 1955 proved to be a worthwhile romp through recent bygone years. So much so that I almost forgot to beat a fast shimmy outside and put more quarters in the meter. My timing was perfect. I'd dropped in the last quarter when the small white station wagon with the yellow beacon on its roof rounded the corner in search of a car to ticket.

I smiled at the serious minded meter maid as she slowly cruised by looking determined to write out a few parking tickets before her shift ended. I continued my search through the dailys, stopping to print anything that appeared to be remotely interesting. When I finished nearly two hours later, I had several pages of events, incidents and other miscellaneous activities that contributed to 1955's year of individual recognition and distinction.

The first seven pages contained information about that side of Detroit known as 'Blackbottom'. A highly visible area of black businesses, churches and laborers working in the automotive plants that was known as much for its good times as well as its hard times. During Detroit's industrial growth period of the 1920s, thousands of blacks migrated from the southern states in search of economic and social freedom in the automotive paradise of the north. The price for that freedom was restricted to a 4 square block area in which a number of black businesses grew and flourished. Anything obtainable legally and illegally could be found somewhere within that area. It was there The Sentiments, individually and collectively, grew up.

Despite all the change that occurred there over the last forty some odd years, there was sure to be something there that was still constant. I'd check the 1951 list against the regular yellow pages as well as the minority businesses listed in the Black Yellow Pages. I figured there had to be someone still around who could give me some insights that might help me determine why they fled.

The last page gave me some background information on the now defunct Shadowcast Recording Company. The company didn't survive past 1955, but the owner's name had been cross referenced and he was still alive and living in Detroit.

His name was Morgan Rivers and he had come to the music business like most people of that time; he sang in his Baptist choir, a choir he helped organize as part of the all-black supply group responsible for transporting supplies to troops on the front line during World War II. He came to Detroit after the war, determined to make it in the music business. He started the Shadowcast label with the investment help of friends and relatives. He scoured the Detroit scene in search of talent and his efforts landed him The Sentiments, among others. Apparently the company went belly up for a number of reasons. Morgan Rivers stayed as close to the business as possible, but never really returned to its core.

I went to the library pay phone and found three Morgan Rivers in the phone book. I got the one I wanted on the second try. The anguished years of dreams unrealized flowed like a wave through the aged voice that greeted me. I introduced myself as a freelance writer doing a background piece on Detroit music prior to Motown. I asked if he could spare a few minutes.

He said he didn't mind, so I asked him a few background questions. He was quite forthcoming. Nostalgic in a way that's painful and pleasurable. I asked if he remembered The Sentiments.

He sure did. "Next to losing my company, they were my biggest loss. Talented boys. All of them. Saw them at a show at...Estelle's Back Room, musta been 1952. Nice, beautiful voices. I knew they had something special. I signed them to my label that same year. Cut an album. Great songs. They woulda' been big."

"Seems like they fell off the face of the earth in 1955 after appearing at a place called Johnny's Lounge. Any idea where they went or what happened?"

He paused. "I booked 'em at Johnny's Lounge. Best bar and music club in the 'bottom', hell! in the city. They were good. Real good."

"So what happened?"

"Don't know. They's just gone. We had a contract. I woulda made 'em big. Don't know, just gone."

"But you must have asked around. Anybody tell you anything?"

He wheezed away from the receiver. "I askt. I askt everywhere and everybody. But nobody could tell me nothin'. Not one thing. Like they was never here."

"Since you booked them into Johnny's that night, wouldn't you have been there to watch them perform?"

"Didn't need to. They were good. I had other lesser known acts appearing around the 'bottom' and I needed to see how they were doing..." He coughed. "...I wasn't there that night."

"Didn't you ever wonder why their disappearance was so abrupt? If they were your top group, it seems to me you would have moved heaven and earth to find out what happened."

"I did! I did what I could, but soon the demands of running the company took more of my time until finally, I had to shut it down. I didn't have the money to keep it running. I lost it all."

I never intended to cause additional pain to a painful memory, so I thanked him and started to hang up.

"You ever find out what happened, you tell me please," he interrupted. "You ever find out what happened to my boys, you come tell me. I gots to know...okay?"

I gave him an emphatic yes and wandered back over to the desk where printed copies of the articles I'd located on microfiche laid unevenly scattered.

The question of what to do with what I learned would have to wait and be dissected along with everything else that didn't make any sense. I wondered why Morgan Rivers hadn't been included in Erotica's initial folder of information. If I found him in the phone book so could she.

Throughout my search I became curiously in awe of a year in which I was a mere biological diminutive devil completely oblivious to the greater world around me. Some would argue that I'd maintained that quality, only more so, in my adult years. There was a headline for everyday and an explanation as to why it was there. The world had changed dramatically in forty years and that was an understatement not worth mentioning. It was interesting scanning the *Detroit Free Press* as a way of getting some sense of what the world was attempting to do as I moved from toilet mastery to a world of recognizable sights and sounds brought to you every evening on one of the big three networks. I flipped over page after printed page of notes, hoping that my hieroglyphics would open up a possibility that I was unable to see.

It was a hope.

Eye weary and shoulder cramped, I emerged from the library during the latter part of the morning, just a tad bit on the hungry side. The sky had become overcast with white and gray clouds jockeying for the lower ceiling. Knowing that morning traffic would be manageable, I decided to tap into a resource that for over a year has been an emotional roller coaster made easier by the fact that we seldom tried to get in each other's way.

***

I motored down Jefferson Avenue into downtown Detroit thinking of what I'd say to my on-again, off-again love interest who spends her non-Lincoln Keller hours as a homicide detective with Detroit's finest. Our latest argument dealt with commitment. We settled it by making love on her beige carpet. Every pent up frustration, need and desire burst through sweaty pores and intermittent gasps. We rolled inside each other like grains of sand falling through an hour glass, filling up only to bottom out and refuel. Commitments were starting to be made as we rested from the second offering. Before we started a third round, she was called to investigate a homicide. That was six days ago. Our answering machines had filled the communication void since that time.

I caught a metered parking space just as someone was pulling out into traffic. My day for parking spaces. I was on a roll. Why can't I have this kind of luck with the Lottery? There was still fifteen minutes of time left in the meter, so I popped in another quarter and walked the remaining half a block to the granite stepped entrance of 1300 Beaubien Street, Detroit's famed First Precinct.

The 1922 constructed gray gothic fortress struck me as an embarkation point for the tired, the poor, the hopeless, the downtrodden and abused. Those hapless who sought help from Detroit's last Calvary...and first line of defense. The building had weathered every social and economic change to hit Detroit and stood steadfast in utter defiance of city planners who'd like to see it demolished. It was a perceptual conflict to the sleek and modern marble walled Frank Murphy Hall of Justice that sat on an adjacent corner. The overworked, understaffed and sometimes disenchanted men and women in blue spent each day trying to restore some semblance of order to a growing social cancer. It reminded me of my days as a patrol officer in Oakland, California. The only difference being the weather and the Pacific Ocean. I came back to Detroit because I didn't like what was happening in Oakland. In Detroit, I liked it even less.

I walked through the tiled floor reception area past the people who sat waiting, welded together in unmatching color vinyl seats. The reasons were endless; report a theft, a mugging, identify a body or just have someone listen to their complaints. An elderly blind woman with her leader dog stood at the chest high, V-cornered mahogany front desk waiting to fill out a complaint form. Several monitors hung from the ceiling, behind the waiting denizens, and provided a panoramic view of all activity in and around the fortress. It was a way station for the dispirited. The elderly woman was being serviced by Sergeant Manfred Stovic, a thirty year veteran assigned to the desk because of a bullet he took in the hip ten years ago. He had a hip replacement and every week threatened to retire. His fair complexion showed the wear and tear of a street cop's life. Vertical facial lines created an imaginary barrier around his face. There were enough crows feet around the corners of his light blue, baggy eyes to merit the attention of the Audubon Society. But he was clean shaven with a pair of false teeth to bring life to a tired smile. He was affectionately known as 'Gabe': his ears looked like they'd been removed from the head of Clark Gable. He had a beer belly, a drinker's nose with enough gin blossoms to make a bouquet, and wore a pair of brown reading glasses that never seemed to fit.

"Gabe," I said as I signed in on the visitor's log. "Malone upstairs?"

"Yeah, Keller. Busy night. Try not to take up too much of her time," he replied as he handed me a visitor's badge.

"Nurturing doesn't suit you, Gabe. Irritates your glands. Last time I checked, Malone had a mother."

Gabe was caustic and rude. A borderline bully with a cynical manner. I liked him. He was the father I never had. I was grateful for that.

"I got a bullet with your name on it, Keller, and you'll never hear it coming."

"You write it out yourself or did you have help?"

A youthful officer answering the phones suppressed a laugh. I smiled at Gabe and eased through oak paneled doors and up the stairs to the Homicide Unit on the fifth floor, opting to avoid the usually laggard elevator.

Homicide was busy for that time of the late morning. The obvious un-rehearsed, unchoreographed noise of phones, voices, computer terminals and a few typewriters bounced around the room like frequent echoes in a canyon. The standard, institutional, metal desks showed signs of burns from forgotten cigarettes and round coffee stains formed from the bottoms of Styrofoam cups just needing eyes and a mouth to form happy faces. The initials of previous investigators were scratched into the painted black surface and coat hangers were twisted into the holes of broken drawer handles. Piles of reports lay strewn across several desks, unmatched and unbalanced wooden four-legged and three-wheeled metal chairs sat under the desks as a matter of practical necessity while Little Caesar pizza boxes were stuffed in the round metallic trash cans. Everyone seemed too busy to notice their standard chaos.

Off to my left a placid faced detective was listening to comments from a distraught elderly woman. Through her labored statement, I surmised that her husband of many years had been found murdered and she'd just identified the body. A blond female detective was yelling into a receiver as she was jotting down information on one of the many standard forms that plague a police officer's life. I also overheard two other detectives discussing a case in which three people were found shot each in the back of the head. Phones rang, chairs scraped across the floor and desks overflowed with stacks of paper, file folders and different culinary debris. I suddenly

became aware of the motion. It seemed that there was this constant movement of bodies in an unorchestrated collage of exploding energy. None of
the motions seemed connected, but bound by a collective purpose. I felt
like I was watching a Steven Spielberg action drama without the John Williams soundtrack. During all the years I'd spent as a patrol officer with the
Oakland PD, working the streets, securing crime scenes and supposedly
making the community safe, I never thought I was part of an on-going mini
drama whose ending was no more obvious than an afternoon soap opera.

I walked past the row of desks toward the back of the room. The dis-
embodied, scattered voices became more amplified and focused. Two detectives stood near the burnt coffee pot, drinking the sludge and discussing
their theory on a recent homicide. Another veteran detective rummaged
through a series of reports. He yelled, "Where's the goddamn Putman file?"
it seemed to no one in particular.

Over at the right hand desk, Detective Candy Malone was busy writing
out a report. No, not Candice. Candy. She pushed her hand through her
medium length jet black hair and released an exasperated sigh. There were
two fans blowing to try and minimize the heat, but she seemed unruffled.
Her dark blue, sleeveless halter top showed no sighs of perspiration. She
wore light beige casual slacks and no jewelry except for the thin banded,
small diamond on her right second finger. She stood taller than her five-
feet, eight inch Nautilus crafted frame.

Her almond beige complexion highlighted inviting dark eyes and sharply
edged black eyebrows. Her round small nose brought balance to a full lipped
mouth and teeth that a dentist would love to have as a model for patients.

Had it really been six days since I'd melted into her flesh?

Focus was going to be a problem.

She concentrated hard enough to not notice me approach her. I sat down
on the edge of the desk.

"Guess what I'm thinking and win the prize."

Those were tired eyes that glared back, momentarily surprised by my
appearance. "What you're thinking is hardly a challenge. It's interactive,
dirty and rhymes with luck."

"Which I haven't had much of lately. Except for parking. Otherwise,
it's been six days. Some monk called me and asked how I manage to stay
so focused. I'm worried."

"Normally I'd love this banter, Linc," she said after a long sigh. "But
it's summer you know, and a hot one at that."

"Tell me about it. Everybody starts the summer with their fuse lit. The heat just makes it burn faster." I was blocking the flow of air being blown by the small oscillating fan as Malone pushed a stack of papers to one side of her desk.

"All shifts are on overtime. Last night alone we had four domestic shootings, three vehicular homicides, two stabbings..."

"...and a partridge in a pear tree," I said in melodic sarcasm.

She grinned slightly. "With his feathers plucked. What brings you here, Linc?"

"Testosterone build up. Detroit may become a wasteland any moment now."

"Take two cold showers and call me in the morning." She pulled out one of those standard institutional forms and began filling in some blank spaces.

"Okay, sweetheart. You win. I need information...forty years old...something from the Fifties."

Her look said get real. "Try the Internet."

"You're more interactive. Thought maybe you could up the info on your computer and save me some research time."

"Even if I could, Linc, I'd have to wait in line. Besides, I'll bet it's not even in the data base. You'd probably have to look through the archives for a case from the Fifties."

"Well, couldn't you...?"

"...No, I couldn't. I'm up to my ass in present day murders. Going back forty years would be stretching my caseload just a little too far."

"Let me tell you what's happenin'." I spoke quickly and covered as much of what I knew without being too revealing, especially about my client. I explained that most of the usual avenues for finding missing people had already been pursued, so before I pushed it any further, I wanted to get a handle on the possible murder scenario. "So all I need to know is: what, if any, missing person reports were made on these guys between August and October of 1955? Is that too much to ask?"

"Normally, no. But this is a bad time, Linc. I can't promise you a day or time because we're really catching it from all sides. This has not turned out to be a fun summer. Plus, another homeless person was found out on Belle Isle this morning with his throat slit. Looks like our annual visit from that murderous creep. Me and Constantino are primaries, but that won't last but a minute." She glanced over to a glassed cubicle with Lieutenant

Ray Steen in black letters on the door window. "Lieutenant's in there now discussing the case with the detective he partnered with when this thing first broke six years ago."

I peered into the office and saw the standing profile of a man who looked to be about two inches taller than me. He was a shade darker, more mahogany than chestnut, with an evenly trimmed beard and mustache and dressed out of GQ casual. "Who is he?" I asked.

"Garrison Brock. Actually, Dr. Garrison Brock now. I worked with him just before he retired. Good detective. He and the Lieutenant had the highest clearance rate of homicide detectives. He's teaching criminology for the State University at Detroit's downtown campus."

"Sounds like a smart man. So, you gonna help me?"

"No promises, Linc. But I'll see what I can do." She snatched the list of names and placed it next to her phone. "Now beat it, lover, before I have you arrested for loitering."

"You want to plan to get together sometime before this century is over?"

"Just need a little time. You know how this job works."

"Yeah. I know. Maybe I'll surprise you and one night when you least expect it, I'll strip nude, dip myself in honey and jump your bones just as you're coming through the door."

"Try not to drip any honey on my rug," she said grinning slightly.

"We already did, babe. But that was six nights ago."

She promised to call me later, but she never said what later meant. I left figuring I had several stops to make before the day ended. I just didn't know then how long the day was really going to be.

Chapter 5

I took the John C. Lodge from downtown to the West Grand Boulevard exit and followed the three-laned street for four blocks until I reached the home of WHIP AM.

The station is nestled on the second floor of what used to be a two-story home similar in design, style and dimension to a number of homes that sit on both sides of the Boulevard. The homes are spacious for their location and make for an odd mixture of residences for families and businesses.

I parked on the wide street and walked through the brass framed entrance to a small, dimly lit lobby where a late twenties, copper toned woman sat behind a windowed reception area.

I walked to the window and spoke through the circled opening. I asked for Roosevelt Keller and showed her my ID.

She called upstairs, mumbled something and motioned me toward the stairs.

I skip-stepped the partially carpeted stairs until I reached the top landing. Ignoring the black backgrounded kiosk, I turned left and followed the narrow hall to the last office on the right. A small wooden speaker was attached to a corner of the wall and I could just barely hear the music being played by the disc jockey working his shift.

I tapped on the open oak door and stepped into the office cluttered with Billboard magazines and a number of music dailies piled on top of a large, round coffee table. Two hard back, green and white cushioned chairs sat adjacent to the table. The walls were a pictorial display of the WHIP FCC license, Rosie's diploma from Michigan State, certificates of community service and pictures of Rosie with some well known music celebrities.

Rosie was leaning back in his swivel chair staring at the blue background IBM computer screen, seemingly oblivious to the world around him.

"Seeking inspiration from the guru inside the processor?" I asked as I pulled up a similar chair next to him and sat down.

He continued staring at the screen, finally pushing a hand through his hair and sighing as if he'd come to the end of a long road. "It's not inspiration I need, but an opening paragraph for this on-going gambling issue between Detroit and our moving-toward-the-national-spotlight governor. I need it for my five minute afternoon CityBeat commentary." He turned toward me with a slightly curled lip. "There's only so many ways you can say 'the trials and tribulations of conservative politics' blah, blah, blah."

"Open with the blah, blah, blah part. I think it's more colorful. And informative."

He ignored the comment and used his mouse to pull down a menu page. "I went into our data base to see what I could find, and as I suspected there's not a whole lot of information on black singing groups from the 1950s. The few music magazines there were at that time didn't want to give a lot of coverage to 'negra' singers. Plus, Elvis was starting to hit it big about that time." He pointed, clicked, tapped keys and did whatever it is people do to get a computer to sing the right notes. I hadn't quite given my soul over to a computer. I still owned an IBM Selectric and it worked fine for me. Although it was becoming increasingly difficult to get parts. "Here's something." A computer-generated black and white picture appeared on the screen with an accompanying article. It was a short piece written with less style than a Sixty's beach movie and enough facts to make an arrest. The Sentiments were making an appearance at Johnny's Lounge the night of September 16, 1955 to celebrate the release of their first album entitled 'Sentimentally Yours' and the single with the same name. "Looks like they were starting to make some noise," Rosie murmured. Without asking, he pulled down the menu page and clicked on the print command. "I'll make you a copy of the article. So tell me, Linc, what's really going on here?"

"Just like I told you last night. My client said The Sentiments just disappeared and didn't leave a forwarding address. I'm trying to find out why. Best as I can tell, her husband must have a thing for nostalgia."

"Uh-huh. And why do I get the feeling that there's a story here?"

I shrugged. "The need to search for truths where there are none. It's a flaw of true journalism."

He gave the printed article to me, casting an arched eyebrow. "You know, if I had time I could find out what's really behind all this. If I really wanted to know, I could find out. You know that. So why try and hide it?"

"I wouldn't want to inhibit your search by revealing the truth before you've had the chance to pose the universal question."

"Which is?"

I folded the article, stood up and leaned forward, staring directly into Rosie's tired, red shaded eyes. "Is that all there is? It's a philosophical classic sang with seductive curiosity by Peggy Lee."

"Well, fortunately, music is my life and the search for hidden truths shall forever inspire me onward."

"Thanks, Rosie."

"What's your next move?" he asked as he clicked back over to his article.

"I hit the streets in search of answers. Best place to start is Johnny's Lounge. That was their last known location."

"That was forty years ago, Linc. Is that place still around? And if it is, who'd still be around that would remember anything about a singing group called The Sentiments? Or any group, for that matter?"

"Good questions that can't be answered sitting here jawboning with you."

"One other thing, Linc," he said as he ripped a sheet of paper from a yellow memo pad. "You remember 'Michael Cross, The Ladies' Boss'?"

It didn't require a moment's run through the memory files. "Sure. He was the morning DJ on WJMB when we were growing up. Why?"

"He still does his Sixties salute across the street at the Soul Sonata. I know for a fact that he's setting up for the 1960's Soul Cavalcade going on there tonight. He does this mostly to meet with, and be seen by, those of us who grew up to his early morning rhymes and chimes. Might be worth a conversation with him. I can get him on the phone and call ahead for you."

"Why don't you do that, Rosie?" I always appreciate a lead from family.

He nodded. "It's Roosevelt, like the president. Not Rosie like the riveter."

"Mom sure loved her presidents."

While he punched in a phone number, I waved good bye and left Rosie's office to go meet with the celebrated, legendary disc jockey from my days as an exploding bundle of hormones. Michael Cross, 'The Ladies' Boss' electrified the airwaves of AM radio during that embryonic period of white owned stations trying to develop a 'soul' format. His arrival in Detroit during the early 1950s broke the traditional presentation of disc jockeys and the music they played and moved it toward a 'personality' celebrity format. He spoke in non stop rhymes. I suspect that he may have been the only person on this planet to find a legitimate way of rhyming the word 'orange' with something from the English language. There were a lot of us who developed a 'cool rap' because we listened to his night format with eager anticipation. He was a legend.

Just across the street and three buildings over sat the once famed Soul Sonata. Despite its long history, the building with the large yellow background marquee and big red letters has since managed to look like a presentable place for people to meet and cabaret.

I pulled open the metal plated doors and walked through a brown tiled lobby until I reached a large open area that held a mixture of tables and chairs on its parquet floor. I walked past the few people standing around or having a drink at the bar in the corner as I worked my way past the two-level stage that held various pieces of equipment for playing music. Since my mission was also information gathering, I spotted the famed Michael Cross occupying a table and chair near the bar on the balcony promenade. He was partially surrounded by several people who were either laughing or talking with him in a festive atmosphere of memories. Marvin Gaye's recording of 'Stubborn Kind of Fellow' drifted melodically in the background.

Even from a distance he seemed to be the illumination of a thousand lit candles rather than an actual physical being. I think it started with that envious full crop of white hair, pumped, wavy and combed neatly to the back. His emerald green eyes, unruffled walnut complexion and slender physique would have convinced the average observer that he hovered some-where in the mid-forties age range. Only his legion of fans would know that he was at least sixty-five. A good looking sixty-five.

As I stepped around his admirers, I was impressed with how well his combination of a white suit and shoes with a blue ruffled shirt and white tie clung to him like a second layer of skin.

"Tailored tough," I mumbled.

He'd just finished whispering something to a svelte mid-thirties bomb-shell in a black evening gown with a slit up the left leg that stopped danger-ously close to the point where imagination is no longer a required function. A quick reminder of Erotica from yesterday afternoon.

When he turned to face me, I extended my hand and he flashed a white tooth full smile the likes of which would make a denture wearer resort to thievery.

"Mr. Cross," I began, "my name is Lincoln Keller. My brother is Roosevelt Keller and I've been a big fan of yours for as long as I can re-member." I noticed his fingers were well manicured and three of the four fingers had a ring with a different color jewel as its centerpiece.

"You're most kind, young man. Your brother, THE RK Display just called." His throaty voice still had that practiced richness and enunciation. He removed a gold plated pen in anticipation of my wanting an autograph.

I hadn't heard Rosie called the THE RK Display in a long time. I let it go. "Besides getting your autograph," I said trying to cover for that over-sight, "I'd like to ask you a few questions about your early days in radio."

"I'm sure you have better ways to spend your time than listen to the historical ramblings of my misspent youth."

"I would consider it enlightening."

He motioned to the seat in front of him. "Then please have a seat. Let's see what questions you have that can't be answered in a reference book."

An eager young waitress stopped by and took both our orders. I stayed with water and lime, Michael ordered a rum and coke.

"Mr. Cross..."

"...everyone calls me Michael," came his humble interruption.

"Fine. But you've earned the right to be called Mr. Cross and that's what I'd like to do." He nodded. "I'm conducting an investigation into the disappearance of a group of singers from the 1950s and it was suggested that you might be helpful."

"Mr. Keller," he said after three chuckles, "there were a number of groups from that time who disappeared from the scene as well as soloists both male and female. Just because you could sing didn't guarantee that you'd be heard, especially back in the Fifties."

"Why was that?" I asked as a way of getting into the topic.

"Oh, lots of reasons. Many of which had nothing to do with the artist. When I started here back in '52, black music or soul or rhythm and blues, sometimes known as that evil 'negra' music, didn't have very many outlets in the first place. Radio stations were limited in what they could play and they typically stayed with the sure-bet, white pompadour groups and singers than take a chance on black artists. Artists like Nat 'King' Cole, Dinah Washington, Dakota Staton and others were the exception among black entertainers that received any kind of consistent airplay. People like Louie Armstrong, Duke Ellington and Count Basie were gifted musicians and song writers who showcased their music through the seamless blending of a talented band. I'm only citing those obvious examples because they're probably closer to your understanding of music of that era. But make no mistake, Mr. Keller, the talent you heard was only a small portion of what was there."

"Let me state the obvious: you've seen a lot of talent come and go."

He paused and flashed that ivory smile. "More than I care to remember and some that I wish I could."

"In the early Fifties there was a local group that everyone seemed to agree was a sure winner. They were known as The Sentiments and seemed to do quite well among the local crowd."

"Saywhat!" he exclaimed after an unblinked momentary pause. "The Sentiments! I haven't thought about them for years now. Charles Treadwell was the lead singer although they could have been the first group to boast of having five lead singers. Those boys were good. I used to wonder what happened to them."

"Then you've heard of them?"

He leaned back in his chair seemingly talking to the ceiling. "I first saw those boys sing at a talent contest we sponsored back in '53 and it was at one of the local union halls we used to rent for dances, shows and other kinds of events like that. They beat out a guy named Tico Robinson, T.R. everybody called him. Boy ended up strung out on drugs, but The Sentiments were good. You could tell that they were taught under the careful hand of a Baptist Church Youth Choir leader. Most people in the business didn't know that the Baptist Church was the place you went to hear talent in its purest form, because they were taught to sing to the deaf lady in the last row of the balcony. Those boys were good," he said shaking his head. "It's too bad they were never recorded."

"But they were!" I said. "I have a cassette tape of an album they recorded entitled 'Sentimentally Yours'. They recorded on the Shadowcast label."

"Shee-it. No wonder they weren't heard. That group of fly-by-night losers didn't know how to grease the palms to get those boys airplay."

"As in payola?"

"You don't win if you don't grease the skin," he said coyly. "Remember, the Fifties was basically AM radio. Low band, low frequency and not a lot of licenses. For those that did own a station, they had to make money. They didn't pay the best salaries at that time and in a big market like Detroit a group's popularity could skyrocket. So how did competing companies ensure that their groups and music were heard? Envelopes of cash under the table to the DJs and Program Directors. That was the way of the world. The bigger record label companies had it down to an art. Cash was openly flaunted. It was just an accepted practice. Smaller companies had to work harder to get their groups heard. Shadowcast records didn't work hard enough or smart enough."

By now the waitress had returned with our drinks. "So the larger companies could just out-pay the smaller companies to make sure their artists were heard."

"Or to make sure certain artists weren't heard."

"What do you mean?" I asked, knowing the answer, but I wanted to keep him talking.

He took a sip of his drink. "Goes on in athletics all the time. Sometimes a coach will offer a kid a scholarship not because he intends to play him, but just to keep another coach from getting him. Worked the same back then. Record companies would pay big money just to make sure a certain group or singer wasn't heard. Usually because the singer or group they wanted to stifle was more talented than the ones they had. They couldn't afford to risk the head-to-head competition. So a budding young DJ looking to make a name for himself could earn a fair share of money by giving the appearance that he might favor some up and coming group over the already established ones."

"Makes you wonder how Berry Gordy pulled it off."

"Read his autobiography. It's all in there." He paused again to take a swallow from his drink. "You know the real irony? Had Shadowcast hung in there and just played the game a little harder, they might have beat Berry Gordy out of the box. Motown records was only a few years away. Wouldn't that have been something? Two black owned record companies doing battle in Detroit. Man, talk about some of the talent that could have made it."

"The Sentiments disappeared in 1955 and no one seems to know why," I said. "What do you think happened?"

"Well, if they didn't go through that thing of egos, drugs and women, then maybe the timing of their voices just didn't fit the moment." He paused slightly, then continued, "The Temptations. Their blend of voices and style were perfect for the trends being set in the 60s. Had they been five years earlier, they might not never have been heard. Maybe that's what happened to The Sentiments. Maybe their voices were ahead of their time."

"Yeah. Maybe," I said with deliberate emphasis on the maybe.

Michael's shoulders relaxed and he looked remorseful. "Sorry I couldn't be more help to you. There's no doubt in my mind that those boys were talented. But, quite frankly, I was too busy trying to carve out my own career to be concerned about theirs."

"I understand." I left a ten dollar bill on the table and stood up. "I appreciate your time and your insights. It did prove to be most enlightening."

We shook hands. "Linc. I have a couple of questions to ask you. Actually, they're more of a favor than questions."

"If it's within my power...sure."

"If you ever find out what happened to those boys, I'd like to know." I nodded. "And...I'd like a copy of that cassette you have. I'd like to hear them again," he added.

"I'll see that you get one," I said to ease the sentimentality of the moment. I made a mental note to ask Rosie to make another tape for me.

Michael Cross thanked me and returned to the admiration and conversation of his loyal legions.

I said good bye and I made it back outside to my Nova. Michael Cross was convinced that The Sentiments would have made it big if not for

Shadowcasts Records' inability to handle the payola angle. I imagined a young energetic Morgan Rivers trying desperately to grab a foothold on the R & B market at a time when the record industry was starting to value blacks as singers, not as owners in the business. If Morgan was bitter, it made sense to me.

I had the address for Johnny's Lounge. It was still in the Yellow Pages. So, I also knew it still had its door open. Less glorious, I supposed, but still open for business. I was counting on Johnny's having a history of good customer service that supported a group of long term customers.

***

Johnny's Lounge still occupied a prehistoric spot on the east side in the heart of what is still called the Blackbottom by some. It was a two-story brick building with blue tainted windows and a brass handle wooden door with major discoloration at the bottom and top. Above the door, a yellow back marquee with black letters announced to the world the names of local entertainment currently gracing the stage. Ben Black and Blue was appearing in a repeat performance. An open, litter strewn field surrounding the decaying lounge, provided parking where homes and lives once thrived.

I parked adjacent to the building, and after entering, followed the worn red carpet to an area where soft brown vinyl chairs where turned upside down on tables just large enough to accommodate a four hand game of bid wist. There was a black painted stage that held microphone stands and the wiring typically found running down the leg of any would be singer.

Johnny's was open for business, what little there was. Two sullen faced cadavers sat hunched over the L-shaped bar drinking a glass of beer and being serviced by a bartender who looked like every drinker's nightmare on the morning after. It wasn't quite noon yet.

The bartender'd seen better days. Her red rouge on puffy cheeks against her chestnut complexion was an invitation to be sinful. She had a 'healthy' figure and a bosom that looked like two moons on a collision course. An obvious silver haired wig rounded out the silver eye shadow on almond shaped eyes. She was a full size model stuffed into a compact silk blouse and waist tight black slacks.

"What'll you have, sugar?" Her voiced rasped through the dead silence and a ready-to-sin smile.

I eased down on the rickety bar stool. "Beer for one. Information for two."

"Those we got plenty of, sugar." She batted her long false eyelashes. "On tap or a bottle?"

"Whatever you got cold on tap," I said. While she poured the drink I took out one of my business cards. She placed the drink on an octagonal coaster with a picture of a guitar in the center. "Name's Keller." I slid the card over to her. "Lincoln Keller. I'm a private investigator."

She read the card and nodded. "Private dick, eh? Never met one before. You lookin' for someone, something or some trouble?"

"I'll take the lesser of the three evils."

"Well, that takes care of your night with me." She smiled. "What do you need?"

"Have you worked here long?"

"Only since the seventh day of the creation."

"From what I remember, God rested that day."

"I know. He came here for a malt liquor. I served it to Him. He was a great tipper."

"That's a lot farther back than I want to go," I said. "How about I stick with information needed from this century?"

"Don't know, sugar. My short term memory tends to short circuit, but I can recall certain long term events in specific detail."

I took out the black and white picture I had of The Sentiments and slid it across to her. "Any chance you remember these guys?"

She studied the picture for a few moments.

"Hey, Stella!" called one of the barflys. "My glass is empty."

"So's your head, Willie." She glanced up at me. "Hang on a sec." I watched her saunter down to the end of the bar, twist off the cap from a bottle of beer and drop it down in front of the now satisfied customer.

She picked up the picture and stared as if she were trying to recall some thought locked away among the millions that are part of her history. "This looks like one of the acts we used to draw back during the days when this lounge was on the places to be. When my dad opened this place back in the 30s, hardly a night went by when our entertainment didn't play to a packed house. We drew them from all over. You should have seen this place back then. Any singer or group trying to break into the big time had to come to Johnny's Lounge."

Early in an interview is often tricky. Do I listen and let her reflect, or do I ask a question that focuses her attention?

She answered the question for me. "I remember this group. They were headed to the big time. Beautiful voices. Nice stage presence. Good show-manship. I think they even recorded an album. Played here about two or three times." She stopped her reflective journey and gave me a curious look. "What's your interest?"

"Strictly professional. I have a client trying to locate any of the members. According to her they played a gig here, and then promptly vanished. No one's seen them since. My client is interested in why."

"Who's your client?"

"Confidential," I said as I took a swig from the cold, foamy glass. "Any idea what happened that night?"

She squinted. "Probably performed three sets like most acts did during that time. Got their applause and pay and went home. We usually shut down about two in the morning back then."

"You said probably."

Sighing deeply, she said, "That was a long time ago, Mr. Keller. I was a lot younger. Seventeen to be exact, a lot thinner and not needing a wig that's hotter than salsa on a devil burger. I worked here because my dad didn't have a son and my mom was too busy asking the Lord for forgive-ness for living off the wages of sin. I turned a few heads back then. Now when I turn a head it's only because he wants his mug refilled. Anyway, there was one head I turned during that time. Wavy hair, light tone, pencil sharp mustache and drove a Cadillac. Always wore a diamond stick-pin in his tie. Everybody called him Diamond Jim. He was ten years older than me and just as experienced."

"You said all this to say what, Stella?"

"You're cute. Keep the old lady from rambling." She leaned forward on the counter. "I said all that to say that I can recall The Sentiments' last night so vividly because I wasn't here. I lied to my father and went to be with Diamond Jim. I didn't make it back that night. I was scared to death of what my father would do. He could be a real hardass sometimes. But when I tipped in that morning, my dad hadn't returned home yet. My mother was asleep and later on that afternoon when I finally did catch up with my old man, he didn't say anything. He seemed distracted, like something was on his mind. I didn't think about it. Just thanked God for the lucky break. I remember asking my dad how it went that evening. He just mumbled some-thing and that was the last I heard of it. I never thought to ask about The Sentiments until weeks later and then I was told that they were going out on the road. I didn't give it much thought after that, especially when I found out that I was pregnant."

"I don't suppose your dad is..."

"...died in 1975. Found him laying in an alley several blocks from here. Someone had beat him to death. We suspected it was some of the local low-life, but nothing we could prove. I inherited this place and all its clientele."

"You know anybody I might be able to talk to?"

She thought for a moment. "This old neighborhood sure ain't what it used to be. You might try Mable's Beauty Salon over on Clay. If anybody knows something, it would be Mable Johnson. If not, try the guy next door, Joshua Hazelton." I thanked Stella and left a twenty on the counter. "Beer's not that expensive."

"But the information is. And it's appreciated."

"No problem, sugar. Next time you come around bring your party face. We don't pull 'em in like we used to, but we never forgot how to make a person feel good."

After I removed the 'Club' from my steering wheel, I fired up the engine and eased into the thickening traffic and headed to Mable's Beauty Salon. I promised myself I would return to Johnny's Lounge. Stella had a lot of history that needed to be told. By then I'd be in a listening mood.

***

Stella had said there were two businesses from that era still open and run by the same owner and in the same three-story ash gray 'attached' building. Usually the owners lived upstairs in the apartments over the business, thus making the cost of commuting a negligible item. Mable's Beauty Shop was one of them, and that's the one I entered first. The yellow background of the dingy marquee listed styles, prices and hours for all who entered. No appointment was necessary.

I opened the steel bar covered door and stepped into a large open area complete with waiting chairs of indistinguishable name and origin lined up against one wall, sometimes separated by wide top wooden coffee tables with an assortment of magazines, many of which predated Sojourner Truth.

There were four women, who I assumed to be beauticians, all engaged in various stages of talk and hair design with their unstrapped customers.

I walked across the black and white checkered floor to the first chair in the row. The red haired beautician was adorned with freckles against her light tan complexion. She had brown eyes and four jeweled studs piercing each ear lobe.

"Excuse me," I started. "Is the owner around?"

"Who's asking?" she asked with a wink of her left eye.

"Lincoln Keller. I'm trying to find out some information on some guys who lived around here years ago. Nothing dangerous or sinister and I'm not with the government. I'm a private investigator."

"Not like any of the dicks I've seen," she said with a short laugh, exposing her front gold tooth. Her comment drew several cackles and cat calls. "Well, Mr. Keller, you go right over there to that door, knock and ask for Mable." She nodded toward a walnut covered door with a brass doorknob.

I thanked her and walked the path between the women having their hair done and the one's who were waiting. I didn't know if it was me or just a stereotype, but it seemed quieter than I would have thought.

I knocked twice on the door and a phlegm voice said to come in.

I entered the small office, made smaller by an unusually large desk with a veneer top and metal legs. The room was filled with bottles, jars and tubes of various hair products and calendar advertisements. A brown metal shelf stood tilted against a wall loaded with an assortment of books, magazines and journals.

"May I help you?" asked the woman whose laugh lines were deeply etched like cuts that never went away. She peered up from an accounting book, gazing at me through her half moon glasses. Her gray hair hung shoulder length and she was dressed in a multi-colored kimono. She was sixty-five if she was a day, but I'd never say that to her face. A square shaped ashtray sat within inches of her lank arms and was filled with lipstick covered cigarette butts. There were enough filter tipped butts to stuff an elephant's mattress.

"Are you the owner...Miss Johnson?"

"That's right," she replied with a raspy caution.

"Hi. I'm Lincoln Keller. I'm doing some investigative work and I wonder if you'd mind answering a few questions." I had already removed a business card and gave it to her.

"Depends," she replied while she read the card.

I removed a cut-out copy of The Sentiments and placed it on her desk. She picked up the picture, holding it by the edges. "That's a 1955 photo of a group known as The Sentiments. They were all local boys who grew up in this area. Do you recognize any of them?"

She studied the photo, taking off her glasses to squint at the picture. "1955? That's a long time ago. I didn't open this shop until '53 and that's been...," she paused, "...much too long. They in some kind of trouble?"

"Not as far as I know. They vanished sometime in October of 1955 and no one's seen or heard from them since.

"Oh?" she said. I nodded. "I don't recognize their faces. They got names?" I smiled and told her all five of their names. "Thought I might recognize the last names. Not many of us left from the old days. Highway ran most folks away, poverty got the others. Them that's left got broken promises." She sighed. "Sorry, son. I don't know any of those boys."

I wasn't deterred. It was still early. "I appreciate your time. I'm going to check with Mr. Hazelton next door. I understand he's also been around here for a long time."

"That was true until two weeks ago, son. Mr. Hazelton died two weeks ago Thursday. Went in his sleep." A slight mist briefly came to her eyes.

"I'm sorry to hear that. I'm sure he was a good man...and a good friend."

She nodded and quickly changed the subject. "Tell you what, son, if I happen to think of anyone who might be helpful, I'll give you a call."

I thanked her and strolled back outside.

I checked those two names off my list and drove to the next place of business. I was optimistic that someone would know something that would prove helpful.

Chapter 6

As I rolled into the third hour of my search, my optimism was starting to wane. It's very normal for an investigation to run into major dead ends, especially those that have been forty years in the making. Still I hoped my luck was running better than it had thus far. I checked with several of the remaining businesses and churches, speaking with anyone who might remember something about the group or its individual members. I spent more time listening to the recollections of people to whom I wasn't interested and nothing about The Sentiments.

The breezy cool morning's partially clouded sky turned into the afternoon's overcast sky with an 80 plus temperature and very little breeze. I wiped the little beads of sweat from my brow as I exited the local liquor store and stepped back on the sidewalk. My conversation with the patronly owner was particularly difficult since we tried to conduct it through the thick bullet proof plexi-glass common to so many establishments.

I was leaning on the hood of my Nova, crossing off the store on my list when I felt a sharp jolt to my back. I quickly looked up only to be greeted by a gap toothed, bearded behemoth with wavy black hair and dark glasses.

"Look, bro," I said, hoping the appeal to the brotherhood would soften his disposition. "My wallet is in my back pocket. There's only a few..."

He shook his head. "You're wanted." He motioned to the blue Lincoln Towncar parked in front of my truck. "You'll ride in the back."

"Hey, I'm kinda busy right now." He dug the circular shaft farther into my side. "But it's nothing that can't wait."

He smiled. "You carryin'?"

"Is that a trick question?" He smiled and jabbed the gun's barrel deeper into my side. ".38 shoulder holster, left side."

He removed my gun and stuck it in his jacket pocket. I was led to the Lincoln Towncar. I opened the passenger side of the two-door luxury ride.

"Figures it would be a two door," I said sarcastically of my name-sake vehicle.

Gap Tooth flipped the front seat forward. I climbed into the spacious back seat with the light blue plush velour wraparound seating, a side panel loaded with buttons and a CD-ROM system better than anything I've seen.

When my abductor climbed into the driver's seat, he made a quick adjustment of the rearview mirror and zipped away from the curb, completely ignoring any possible coming traffic.

"You got a name?" I asked.

He glanced into the rearview mirror and then looked straight ahead.

"Is it fair to ask where you're taking me, or to whom?"

He said nothing.

"How about them Tigers?"

He turned up the volume to the CD I recognized as Grover Washington's 'Mr. Magic'. Obviously he wasn't in a talkative mood. I leaned back against the seating and watched the scenery through the outside tinted glass.

"How about turning down the air conditioner?" I asked.

He touched a button on the front panel and the cold air flowed a little slower.

"Thanks," I said. "How about...?"

He pushed a button that rolled up a glass panel between he and I. I caught just a trace of a grin as the panel sealed shut.

"I can take a hint, buzzbrain," I said while smiling. It seemed my only options were to scream unmercifully and hope someone heard me through the sound proof windows...or sit back and enjoy the ride.

I wasn't a very good screamer, so...

***

It was a short ride. We came to a stop outside a one-level building known as the Wayne Turner Community Center. The painted yellow brick building was designed like a ranch home only longer and with office space. There was an assortment of activity around the building from children rollerblading to elderly gentlemen engaged in a fierce game of checkers.

I was let out of the car and thought this was an odd place for an abduction.

"This way," the driver said pointing to an area behind the building.

"Try not to talk so much," I said. "It doesn't fit your style."

I followed him as he followed a sidewalk past the side of the building. Once I was able to focus on the noises coming from the back, I knew something about where we'd end up.

It was confirmed when we came upon an excellently designed basketball court that featured ten men of various ages and shapes engaged in a full court, take-no-prisoners, run-and-shoot game.

The outside court was encased by a green fence about eight feet in height with an additional section on the top for, I suspect, preventing basketballs from bouncing, or being thrown, off the court. There were eight baskets with glass backboards, but only two of the baskets were being used. The poles holding the baskets were painted black and the pavement featured all the appropriate basketball lines with a large fist and dangling chain painted in the center of the court.

"I hope you didn't bring me here because one of the teams needs a sixth man."

No reaction. This guy would have made a terrific guard in front of London Castle. He pointed to the lowest bench of the gray painted viewing stands. "He'll meet with you over there."

Who will meet with me? was the obvious question. I didn't think asking Gap Tooth would help much. I grunted, wandered over and sat down as one fleet footed gazelle with a slight paunch attempted a sure two-handed dunk only to have it blocked by a sixteen or seventeen year old seven-footer.

The raucous taunts suggested an end to the game and the ten players began picking up their various athletic bags and drinking from their water jugs. At that point it seemed like the walls opened up because teenagers and other young adults began pouring in from all directions armed with basketballs and dressed in their sleeveless pullovers, hightops and sweatsocks. It was a matter of moments before every basket was occupied and the dreams of NBA stardom kicked in.

As the previous players began to dissipate, I was approached by a sinewy man of mocha skin, gray eyes and about six feet two inches in height. He had a black towel hanging across his bare shoulders and a smile that I couldn't immediately interpret. It looked like the same smile Senator Bentson gave Vice President Dan Quayle during their debate after the Vice President mistakenly compared himself to Jack Kennedy.

He used the towel to wipe the sweat from his forehead, and as he came closer I stood up, not wanting to be in the sitting down defensive position with someone I now recognized.

He extended a sweaty hand and I hesitated. "They won't mistake it for a sudden move will they?" I asked. I pointed to the four men I spotted sitting or standing in close proximity of our encounter.

"No, we already know you're unarmed," he said matter-of-factly. "Keller, isn't it?"

"In most instances. However, friends call me Lincoln." His grip was strong and sure.

"I won't presume a friendship until after we've talked." He nodded to the bench. "Please let us both sit down."

"Your muscles might stiffen," I said.

"Yeah. The things I never worried about in my youth." He stretched out his legs and folded his arms across his chest. "You have spent the morning on my turf asking questions, Mr. Keller, about people who are not here. I have to ask myself why. And since I don't have the answer, I thought maybe you did."

"Night Life. That is who you are, isn't it?" I asked knowing the answer.

"We've met before?"

"No. I only know you through reputation and some of your activities during your...misspent youth."

Jon 'Night Life' MacDonald was the quintessential con man, rogue and hustler who had a long history of time spent in youth homes, juvenile centers and minimum security facilities. He was smart enough to never draw hard time, but had made a series of bad moves which resulted in his having to spend time in one of the state facilities. The sheet on him went as far back as his twelfth birthday when he was picked up for stealing a car and joy riding around a neighborhood before crashing it through the front door of an elderly couple's home.

After he turned thirty-five he didn't seem to be mixed up in anything illegal, at least nothing proven, and over the last twelve years he was supposedly a model citizen engaged in a number of entrepreneurial activities in and around the 'bottom'.

"You flatter me, Mr. Keller, but it doesn't answer my question."

"It's no secret since you've obviously been informed that I'm here."

He smiled a knowing smile. "There's little that goes on here that I don't know about. You were saying?"

"Back in 1955, five men from this part of town formed a singing group called The Sentiments. Everything I've read thus far suggests that they were headed to the top. And then one day they mysteriously vanished. No one seems to know why and no one's heard from them since. I've been asked to do some checking around to see if I can determine what happened to them."

"Who wants to know?" he said looking straight ahead.

"That's confidential."

He wiped more sweat from his head and chest, stood up and stretched. He turned toward me, his mouth drawn tightly together as if he were contemplating the meaning of the universe.

"What happens if you should learn something?" he asked, signaling to one of his corner observers.

"I tell my client. From there the client decides what to do next."

"Maybe I can help," he said. He whispered something in the ear of the medium height male whom he signaled.

"I'd rather you didn't," I quickly replied.

He gave me a questioning stare as if my remaining brains had fallen out on the ground. "You're refusing my help?"

"No, just saving it for when I really need it." I looked over to the men watching us. "I'M STANDING UP, GUYS!"

"Unnecessary, Mr. Keller."

"Call me overly cautious." I stood up. "Look, if I accept a favor from you now, then I'll owe. I happen to know that when people owe you a favor you expect it repaid double or triple what you gave out. I'm not going to risk that kind of relationship on this activity. If I'm going to owe you, I'd rather owe you for something worthwhile. Something that will allow me to live with how I'll have to pay it back."

"Sounds like you don't trust me to be fair," he said incredulously. I couldn't tell if he was pretending.

"I trust myself to be fair if you owed me a favor. Beyond that, I don't know. It's apparent that people around here owe you or they wouldn't have been so quick to contact you when I started making my inquiries. I figure you have a stake in a number of businesses around here, all legitimate I'm sure, and that's how you're able to stay within the information flow. People owe and they look for ways to pay you back. Calling you about me was one way for someone to have a marker removed from the debit column. So please don't be insulted by my refusal. As I said, I rather save it for something I really need."

He signaled to Gap Tooth who ambled over with all the loyalty of a Great Dane. Night Life whispered something in his ear. He nodded and moved back to the end of the bench.

"Mr. Keller, my driver will return you to your car. Good luck with your inquiries. I'm sure we'll talk again."

We shook hands one more time and he moved toward the back door of the Community Center, closely shadowed by his four bodyguards.

I was escorted back to the Lincoln Towncar and driven back to my last location. The driver didn't say anything until I was ready to get out of the car. He handed me a sheet of paper before unlocking the door.

"Go to this address. She'll be expecting you."

I took the sheet of paper. "That's a pretty long sentence. You may be drained after that. Are you going to be okay driving back?"

"Have a good day, Mr. Keller," he said as he slipped on a pair of dark shaded wraparound sunglasses.

I climbed out of the car and watched as it sped off and whipped around the corner as the light was starting to change.

I shrugged and walked to my Nova.

After I climbed inside, I opened the sheet of paper. There was a name, an address and phone number printed in blue ink.

"Pearl Dibell," I read to myself. "And I'm expected." I fired up the engine and turned on the radio. The DJ for the 'mix' was playing the Spinners 1970s hit 'I'll Be Around'. I thought it an appropriate song given my encounter with Night Life.

"And that's why I love America," I said humorously as I pulled away from the curb. I had a lead that I didn't have before meeting Night Life. I wondered why he did this for me.

Chapter 7

The address I sought was in a neighborhood where the brick, two-family flat seemed to be the architectural trend. I drove down the tree lined, two-laned street with parking on one side and a gas powered security night light located on each lawn until I came to a large home on a corner; a two-family flat with brown and white awnings, a large front porch and rows of multi-colored flowers surrounding the base of the foundation.

I parked on the street, locking my 'Club' across the steering wheel like a habit.

The sidewalk leading up to the porch was split with grass growing between the two pieces. The four steps leading up to the door were con-crete and there were two almond colored wicker chairs and a wooden table sitting on the front porch.

I checked the two addresses and pushed the button that rang the bell for the bottom flat.

"Just a minute," came an elderly voice through the screened open bay window.

I heard the hall door open followed by the thick wooden door with the glass interior.

Standing between me and the screen door was a white haired elderly woman wearing thick bifocals and too much eye makeup. She was wearing a blue and red sundress, exposing the flaccid skin on her arms. She was all of five feet tall but I had a hunch that she walked taller.

"Mrs. Dibell?" I asked.

"Are you the man Jon sent over here?" she asked back in a manner that said I'd better be him.

"Yes, I am."

"Please, please. Come in, come in." Her manner became cheerful.

I followed her through the foyer and into her flat. Her living room contained a camelback sofa, loveseat sleeper, armchair and ottoman deco-rated in a blue and white awning stripe and covered with the kind of plastic that was so popular in living rooms back when I was a kid on the north end.

There were two large lamps with shades big enough to cover Captain Kirk's ego. There were also a series of throw rugs scattered on top of an orange wall-to-wall carpet. An octagonal shaped coffee table with cabriole legs and scroll feet held a number of plaster knickknacks of female animals leading their young by a gold leash. On a wall above an antique upright piano was a picture of Jesus on the cross, prominently displayed in a metal frame with a bottom light. Across the white mantel of the fireplace was an assortment of pictures, black and whites as well as color.

It was a deja vu that had me feeling like I was ten years old again. That was a horrifying thought.

"Sit down, young man," she said pointing to the white plastic covered bergere armchair. "I hope you like iced tea. I'll bring us some from the kitchen." She turned and walked through the dining area into the kitchen located in the back.

She moved rather easily for someone I guessed to be in her eighties.

I started to sit down in the armchair and suddenly stopped halfway when I heard the voice of my beloved Aunt May ringing in the background of my conscious, "Lincoln! This room is for looking. Not for sitting or playing. You hear me?"

"Yes, ma'am," I answered to that part of her that will live forever.

I was still standing obediently when Mrs. Dibell returned with a tray that held a pitcher of iced tea, two glasses filled with ice, two silver spoons, a bowl of lemon slices and several packs of Sweet-N-Low.

"Young man, you're not sitting?" she asked more than said.

"Well, I was just, uh...I'll just sit on the piano bench if you don't mind."

"Long as you're comfortable, son." She poured tea into both glasses and dropped in a lemon slice. I stirred in one pack of sugar and she took hers straight. "Now...," she said settling back on her plastic covered white chesterfield couch, the plastic popping with each movement. "...I was told that I might be able to help you."

"Yes, ma'am," I said. I opened my briefcase and took the picture of The Sentiments. "Do you recognize any of these men?" I asked as I walked over and handed the picture to her.

She took the picture in hand, leaned forward and adjusted her bifocals. She studied the picture for several seconds. I watched her face. There was a subtle shaking of her head and just the slightest tsk from her lips as if there was a lot more in her hand than just a picture. She stopped, put the picture down on the coffee table and gazed out the open bay windows.

She sighed heavily before she spoke. "I know them all. I haven't seen or heard from any of them in over forty years."

I was happy to hear that statement, although I wasn't sure she was happy to share it. "How well did you know them, Mrs. Dibell?"

I could see the remorse in her eyes as the flood of memories started to burst through to the surface. "Very well. I was the Youth Choir Director at First Missionary Baptist back when they were youngsters first learning how to sing. That would have been oh...1938. None of them were more than nine or ten at the time. They were all part of a very talented Youth Choir, but their voices were exceptional. I could hear it the first time each of them opened their mouths. They were all born to sing. God personally molded their voices." She stopped to take a sip of her tea, and then continued, "I worked with them until I had to step down as Choir Director. I had a bad case of pneumonia that left me bedridden for a long while. They were all ready to enter high school about that time. How I missed working with them." She sighed, then looked at me. "Whatever happened to those boys?"

"That's what I'm trying to find out, Mrs. Dibell. No one has seen or heard from them since 1955. Tell me, what happened to them once they got to high school?"

"There was a music teacher there named Matt Stewart who took an interest in their voices. Charming fellow. He took them under his wing."

I remembered seeing Matt Stewart in that old high school picture. He was the one playing the piano while The Sentiments were practicing. I wondered how Julie was doing with him.

"From what I understand," she continued, "he taught them some of the refinements of singing. How to breathe, changing pitch...things like that. They really learned under him."

"And you as well, Mrs. Dibell," I said reassuringly.

"That's kind of you, young man," she said offering to refill my glass. I thanked her and poured it myself.

"What happened after that?" I asked.

"Oh, they would stop and see me from time to time, but they had dreams of pursuing the man-made stage lights in nightclubs and auditoriums and forsaking the gospel light God had shined for them to follow. Between my being a nurse and helping at the church, we never saw each other that much."

"What were they like?" I asked trying to steer the conversation from a memory of unrequited hope.

The question triggered a wave of memories that were sitting tucked away in a far corner waiting for someone to display an interest.

I'm not sure if it was the pleasure or the pain of the memory that contributed to her reflective animation, but it did help me in ways I wouldn't realize until later.

She laughed at the memory of Lennix Williams as a classic cut-up. He was always telling jokes and doing impersonations of voices he'd heard on the radio. She described his voice as a 'pure falsetto', soft and gentle to the ear. She saw Adam Carter as the shy, short angel with a mischievous streak. He played pranks and could innocently look like he didn't know what they were talking about. She laughed some more when she described some of the pranks he played on various members of the Youth Choir, but he could always be counted upon to blend his second tenor into the flow of the combined choir voices. Michael Parker was the reader. He loved historical books and books of historical fiction. He dreamed one day of writing a history book on the black cowboy. He could jump easily between a soft and hard baritone depending on what the song needed. He often took the lead on some of the more difficult gospel songs. She said he could make the rafters shake and move the spirit from the soul whenever he got to feeling the 'Holy Ghost'. Henry Hill was the real athlete of the group. He was especially motivated to play baseball after Jackie Robinson made his debut with the Brooklyn Dodgers. He would always read the daily boxcars to see how Jackie did during a game. He trained himself to sing in a bass that Joshua would have used at the battle of Jericho. "Had he sung, those walls would have truly come tumbling down." Charles Treadwell was the natural leader of the group. He was the one who made sure they came to rehearsals, kept them focused, joked with them when they were being too serious and scolded them when they were being too silly. He had the most versatile voice. He could move easily from bass to first tenor and back again with minimum strain on his vocal cords. He was the one who made sure the blend of voices was perfect.

"Sounds like they were born to sing together," I remarked.

"Yes," she replied softly.

I put down my glass of tea, having just raised it to take a sip. "Is there anyone around who might know where to find him?"

She removed her bifocals and squeezed the bridge of her nose. Sighing heavily at the unrestrained flow of memories, she said, "Pastor Ezell Jordan down at the First Missionary Baptist Church knows as much about the comings and goings of people in this area. Other than him, I'm not too sure. Probably too tired. It gets harder to think."

"Of course, Mrs. Dibell. I've taken up enough of your time." I stood up and carried my glass over to the tray. "I'm grateful for the time you've given me. It's been real helpful." I motioned for her not to get up. "I can see myself out."

She leaned over and grasped my hand. "Thank you, young man. I do hope you find out what happened to my boys. All of them."

I shook her hands reassuringly and left her sitting on the couch.

Thinking.

And remembering.

After I removed the 'Club' from my steering wheel, I paused and remembered passing the First Missionary Baptist Church during my drive around the area. If memory served me, I knew it would be located about eight blocks from where Mrs. Dibell resided. I started up the Nova and pulled into traffic.

As I came in sight of the church I made note of its size and knew immediately that whoever was its Pastor, it was a large, charitable and busy congregation. Which meant Pastor Jordan's time would be zealously guarded by a matronly church secretary who ruled with a warm smile, a soft heart and an iron will. The likes of which fit my late Aunt May, who also served in that function with Second Union Baptist for twenty years. She was so fond of reminding me of one of the many truths in Baptist Church culture: "Our Pastor's job is to save our souls. Mine is to save this church."

I smiled knowing her wisdom from on high would guide my next steps.

Chapter 8

Located in an area of the 'bottom' of mixed blessings, the First Missionary Baptist Church was a red brick monolith adorned with stained-glass windows, white trimming and a brass enclosed tower atop its five story structure. Etched in gothic lettering on one of its white cornerstones was the year 1955 arched above two clasped hands holding an olive branch.

I parked my car in the large, semi-vacant parking lot and walked around to the front of the building where a glass encased, white bordered kiosk held the weekly declaration in bold black press-on lettering.

"Jesus is on the main line,
    call him up and tell him what you want."

"Nobody says it better or with more flair than we Baptists," I said, smiling slightly.

Once I cleared the fourteen concrete steps, I eased through the double glass doors into a lobby with a tiled floor, bright colors and a kiosk listing the names and locations of the church staff members.

Pastor Ezell Jordan had an office located somewhere near the back of the church. I also noticed a Mrs. Winona Holton occupied an office next to Pastor Jordan. Appropriate since the title next to her name read Church Secretary.

"Ah. The protector of the jewels," I muttered.

I followed the lobby until I rounded a corner and came to a beige carpeted hall of offices with large windowless doors evenly spaced apart with numbers located on the jambs. The hall, in fact the church, seemed unusually quiet and subdued. Maybe it was the time of day. Maybe I was just on the quiet side of the building.

Office number 205 was the habitat of Mrs. Winona Holton and the place where I needed to start my inquiries.

The door was open and I stepped into an immaculately ordered office, the likes of which should have been packaged and sold to the Federal Government. Sitting at a large wooden desk with hand carved trimmings was a round faced, bronze, smooth skinned woman with salt and pepper hair tied in a bun. She was talking on the phone in a sweet, even keeled voice that could melt an icy heart. She was conservatively dressed in a matching green dress and jacket with green and white checkered trimmings on the sleeves. A pair of round framed glasses hung from a purple string around her neck. She glanced up and saw me standing in the doorway. She signaled that she'd just be another minute and motioned for me to come forward.

She had to be Mrs. Winona Holton or I'd be sadly disappointed.

The top of her desk would have made Felix Unger jealous. There were no scattered papers or an overrun In and Out box. There were two books stacked on top of each other on a corner of the desk. I couldn't see the titles, but 'Neatness Is Next To Godliness' struck me as one of the possibilities. The four file cabinets, credenza and two wooden side-chairs looked as if they always belonged there on top of the spotless light gray shag carpet.

She mumbled a few more statements into the phone and assured the caller that she'd send out those items during the afternoon mail pick up. She returned the phone to its cradle and cast her brown nurturing eyes in my direction. Her smile was wide. Not Cheshire wide, but wide.

"What can I do for you, young man?" she asked with barrier breaking charm.

Young man? I liked her already. "Mrs. Holton?" She nodded. "Good. My name is Lincoln Keller and though I don't have an appointment, I would very much like to talk with Pastor Jordan, if I may."

"He's extremely busy. May I ask the nature of the problem? Perhaps I can be of assistance."

Thoughts raced through my head; 'She's at the first level of protective resistance. Charming, curious and filtering what is and isn't important. Make your next steps count Lincoln.' "Perhaps you can," I said with a smile. "My late aunt, Mrs. May Williams, who was the Church Secretary over at Second Union Baptist for twenty years used to always tell me that if I needed to have something done in a hurry, go to the person responsible for getting things done."

Her eyes widened. "May Williams was your aunt?"

"Yes, ma'am."

She crossed herself. "Your aunt was a sainted woman. Heaven became a better place when she was called home. She was so helpful to me when I started here for Pastor Jordan. Lovely, lovely woman."

"Yes, ma'am, she was." I'd always thought that about my aunt. I also thought what a small world this can be. I was out of leads until Night Life helped out. Meanwhile, here was somebody I never knew that knew my aunt apparently pretty well.

"Now how can I help you Mr.-"

"-it's Lincoln, Mrs. Holton. I'm a private investigator and I'm looking into the disappearance of five men that Pastor Jordan may have known several years ago. Mrs. Dibell suggested I talk to him."

"How is she?" she asked while picking up the telephone and punching in four numbers.

"She seems fine. Tired, but with a streak of feistiness."

"That's our Mrs. Dibell. I don't know where she finds the time to help at the church, assist our day-care center, teach Bible classes and tend to that garden of hers. Oh, she keeps a lovely garden in her backyard." She spoke into the phone. "I have a private investigator, a Mr. Keller out here who'd like to speak with you for a few minutes. No, you still have an hour before that meeting...they've already been called...they'll be here at six this evening...probably in the second drawer on the left, where you usually keep it...not until Friday." She hung up and looked up at me. "He's in the next office down. He can give you twenty minutes...but no more."

Her subtlety was not lost on me. "I'll not go a minute longer, Mrs. Holton."

Her smile brightened and she waved me away.

I began my mental calculation of the time the moment I stepped into the hall. The carpeted hall muffled my approach, but I found the heavy wooden door ajar, tapped on the jamb twice and a barrel toned voice hastened me in.

Perched behind a long, shiny wooden desk with two gold stemmed lamps on each corner and possessing a regal bearing accented by the gray streaked temples of his medium coifed hair sat the person who I assumed to be Pastor Ezell Jordan. He looked up from a thick leather bound Bible and motioned me to come forward.

As he stood to greet me, I felt the sense of eternal caring radiate from the tall, angular man whose brown eyes and age lines on a cleanly shaven face were the only indications that he was more than just elderly.

"Come in, young man. Come in," he said graciously as he extended his hand to mine. His grip was strong as he towered over me by a few inches.

"Thank you for seeing me on such short notice, Pastor Jordan. I know you're busy and I'll try not to be too intrusive." He was wearing a dark blue two-piece suit with a basic white shirt and dark blue tie. I took it to mean that he made no effort to stand out. "I'm investigating the disappearance forty years ago of five young men who lived in this area. I just recently spoke with Mrs. Dibell. She was very helpful and suggested I contact you."

"Sistah Dibell has been a member of our congregation since before I became Pastor," he said as he motioned toward an area where a brown leather couch, hand carved coffee table, embroidered throw rug and black velour recliner added an informality to the formal surroundings. "She's one of the few who remembers the first church we had over on Riopelle Street. Still makes it to church every Sunday. I don't get to visit with her as much."

Behind the couch were several floor-to-ceiling oak bookshelves that covered the entire back wall. Each shelf was filled with books on religion, philosophy, political science, social science, law primers and autobiographies. The walls were a collection of brass plated plaques of varying sizes, each commemorating Pastor Jordan for some service. There were pictures of him with various political and spiritual officials as well as artists' drawings of both Kennedys, Martin Luther King, Harriet Tubman, John Brown and other historical figures.

"That's quite a collection of books you have there Pastor Jordan," I mentioned as I lowered myself into the enveloping comfort of the leather couch. "There are titles here I haven't seen in years."

"I enjoy the variety, and the knowledge adds many a helpful perspective to my teachings," he responded pleasantly as he took his place behind a cherry wood desk that suited him well: large, solid and built to last forever.

"I notice you also have books on the various criminal justice branches of the government. You're not planning a massive overthrow are you?" I hoped I sounded funny.

I guess I did. "Not likely," he chuckled. "It's just a passing interest. Although knowing how the system works has been helpful in some of my prison reform efforts as well as getting certain cases reviewed. But I don't think you stopped by to discuss my literary interests. Why don't you tell me what's on your mind, young man?"

Young man. Again. I gave serious thought to switching my loyalties from my church of many years to First Baptist. I quickly reiterated, "My client has asked me to locate several people who disappeared from this area years ago. I discussed it with Mrs. Dibell. Like I mentioned, she was very helpful, but she didn't have all the answers. So she sent me to you."

"Just who are you trying to locate?" he asked.

"Five men who, for a short period of time, were a singing group known as The Sentiments." I rattled off all five of their names and the little background I had. He listened with keen interest. As I spoke he gave me no indication as to what he was thinking.

When I finished he leaned back in his recliner, then gave a big indication of what he was thinking. "I baptized all five of those boys. Watched them grow into manhood. Mrs. Dibell was the first one to recognize their gift. She taught them the basics of breathing, pitch and delivery so when they sang with our youth choir, it was like they were singing to the Angels." He sighed, remorseful. "It would be a sin to say I haven't missed them."

"Didn't it strike you as odd their just vanishing like that?" I asked.

"Not at the time, no. When they decided to try their luck in show business, much of their time went to singing in the various clubs and night establishments. Their attendance in church declined, though not completely absent. Along that time, the needs of my congregation started to increase.

So I didn't see them as much."

"Is there anyone around here who might know where they went?"

"Hard to say." He chewed his bottom lip. "This neighborhood has changed so much over the years that it's difficult to know. I've performed a lot of weddings, christenings and funerals. A number of people from that time have moved away, though some still come here for Sunday service. I could ask a few of those from the congregation who grew up about the same time as The Sentiments. See if they know anything."

I removed a business card. "That would be helpful, Pastor Jordan. Feel free to contact me at any of those numbers."

He took the card and eyed it for a moment. "Why is your client interested in knowing what happened to The Sentiments?"

"Not really sure. Closure, I'd guess. I just fell into it."

"Or perhaps your involvement is the result of a powerful, spiritual intervention. The Lord does moves in mysterious ways," he said with an unarguable certainty.

"Amen to that, Pastor. Amen to that."

"What have you surmised so far?" he asked.

I rubbed my hands together. "Well, if I were to use the journalist creed for gathering information, I know Who is missing and I have a pretty good idea When they turned up missing. I don't know Where they've gone, Why or How and I sure don't know What happened. Every known source of information gathering so far has come up short. I'm not sure yet, but as best I know they haven't used their social security numbers, nor has anyone else for that matter. No previous paychecks to go on, no credit cards, no income tax returns, no nothing. I'm smart enough to know that this is more than just a coincidence, but...I'm drawing blanks." I made a mental note to get back with Julie soon and see what her magic computer had to say.

"That does sound odd. Almost thorough." He glanced at his watch. "But I'm afraid the time is getting away from me. Sorry I couldn't be more helpful."

We stood up at the same time and shook hands. "Oh, but you've been helpful, Pastor Jordan. Maybe someone in your congregation will remember something." At this point I was willing to accept help from anyone.

"Possibly. All I can do is ask. But please, if you find out anything concerning their whereabouts, would you let me know?"

"Yes. My pleasure."

He escorted me to the door and wished me luck. On the way out I made sure I stopped in and thanked Mrs. Holton for her help. She smiled and reminded me how much of a loving person my Aunt May was.

I needn't be reminded.

During my stroll back to my car, I found myself struck by the character of Pastor Ezell Jordan. In many ways he was like a number of Baptist Ministers I'd met and known over the years. Engaging, articulate, passionate convictions, strong sense of right and wrong, well read and a fearless representative of the downtrodden. However, I did think his choice of readings provided a greater breadth from which to draw inspiration. Probably not that unusual, but definitely...interesting.

Night Life MacDonald turned out to be quite helpful...without his usual strings attached.

I crossed the street as a black Buick stopped for me, and upon entering my car, I quickly dismissed the thought of Pastor Jordan's literary collection when I checked the dashboard clock. It was early afternoon and my luck was running south. There was a great deal of peripheral information, but nothing came into focus. I decided to stop and head back to my office. There were a couple of open loops from two previous cases I wanted to close, and I wanted some time to prop my feet up on my desk and think for awhile.

I did a quick U-turn and sped back to the freeway.

This mystery had just become a little more complicated.

So, what else was new?

***

The drive back across town was uneventful, which worked out well for my overly active imagination. I must have put the Nova on automatic pilot because I don't really remember stopping at corners, yielding for pedestrians or speeding onto the highway. My mind was a million light years from the present, looking at the large puzzle called the universe and trying to make sense out of its make up. I didn't feel like I had all the pieces, and what pieces I did have didn't fit.

If five members of an up and coming singing group suddenly vanished, at what point in time did members of their families or friends and loved ones from the 'hood' start to notice? Did anyone file a missing persons report? Are all the family members being truthful when they say they've received no contact? Where is Matt Stewart?

I made it back to the office and had just sat down when the phone rang. I answered. The voice asking to speak to Mr. Keller brought me back into focus.

Erotica.

"Mrs. Tremaine," I said in an even strain. "What can I do for you?"

"I was wondering if you found out anything. I'm a little anxious and I don't mean to be bothersome."

"Not at all." I told her everything I'd learned so far. Which didn't amount to much. It had been less that 24 hours so far.

"Well, they've been missing a lot longer than you've been looking."

"Once I know more, I can do more. Until then, all I can do is keep you posted."

"That's a very limited view of your abilities. I think there's a lot more you can do besides keep me posted."

I paused. "I'm not quite following you."

"Well...," she said stretching the moment. "...you could invite me to a nice restaurant tonight where we could enjoy a quiet dinner and drinks."

"You have a rock the size of New Jersey on your left ring finger that in my mind limits the kinds of invitations you receive."

"I'm not looking for a marriage proposal, Mr. Keller, just dinner."

"And I'm not looking for trouble, just The Sentiments."

"Since we have that in common, it should make for a stress-free dinner," she replied.

I ignored all common sense. "You like Italian?"

"Love it."

"How about Appolonia's on Woodward?"

"Love it."

"Say...seven-thirty?"

"Love it."

"Where shall I pick you up?"

"I'll meet you."

"Fine," I said. "I'll be the guy with the silly schoolyard grin."

"I like schoolyard grins. I haven't seen one in awhile."

After we hung up, I checked the time. It was close to three o'clock and my stomach was sounding like a California avalanche. I couldn't wait until seven-thirty. The burger joint next door would ease some of the rumbling, the rest would have to wait until after dinner.

Chapter 9

I came back to my office with a to-go bacon burger and chili fries from the 'grease and grime' fast food fatality next door and made a few phone calls to other clients waiting for important information. I was contributing to the rising divorce lawyer industry based on my surveillance of a husband and a wife. Two separate cases, the same result. Carnal pleasures that dictate social realignment. What a life.

Intercepting a pass from a strong armed quarterback to a fleet footed receiver was a lot easier to handle than some of the stuff I'd seen of late. The phone rang and disrupted my biased moral judgments. I answered on the second ring.

"Hello, Lincoln Keller please?" the male voice on the other end had the seasoned tone of age and wisdom.

"Speaking."

"Mr. Keller. How are you today?"

"I'm fine, thank you. To whom am I speaking?"

He coughed and cleared his throat. "My name is Wilbur Harris. I own and run Harris' Barbershop. Been in business since 1950. Same store on the same corner for over forty years."

"Yessir," I replied remembering my father's adamant belief in respect and courtesy.

"I understand you were asking about some boys that used to live hereabouts. My friend, Mable Johnson gave me your name and number; said I should talk to you."

"If you can be helpful, sir, I would appreciate it."

He coughed again. "Cain't talk just yet, got customers coming through the door. I close at seven."

"How about if I came there right now?" I asked anxiously.

"That'd be alright. I can talk while I work."

Either the word had gotten out that it was okay to talk to me or he was someone who didn't owe favors to silent investors like Night Life. However, it was a break I welcomed. "I'm looking at three thirty right now. I can be there by four and I promise I won't take too much of your time."

"I can give you all the time you need until it's time to close."

We both hung up.

I stood up, stretched and shook the cobwebs from my mind. The first wave of afternoon lethargy had started to set in before I received the phone call.

My energy level was restored.

I looked forward to hearing whatever it was Wilbur Harris wanted me to know.

***

Harris' Barber Shop was located at the corner of Chene Avenue and Theodore Street, just east of the I-75 freeway. It was your basic storefront in a two-story brick building with a vacant area on one side that served as a parking lot and general meeting place. An infamous yellow background marquee was posted above the door listing the prices for cuts, styles and mustache trims. There were steel painted gray vertical bars on both front windows which were divided by a small one step porch that led to the thick oak door.

I got lucky again with the parking as I just beat a black Buick to the last parking spot, and then jaywalked across the busy two-laned intersection. Once inside, I noticed the standard, typical, predictable layout customarily found in African-American barbershops across the country.

A row of unmatching cushioned and uncushioned chairs lined the walls providing an unobstructed view of the three barber chairs where the barbers were engaged in separate and distinct dialogue with each chair's occupant. A row of mirrors filled the back wall and its shelving held the various sprays, liquids and powders each barber uses to give his customer that special 'look'. Various sizes of clip-on electric clippers were within reaching distance of the gifted hair designers and general conversationalists. A small color television was propped in the top corner of a far wall providing an unobstructed, and usually uncomfortable view of the show's program which was turned on but unheard. Two magazine tables broke up the pattern of chairs and held an eclectic collection of men's magazines with a decidedly afrocentric bias. Ebony, Jet, Essence, GQ, Black Enterprise and Emerge were some of the obvious titles. Clumps of hair lay scattered around the three chairs.

A collection of African-American men of distinct ages and manners, clad in the clothes that represented their respective generation, sat calmly in the chairs, engaged in various arguments and discussions.

My entrance was basically unnoticed now that the traditional topics of sex, sports and politics had returned ever since the O. J. Simpson trial was over.

The barber working at the chair farthest to my left looked to be in his late twenties, favoring a 'fade' haircut to go with the gold ring in his ear. The middle chair was being serviced by a man I took to be about my age. Middle thirties, modest medium cut, some graying in his mustache and a slight paunch. The chair directly in front of me had a gentleman whom I took to be in his late sixties, although you wouldn't know it by looking at him. His face was still smooth as the day he turned twenty-one. His brown eyes looked tired, but not worn. His medium haircut was evenly salt and peppered, and he seemed quite engaging.

"Mr. Harris?" I asked just loud enough to be heard but not impede the current debate.

He stopped trimming the older gentleman's hair. "That's me, son," he replied in a manner that was quite disarming. "What can I do for you?"

"My name's Lincoln Keller. We talked earlier."

He turned off his electric clipper and extended his hand. "Glad to meet you, son." His unlined hand still had a firm grip. "Just let me finish this back area here and we can talk."

"Whatever works for you, sir. I'm on your time."

The hum of the clippers started and I sat in a ladderback hard chair just to his left.

Wilbur Harris, I surmised, was a pictorial historian. The walls in his area of the shop were filled with those wallet size black-and-whites of well suited men and women posing for their high school graduation picture. Each was signed and dated. I assumed some comment of thanks and adulation to Mr. Harris was written on the back. It was an interesting chronology of photographs from the early 1950s on up through the 1990s. Mr. Harris had obviously served a number of grateful clients. If nothing else, it was interesting watching the mens' hairstyles as they slicked, grew, curled and shrank to signal the beginning of each new decade.

Mr. Harris unloosened the white and black striped barber's sheet from the slick haired elderly gentleman, shook off the hair and signaled to the next waiting customer.

"Bug," Harris said to the just finished customer, "you might want to stay around. I'm gonna help this young man with somethin' I know you know about."

Bug shook his head to get rid of any residual hair cuttings and sat down in an empty seat just to my left.

Mr. Harris turned to me as he prepared his next customer. "Just who are you lookin' for, son?"

I removed the picture of The Sentiments from my briefcase and showed it to him. "You recognize any of these boys?"

He held the picture near a tubed light and smiled. "Sho do." He then went to five locations on his wall and pointed to their individual pictures. "Tha's all of them right chere." He gave the picture to the elderly gentleman. "You remember these boys don't you, Bug? They could sang, ummp, they could sang!"

Bug looked at the picture, rubbing his round tipped nose. "I remember 'em when they sang down at Johnny's Lounge down there on Chene. They was too young to drink, but boy, they could sang. Yeah, I remember 'em."

He gave the picture back to me and I held it loosely between my thumb and finger. "Mr. Harris, my client is interested in knowing what happened to them. They vanished in October of 1955 and no one's heard from them since that time. I'm checking around to see if anybody remembers anything that might be helpful."

"Who's your client?" he asked.

"Sorry. I have to keep that confidential." Mr. Harris and Bug exchanged a look. It was a quick signal. Subtle. Revealing. I didn't want them to clam up having just made some progress. "But I can tell you that my client is young enough to be one of their daughters."

"Well, that tells us who it isn't," Bug replied with a faint cough.

"That important?" I asked.

"Yeah, a might important." Mr. Harris started combing his customer's hair. "Any of us still alive from back then remembers that they came up missing. We all thought it was peculiar. Them just leaving like that and then not contacting anyone, not even their families. Shame."

"Well, that's just it, Mr. Harris. It was peculiar. You know that none of the family members filed a missing persons report. There's nothing on record with the police." I wasn't really quite sure of that yet. I needed to speak with Julie. But, so far it seemed like a safe assumption.

"I'm not surprised," he said picking up his electric clippers.

"Why not?" I asked.

"Tell 'im, Bug."

Bug was also in his late sixties or early seventies. He was clean shaven except for some gray stubble. His hair was white and combed back. A small bald spot shined on the crown of his head where hair once ruled. "When you lived in the 'bottom'," he began to relate, "the last thing you did was report something like that to the police. Back then they weren't very helpful. They just drove around trying to keep us under control. If something didn't end with a shooting, stabbing or somethin', they just let it go. So five colored boys turn up missing one day and no one knows where they are. So what?"

"Had they done anything that might have contributed to their turning up missing?" I asked the question though I still dwelled on what Bug had just said.

"None of us knew one way or another," Mr. Harris said," but somebody thought so."

"Who thought so?" I asked.

"Some white boy police officer who used to come around asking questions. He was real interested in wanting to know where they were."

I stopped, not expecting that bit of information. "A police officer? Uniform or plainclothes?"

"Well, he wore a uniform most of the time, but sometimes he came around without his uniform. Used to get real nasty with some of us. Would say we were lying and we'd better tell him where they were. Even cracked a few heads trying to find out. Just waltz into any of our stores and start asking questions. Remember when he slapped around old Charlie the Pencilman?"

Bug nodded.

"Why was this police officer looking for The Sentiments?"

"He never said why. Just asked questions and knocked some of us around if he didn't like the answers."

"Who was he?"

"Officer Roberts. Craig Roberts. Hard one to forget. Big bruiser type. Thick neck. Deep set eyes. Like an assassin. He used to come around pretty often. Then he'd stop for awhile. Then he'd show up again. We started to see less of him around '62, '63. Then from time to time, somebody else would come around asking questions. There was less head-cracking stuff when Mayor Young came into office. Then questions about The Sentiments stopped. That is until today when you showed up asking questions. You riled things up a little bit."

They went on to explain why no one knew anything this morning and why Night Life questioned me. I was being checked out.

I noticed that several other men were starting to listen to bits and pieces of our conversation. "But I am curious about this police officer who was also looking for them. Craig Roberts. Why would he be interested?"

"Don't know, son. Back then we weren't allowed to ask a lot of questions. You'd risk having your business taken away or being thrown in jail for some no good reason." He turned to pick up his scissors. "Don't remember too much about him except his name...and that he was a real son of a bitch. White boy, low haircut so you really couldn't tell what color his hair was. Like the crewcuts they used to wear in the army." He stopped to raise the barber chair. "We used to call him 'White Death' cause he always looked like he could kill someone."

That made sense. It was a pretty standard look for police organizations of that era.

He asked me to stand up. He eyed my height. "I'd say a little shorter than you, but stockier, like he was a wrestler. Usually wore dark glasses..."

"...eyes was blue," Bug said assuringly during his interruption. "Saw them once when he was giving Mack a ticket. Had another officer with him at the time."

Not certain as to what it all meant, I said nothing. A police force can be a mighty secret society, but in this case I knew who to ask.

"I can look into it," I offered. I was writing down what little information they'd given me. I thought I'd drop a dime and see who picked it up. "Mr. Harris, what do you think happened to The Sentiments?"

He stopped trimming the back of his customer's neck. It was a slight, knowing pause. "Trouble. Some kind of big trouble. Back then there was less kinds of ways to get into trouble than there is nowadays. But back then, even if you got into a little trouble, they made it a big deal."

"Who is they?"

He continued trimming his customer's hair, allowing a moment to set between us. I knew what he wanted me to say, but I needed to hear him say it.

He finally sighed. "Police officers who patrolled the 'bottom'. They used to call this area Paradise Valley. Most were okay, decent enough, but a few weren't. Those were the ones who went out of their way to remind us what they could do. For those of us who owned businesses, it was always a threat. First time a colored officer showed up, we began to feel a little easier. 'Course that didn't stop the other officer from coming around asking us again and again, where were The Sentiments? Who's hiding them? Didn't we know he could make life tough for us if we didn't tell? Things like that. I think we all knew those boys ended up in some kind of trouble.

The fact that we didn't know what kind of trouble probably saved us a lot of grief."

I took out my business card case. I gave a card to Mr. Harris and one to Bug. "If you happen to remember anything else, don't hesitate to call me, okay?"

I shook his hand, thanked him and left the barber shop having finally gotten some information that would at least focus my investigation. I crossed the street to my Nova just as a familiar Lincoln Towncar went cruising by.

I waved to the stoic driver. His returned glance revealed nothing.

It told me a lot.

Chapter 10

The afternoon started to wear on me like a lead vest. I had pages of notes I wanted to review and a few more leads to follow. Specifically, Officer Craig Roberts.

I stopped and called police headquarters, asked for Gabe and was put on hold. He finally answered. Gabe growled into the receiver, just as curmudgeonly as the uncle every family keeps locked in the basement.

"Gabe, it's Keller. How's it hanging?"

"Barely noticeable over a healthy waistline, gumshoe. The lobby's gettin' crowded and my day's about to end. Make it quick."

"I could add inches to that waistline buyin' an early dinner."

"You tryin' to corrupt a veteran of the blue?"

"Naw. I just thought I'd buy lunch for a friend."

"He turned you down so you called me? I'm out of here in twenty minutes. Meet me out front on Beaubien."

He hung up.

I made it downtown and found a parking spot around the corner from Beaubien. I hurried into the precinct lobby and saw Gabe talking to some youth with his cap turned backwards.

Gabe glanced up and looked relieved. "Keller. Man, I thought you stood me up. I'm outta here." He said something to one of his assistants, an eager young officer with a hairless face, opened the access door and we headed through the lobby, past the sad faces as they waited for someone to tell them something they didn't want to hear.

Once outside the brass lined doors, Gabe pointed to a small diner notorious for its beer belly size burgers that dripped grease by the bucket and

French fries that when they weren't being eaten, could be used as saxophones.

"Jeez, Gabe. I haven't eaten there since the last time I had my stomach pumped," I said hoping he'd want to consider another location.

He moved forward with a knowing swagger despite my protestations. "Keller, you've gotten wimpy since you've left the fold. Come on. No salads and water for people who really work."

We crossed the street as Gabe started a nonstop monologue about his retirement and what he intended to do now that he and his wife had finally sent the last daughter off to college.

The inside of the diner was a mixture of present day reality and the best of a previous era diner architecture. It reminded me of a small barracks where everything was divided by the long line down the middle of the building. A high, white formica top counter with those round backless seats and red vinyl covering that forced its occupants to lean forward and relax on their elbows dominated the scenario.

The booths were a fixture against the walls and came complete with the typical table condiments, a red and white plastic checkered table cover and a miniature juke box with a selection of music that only a greaser from the 1950s would have recognized.

We wandered back to an open booth and eased onto the long cushioned covered seats that some designer felt only needed the barest of inches between the table and the human chest in order to experience true dining comfort.

"Gabe, wasn't this place condemned during prohibition?" I said picking up the tattered printed menu.

"Don't complain, Keller. They're able to splurge on food because of their low overhead." He didn't bother opening a menu. "Try the 'Suicide Watch', it's their best burger."

The waitress who took our order was a veteran of the diner wars. Her waxed hair was pulled back in a bun and she had rouge dripping out of her age lines. She traded barbs with Gabe and then wrote down what we wanted.

The killer bacon burger from an hour before was already burned off. I opted for an gastronomically acceptable chili dog and root beer. I had to go easy; I had a dinner with Erotica coming up this evening.

Gabe went for the 'Suicide Watch' and 'Fearless Fries'.

"What's on your mind, gumshoe?" Gabe asked taking a toothpick out of the small jar on our table.

"How long you been wearing the 'blue', Gabe?"

"Started in July of '58. I was twenty, full of piss and vinegar and ready to instill my own form of law and order."

"What was it like being an officer back then?"

He paused. "'Bout like now only less so. The way of doing things seemed clear, not so complicated. You knew what you had to do and you did it."

"Officers had a lot more leeway back then?" I asked.

"Only in that we spent more time in certain communities. You came to know the people a little better than you do now." He stopped, his blue eyes searched the files of forgotten memories. "'Course we were starting to transition from being foot patrol to mobile. We knew less about the people so we had to rely on the enforcement of the rules." He flipped the toothpick over and bit on the other end. "You were a pretty good defensive back and rumor has it that you were a pretty good cop with the Oakland PD. You got something you want to ask me, don't beat around the bush. We don't have the time."

I sighed and leaned back. "There's something I need to know and I would appreciate your being honest with me."

"Hey, you're buying."

"I've been doing some research over in what used to be known as 'Blackbottom' and I've been hearing some things that are...disturbing."

"Like what?" Gabe asked neutrally.

"Things like officers carrying the power of the uniform farther than it was intended. Especially in the area of physical intimidation of local residents."

By now our food had been brought to us and Gabe proceeded to drown his 'Fearless Fries' with a bottle of catsup. He was cutting his burger as he spoke. "Keller, if you're asking me if officers took the law into their own hands by sometimes breaking a few heads, then the answer is yes, it happened."

"Why?" I asked flatly.

"Because at the time, they could." He took a bite of his burger. "During the Fifties, officers weren't bogged down by all these laws that protect the rights of criminals. There were no rules on search and seizure, no Miranda rights and criminals didn't walk due to legal technicalities. There was the Law and God's backing, so if heads needed to be cracked to get at the truth or restore order, then a lot of incidents were ignored."

"Ends justifies the means?"

He continued undeterred. "I didn't say it was right, gumshoe. I said it was done. Sometimes promotions were made according to how much you did. What didn't matter was whether or not someone got hurt in the process."

"Especially if that someone hurt happened to be black."

"It may have looked that way if you were working the 'bottom', but it wasn't limited to that area. Heads were cracked all over the city. We were equal opportunity head crackers."

"So, an officer could just roust a citizen any time it damn well pleased him and the brass looked the other way."

"Only in severe cases was action ever taken," he continued.

"Like someone accidentally dying?"

"That would be severe," Gabe replied. He took a sip of his ice water.

I used my fork to unconsciously slice my chili dog into little pieces though it never made it to my mouth. That killer bacon burger wasn't as far gone as I thought. "I heard something that may involve a former officer who worked the 'bottom'."

"Who?"

"Craig Roberts," I said.

Gabe swished his drink around for a few seconds. "Yeah, I heard about him. Mean tempered. Usually couldn't keep a partner too long. Spent most of his career on patrol. Got a desk job and finished his last five years. I think he'd gotten his shield by the time I started. Lot of the old timers back then said he was a 'Shine Breaker'."

"Meaning?"

Gabe wiped the corner of his mouth with a small paper napkin. "I have to spell it out for you, Keller? Okay. His street methods for getting the truth out of 'coloreds', that's what you all were back then, were effective. He was admired for his results."

"Gabe, the matter-of-fact way in which you say this bothers me."

"I'm sure it does, but that's pretty much the way it was back then. That's one of the many reasons why blacks started getting hired in the department. We had to break it up somehow. Guys like Roberts were given a free hand as long as they got results. Who the hell cared if a few heads were kicked in along the way? They were just 'colored' heads." He stopped and leaned forward, his eyes dancing with an intensity I hadn't seen before. "You getting my drift here? Officer to Officer?"

"Yeah. I got it."

"Lot of guys rode with him, but not many really partnered. There was one guy though. Name of Ron Brickham. Joined the force in the early Seventies. Roberts was his training officer and they seemed to hit it off. Stayed partners for several years. Brickham was a physically younger version of Roberts. Built to wrestle trees and piss on the roots."

I took another swallow of my not-bad root beer. "Maybe I should talk to this Brickham guy. Is he on morning shift?"

"I suppose so. But not with the department. He got bounced several years ago. He wasn't as sensitive to the community like some of our new college graduates." He stopped to chew. "Last I heard, he was running his own security firm somewhere on Eight Mile Road I believe. Brickham Securities, or some piece of shit name like that."

"Worth my time?"

"You're the PI. I'm just a public servant. What do I know?"

"More than you let on."

"Keeps my ass clean." He took the last bite of food and pushed the bill toward me. "Well, I gotta go. Taking in a grandson's junior football game tonight, although I don't need the grief." He slid out while I decided to sit for a few more minutes. "You might not like what I had to say, Keller, but I'm not gonna lie to you or sugarcoat the truth. I got too much respect for you to do that. You and others before you made it easier for others to get fairness and justice." Then he said something way out of character for him, but I'm glad he said it. "I gotta admire ya."

I nodded my acknowledgment. "This guy Roberts still around?" I really wanted to know.

He stopped and looked at me suspiciously. "You figure you're gonna balance the scales of justice?"

"Just like to ask him a few questions...nothing more. It's related to this case I'm working on."

He thought for just a second. "I'll see what I can do. You still know how to use a phone?" I nodded. "Use it tomorrow. Make it late morning before you call me." He rubbed his hand across his scalp. "Don't do nothing foolish Keller...you hear?"

"I hear." Before Gabe left, I called out to him. "Gabe. Did you ever have to crack a few 'colored' heads?"

"You should know better than to even have to ask that question. Like I said, I was an equal opportunity head cracker. I never saw color, just the crime. See ya around, gumshoe."

I watched as he swaggered passed the counter and booths through the door and back to his post where after thirty plus years of civil service he still showed up for his watch trying to make a difference in his own way.

I paid the cashier and strolled back to my Nova. The afternoon had proven to be informative as well as draining. I eliminated The Sentiments from the unsolved, unclaimed category of human disposal. I also had a little more substance to the story told to me by Mr. Harris and Bug. I needed an early picture of Craig Roberts to show both of them and I needed to know if Roberts' interest in The Sentiments was purely as an investigating detective or was there more? Once I made a copy of his picture from the police academy yearbook, I'd show it around to get a confirming ID.

I'd also been given an instant look into life as seen from someone who knew enough about the way it was to accept it as part of his youthfulness around a job he wanted. Gabe also reminded me of why certain things had to change if the true notion of justice was ever going to be realized. I think he realized it, too.

I decided to drive home and park my carcass in my apartment. Maybe I'd begin to make some sense of all that I had gathered. Maybe I'd suddenly get hit with a flash of brilliance.

I wasn't lucky enough to avoid the swelling rows of end-of-work commuter traffic jamming up every possible lane in an Olympic record setting pace to leave the city before it descended upon their innate paranoid feelings.

Music from the WHIP softened the mental anxiety. The Temptations sang 'The Way You Do The Things You Do' and I felt a kindred connection to a bygone era.

The slowness of the traffic, combined with the summer heat and no air conditioning in my car left me with an undesirable sweat funk complete with stained underarms and wrinkled pants.

Not the best look for a dinner date at Appolonia's.

Back inside my homestead, I was sipping the last dregs of an ill advised concoction of frozen lemonade mixed with cranberry juice and belched several choruses of 'My Way' in G minor. Despite my defilement, the brief respite had produced some interesting developments.

An immediate distraction was needed. I had spread out the notes from this morning's time in the library.

When I was at the library that morning there was something in the research of 1955 that didn't strike a particular chord at first, but now seemed like a related point. On a hunch I took note of it. An obscure article tucked away in a corner of the fifth page and written by a *Free Press* reporter named Peter Kindersley dated March of 1955 concerned itself with the apparent disappearance of a Union activist named Charlie Frey (pronounced fry). At the time of his disappearance, Charlie had been the first of a new breed of union activists. He was college trained and had worked in the plants 'on the line'. Charlie served in the Army during World War II, and upon his return, he jumped heavily into the inner workings of the Unions. The article went on to say that Charlie's views, at times, were more radical than the usually vocal union leadership and over time came to be viewed as someone whose philosophies eventually caused a rift between him and his union brethren. So much so that during the Communist 'witch hunts' of the McCarthy regime, he was singled out as a possible sympathizer.

Charlie never confirmed or denied any association with a Communist philosophy, but so much pressure was brought to bear that he was eventually harassed out of the union and the possibility of an indictment loomed on the horizon. I looked carefully at the rather faded black-and-white picture of him addressing a group of people gathered at the new building for the First Missionary Baptist Church. A young pastor Jordan stood to the right of the podium.

Charlie Frey vanished in September of 1955 and months later Peter Kindersley's article was a journalist tongue-in-cheek reflection on a person no one seemed to miss. The article was entitled, "When will Charlie Frey?" and was equally as comedic as it was condemning.

Charlie was alleged to have vanished without a trace. Just like The Sentiments.

Interesting, I thought. Possibly connected. Admittedly, it would be a stretch.

I called the office and checked the answering machine. There were four messages waiting to be heard.

I pressed the play button. The digital voice spoke. It irritated me like it always does when it mechanically reiterated that there were four messages before it beeped its way to the first one.

El numero uno wanted to talk with Jefferson. His voice had that pained fear of a bail bondsman who lost one of his wayward sheep.

The second caller was also for the elder Keller, a salesperson wanting to send him a copy of the new *Guns* catalog.

The third message filled the restless void with the voice of my on-again, off-again homicide detective love-interest. Candy Malone. She wanted me to know that she did run those five names through Missing Persons and no reports had been filed. She even went a step further, logged the names onto the computer and found nothing in any of the other data banks. Among those information sources were the names of those men currently keeping state employees happy being locked up for various crimes.

None of The Sentiments were among that illustrious group.

The message ended with me being assured that she'd check in later. Although I didn't know what 'later' meant.

Number four was from Stella. She left a number and told me to call anytime.

It seemed like the right time, so I called.

Her saucy voice supplied the greeting from Johnny's Lounge.

I said I was returning her call.

"Yeah, sugar. I know someone who might be able to help you. Still interested?"

"In you? Always. For information? Of course."

"You sweet thing. If only you were a half a century older."

"Then you'd be too young for me."

"Get outta here. Anyway, you may want to contact a guy by the name of Tyrell Stubbins. He works at a bar out at Metro Airport. He's been around awhile. I think he can help you. I have his number at work."

I wrote the number down on a memo pad I carry in my case. "Thanks, Stella. What do I owe you?"

"Just tell me I'm the love you lost in this life."

"This one and the previous three. I don't intend to mess up in the next one."

She cackled. "Come by sometime and let me buy you a drink."

"It's a date, Stella. And thanks."

I punched in the number and after the second ring, I asked for Tyrell Stubbins.

He wasn't available so I left my office number and asked if he would call me when he had a moment.

I yawned, wiped the water from my eyes and picked up the phone.

"What next?" I asked myself.

"Assuming none of these guys went off to college," myself answered, "that leaves two other possibilities for African-American men born and raised in the Motor City."

Since it was that time in the late afternoon, I figured I stood a better than even chance of catching up with the youngest of the Keller clan, Truman, Ford Motor employee extraordinaire, blue collar union activist second to none, and one of the principle forces behind Local 721, one of the more aggressive unions to ever grace an auto plant.

More than likely he was somewhere in one of the plants trying to resolve an employee/management problem.

I punched in his beeper number, waited for the signal and left the office number for him to call.

I stepped into the bathroom to throw some water on my face. The cold drops against my skin felt revitalizing. I was wiping my face with a paper towel when the phone rang.

"Keller Investigations," I said.

"Damn people are going to drive me crazy, Linc. I'm serious. They are going to drive me straight out of my mind," Truman barked over the sounds of machines running in an enclosed environment.

"What have the wealthy, palatial hill dwellers done this time in their continued oppression of the lumpen-proletariat?"

"Not funny, Linc. Jobs are on the line. People are running scared. I have a mitt full of grievances just waiting to be resolved and there aren't enough hours in the day. Speaking of which...why are you taking my time?"

"Case I'm working on. I'm looking for some guys and I want to see if they spent any time as employees in the auto plants. I thought you might have access to a data base."

He hesitated for just a moment. "How recent were these guys employed?"

"As recent as 1951 through 1956. Give or take a day or two."

"You're serious?"

"As a grievance," I answered.

"Well, I'm only up to my neck in work and you want to pile it up a little higher. The 1950s. We didn't have the best record keeping back then. I can check some of the files and maybe talk with a few people who were working back then. The problem is, I can do some things with the Ford side, but they could have just as easily worked for GM, Chrysler or AMC, though it no longer exists."

"Couldn't you work your UAW network?"

"Yeah. For UAW business, of which this request doesn't qualify."

"All right, robber baron. I have two tickets to the Lion's game with San Francisco this Sunday. Their yours."

"Good. I always enjoy helping out a brother."

"One other thing; I have a question that couldn't wait until tomorrow," I said faking sincerity. "You once mentioned that part of your training as a Union representative included the history of how unions began with a specific focus on the events in the Detroit area."

"Is this a quiz?"

"Funny. Listen. I'm particularly interested in the events surrounding a guy named Charley Frey. He vanished sometime in 1954. Apparently he got some heavy backlash from his supposed beliefs in communism. I got the impression it created quite a division within the ranks."

"Charley Frey? Damn, this is a quiz," he yawned into the receiver.

"So, you do know about him."

"Only through reputation. He was long gone by the time I showed up in the plants. But for a lot of the old timers he's still revered. From what we were told, Charlie was a strong believer in the union but really questioned its focus on seniority as a way of determining who received the most benefits or favors. He thought it created a hierarchy among supposed equals. Apparently, there was a strong faction of support and it was creating a split among the brotherhood."

"How so?"

"On the surface you could say it was people in the trades versus the people who worked on the line."

"What was underneath the surface?"

"Black versus white for all practical reality. Charlie didn't like the fact that there was this informal system among the trades to move more whites into those positions than blacks. He was the first person to actually call the union to task. Somehow his actions became interpreted as consistent with a communist ideology. Given the closeness to that whole McCarthy thing and the country's general paranoia in the Fifties, that made Charlie a marked man. I think what sealed his fate was an interview he gave in which he said he understood how communism would be an acceptable philosophy for maintaining equity among the working masses. When it hit the press, the interviewer took a lot of liberty with Charlie's words and the next thing you know, the public lynching had begun. I think the powers of God and McCarthyists were brought down on Charlie. According to some of the guys who knew him, he talked about being followed, having his mail opened, hearing footsteps outside his home and a lot of other things that were designed to make him look ridiculous. The article also triggered his alienation as a union member and virtually assured his being silenced from that point on."

"What happened after that?"

"I'm a little vague on the actual events, but I remember reading somewhere that Charlie was being investigated on other matters, but it was well known that it was really about his political beliefs. Next thing we know...poof! He's gone. Vanished."

"Any idea what happened?" I asked, suspecting this story had an interesting parallel.

He suppressed a yawn. "At first it was thought that he was 'offed', him being so outspoken and everything. The union has certain ties that would have made it easy for him to end up in the cornerstone of somebody's skyscraper. But about...oh, ten, maybe fifteen, years ago it was rumored that he was seen at some mall in Montreal. 'Course, that's a lot of years in between sightings. People change. Could have been him, but who knows?"

"Anybody try to find out?"

"Communism wasn't exactly a politically correct word back then, Linc. Plus the union did make some strides in terms of blacks becoming more involved in the politics. I think over time, old Charlie became a forgotten incident in the union's history."

"Just one other question, Truman. I checked the archives and found references to Charlie in the *Free Press* and *News* back in '54. But there are no pictures or written references to his color. Was he a brother?"

"Was Capone a mobster?" He snickered at his question. "I'm not surprised at the lack of reference. Try the *Michigan Chronicle*. You'll probably have better luck."

"Thanks, bro. I owe you."

"Payment will be taken out of your hide the next time we're at a family gathering."

"Love those peaceful family outings."

He laughed heartily. "Yeah, don't I know it. Fax those names over to my office and I'll look into it when I get back over there. And get me those tickets to the 49ers game."

I jotted down the fax number, thanked him, hung up and immediately faxed over the names with a cover letter that said 'No info, no tickets'.

My overly stimulated mind and dog-tired body were left to work out the conflict over a simple, but important question. Do you believe in coincidence? In 1955, six black men suddenly vanished from the Detroit scene no more than a month apart. One was, more or less, a political fugitive, the others...? Was there a connection? As a police officer with the Oakland PD, we were trained to look for the story underneath the surface. To not be completely convinced by the obvious. Even when the obvious is irrefutable.

The connecting lines were showing me the back of the picture. So, to further assist my efforts, and due to my need to not waste time, I called Julie over at INFO-SEARCH, knowing she'd work late just to avoid driving through the slow traffic.

She answered on the second ring.

"Hey, Jules. It's me." I'm one of the very select few in all the universe who she'll let call her by that name.

"Hello, me."

"Cute. What do you have for me?"

I heard papers being shuffled in the background. "I was able to access the insurance carrier for the Detroit Board of Education. I did find that information you wanted on Matthew Stewart. I've got it summarized on one sheet. You want to write it down?"

"No. Just fax it over."

"It's on the way."

"What do I owe you?"

"Since you aren't available, which one of your brothers is single and in reasonable control of his faculties?"

"That would be Jefferson."

"The bounty hunter?"

"He does marvelous things with handcuffs."

"I can hardly wait. I'll send you a bill."

My next request probably meant nothing but I thought I'd ask anyway. "Hey, Jules, just one other thing."

"Your meter's running."

"See what you can find on a Pastor Ezell Jordan of the First Missionary Church."

"I've heard of him," she said neutrally. "How deep do you want me to look?"

"Skim the surface first. Probably nothing there anyway."

"Then why look?"

"Because it occurred to me to look."

"Okay with me. It's all billable. Listen for your fax."

It was only moments before the fax machine rang and the one-page info on Matt Stewart fell into the tray.

I sat down, propped my feet on the couch and read the paper.

Matthew Stewart was born October 8th, 1922, the son of an Army Major in Waco, Texas. His father's name was William and his mother's name was Sarah. He spent most of his adolescence living with his parents on a series of military bases in the U.S. and Europe. He came to Detroit in 1945 after a tour of duty with the Army and after having spent time during World War II fighting in Europe. He was immediately hired by the Detroit Board of Education where he was assigned as a Music and Science teacher at Miller High School in the area known as 'Blackbottom'.

He retired from the Detroit school system in 1965.

According to Julie's summary, Matt Stewart lived at the same address until his retirement, then he spent the next ten years living at various addresses in and around the Detroit area. Apparently he left Detroit in 1981 and was using a post office box that Julie had traced to Lakeville in Missaukee County which was about three or four hours northwest of Detroit. It seems that Matt's retirement checks were still being sent to that post office box. There was no phone number listed. Probably not unusual for that part of Michigan. Julie also confirmed Matt Stewart's location through the *Detroit Free Press*. It seems that he never canceled his subscription. So a daily paper as well as monthly retirement checks were pieces of his connection to the rest of the world.

There didn't appear to be a distinct employment pattern after his retirement, though he did stay in Detroit for several years. I wondered what he did after he left the school system.

I stood up and stretched, unloosening every tight muscle in what could have gone for a Tarzan call for elephant help. It felt good.

I stepped into my bedroom to check through my closet for something appropriate to wear to my early evening rendezvous with Erotica. I wanted, and needed, the break from my investigation to meet with this mysteriously attractive woman for whom I'd generated a subtle sweat and experienced tightened muscles in certain critical areas of my body.

"Focus, Keller. She's a client," I muttered, thinking about Detective Malone as well.

My search was interrupted by the familiar cat-claws-on-a-window sound in the living room. I walked in there and saw my buddy Free Ride pawing at the window. I thought it was strange since he rarely shows up for breakfast and dinner on the same day.

"Rodent supply must be short," I mumbled. I strolled over to the window and peered into his seemingly pathetic eyes. I rolled open the window and he quickly bounded into the room and onto the floor. He did a quick circle and immediately fell to his side. He glanced up with that look only cats have mastered. The one that says 'ain't I cute and wouldn't you just love to pet me?'

I glanced down at him, reluctant to play the game, but like most fools taken in by these feline phenomenons, I couldn't resist.

Within a split second of bending down to rub his side, I heard the loud crash of exploding glass. Time seemed to move slowly as I dove to the floor. Shards of glass bounced off me as another explosion broke another pane of glass. Instinctively, I rolled closer to the wall trying to cut down any visible angle. Another explosion caught me melding as close to the wall as possible, literally crawling underneath its coat of paint. Glass continued to bounce wildly around my living room as I waited an eternity for an end to the timeless chaos.

It ended as abruptly as it started. The silence was magnified as I listened for other unusual noises. Other than the loud, rapid thumping in my chest, there were no other noises of substance or concern. I peeled myself off the wall and surveyed my immediate surroundings.

The pieces of glass, like snowflakes, all had their own distinct shape and lay scattered across my carpet and couch. I rolled over into a sitting position keeping my back to the wall and waited. Had my senses not been on full alert I might not have realized that I had my arms folded in a protective embrace around Free Ride. His head was cradled on the inside of my elbow and he seemed perfectly content to lie there and be held. He looked up at me as I looked down at him.

"I guess next time you'll eat out," I said while rubbing his head. "Looks like I owe you, boy."

I felt my breathing return to normal as I slowly rose to a standing position away from the window. From outside in the hall I heard a nervous shrill of a voice ask, "Is everyone alright in there?"

"Who's asking?" I yelled back.

"Mr. Greenway from across the hall." My neighbor, who spends most of his time walking around the parking lot picking up litter and other memorabilia, is a retired dock worker who fancies himself as quite a catch for divorced women or widows between the ages of thirty-five and sixty. "Are you okay in there, son?"

I opened my front door and saw the white haired, flaccid muscled Mr. Greenway clad only in a thick maroon robe, white bottoms and slippers, standing among a growing crowd of onlookers.

"Hello, Mr. Greenway." I waved slightly.

"Jesus, Mary and Joseph, son! Were those shots we heard?" he asked with wide-eyed exclamation as he inched toward the window.

I glanced around my apartment, quickly checking for traces of evidence besides the broken glass. It didn't take long to spot the conclusive evidence that was embedded several feet away from me; three holes in the wall, each about the same size and circumference, placed about three inches apart in a loosely diagrammed triangle. The shooter wasn't very good.

Or I was lucky.

"Yes, those were shots you heard, Mr. Greenway," I said motioning for him not to come any closer. He hesitated. "This is a crime scene, Mr. Greenway. You won't be helping the investigators by coming over here."

He stepped back with the rest of the gathering crowd as the increasing blare of sirens signaled the approach of the patrol unit closest to the area when the 9-1-1 call was phoned in.

Someone believed that I knew something and was willing to risk it all to be sure I didn't tell. Only what was it they thought I knew that they didn't want told? And which of my several on-going cases were they particularly interested in?

I assumed I was working on a simple missing person case that went back forty years. My assumption had been my first mistake. I assumed I shouldn't make another.

Turns out that next to my first assumption about Erotica, this was the best assumption I made throughout this entire case.

Chapter 11

I recited my story several times to the first, second and third wave of officers, staying basically with the facts as I knew them. Each time I told the incident, it actually gave me new insight as to what might be going on.

Even more unusual than having someone rip three bullets through my bedroom window was having a Lieutenant from Homicide show up as an investigator when there was no supine body to examine. This crime scene orchestra done in 'D' minor was being coordinated by the equally competent, and not too amiable, Lieutenant Nick Knackton. A hog jowled, burly twenty year veteran with curly prematurely salt and pepper hair and a walnut tone skin, he prowled the scene like an irritated bulldog ready to take a bite out of anything within snapping distance. We've known each other from before and have crossed swords one time too often. As he lumbered toward me, I tried to keep in mind that the real reason for our dislike of each other was a certain homicide detective for whom we both shared similar lusts.

"I see you're still a popular guy in this city, Keller," he said with obvious disdain. "Someone must still be upset with you for all those missed interceptions during your heyday."

"Your concern is underwhelming, Lieutenant."

"Who've you pissed off lately?"

"Just you. But this doesn't have your subtlety."

The crowd of onlookers and officers paid little attention to the normal exchange that was part of our brief and wonderful history. Our banter wouldn't make it any easier on Malone. She had to work with this clown.

"What aren't you telling me, Keller? You want me to believe this was just a random shooting? This ain't your typical driveby."

"It's more like a drive in shooting, but let's not play semantics."

He glowered. "According to what we dug out of your wall, you were fired upon by someone using a Glock. Most likely a 9 millimeter. The pattern indicates that it was willful and deliberate, not random. This was not a driveby. Someone was using that melon on your neck for target practice. The question is why. So now I'll ask again; who have you pissed off lately?"

I wasn't aware of anyone who'd go through this much trouble just because of my investigation to determine what happened to The Sentiments. Besides, it could have been from another case, past or present. But I thought I'd give him an answer. "Just the usual crowd of repressed, uptight signature killers upset by the new zoning laws."

"It's your funeral, wiseass. I'll make sure I come around and ID the body. But somebody shot at you from across the street."

"I know, Lieutenant. I already checked out the angles before your crime techs arrived." I slid out from the kitchen chair and walked over to the small window that looked out onto the street side of the building. "I figured the shots were fired from the fourth or fifth floor of that apartment building." The building I pointed to was an eight story apartment dwelling originally constructed near the turn of the century as a hotel endearingly known as St. Peter. "There are two apartments on the fourth and fifth floors that I know are abandoned. Getting in and out of that place is an insult to any second story man. The shooter must have set up shop over there and just waited for the right moment."

From where we stood, we could see through the dingy windows, the outlines and movements of investigating officers looking for available clues.

"You're lucky that cat showed up when it did," Nick stated.

"Yeah. He's a regular Saint."

"You sure you've told me everything I need to know about what you're doing?"

"I've told you everything you need to know," I said trying to display a convincing streak of sincerity.

His tilted head and the straight line formed by his mouth told me he wasn't buying it. "That doesn't mean you've told me all there is. Don't worry, Keller, if you're lying to me, I'll find out."

Nick hung around after the investigating team had finished collecting their evidence and gathering statements from people near the scene.

He waited until we were alone. He fastened the bottom button of his tweed jacket and headed for the door. His burly right hand completely covered the door knob when he turned back to me. "Let's get one thing clear, Keller. In my book you're just a two-bit, penny ante, key-lock peeper living off your supposed gridiron glory. In my mind that makes you one step removed from sewer slime. I'd just as soon step on you than give you the time of day. Unfortunately, in this town, athletes, no matter how untalented, are revered so they get advantages not available to the average slob. I don't know what you're up to, but it stinks short of waste deposits. You'll trip up and I'll be there to grind you into the ground."

"Lieutenant, is this what's known as constructive feedback? Something they teach you in your managing human relations seminar?"

"Long as we understand one another, peeper," he growled.

"We do, Lieutenant." He turned to walk out the door. "Oh, Lieutenant," I called out. "So tell me, how are you spending your nights these days?"

I thought one of his eyes would roll over. "Don't fuck with me, peeper. You couldn't take the screwin'." He pivoted and started down the steps.

"I'll mention to Malone how helpful you were."

He stormed down the steps and I closed my apartment door.

When I had the place back to myself, I surveyed the damage, walked back to my bedroom, showered and jumped into a clean set of casual clothing, strapped on my shoulder holster, placed the .38 in its holster and grabbed my black jacket out of the closet. I glanced over at the pieces of cardboard taped over the broken windows by the creative and industrious property management representative who was so concerned for my safety that he swore he'd have the windows replaced by the end of the week. Fortunately, I wasn't armed when he made the offer.

Despite the other cases I was working on, I couldn't help but feel by some sixth sense that this shooting came from a full day of asking a lot of people a lot of questions about The Sentiments. And the further I went into this investigation, the more someone kept changing the rules. This most recent glass shattering experience convinced me that I wanted answers and in order to find out what I needed to know, I'd have to forsake the soft inquiring approach and play by my own rules.

I knew exactly where I'd start. I had a dinner date coming up with her real soon anyway.

Chapter 12

I kept the radio off for now as I endured the stop-and-go evening traffic of Detroit's over used streets. Streets that were laid out by city planners from a long-ago generation from a far-away world that had no way of knowing how many vehicles would be on America's roads in a short six or seven decades into the future as they knew it. What a testament to Detroit! The fruits of her labors now hang heavy on her own branches. Her astounding and triumphant success against tough odds in becoming the undisputed Queen of the Auto Industry, and thus spearheading the mass transportation revolution, has changed the world forever. Some for good, some for not, and Detroit has plenty examples of both. I couldn't help but realize what a dramatic and pivotal piece of world history was passing beneath the tires of my quick and reliable Nova.

Love it or hate it, Detroit is here to stay. One way or another. She'll continue to grow, to adapt, to evolve. I won't say it often, but sometimes I have to let myself realize that I really love this town. If you know where to look, there's *a lot* of good going on.

As I made the turn onto Woodward Avenue, I decided I wasn't going to say anything to Erotica about my recent and impromptu interior decorating project. At least not yet. I'd been thinking: who threw the lead at me and why?

The idea that maybe it was because of another case wasn't cutting it. Something told me that the most recent addition to my list of clientele may be into something a little deeper than a nostalgia thing. I had questions. A number of questions that might help me understand why The Sentiments were so important to her, and why, damnit, would someone want to shoot me over it? They were questions that could have easily been answered in a more professional environment, not on a dinner date in one of Detroit's better examples of class and elegance. But like the moth attracted to certain death by the flame, I was drawn to her in ways that an office conference could not satisfy.

It was a dangerous attraction.

Especially for someone in a state of semi-commitment to an equally attractive homicide detective.

A woman licensed to carry and discharge a firearm.

It was only dinner and conversation. Conversation that might help move the case along.

No harm. No foul.

At least, that's what I rationalized as I pulled into the narrow parking lot.

At least the meal was Italian.

***

Appolonia's on Woodward Avenue is the last of the real Italian restaurants with an authentic Italian atmosphere, not the commercialized, franchised and homogenized substitutes that seem to delight the taste buds of millions of Generation X'ers.

Housed in a two story, pink and green stucco building with green and white awnings and shingled windows, Appolonia's is the last holdout in an area in desperate need of urban renewal and additional parking. A classy place where people go to feel important and sensible.

The food is second to none.

I squeezed my Nova in between a Jaguar LX and a Cadillac DeVille. Both cars tried to take up two spaces, but I managed to just squeeze in. My car was safe from any car jacker because given the three choices, where would you put your money?

The parking lot was well lit and employed the usual half-blind, over-weight, five dollar an hour rent-a-cop to provide additional security.

Right.

Once inside the double glass doors, I walked down the blue carpeted steps until I found myself standing next to the brown lectern being greeted by a middle age gentleman with advanced graying hair, dark eyes and a luminous smile.

The blue draped, moderately chilled restaurant was lightened by glass encased candles placed on top of the white clothed tables. The walls were adorned with pictures of famous Italians. Frank Sinatra, Tony Bennet, Dean Martin and Joe DiMaggio led the celebrity display along with scenes from Italy-looking places taken during the early part of the century.

The smiling greeter's name, not surprisingly, was Antonio. I gave him my name and said I was supposed to meet someone.

"Ah. A Miss Tremaine instructed me to bring you to her booth the moment you arrived." 'Miss' Tremaine? His high pitched voice had an undertone of lust. "This way, Mr. Keller."

Through the finely carpeted maze, with music from the home country serenading through hidden speakers, I was led to the corner booth where 'Miss' Erotica Tremaine sat, finely sculpted in a dinner outfit that spoke more of desserts than appetizers.

She wore black espresso riding pants and a wool ribbed short sleeve turtleneck that hugged and accented her slim figure. A four button, fuchsia, wool cardigan jacket with a brown leather trim hung loosely opened, ex-posing the diamond necklace nameplate that had captured my attention the first night we met.

Seeing her had a relaxing effect. My blood was still pumping faster than usual from the fireworks a short while ago, but seeing her smiling there in the elegant surroundings was like I just stepped into a warm and calming breeze.

I extended my hand in a formal greeting, but foremost in my mind was how was I going to maintain a civil conversation in a cultural atmosphere designed for opening forbidden passages and probing untouched areas.

"Mrs. Tremaine."

"Mrs. Tremaine," she repeated in a playful mock. "Such formality. Please call me Erotica so that the conversation isn't too stilted." I nodded my agreement. "Please sit down, Lincoln."

I slid into the leather covered booth, sure that all eyes in the restaurant were watching my every move.

"I took the liberty of ordering white wine, a Chardonnay. I hope that was alright."

"Fine. White wine only makes me goofy."

"Then I'll order two bottles," she said as she unfolded the laminated covered menu.

I opened mine. Tall menus with numerous items are great for providing a natural gap in awkward conversation. Gives the mind a chance to regroup and think of the next thing to be said.

I thought of a real good one. "How about an appetizer?" I asked. "See anything you like?"

"Yeah, I do. There's even some things on the menu as well."

Outwardly, I ignored the comment. Inwardly, I strained to keep my composure.

We agreed on steamed mushrooms just as the waiter, a latte-toned, black haired man in his mid-twenties returned with the white wine.

He poured the customary sample. I did the customary swish, taste, eye roll and head nod. He filled both our glasses and took the order for appetizers.

"Shall we make a toast?" she asked, already holding her glass over the table.

"What shall we toast to?"

She paused. "Hmm...how about lost lives recovered and nights that have no boundaries?"

I shrugged with a smile, tapped glasses with her and we both took our obligatory sip.

"Erotica," I said as the effects of the wine danced in the back of my mouth. "I'd like to give you an update on what I've learned and there's some questions I'd like to ask."

"There's no rush...is there?"

I eased the wine glass onto the table. "I'm on your time. Aren't you concerned as to how it gets used?"

"You don't appear to be abusing it."

"You're my client. Don't you want an update?"

"Lincoln, do you know that in certain cultures it is considered rude, even disrespectful to discuss business without first spending time getting to know one another? Inquiring about each other's family? Getting some sense of the person's history?"

"I don't get out much."

"Then consider yourself properly chastised," she softly scolded.

"So, Erotica. In the spirit of respect and social discourse, who are you?"

"In what sense? The existential Who Am I or the general Who Am I?"

"Try the practical..." I glanced at my watch. "...7:53 p.m. Tuesday night Who Am I?"

She sighed, glanced upward and began to tell me the summarized version of Erotica Tremaine.

She talked and I poured more wine. Between the appetizers and the main course of Vegetarian Lasagna and Shrimp Fettucini, she talked about growing up as the only child in a middle class home on Detroit's west side. There was nothing outstanding other than her genuine love of music. She'd spent time singing in a gospel choir. Rarely as lead vocalist, but was told she had a soothing falsetto. After graduating from Northwestern, she headed west to UCLA to study music and hoped for a break in the budding west coast music industry. She received her master's in Fine Arts, hired an agent and spent the better part of her twenties moving from one gig to another. After a couple of bands, two singing groups, some commercials and one ill fated solo attempt later, she wound up back home in Detroit doing contract work as a background vocalist for a variety of commercials.

"You know the voice-overs for WALT FM smooth jazz?" she asked while wiping the lasagna sauce from her bottom lip.

"I'm sure I've heard them. I usually tune in and out of what's being said unless it's an old Temptations song."

"Well, my voice is mixed with the other two. Those voice-overs really helped the stations ratings. Soft and serene with just a subtle hint of sexual longing."

Two years ago while rehearsing a commercial, the client happened to be in the studio, heard her voice, saw her style, asked her out...and the rest is history.

"You still do contract singing?" I asked.

"From time to time. Not as much as I'd like."

"What's your interest in finding The Sentiments?"

My question was followed by a wide eyed stare. "Well, that certainly was an abrupt turn. I suppose the social amenities are over?"

"I'm not giving you an update. I'm just getting information."

"Okay. Tell me what you have so far and I'll tell you why I'm interested."

I gave her everything I had, which didn't amount to much as long as I skipped the part about the bullet holes in my apartment. She listened intently, stopping only to sip the wine. I noticed that she was particularly attentive when I mentioned the police officer, Craig Roberts.

"So that's the long and short so far," I concluded.

"What about this police officer? Any idea who he is and what's his interest?"

"Not yet. I have a contact who might help me. I hope to have a better idea tomorrow." The waiter came and removed the uneaten food and dishes. We asked for a few more minutes before deciding on dessert. "Anyway, I'm obligated to ask you that given what you know, do you still want me to continue looking into this matter?"

"Yes, I most certainly do."

"Why?"

"Back to that again, are we?"

"Yep."

She opened her black velvet purse and removed an opened pack of Virginia Slims. I'd noticed how she refrained from smoking until we came to this point. She flicked open her lighter, took one drag and blew the smoke toward the ceiling. Faye Dunaway couldn't have done it any better. "About a year ago, someone very special to me began talking about his involvement in the music industry in the late Forties and early Fifties. Some of the stories he told about black groups, the record industry, the travel and the clubs are laced with happier memories of what was a tough time for black groups. Anyway, the more he talked, the more he talked about The Sentiments." She paused to take another drag on her cigarette. "I began to get the sense that there was something unresolved. So I started making discreet inquiries. I know a few people in the industry, so I was able to gather some information which I've given you. I tried to trace their families, but they've scattered over the years. Most of them don't live in Detroit, or are too young to know anything or have since died. I hit a brick wall, didn't know what else to do. That's when I was given your name. I called your office and got your answering machine. On a hunch, I drove by and went to your office. Naturally, you weren't in. I must have looked distressed because one of your neighbors told me to try Artie's. So I did and there you were. The rest you know."

That helped. But I wanted the real. "If you don't mind my asking, who's the special someone?"

"I'd rather not say just yet. I'd like to see how far this investigation goes."

"Erotica, it doesn't take much to figure out that you have more than just a passing interest in finding these men. Now, given what I assume to be their ages and what I assume to be your age, it stands to reason that you may be a blood relative or an interested friend of someone's family. To be honest, if I really needed to find out, I'd just run your license plate number through a someone I know at DMV, pull up the basic information and through another source, cross check the information with credit reports, college records, birth certificate, marriage certificate and on and on. Catch my drift?"

She smiled like someone relieved of a secret. "I'm impressed. I had no idea I was hiring the world's greatest private detective."

"You have me confused with a colleague of mine named Elvis Cole. Just simple deduction ala Sherlock Holmes."

"Well, I didn't realize my life was an open book. Aren't there privacy laws?"

"Sure there are laws. Written by lawyers looking to specialize. In this information age, law or no law, privacy is a meaningless concept."

She sat back in her chair, her red tipped, manicured fingers steepled on her lap. "Then it would be easy to find out if it's possible that, say, Adam Carter is alive and he's my husband."

I stopped my attempt at showing off to let the words settle in. I wanted to ask WHAT!?, but it came out, "Is Adam Carter your husband?"

She blew a self satisfying cloud of smoke toward the ceiling. "Yep."

Chapter 13

Adam Carter was Leonard Tremaine!? Alive and living in Detroit!? As his wife put it: yep. As I sat across from her and noted how beautiful she can even make a cigarette look, I remembered what Mrs. Dibell said about Adam Carter, and how she smiled when she called him the prankster and how he was the shorter of the group but just as handsome as them all.

And now he pulled off another prank. One that's worked like a charm for forty years. Geographically, he didn't go far when he 'disappeared' those many years ago, but socially, economically and culturally...he moved light years away. As I would later find out, he went about 30 miles north of

Detroit to a place where no one looking for a black man would ever think of looking: Oakland County, Michigan.

And look at him now. Tremaine Home Improvement. Thoughts swam through my head. There had to been some, not much, but some plastic surgery or something at some time. Going on television and starring in years of tacky but amusing commercials was not a good way to go on the lamb. Or was it? He sure fooled me pretty well. I'm sure I'm not the only one.

"Your husband!?" I said/asked. "The guy in the center in the picture you gave me yesterday. What's going on?"

The show of unbelievablility on my face must have shown through like a beacon. "Lower your contempt, Lincoln. Despite the thirty year difference in our age, I happen to love him very much. More than his four ex-wives."

"I wasn't thinking *that*. It's that you deliberately deceived me. Why?"

"Okay." She lifted her hands slightly in a conciliatory gesture. "Sorry. But there's two reasons why I didn't tell you right off: one, I don't want him to know that I've hired a PI, and; two, I was afraid it might prejudice your investigation."

"I thought he looked familiar, but I sure couldn't place him...until now. 'Tremaine Home Improvement'. He used to advertise on Bill Kennedy At The Movies. Channel 9 on Sundays. I can still see his face staring at the camera using his classic line; 'Remember our name, we're Tremaine. We say, Don't Remove, Improve. Call us at Tyler 65000'. That's the client you met two years ago."

"Yeah. That's my husband. Surprised?"

"Of course, I'm surprised! I'm surprised by a lot of things," I said to her and myself. Pausing to look at her, I asked inquisitively, "What the hell's going on here? You only want to find his friends. I can understand that. But why'd you want me to think he's among the missing? Besides, he should know where to find his friends. Why waste your money? If you really wanted me to find the other four members, he'd be one of my first leads."

"That's just it. He really doesn't know. Says he hasn't got a clue. Look, I'm sorry I can't tell you everything. I don't even think *I* know everything. But please understand this much: he really doesn't know where the others are and there's something about it that he really needs to resolve. I want to help him resolve it. " She paused. "For the last two or three weeks, he's been talking...no, make that obsessing on the time when he sang with The Sentiments. So much so that he's neglected the business, he doesn't return phone calls and spends most of his day sitting in our den listening to music from the 1950s. Yesterday, not too long after dinner, I walked in on him sleeping in his favorite lounger listening to The Platters. I started to cover him with a blanket when I noticed lying on the floor next to him was an exact copy of the suits they wore when The Sentiments were starting out."

She didn't answer why she led me to think Adam Carter, aka Leonard Tremaine, was also missing. I'll follow that one up later. But now at least I knew who her someone special was. I couldn't think of what to say just at the moment so I suggested meeting with her husband to discuss his blue funk.

"No! I don't want him contacted at all. That's why I didn't want you to know who he really is. He can't be helpful. This is my request and I'd like it honored."

"It seriously limits what I can do."

"I'm your client, Lincoln; not my husband. I pay your fee so I call the shots."

"I don't need this kind of business. You want to pay me to do a job, fine, but I work by my rules, not yours."

Her retreat was immediate and strained. "I...I didn't mean, I just...Sorry, Lincoln. I don't want to limit you, but my husband can't know about the investigation...please."

"He's certain to be helpful."

"I don't want to get his hopes up only to have them ripped down like old curtains. I want something concrete before I approach him. If you don't find out anything, then he's no worse off than when you started."

I waved to the waiter, told him we'd pass on dessert and to leave the bill. The level of tension had risen somewhat and I didn't feel a need to push it any farther. "I appreciate the fact that you're trying to protect your husband. It's probably none of my business. But in order to conduct a thorough investigation, I need access to all the resources...of which your husband is one."

"Are we leaving?"

"And if I'm really going to be of any real help to you," I continued, ignoring her question, "I need you to be absolutely forthcoming. I protect client confidentiality like a shrine." I took out my wallet and dropped the cash plus the generous gratuity on the bill tray. "I'm leaving. I have work to do. You want to stay, that's your business. I can check out other leads while it's still early."

"Lincoln. I didn't mean to..."

"What you meant is none of my business. You're paying me to solve a mystery and find, now it's four and not five, guys who sang together way back before you and I were born. One of whom is your lawfully wedded significant other. I'll do the best I can and send you a bill for my time and expenses minus tonight's meal. That's just me being a nice guy." I slid out from the booth. "I'll call you tomorrow, Mrs. Carter."

"Back to Mrs. again. Wait, Lincoln." I stopped just to fill the moment. "How about staying a nice guy and walking me to my car?"

Basic gentlemanly manners 101 as taught by my late Aunt May burned like a cattle brand upon instinctive cognitive responses. Sure I'd walk her to her car. What gentleman wouldn't? I nodded, almost imperceptibly, as she slowed to where I stood and eased her arm through mine.

We stepped into the calm night air like disagreeable lovers glad that the night had ended.

She directed me toward a two-toned silver and black Lexus. I tried not to be too impressed with the choice of Raider colors. I figured it to be a coincidence. Despite its rarity, a coincidence sometimes does occur.

The familiar beep of a car alarm being disengaged brought reality back to the moment. She unlocked the door, slid into the gun metal gray interior like a royal seductress and I closed the door behind her.

"Good night, Mrs. Carter," I said as I heard the door lock in place.

She started the noiseless engine and powered down the driver side window. "Linc. Wait a minute please."

I'd put a few feet between us when I stopped. "Yes, Mrs. Carter?"

"I just wanted to thank you for dinner and...for all you've done so far."

"When I'm done, you'll get my bill."

Her returning gaze read caution and hurt, the one used on every sap who is vulnerable in the two places that hurt the easiest. That brought my attention back to her car. I knew I was close to the flame. Close enough to be burned. "I have my reasons, Linc. I don't think my husband can be helpful and I don't want him involved. Please try to understand."

"It might have saved me a lot of leg work."

"And it might not have."

"But I'll never know...will I?"

She sat back in the leather covered bucket seat and released an exasperated sigh. "I just don't want him involved."

I stood away from the car door. My hands held chest high as if I was surrendering. "It's your ticket. I'll do what I can. Drive safely."

"I had a nice time, Linc. Really. Thank you."

I waved good bye and watched as she backed out and eased out of the parking lot and onto Woodward Avenue.

Once inside my Nova, I fired up the engine and pressed the button to automatically jump to WJAZ. My mood was rewarded by Grady Tate's rendition of 'Sack Full of Dreams'.

I suppose anyone else would have driven home, flipped on the twenty-four hour Monster channel and watched an endless parade of Godzilla versus anybody movies while drowning a pint of Jack Daniels until you or the cable channel gave in.

I eliminated that option. For two reasons; I'd seen all the Godzilla movies and I was out of Jack Daniels.

It was still early enough to catch a drink and try and figure out what the hell was going on with me.

***

My careening spirits ceased its broken winged flight and landed me at a windowless drink-and-die hole known as Mellow Yellow's near the soon-to-be completed Davison freeway. Prior to reconstruction, the three-laned, shoulderless, grassy hole was a place where old mufflers and tires went to die.

Inside the smoke tinted, clattery den of ladder chairs and red vinyl covered bar stools, an aging crowd of players and dealers, use-to-be's and might-have-been's, gathered in a weekly ritual of story telling and anecdotes in a valiant attempt to hold back the years, despite the abundance of sweat stained stingy brims and wigs from a previous decade.

I found an open stool near the end of the bar, parked my carcass while Johnny Taylor's 'Cheaper to Keep Her' blared from an old Wurlitzer juke box.

The bartender, an ebony toned bulk with sleepy eyes and a scattered outline of unshaven gray hair cast a shadow across my end of the bar.

"What can I get you?" he asked in a raspy smoker's throat.

I ordered a gin and tonic with a twist and while he put together the drink, I put together what had happened.

A blind man, in a dark room, staring in the opposite direction with one eye tied behind his back would have seen it.

I'd crossed the line.

That invisible barrier that separates business from everything else and demands professional behavior so as not to mess up the results, had been cracked.

There was an opening and I put my hand through.

From the moment Erotica approached me at Artie's I focused on the doughnut and not on the hole...so to speak.

I wanted something beyond what she asked and I hoped she wanted it too.

Maybe she did. Maybe I just read too much into what I believed to be flirtatious behavior.

Maybe I should have thought more with the head on the fence and not the one in the tower.

I'd just gotten into a nice round of self-maligning and a second drink when I was tapped, not so gently, on my shoulder.

I turned and standing next to me was a bearded, slick haired extensive work of bronze flesh in a too tight Irish green sharkskin suit.

He was weaving.

I immediately thought of the essay question I missed on an undergraduate Anthropology exam. We were asked to describe the 'Missing Link'. I couldn't. I'd seen enough offensive and defensive lineman over the years to know that the 'Missing Link' was possible. Now after years of intensive searches in some of the far off regions of the world, here he was. In Detroit, at Mellow Yellow's.

Drunk.

"You're in my seat," he said, slurring the s.

I turned my head in the direction of the slurring s and came face to face with Big Foot's drunken twin. Not my idea of an eventful evening. So I nodded and moved over to the next open bar stool.

That's when I noticed the room becoming less riotous.

That's also when Chewbacca tapped me again.

"Yes," I said spotting him with my peripheral vision.

"You're still in my seat," he slurred in stereo. I glanced around and noticed the crowd becoming amused by the unexpected entertainment.

Game time. And I'd wandered into the arena.

I looked up at the bleary eyed Colossus, now sporting a gap tooth grin.

"Look, Ivan. Kindly point out to me the one seat in here that doesn't have your name on it and I'll go sit there."

"They're all mine. I own the bar. Want to make something of it?"

I didn't want to. If this guy's skin was green instead of white, he could've passed for Godzilla. I asked for my bar bill, dropped a twenty on the counter and tried to walk around the Great Wall of Chatter.

He blocked my path and the entire room quieted, the only noise came from the drifting smoke.

He pointed a beefy finger. "You're a stranger in my bar. I don't like strangers in my bar and I should kick your ass for coming in here without my permission."

I folded my arms across my chest. "You don't want to do that."

"Why not?"

"Look into my eyes, hamhock. Look close. Tell me what you see." He stared for just a brief moment. "Right. There you go. You see it. Total unconcern for whatever happens to me. You see, I don't care. You know what that means. It means I just became the most dangerous event in your life and I know it's something you're not used to."

He breathed heavily and I sensed an uncertainty among the patrons.

I had more to say. "Here's what really makes it dangerous for you, Beef Man. You have now had too much time to think about this. You've hesitated and you're uncertain despite the alcohol on your breath and in your blood, your head is fighting to make sense of what's happening. You see, I'm someone with nothing to lose. You and I start something right here and right now and there are four outcomes, all of which favor me."

He looked around the quiet room. Probably for support. Maybe trying to find a way to lightly pass it off. I watched his hands and pressed on.

"Option one: You kick my ass. Your rep remains intact, but I don't lose anything because I wasn't expected to win. Option two: We fight to draw. No winners or losers, but your rep is hurt and mine is established. Option three: We battle and I win. Your rep's shot and I'm the new king of the hill. How do you like that so far from a man who has nothing to lose. Care to risk it?"

"You said there were four," stated the bartender through ever watchful eyes.

"Oh yeah. Option four: We can forget about this nonsense, you let me buy you a drink and you agree to listen to me talk about my already frustrating evening."

He blinked intensely. "Does it involve a woman?"

"What doesn't?"

"You just bought a listener."

We slapped five, the bar members cheered and returned to their business with one more story to tell.

"What's your name, bro?" he asked as we slid onto the bar stools.

"Keller, Lincoln Keller. But tonight you can call me mushface."

The bartender brought us a round. I had the gin and tonic, he had a tall malt liquor.

"Everyone calls me Tank."

"Respectfully, I'm sure."

We toasted and he took off the first half in one gulp.

He wiped his mouth and set his drink on the counter. "So, Lincoln, what's her name?"

"Erotica."

"Really?" Tank was a good listener as most drunks go. I bought three rounds, thanked him and we exchanged business cards.

He'd never met a private investigator.

I'd never met someone of his...demeanor who was a florist.

We laughed about each other's chosen profession and wandered out of the bar and across Woodward Avenue to our parked cars.

Tank drove a blue Econoline Van with a blue lettered advertisement that said. 'You Order Flowers, We Deliver Love'.

"Keller, you drunken bastard, you're all right."

"You're not so bad yourself, Tank." What else could I say?

I yawned, shook my head and slid the key into the driver's side door of my Nova as Tank roared onto a clear lane on Woodward. I thought about the path back to my apartment having remembered that the Davison Freeway was unavailable for travel.

It was during those few inattentive seconds that I felt the sudden jolt on the space that separates my shoulder from my neck, like someone had just dropped a brick from a three story building onto my right side.

Chapter 14

I grabbed the spot were the pain was sharp and wincing. I didn't have time to think about what was going on when I was spun around and punched solidly in the stomach.

I might have succumbed to the pain of that blow if not for the fact that I instinctively tightened my stomach muscles and while my attacker had leaned forward to follow through, I headbutted him.

He immediately grabbed his forehead. Someone else kicked me in the ribs. I took the blow, quickly spun around and smashed his face with my clenched forearm.

It was all happening too quickly.

Someone grabbed me from behind and threw me into my car. I braced for the impact and was able to ward off some of its sting.

My solar plexus collided with the driver side mirror. I doubled over. I felt a kick to the back of my left knee and another sharp pain in between my shoulders.

My head buzzed as I fought to stay on my feet. Memories of being trampled by huge offensive linemen who ran like Airedales and stomped like wrestlers triggered the adrenaline I needed to keep from falling on the ground. Another blow caught me on the side of the head and I thought the back of my eyes shifted.

The blow must have sent me to the outer reaches of comedy heaven because I thought I heard unmistakable laughter.

Someone was laughing. A staccato laughter of intense amusement.

I felt no further pain, but I heard other sounds. Like flesh being smashed against more flesh.

Some grunts and more laughter.

I managed to pull myself up. I tried to focus my vision against the images that seemed to scatter back across Woodward.

One image still loomed in front of me. I couldn't see his face, but I managed to raise both arms, with my fists clenched, ready for action.

"Hey easy, Keller. We already decided not to do this."

I recognized Tank's voice. I exhaled deeply and leaned against the hood of my car. "Tank? What the hell happened?"

"As I was pulling away, I just happened to glance in my rear view mirror and I saw those three guys come after you. So I doubled back."

"There were three of them?"

"Yeah. Not very good though. Looked like rank amateurs. Probably why there were three."

"Jesus."

Tank's image became clearer and I felt the adrenaline pump a little less. "You get a good look at them?"

"Overage beefcakes high on fat content. Two rare, one well done. They each ran off in a different direction. Didn't see any car."

"Doesn't sound like anyone I know," I said.

"What was all that about, Keller?" he asked.

I leaned forward. I began to regain my normal breathing. "Damned if I know."

"Piss anybody off lately?"

"Only everyone who loves me."

"This got anything to do with that woman problem we talked about?"

"It shouldn't, but it's possible."

I stood up stretching each muscle that had an obvious pain.

I couldn't think of anyone who'd have reason to jump me at this time of night having just come out of a bar. However, the coincidence of the bullets through my window and now the attempted mugging. Hardly a co-incidence and I'd be a fool to think otherwise.

"You sure you're okay, Keller?"

"Yeah, Tank. Just a bit shattered on the manly front side, but I'll live." I looked at that walking building and attempted a minor grin. "I owe you one my man. Thanks."

"Forget it."

I eased over to the driver's side door, found my keys still in the lock. Before I stepped into my car, I hesitated.

"Tank. Was it my imagination or did I hear someone laughing?"

"Oh, that. Yeah, that was me. I always laugh when I get into a fight. The more people there are, the harder I laugh."

"So a fight is funny to you?"

"I enjoy a good fight. It's better than old reruns of Amos n' Andy."

"So if you and I had thrown down in the bar, you would've been laughing through the whole thing?"

"Yeah. It makes people nervous. Then they're not sure what they've gotten into."

I nodded. "Tank. I don't think I could've handled you laughing while I'm trying to take you down."

"I wouldn't have fought you anyway, Keller. All I wanted was some-one to buy me a drink. You were new in the bar and the best target."

"Why didn't you just ask?"

"And miss all this fun?" His smile showed the mischief in his eye and then I realized I'd been had. I couldn't help but like him. "Can you make it from here?" he asked genuinely concerned.

"Yeah. I'm fine," I said, almost telling the truth. "I'll see you around."

I picked up where I last left off. My keys were still hanging in the door lock. After unlocking my ever-present Club, I fired up my always reliable chariot and peeled into traffic. I drove the main streets, cutting as straight a path as possible back to Livernois Avenue.

My senses were operating on overdrive. I made a quick mental examination of some of the happenings that happened lately and realized that just a little over the last 24 hours I'd become reacquainted with marijuana, was escorted by 'Night Life' and his silent henchman, had one of my windows taken out by hot lead, found out I was lied to by one of two of the world's most beautiful women, was mugged and drank a little too much with some manic white dude wide enough to be a building. My thoughts were extended to another topic when I instinctively glanced into the rear-view mirror: that black Buick again. Now what? I was certain the two men in it have been following me since earlier in the day. I think I saw them first maybe when I was leaving Pastor Jordan. And did they have anything to do with the shots fired though my window? And/or the little altercation with me and Tank just a few minutes ago?

Paranoia. No doubt. Coincidence. Not bloody likely. I removed my .38 from the shoulder holster and placed it on my lap as I made a turn down a residential street. The headlights of the Buick followed. They were lousy at tailing, which meant they weren't professionals.

I did some deep breathing and shook my head in an attempt to shake loose anything that might be stuck.

I didn't like being followed and I wasn't about to lead them back to my apartment.

I came to a corner that lead onto Hamilton Street.

I waited, hoping they'd think it was the traffic that held me up. Actually, it was. I spotted the Hamilton Bus making its way down the street and paid attention to its speed and pace. Just as the Buick had inched closer, I ripped onto Hamilton, just a few feet in front of the bus.

The bus driver slammed on the brakes, inadvertently creating an immovable barrier for the men in the Buick. I floored it, racing across two lanes to a stop light that had just turned red. I made a sharp left, scaring the oncoming drivers, and sped over to the Lodge Freeway.

I made it to the on ramp without being followed. Gunned the engine, accelerated into the third lane, checking my rear view mirror for unwanted guests.

I didn't see the Buick. I was left wondering who'd want to follow a slightly inebriated PI other than the local constabulary. It was a question I'd consider later.

With my gun back in my holster and my adrenaline back to normal, I drove back to my apartment, happy to kick back in my LA-Z-BOY and listen to the sporadic traffic on Livernois Avenue.

I checked the answering machine and saw that there were four messages waiting for me.

And wait they would.

I waltzed into the kitchen, opened the fridge and removed an ice tray. I cracked loose several cubes of ice and wrapped them into a dish towel. I placed the wrapped cubes behind my neck and the cold sting felt quite soothing.

I plopped down in my LA-Z-BOY and tilted back with my feet upheld by the footrest. I felt like I'd been dragged through the small end of a funnel.

I searched for some clarity of thought. Erotica Carter is married to Adam Carter, a popular home reconstruction magnate who had a brief singing career with the other four missing Sentiments. Considering his local popularity, it also stood to reason that the people I talked to must have recognized him as well. Yet no one said a word.

Was it because I didn't ask the right questions, or was I being lead somewhere?

Everyone I talked to had to know that the Adam Carter in the picture, youthful and clad in 1950s singing attire, was the same one who'd become a local commercial celebrity of Tremaine Home Improvement.

I hadn't thought about him since I'd left Detroit on a football scholarship with a small black college in Texas. That was 1975. In 1980, I was a rookie defensive back with the then Super Bowl Champion Oakland Raiders, learning my craft from some of the best in the business.

That was a long time ago and Adam Carter was not the most pressing thought in my life. No wonder I didn't recognize him.

Now, what to do about it?

I had to find out why everyone else lied. A lie by omission was still a lie. And why was I suddenly at the center of someone else's world?

The phone rang. I checked the clock. It was 12:45 a.m. so it was either family calling about an emergency or Elvira, Mistress of the Night calling to tell me she had an opening.

I was tired. I hoped the caller would hear the reluctance in my greeting. "Linc. It's Erotica."

"How'd you get my home number?"

"I just did," she said matter-of-factly. "Didn't you get my messages?"

"I haven't checked my answering machine."

"Oh." I let the pause drift between us. It was her nickel...or thirty-five cents. "My husband would like to meet with you. Can you come by tomorrow morning? It's usually the best time for him."

"That was a quick change of heart. But sure. How about an address?" I wrote it down on a pad by the phone. It was a Palmer Woods address. "Would around nine o'clock be okay?" I asked.

"Should be just fine. And, Linc, thanks. For everything."

"I haven't really done anything, but you're welcome." I caught her before we hung up. "Erotica, who else knows about what I'm doing for you?"

"Up until tonight when I mentioned it to my husband, just you and me."

"You know anyone who drives a black Buick?"

"Not that I'm aware of...why?"

"No real reason, just asking. See you tomorrow."

Even though it was close to one in the morning, it had been a very active day and I was too pumped up for bed. It all had me in a talkative mood and feeling gregarious all of a sudden, so I figured I might as well find out what other secrets were behind the digitized voiced intro of my office answering machine. I punched in the number, listened to my greeting and then punched in the numerical code to play my messages. There were four.

Two from Erotica, which I deleted, one from Tyrell Stubbins calling me from the bar out at the airport which I saved, and the last from someone named Diane Bristol, leaving me a number and instructions to call her anytime tonight. She said it concerned The Sentiments. I saved the message and punched in her number. She did say anytime.

A woman's voice answered after the third ring.

I introduced myself and asked for Diane Bristol.

"Hello, Mr. Keller." Her tone was tired, almost flat. "You don't know me. My name is Diane Bristol. I was in the beauty shop when you came by. I understand that you're trying to find out some information on some men who used to live around here."

"As a matter of fact, I am."

She hesitated and then said, "Well, I think I might know something. Interested?"

"What is it that you think you might know?" I asked, not completely convinced that she was on the level. Besides, after all that's happened today, I was naturally cynical. Even still, there was something in her tone that didn't settle my restless spirit.

"Well..." she said dragging the word before filling in the gap, "...one of those guys, Charles Treadwell, used to date my aunt. I'm almost certain they've kept in touch."

"Think she'd be willing to talk with me?" I tried to not let her hear my growing excitement at the possibility of catching a break.

"That depends on how willing you are to talk to me," she said.

"I assume you mean in person."

"As well as tonight. In the next hour." Her tone suggested that there was no negotiation.

I waited.

I hoped to get a feel for what she really wanted. I didn't like the idea of running off in the night to meet some mysterious person I didn't know, but I couldn't imagine why she'd want to deceive me.

"Mr. Keller?" she queried.

"I'm here. Where do you want to meet?"

She gave me an address and described the place as a corner townhouse in a low rent cooperative. In my day, we used to call those places The Projects. Now they're called cooperatives. She told me she'd leave a light on and she'd expect me in an hour.

"Okay, Miss Bristol. I'll be there."

After we hung up, I pulled the Metropolitan Detroit phone book and looked up Diane's name and address. I didn't see a listing. She could have conceivably had an unlisted phone number. People do it all the time. So I made a phone call.

I knew Julie, and I knew she'd up at this hour. She's gotten calls from me at the wee hours of the morning before. When she answered, I heard Nikki and NaShan, her two-year-old twins, yelling in the background.

"What are those girls yelling about?" I asked to start our conversation. I knew better than to ask why are they up at this hour and isn't this a school night?

"Hi, Linc. Oh, Nikki and NaShan are helping me with a recipe for Jambalaya that I pulled off a Web page this evening." There was a momentary lapse as she stopped to ask the girls to quiet down. "What do you need, Linc?"

"Wait a minute, isn't it a little late for the twins to be up?" I just had to ask.

"Not if they're Vampires. I'm waiting," she said unsympathetically.

"Can you run a name real quick?"

"What am I working with?" she asked as she whispered something to the girls.

"Only a name and an address."

"When you don't give me much, don't expect much. Let me get the girls calmed down and I'll see what turns up on my database. It may take a while. I don't have access to as much here as I do at the office. How soon?"

"Half an hour?"

She tsked. "Lincoln, you're something else."

"Comes with being charming."

"Irritating is a synonym for charming. I'll call you back."

I decided to use the time for her call back to change into something more appropriate for visiting strangers when the rest of the sane world is sound asleep. I slipped on my Levi's faded blue denims, my blue jeans shirt and my white, blue lined running shoes. Anticipating some coolness in the air, I also grabbed my lightweight black Players jacket.

Given the recent events in my evening, there's a certain rush that comes when the mind, body and spirit anticipate an unknown action. It's as if all your senses move to the next level of awareness and the adrenaline begins to surge through you like a giant wave looking for an unprotected shore. Kind of like playing defense when the offense has second and short. Any number of things were possible, and not easily defensible.

Which also meant: be cautious.

I had no reason to believe that Diane Bristol wasn't legit and that she had some helpful, maybe even vital, information. But sometimes a subtle shift in tone and manner can provide just enough of a signal to let you know that you're waving a red flag at a charging bull.

I hoped Julie could help me determine if I was dealing with a charging bull, an out of control truck or a rabbit just trying to find a place to hide.

The phone rang in ten minutes. I quickly answered. "Yeah, babe. What you got for me?" I asked anxiously.

"Assuming you mean me, a good time. A hard time if you meant any-one else. Who's babe?"

My love interest Malone caught me unexpectedly. "Hello, Detective. Why the call during the witching hour?"

"I'm rotating off for the next two days so I'm calling to see if you have any plans. Who's babe?"

I knew what it means if she asks something twice. "Just an associate who's supposed to call me right back about a lead. I'm just working for a living."

"At this hour? Hard working man like you needs to relax. Tension can be so debilitating."

"Know where I can find a good physical therapist?"

"You know my address. Make sure your lead brings you this way to-night."

"You're on. Shouldn't take longer than an hour."

"Good. What I have in mind will take much longer than an hour."

"Sounds like my kind of therapy."

"My fingers are anxiously waiting to do the walking. See you soon."

The phone rang again the second I set it down. I decided to use socially acceptable greeting and not risk further embarrassment. The voice was Julie's.

"Best I could do is a Diane Bristol who works at Mother Town's Kitchen. Forty-four years old, born in Detroit and has lived all of her life on the northeast side. No kids or spouse from what I could find out. Couple of early drug busts but apparently she's been clean for awhile. No current address listed. Previously lived on Mt. Elliot Street with a former boy-friend named Lester Jones. He's had a couple of misdemeanors and the one B and E sentence was timed served. She put up his bail."

If you don't give much, don't expect much. Yeah, right. "So what's her sun sign?" I asked.

"Virgo. Why?"

"Never mind. Any red flags?"

The rustling of paper in the background told me she was quickly skim-ming what she had. "Other than her questionable taste in boyfriends, noth-ing really jumps out."

It might mean something and it might not. "I suppose that'll have to do."

"This was short notice Lincoln...and while I'm at home," she replied as if insulted.

"I know. I'm a cad. How can I make it up to you?"

"Pay your bill and don't call me for at least a week."

"Madam, you insult me."

"Not enough. Bye."

Diane Bristol was part of a partially completed puzzle with several of her pieces lying around the table. I checked the address she'd given me and decided I'd proceed with optimistic caution. My .38 felt snug in my holster. Security against an unknown caller...and a persistent Buick.

***

The drive across town took all of twenty minutes. I cruised on Conant Street, passing through a neighborhood of two family flats until I came to a driveway with a sign announcing the entrance into the East Village Cooperative. I drove by the plain, similarly designed apartments. On the east coast, they'd be known as row houses. In Detroit, the walnut paneled, two-level apartments said a lot about our lack of creativity when faced with an opportunity to earn more by doing less.

I walked the open driveway listening for the movement or sound of an unadvertised dog until I came to a screened storm door on the side of the apartment, near the back. The smaller numbers plastered at an angle across the exterior reinforced the fact that I had indeed come to the right location.

After I'd knocked three times, I heard locks being unbolted as the red painted interior door was opened revealing a woman whose dyed brown streaked hair was an unintentional endorsement for keeping the 'natural look'. Her brown eyes and the tight line across her lips reflected the caution endemic to much of the urban experience.

"Diane Bristol?" I asked. She slightly nodded. "I'm Lincoln Keller. You called me earlier."

"May I see some ID?" she asked standing partially concealed behind the interior door.

It wasn't an unusual request, given the circumstances. I pressed my pictured license against the screen and she silently matched the picture with the person.

"How'd you managed to smile?" she asked flatly.

"Timing. I started smiling while I filled out the written test and kept smiling until the picture was taken. I figured if I have to live with this picture for awhile, I didn't want people yelling and showing the Catholic cross every time I had to show it."

It seemed to lighten the moment as her mouth moved toward a half grin. "You haven't felt terror until you've seen that horrible picture of mine," she said. She unlocked the screen door. "Come in." After I stepped inside, she motioned toward a set of steps. "Down those steps."

The wooden, partially creaky steps led to what I knew was a reconverted basement that now was passed off as an economical way to beat the high cost of living.

Diane's domicile away from homelessness was decorated to satisfy basic creature comforts, not to entertain an undersecretary to a prominent cabinet member. At least I didn't think it was.

An alpine rattan and wood armchair and coffee table were the accessory pieces to an auburn sofa and sleeper. A small screen television with a cable box on top sat on a sagging metal stand with four plastic wheels. There were a few pictures displayed on one of those easy to assemble wooden shelving units. A portable closet was located in a far corner, its metal base causing the supporting racks to lean ungraciously to one side. The room smelled of mildew and smoke. I supposed that the various pipes that ran along the ceiling became less noticeable the longer you lived there.

"It ain't much, but it's mine," she said from behind me. I thought the comment was unnecessary given some of the bodies I'd seen in places that made this room look like the inside of the Taj Mahal.

"It's quite nice," I said dismissing the comment.

She pointed toward the armchair. "Sit down." I did. The squeaky rattan finally quieted after it adjusted to the shape of my selfishly regarded posterior. "I'd offer you something, but I'm afraid you caught me a little short this week."

"Don't apologize, Miss Bristol. I'm fine."

I took in the full view of Diane Bristol as she settled into the farthest corner of her sofa crossing one thin leg over the other. She's seen and lived on, or near, the roughest edge of urban survival. The stark age lines were road maps that led through the chapters of her unrealized dreams. Her soft honey complexion probably worked as a magnet once upon a time, attracting the slickest and the sleek to her once buxom and long since abandoned hourglass figure. Her red, tired eyes contained the stories that every mother dreads and every father fears. She wore a white uniform with a name tag that advertised the renowned restaurant chain where she was employed.

The tight dress stretched around her fading figure and the hem line stopped just above her thin knees. If I hadn't known from Julie that Diane Bristol was forty-four, any guess of her age would have been wrong and a shame.

"Why'd you contact me, Miss Bristol?" I asked to focus the discussion away from apologetic remarks about her dwellings.

She pulled a pack of Kool Lights from her pocket and offered me one. I declined.

She tapped the bottom of the pack against her palm, forcing out one of the filter tipped cigarettes, flipped open the lighter on the coffee table and after she drew in her first breath, released the smoke toward the ceiling before she responded to my question.

"As you can see, Mr. Keller..." she said using the hand holding her cigarette in a half sweeping gesture, "...I don't have very much. My life is tough and I don't care what you or anyone else thinks about it."

"Why should you?"

She hesitated for just a moment before continuing. "Well, I don't. But it is a struggle trying to pay the rent and eat. Some days I can do one and not the other."

I nodded as an acknowledgment of what she was saying.

"I haven't had the luckiest breaks in the world with money or men, so I have to do what I can to survive."

"How does contacting me help you survive?" I said, already knowing the answer to the question.

She took a drag on her cigarette and held the smoke in while she talked. "I have something that might be helpful to you and I can let you have it, but I want to be paid." She released the smoke into mildewed air.

"If the information is helpful, I might be in a position to provide you with adequate compensation." I leaned forward listening to the subtle cracking of the rattan. "However, it's got to tell me something I don't already know."

She stared momentarily as if that thought hadn't occurred to her. "I think it will be. Can we talk about a price?"

"Not until we talk about the information. Tell me what you got and then we'll talk about a price."

"How do I know you won't try and stiff me?"

I leaned back in the chair, crossing my ankle over my knee. "You knew that when you called me. Now we can go back and forth all night with this game, which I won't do, or we can decide to trust each other and move this along. I didn't come here to stiff you and I didn't come here to get stiffed...so let's talk."

What ran through her head during those few moments of indecision were the thousands of lies and broken promises made to her across a millennium of relationships. Here was one more person, one more time saying, 'Hey, Baby. Don't worry. You can trust me.'

She placed her cigarette into a black plainly designed ashtray, stood up and walked to a shelving unit and pulled down a tattered edged photo album. It didn't really surprise me to notice track marks on the back of her legs.

When she returned to the sofa, she opened the cover and slowly began flipping through the pages.

I don't know what she saw except maybe reminders of the times when her life had a meaning unknown to her at the time. She didn't speak as she moved from page to page. She'd stop from time to time to shake her head regretfully at a pictured memory.

The fact that I was in her apartment didn't mean that I was in the moment. I knew she wanted to wander alone until finally looking up from the path to see me standing there.

She stopped about halfway through the album, turned it around and placed it on the coffee table. "Look at the top picture on the right."

I carefully lifted the album, holding the worn edges and focusing my eyes on the black and white picture of a couple sitting at a table in what I assumed to be a bar or nightclub. I immediately recognized Henry Hill. The bass singer who followed the career of Jackie Robinson. He looked youthful and full of promise, dressed handsomely in a suit that seemed tailored to fit him in a 1950's style. The smiling woman next to him seemed just as full of promise but more so. There was a large corsage pinned on a striking one piece dress that may have been a little risque for the 1950s. Despite Diane's tired eyes and world weary appearance, I could see the resemblance. More sisterly than anything else.

"I recognize Henry Hill," I said. "The woman is obviously your..."

"...my mother Belinda Bristol," she said finishing the thought. "They dated for awhile."

"How long awhile?" I asked prepared to have my assumption validated.

"Long enough to fuck me into existence," she replied harshly. She picked up her cigarette and took another drag. "Don't worry, I can produce my birth record. That bastard is my father, there's no doubt about it. My mother practically wallowed away her life waiting for him and what did he do? Copped a piece and then ran out on her at the first sign of trouble. She loved him and all it brought her and me was years of heartache."

"Actually, Miss Bristol, we don't know if he ran out on her. We do know that he and three others came up missing and that's all we know."

"I know she loved him to her death." Her voice rose sharply. "I know he wasn't there to help us through. I know she married three other piece-of-shit men to fill the void space that he left. I know I never called him 'Daddy'. That's what I know."

For the next several minutes I listened to Diane speak with joy and bitterness of her life with her mother and the three stepfathers along the way. She crushed out her cigarette remarking that she didn't understand why she and her mother had been punished. She railed of how much a good person her mother was, embellishing each comment with an equally charged assault on the men her mother married and particularly the one whom she loved.

I'd seen this happen many times before during homicide and missing person investigations. Oakland, California hadn't been spared any of this kind of carnage. It's a cleansing of the mind and soul in an attempt to find a spiritual and physical equilibrium. A need to explain where explanations do nothing but fill the empty void of time.

When I sensed that she'd said enough, I took the moment to interrupt. "Miss Bristol..."

"Diane."

"...Diane. When was this picture taken?" I tried to walk around the shards of her broken dreams.

She lit another cigarette. "September of '53 at a place called Johnny's Lounge." I nodded that I knew where she was talking about. "Apparently it was a real hot spot over on the east side. My mother used to talk about it as the place to go for music and fun. She met my dad there." That made sense.

"Diane, I already knew about Johnny's Lounge and quite frankly, knowing that Henry Hill is your father doesn't help me figure out where he is."

"There's more," she said. "Look on the very last page of the album." I gripped the remaining pages and flipped them over until I was looking at an open letter, penned in black ink, tucked neatly between the plastic covering. "When my mother died in '85, I was going through her things trying to decide what to keep and what to throw away. I came across that letter just where it is in that album. Imagine my surprise when I read it and saw that it had been written by my father. As you can see on the top of the letter, it was dated August of 1957, almost two years after he supposedly vanished."

Though it was barely readable, the date was there. It was a letter written with a deliberate attempt to say so much on one page. Mostly apologies and a vague reference to someone named 'Swan'. 'Sorry about Swan,' Henry declared.

Who's Swan?

"Diane, this is going to sound like a stupid question but hang with me; how can you be sure that this is a letter from your father, Henry Hill?"

Her sardonic smile agreed with the stupidity of the question. "I can't prove that it's from him, but I have no reason to doubt it either. Why would my mother have kept the letter all those years? I also have three other letters, written by members of The Sentiments over six months back in 1955. Since the letters were in my mother's possession, I took the liberty and read all three. The letters say a lot and then very little. I'm not sure what to make of it and at this point, I really don't care. They don't have much value to me."

"And..?"

"... and I figure they may have greater value to you," she said folding her arms across her chest.

"You mean like artistic, esoteric value?"

"Don't play me for stupid, Mr. Keller. I'm talking duckets."

"And that's what I'm hearing. If the letters are legit, I can probably get you a couple hundred bucks."

"A thousand would work better," she replied, insulted by my first offer.

I could probably squeeze it out of Adam or Erotica if I wanted to, but I needed some greater assurance that she was onto something.

"A thousand dollars for all the letters?"

"A thousand for each letter. Henry Hill's included."

"Four thousand dollars. That's a rather steep price. How do I know it's worth it?"

"You said something about trust."

"Alright. Assuming we trust each other, I don't carry that kind of money around with me. I need to have it authorized from my client. How long can you wait?"

"My rent's due on Friday," she said flatly.

"I'll call my client tonight and see if that price can be paid. If it can, I'll call you tomorrow."

I stood up, leaning forward so as not to bump my head on a low hanging pipe.

She crushed the half smoked cigarette while standing up. She seemed edgy. Almost as if she were standing on the border of another unfulfilled dream. "Don't keep me waiting too long," she said insistently.

I shook her hand. "Thanks, Diane. This has been somewhat helpful and I will call you tomorrow with my client's answer."

"I don't go in until noon. Best to call me at work," she said writing the number on a slip of paper.

I folded the paper and slipped it in my pocket. "Thanks. I'll call you as soon as I know."

I left Diane Bristol's haven greeting the cool night air with an extended sigh of relief and inhaling deeply to clean my smoke stained nostrils.

As I approached my Nova, I thought of all the things I'd gotten to know about Diane Bristol. Her life had been a tale of settling for less than what she wanted. The hard edge of the city's attitude had consumed her through a series of needed but unwanted relationships and turned her once physical advantage into a day-to-day attempt to keep Satan at arm's length.

I knew she'd wait as long as she could for the money.

I knew the money would help her get through the moment.

I knew those moments would take place through the track marks on her legs.

Whatever she knew, and if Erotica paid for it, would eat away at the physical foundation of her person and expedite the moment when she and death would meet on that common ground.

I didn't want to be a contributor and I'd learned enough about life to know when to mind my own business...or had I?

My concentration on Diane's plight almost made me forget that I had a therapeutic rendezvous. It's been one hell of a long, long day. A therapeutic rendezvous would be the perfect way to wind it down.

Chapter 15

In terms of miles, it was a short drive from the dismal projects of Diane Bristol to the comforting haven of Candy Malone on Detroit's northwest side. But in terms of living standards, it was a drive to the other side of the world. My partner in mutual therapy lived on a tree lined, modest neighborhood of immodest appeal. The neighborhood looked good because the people living there made damn sure it did. They liked it that way. I parked outside her two-story Cape Cod.

The quiet was pleasant this early in the morning. I moved silently up the concrete steps and slipped my key in the lock. The darkness wasn't a barrier as I made my way around the familiar setting to the kitchen. As always, a pot of coffee, decaf/special blend, was heating in anticipation of her addiction. Mine, too.

I'd just poured a cup when I heard the recognizable click of a gun's hammer behind me.

"Believe me," I said. "It's not coffee worth dying over."

"You're hardly in a position to be a coffee critic," she retorted.

"Join me?"

She uncocked the gun and eased behind me. "Times are too dangerous to be screwing around, lover. Or is that why you're unfashionably late at this late hour, Linc?"

I turned around as Malone lowered her police issued Glock and gazed at me through those piercing tell-me-the-truth-or die eyes. "I'm just early for tomorrow."

Malone's jet black hair fell loosely around her shoulders. She wore a crystal blue chiffon chemise with a satin trim that cut just high enough to reveal most of her taut statuesque legs and the remaining outline of her step aerobics body that demanded my full attention.

"I'd almost given up on you," she said stifling a yawn.

"Your invitation was too good to overlook." I nodded toward the parquet counter top. "You may dispose of that weapon now. I am a man of peace."

She placed the gun on the counter and we moved toward each other. We locked in a passionate embrace further heightened by the dance of connecting tongues. It felt good to hold her close again. My own heat intensified by hers.

Moments passed before we pulled apart.

"Easy, sailor," she said. "This isn't your twenty-four hour convenient jump, hump and slump. Talk to me. What's up with this case you're working on?"

"Can we talk later?"

"We talk now and let it build."

"It's already built. In fact, it stands erect pointing toward the mother lode."

"Talk," she said. "And pour that out," she added referring to the cup of coffee I just poured. "Let me make you a fresh pot."

"Something flavored?"

"Vanilla Hazelnut."

"You're on."

She made fresh coffee while I talked about the ends and outs of trying to locate the rest of a singing group that mysteriously vanished and no one, including one of the former members, seems to know where, why or how. I took her through every aspect up to my recent visit with Diane Bristol. I was careful to refer to Erotica in the most general terms. Malone didn't like the name, and, thank God, didn't grill me too hard if I thought she looked like her name. Despite the well brewed coffee and my own stimulating conversation, I felt tired. Malone took pity on me and led me away from the table to her bedroom.

"Heard enough?" I asked.

"Seen enough. Sorry to hear Ron Brickham's name come up, but that's to be expected."

"Why?"

She picked up our empty cups and put both in the sink. "I'm not real familiar with what went down, but IAD investigated some of his activities and he was retired, without his number. Must've been about eight or nine years ago."

"What about Craig Roberts?"

"A little before my time, babe." She grabbed my hand. "Come on, tiger. I'm looking at someone in desperate need of a full body massage."

"Can I just have the Headline News version and move right to the Sports Hour?"

"Think you'd last?"

"Just put me in, coach."

"Your spirits revitalized?"

"You have an uplifting effect on me."

The rest of the night became everything we wanted, only taking time-outs to discuss innovative strategy. And for now, Malone crowded out every thought of Erotica. The rest of womanhood for that matter.

***

We slept until seven-thirty, which was good for about 3 uniterrupted hours. My batteries were recharged enough for now. I left Malone lying in bed while I awakened my senses in her recently renovated shower. I'd just finished rinsing the lather out of my hair when I felt the rush of cold air and the soft feel of two hands moving slowly up my back.

"Wash your back, sailor?"

"I don't know if I can afford your rates."

"Then let's barter."

***

While Malone blow dried her hair, I prepared my standard, easy-to-fix breakfast of scrambled eggs, sausage patties, wheat toast and instant grits. There was just enough orange juice to fill two medium sized glasses.

Clad only in a white robe, she plopped down in the leather cushioned chair and waited while I served up breakfast.

"So what's your next move, Linc?"

I spread blackberry jelly on my slice of toast. "I've got a lead on this guy Matt Stewart. His last known address is a post office box up north in Missaukee County. I'm also meeting with Adam Carter this morning to see what he knows."

Malone curled her lip in that contemplative way she has. "So, this Erotica woman, and by the way, who would name their child Erotica? is married to one of the former members and she, for some reason, felt it was important to leave out that little tidbit."

I thought about asking who would name their child Candy? but very wisely decided against it. It was better to just say, "Go figure."

"I don't like it, Linc. Why the secrecy? Why the deceit?"

"That's what I hope to find out." I cut off a piece of sausage patty. "By the way, what are you planning on doing for the next two days?"

"The answer is no, Linc. This has been a hellacious week and I'm going to do nothing but stuff that reminds me that I'm alive and that there's more to this world than dead stiffs and the people who cause it."

"Sounds like you need the ultimate form of day therapy."

"Yes, but you're leaving to go to work."

"I wasn't thinking sex."

"What then?"

"Sak's."

She grinned. "Similar sound, different outcome."

"I don't know. Seems in both cases the outcome is your pleasurable satisfaction." I spotted the blue digital numbers on her microwave. Time's awastin'. "Meantime, I have to run. Don't want to keep the Carters waiting. Who knows what secrets hidden away in their walk-in closets will come rummaging through hanging fashions from Sak's Fifth Avenue?"

"Take care of yourself. If I get lonely, I'll leave a message on your answering machine."

"Too busy to speak personally?" I chided.

"You mentioned Sak's. There goes my day."

***

The address of the manor Erotica described in her directions was one of several that lined the tree enhanced enclave known as Palmer Woods.

The area was a testament to the spoils of a rampant industrial era. Every home had its highly manicured space and circular driveways. The distance between homes showed that Detroit had its opulent side, reinforced by the highly visible security personnel patrolling in their bubble topped Chevy Blazers.

The Carter home was a brownstone Tudor with white pillars and an evenly coifed lawn with an assortment of flowers that provided a multi colored background.

The red brick path matched the steps that led to the huge wooden door with the brass knocker. I suppose class gets defined at some beginning level. It seemed I'd found its origins.

As I came up to the door I thought about when and how I was going to pass on to Erotica the details of my meeting with Diane Bristol, if at all. After knocking the brass to signal my arrival, the door opened and I was greeted by the dream that haunted my subconscious since Appolonia's.

Erotica stood before me. Dressed in a light blue halter top, tight black shorts and workout shoes, her sweat matted hair added another level of allure to an already lusting heart.

"Come in, Mr. Keller," she said, using a blue towel to wipe away the beads of sweat. "I just finished my workout. I love working up a good sweat... don't you?"

"Depends on the activity."

She smiled. "You prefer sweating alone or with a partner?"

"I tried it alone. It's a lot more fun with a partner," I replied as she closed the door behind me.

I stepped onto a shiny parquet floor, evenly covered with multi-colored throw rugs that represented different cultures. The expansive front area walls displayed a number of oils depicting various regions of landscape. A large multi-light glass chandelier hung from a cathedral style ceiling as I was led past a marble stepped, circular stairway.

Definitely not the cheap seats.

"Nice place," I said.

"We like it. Care to follow me?"

It begged of something cerebral. So I let it go. "It's your house. I'm just visiting."

She laughed and led me to a spacious carpeted room lined with floor to ceiling bookshelves, a large casement window with white lace curtains and a fireplace the size of a small apartment. A large wooden desk sat in front of the window with a high back leather chair swiveled toward the picturesque view of the back area.

"Honey," she said in a tone designed to spark a man's interest. "There's someone here I'd like for you to meet."

She walked around the desk to the chair, in a seductive sway that black widows used to draw in their mates, leaned forward and whispered something to the occupant.

When the high back chair slowly came around, I gazed at the slumped posture of the man who was one of the first true entrepreneurs in Detroit's black community. I'd seen his face on a hundred tiresome commercials over the years and his silly jingle was forever carved into a memory bank, subject to unwanted retrieval.

He looked different up close than on the twenty-one inch screen. His age-lined face was a far contrast from the vibrant, fast talking salesman whose commercials dominated a once popular local afternoon old-movie show. It was almost impossible to believe he was the gifted singer and lovable prankster who stood flanked by his friends in the first photo I saw of him. His medium cut, completely gray, slightly curled hair had thinned at the top and his coppertone eyes, once alive with anticipation, had the look of hopelessness. An interesting set of contrasts in a house that radiated optimism.

He seemed thinner. Like the sagging branch of a tree about to topple over, his deep brown skin hung loosely around the jaws and neck. He wore a black cotton robe, opened at the top to expose the gray hairs scattered around his chest like weeds. I swear he could have looked older than Mrs. Dibell.

"Mr. Keller," he said clearing his throat of phlegm. "Please have a seat." He pointed to the matching leather armchair in front of his desk. "My wife seems convinced that I have need of your services."

"Do you?" I asked.

"She seems to think so."

"And what do you think, Mr. Carter?"

He strained a sigh. "I doubt if I do, but I'm rarely able to convince her otherwise. Stubbornness of youth, I suppose." His voice was tired. Resonating away from any emotional message.

"I'm just trying to help you, honey," she interjected. "Mr. Keller comes highly recommended. I just can't bear watching you waste away without trying to do something."

The strong glare he attempted to give her was a strain. Unconvincing, if he was trying to give a message.

"Allow me the pleasure of at least being a proper host, Mr. Keller. What can I offer you to drink?"

"Not really thirsty. But I'll take some orange juice or something along those lines."

"I'll take care of it," Erotica said moving away from the chair. "What would you like, baby?"

"Some of that tasteless mineral water," he replied.

"Fine. I'll leave you two men to talk and I'll be right back."

Erotica didn't just exit a room. Not without taking with her all the unrequited passions and thoughts common to men who lusted for something better.

"She is a work of art...isn't she, Mr. Keller?" he said as he moved slightly forward.

The squeaking leather pulled me back to the moment. "Yes she is, Mr. Carter. But I'm not here to talk about art."

He sighed. "You ever hear of The Sentiments?"

That was a quick change of subject, but I appreciated it. "Not until late yesterday afternoon," I replied.

Carter opened a side drawer and removed a similar folder, only it was more organized than the one given to be by his wife. He opened the folder and removed an exact copy of the black and white picture I had. Five guys smiling. Lined up by height to make a V. Anticipating a bright future.

"The one on the far left, he's the lead singer. Name's Charles Treadwell. He was the one who organized the group. We were all boyhood friends who enjoyed singing and were just starting to get some notoriety." There was a hint of pride in his weary tone. "Things were just starting to break for us when the other four members just vanished. They've been missing since October of 1955."

"I know," I said matter of factly. "Any idea why?"

"No...Yes...Maybe...Oh, I don't know," he replied wearily.

"You forgot definitely possible and clearly perhaps," I said. I was getting impatient. "Mr. Carter, forty years ago, you and four of your boyhood friends were just starting to experience some local fame when four of them suddenly vanished...and no one knows why?"

He considered the question for a moment, then answered the obvious, "That's pretty much what I'm saying."

"They just disappeared?" I reiterated with my palms up.

"That's right," he said, his tone moving toward condescension.

"And not you, or any relatives, friends, passing acquaintances, former lovers or anyone has a clue as to why?" It was more a statement of surprise than a question. "That seems a little farfetched."

"Try living with that fact for over forty years."

I paused, trying to get a handle on what I was hearing. Some of it didn't make sense, but then neither do most of the lunatics who hold political office. "When did you last see them, Mr. Carter?"

He sighed. "We were going to do a gig at Johnny's Lounge over on Kercheval Avenue. The four of them had gone ahead and I was running late because of my other job. Things got kind of hectic, so I didn't get there until after the last set. I remember the cab pulling up in front of Johnny's and there were several police cars parked around the building. No one was being let in or out. I finally worked my way passed the crowd and saw a woman I knew who worked as a waitress in Johnny's. She said there'd been some shots fired in the back alley. It was believed someone was murdered. Blood was found, but not a body. I asked about my group members and was told they had gone home. That turned out not to be true. They never made it home. No one, not one person, relative or friend has seen them since that night."

I could confirm the story through old police records from that night. But the curious thought crossed my mind that Stella at Johnny's didn't mention this. Sure, she was out that night, but news of a murder gets around and sticks around.

There were other things that nagged me. Some meaning underneath the surface of the once handsome face of the gentleman across from me. "What is it that you're not telling me, Mr. Carter?"

He stared at me for just the briefest of moments. "I assume what we talk about is confidential."

"Your wife hired me, but the clause extends to less than open husbands."

"I think I know why they vanished. I'm just not sure where." I said nothing knowing the void was his to fill. "I suspect the reason they vanished might be because of their possible link with an alleged murder that took place that night."

I still didn't say anything. I didn't have to because Erotica said it all when she picked that moment to wander back into the room.

"A murder!" She was carrying a tray with a pitcher of water and a tall glass of orange juice. "Honey, you never let on that they were involved with a murder." She sat the tray on the desk and leaned forward to rub his haggard face. "Oh, baby, why didn't you tell me?"

"I didn't say they murdered anyone. I said it's a possible link with a murder. I'm not sure. All I have are bits and pieces of information."

"You want to tell me what you have?" I interrupted.

"Most of what I have is in this folder. Take it if it'll help." He slid the folder over to me. "The rest are rumors I've spent years trying to confirm or deny."

"You think one, two or possibly all of them may be linked with an alleged murder that took place that night? You just said that there wasn't a body. How can there be an alleged murder without a body as evidence? What do the police say? Have you talked with anyone down there about what happened that night? Do they have any suspicions?"

"All I get is that the case is still open and if I ever have access to additional information I should come forward."

"So they believe there was a murder?"

"They believe something happened. They did find blood. It belonged to somebody. Type A negative. Beyond that. I haven't gotten much help."

"Who's the alleged victim?" I asked.

"I don't know. Rumor has it that it was a white woman everybody called 'Swan'. They used to frequent the clubs down in the 'bottom' back then."

Ala the Cotton Club in Harlem during its heyday.

"I talked to someone who said that there was a cop named Craig Roberts who used to frequently come by and roust people in order to get some information on your former buddies. Does that sound familiar?"

Adam Carter coughed several times before answering. "I suspect it had something to do with the alleged murder that no one seems to know about."

"Including yourself."

"That's right."

Erotica had remained strangely quiet through our discussion. For someone who had such an aggressive interest, she seem unusually subdued.

"Mr. Carter, why the sudden interest in locating The Sentiments?"

"It's not sudden," he said in a defensive tone. "I've been trying to find them since the day they vanished and I've run into one dead end after another." He calmed down and spoke in a more deliberate manner. "Over the years, I'd learned to live with the fact that I'd never see them again and that I'd never know why. Obviously, I didn't pursue my singing career."

Hearts and Flowers was never a song I mastered on the piano and I was less infatuated with it as an emotional motivating piece. Fact is, most relationships have a qualitative endurance that survive the quantitative cycle. That's if they're worth anything at all. So his appeal to friendship long lost was wasted on me. If I continued on, given this possible murder wrinkle, it would be to do the job. The rest of it was theirs to work through.

"Mr. Carter, you're certain you have no idea where your friends have vanished?"

"That's what I said, didn't I?"

"And this alleged murder happened in back of Johnny's Lounge?"

"That's right."

"Wait a minute," I said moving toward exasperation. "You want me to locate members of this former singing group who haven't been heard from since 1955 because of a possible murder that may or may not have happened sometime between September and October of 1955 involving someone we can't identify in back of a place called Johnny's Lounge?" I paused, not sure where I was going with the outburst.

"No. That's where the problem lies," he said as Erotica poured cool water into a glass and gave it to him. "It's my wife who wants to find my friends...not me. I'm content to leave well enough alone. Last night after my wife explained to me what was going on, I only agreed to meet with you to tell you to leave it alone. It's been lying dead for forty years and one more day, week or year won't make a bit of difference."

"But, Honey..." Erotica interrupted, "...their memory has been a worry for you lately. I know it. I look at you every day and I can see it in your eyes. You're a self-made man who has everything except the one thing you've needed most: pure, non-politicized, unconditional friendship. Just like you had with The Sentiments. It's been eating away at you and you wouldn't do a thing about it. So I had to. I had to do something."

I picked up the glass of orange juice and took a long swallow and placed the half filled glass back on the tray.

"It needs to stay buried, Erotica. It serves no purpose now to resurrect the past." His half hearted tone did little to convince her...or me.

"I'll not stop until the questions are answered. Not knowing is killing you...and me as well. I can't stand to see you in anymore pain. I had to do something. You will still help us won't you, Mr. Keller?" Erotica's pleading eyes could have easily been mistaken for something more inviting.

"I don't like getting involved in family disputes, but then I couldn't earn a living. Why don't you two talk it through a little more and then call me." I picked up the folder and leafed through its contents. "Just out of curiosity though, what else can you tell me about the other four members?"

He sighed. "Charles Treadwell was the second tenor and lead singer. Lennix Williams sang first tenor. Michael Parker was the baritone. Henry Hill sang bass. I had the most range so I usually filled the gap where needed."

Nothing I hadn't already found out, but I thought it would be nice to say, "Like Ron Banks does with The Dramatics."

"Talented local group. Our groups had similar styles, although I'd say we were closer in style to The Dells."

"You may have set the mode for The Temptations."

"No. The Temptations were far more talented in ways we hadn't imagined. They really brought showmanship to five part harmony."

I nodded. "Well, as I said, you two talk it over and call me."

"Thanks, Mr. Keller." Carter's tone was one of relief, but I sensed something else going on.

I closed the folder and looked into their eyes. There was part of the story one or both weren't sharing with me and that always made me nervous. However, it was still their call and I had other things to do. "I'll be leaving now." Erotica started to move away from her husband. "Don't bother, Mrs. Carter. I'll see my way out."

"Oh, I don't mind," she said with a certain firmness.

There's an instinct you develop when you spend enough time wrestling with human savagery and deceit. I don't know if it's a sixth sense as much as it's a continuous spreadsheet of facts and information about the human animal constantly available for your perusal. The answers are always in front you. It's the questions that are confusing.

Erotica walked next to me as we quietly approached the front door.

I reached for the brass doorknob when her slender, well manicured hand touched mine.

"Technically, I'm still your client, right?"

"You're the one paying the bills although you've got some resistance here." I nodded toward the room we'd just left.

"Then I want you to continue your search unless I tell you to stop."

"Erotica..."

"...It's my money so I want you to continue. Please."

"You're right. It is your money. Speaking of which..." I started to say, thinking this was a good time to bring up Diane Bristol and her very expensive letters.

"...I'll write you a check to cover additional expenses."

"No, the retainer is fine. However, there's another matter."

I told her about my meeting with Diane Bristol and what she wanted. "So I don't know what the letters will tell us. You have to decide if they're worth going after."

"Four thousand dollars. I can swing the money, but what do you think? Is this woman for real? Just because I can afford it doesn't meant I want to waste it."

"I hear you. I saw the one letter from Henry Hill. It didn't tell me a lot, but it still remains to be seen. And it is a new lead. I've had some experience with negotiating. She'll not get any money until I'm sure she has something worth buying."

She turned and walked toward a small den, returning moments later with a check for four thousand dollars. "Use it if it helps."

I shook my head and asked to use the phone sitting on the teak table in the foyer.

She nodded yes and I punched in the numbers to my office. Jeff didn't answer, but the machine did. There was one message from Gabe. He told me to go to the place where we had lunch.

I thanked Erotica and let myself out.

I left the Carter manor more or less convinced that their interest in finding the remaining members of this lost singing group was itself becoming more interesting. The red zone for me lay in the reasons why.

Once inside my Nova, I checked the clock. Only mid morning. Fifteen minutes of time driving, thinking with the radio on in the background found me back on Beaubien Street in front of the restaurant where Gabe and I choked down a lunch the day before.

I found a parking spot two car lengths from the entrance, just beating out a black Buick, popped some coins in the meter and strolled into the restaurant. I saw the grizzled, sandy haired owner, garbed in a dingy white outfit and wearing one of those uncolorful plastic caps.

I told him my name and he handed me a manila envelope.

I sat down in an open booth near the door, ordered a large Coke and opened the envelope. There were only two items, a hand written address and an old academy picture of Craig Roberts. He looked like a lot of tight faced, militaristic, 1950s black and white photoed men who craved order and discipline. In his case, the eyes looked more menacing than your average psychopath, but then I'm no psychologist.

I sipped from a tall glass of Coke, filled mostly with ice and thought about the best approach to use with this former police officer. Professional courtesy. I'd call first. I used the phone near the booth.

It was time to call Craig Roberts and strategically figure out how to let him lead me to the truth about that night over forty years ago. I checked the address as the numbers beeped inside the receiver.

I was relieved when a woman answered. Her voice was cordial, bordering close to pleasant. I returned the social courtesy and asked to speak to Craig Roberts.

She hesitated before asking the nature of my inquiry.

"I'm an ex-police officer and I'd like to ask him some questions concerning a former case."

She was still hesitant. "My father doesn't see many visitors. His condition can't handle that kind of excitement."

I told her it was very important and promised not to take too much of his time.

"Well, he's taking his morning nap. So why don't you come over now."

I asked for the address and directions, not wanting to make her too paranoid. I told her I'd be there in under half an hour.

Chapter 16

It only took twenty minutes for me to locate the two-story, single family home on the tree lined street just bordering the town of East Pointe.

I parked on the street, shook my head to revitalize the circuits, walked up the wooden stairs and rang the buzzer.

The door was opened almost immediately by a woman whose brown curly hair looked more natural than prepared. She was cute. The kind of cute that's generally the second one to be asked to dance when your first choice is already taken. Her brown eyes pierced through me like I was being dissected for someone's dinner. Her face was round with high cheek bones, pointed nose and small mouth. Her medium height was the outstanding characteristic of her square shouldered body she kept hidden under a red patterned tent dress and one strap sandals. She could have been in her mid-forties or mid twenties. Her face wasn't an obvious giveaway.

I introduced myself as the one who called earlier.

"I'm Melanie Roberts and I know you're a private detective," she stated with some indignation. "You lead me to believe that you were a former Detroit Police Officer."

She cast a look that reminded me of someone who was the most-put-upon-burdened-soul to grace this planet since Joan of Arc's fiery battle with the intelligentsia of her time.

"I wasn't trying to be misleading." I showed her my license and gave her one of my cards. She read it carefully and cast a discerning eye at me. It was a hesitant gesture of letting me into their white two-story woodframe. I stood in the small rugless foyer with a clear view of the uncarpeted wooden steps that led upstairs. "I am conducting an investigation. It's an old case. I hoped your father might be helpful."

"Well, come in. I suppose it's okay." She led me into the front room which struck me as modern gaudy. The unmatching two seater couch and armchair were equally unmatching with crocheted doilies located on the arm and headrests as well as the uncomfortable single buttoned, tassel-end pillows evenly spaced from each other. The dark brown wall-to-wall carpet was covered by several throw rugs and a long plastic runner. On the mantel of the fireplace was an array of family pictures of different sizes, frame colors and designs. Among them was a large black and white head shot of a stern faced Craig Roberts – complete with assassin's eyes. There was a medium size color picture of a uniformed Craig Roberts standing next to a younger, stoutly built officer standing in front of a blue patrol car. It was dated 1973. I assumed the other man was Ron Brickham. Next to it was a color picture of Melanie looking not bad in a one piece bathing suit smiling and being embraced by a blond haired, muscular gentleman whose eyes were shaded by the bill of his cap and shadows created by the sun. They made a rather handsome couple, but his smile seemed strained. It looked like a recent picture. I was particularly struck by a black and white picture of a woman who appeared to be the upscale version of Melanie. I assumed it was her mother.

I didn't take it as a comfortable place to relax and I believe that was the intent. "How'd you know I'm a PI?"

"My father still has contacts in the department. He made a phone call and found out who you were," she said with fading interest. "Have a seat. I'll got get him."

I sat uneasily in the armchair convinced that I'd make it a short interview.

The house seemed unusually quiet for the latter part of the afternoon. All the sound created by foot movement was minimized by the carpeting in all the visible rooms. I heard no television, radio or music of any sort. It was the kind of quiet I'd expect to encounter by a cheating person's secret lover hiding in the closet when the spouse has unexpectedly come home.

It was unnerving.

After a short eternity, Melanie returned, pushing a wheelchair which contained, what I assumed was, the shivery body of Craig Roberts.

There was a smoldering anger behind his squinted cobalt eyes. His forward lean seemed brought on by age as opposed to habit. His hair was snow white with barely noticeable bald lines. He had long age lines that seem to connect his genetically similar nose with his mouth. He wore a dark green cotton sweater and his legs were covered by a blanket, revealing only his white socks and light brown backless slippers. A pathetic picture. There once was a strong, big man underneath that flaccid skin.

Based on what I'd heard, I wasn't sure how I'd feel about the man once we finally met, but I knew I had to stay objective and rational in an attempt to get his side of the story.

I stood up and walked over to him, my hand extended in a courteous greeting. "Mr. Roberts. Nice to meet you. My name is Lincoln Keller."

He kept both hands on top of the blanket. "What do you want in my home?"

Okay. I could go with the direct approach. "I'm investigating something that took place forty years ago and I hoped you could provide me with some answers."

"Who sent you?" His voice was croaked with a permanent patch of mucous.

"No one sent me. I became aware of your possible involvement by accident. So I'm following a lead. Just as you would do if you were in my shoes."

"You're wasting my time, boy."

I smiled. "My name isn't Roy, it's Lincoln," I replied trying to deflect an overt confrontation. "I have it from reliable sources that several years ago you worked the northeast area of Detroit and were engaged in the search for five men who mysteriously vanished." I didn't feel a need to mention Adam Carter.

"Fuckin' shines committed murder." I appreciate a man who comes directly to the point. He slapped his knee. "They murdered my fiancee. Stabbed her to death in the back alley of one of those jigaboo joints. I swore I'd find 'em if I had to break a thousand heads." He stopped and sneered at me. "What are you? One of their bastard offspring?"

"What I am is a former police officer, like yourself, trying to solve a mystery. Did you see any of those men actually stab your fiancee?"

"They were standing over her body when I came back from getting the car. I saw those bastards and I'd arrested them if I hadn't been knocked cold. When I finally woke up, my head hurt like hell, her body was gone and I was at the bottom of a dumpster. Nobody at that joint seemed to know anything about it. But I knew they were lying. Sticking together to protect their own kind."

As he continually tested the limits of my tolerance, Melanie sat very still on the couch. Staring intently at her father and then giving me a momentary gaze. She made no effort to interrupt. I suspect it was a role she was used to playing.

"So, you have no idea what happened to those five men?"

"No! Or else I would have shot them on sight. We were going to get married. I loved her! Do you hear me? I loved her. But she was taken from me by those worthless coloreds."

"Are you sure that's the way it happened?" I asked. I decided he couldn't be anymore intolerant if he tried, so I dropped the general politeness.

"You saying I didn't see what I saw? Get the hell out of my house! Now! Or so help me I'll-"

"-get a rope and hang me? Maybe shoot me in the head? How about a knife wound to the belly? You know, something a little more familiar."

He cuffed his hand over his mouth to cover the series of raspy coughs triggered by his excitement. Melanie rushed to his side, removing a small plastic container of pills from a pocket in her dress. She immediately opened the top and removed two capsules. There was a pitcher of water sitting on the dining table. She quickly poured a glass of water and administered the pills and water while he grasped his chest.

She scowled at me while he regained his breath. "I told you not to get him excited! Now look what you've done. Just leave. Now! No more questions."

"Miss Roberts, forty years ago five men vanished because they believed they would be charged for a crime they didn't commit. Now I think your father knows what really happened that night. If I can find out from him, it might help me."

"Why should we help you anyway?" she asked, calming down her father.

"Because wherever they are, those five men have suffered unnecessarily."

"They've suffered? What about us? Haven't we suffered because of their actions? They took away his fiancee," she said pointing back to a calmer Craig Roberts. "They also took away my mother."

I wasn't as surprised by the revelation as much as I was concerned about what she thought was the truth. I knew what the deal was but decided to goad a little further. People tend to be more revealing when they're yelling and out of control. "How the hell could she have been your mother? Your father just said she was his fiancee. Were you born out of wedlock?"

"I know now I was born a year before she was murdered. I was put up for adoption at birth and spent most of my life in foster homes. When I was eighteen, I left my foster parents and took to living on my own. For about the next twenty years I always wondered who were my parents. I was never allowed to see the records until several years ago when I hired a clever private investigator. He told me who my dad was and I came to him. He opened his heart to me. Took me in. He told me about my mother and what happened to her." She looked over at Craig who had now regained his breath. "We've helped each other so much. Don't preach to me about suffering. Wherever those men are, I hope they rot in Hell! Now get out of here!"

I threw up my hands as a concessionary gesture. "I'll leave, but it won't stop what's been started. The truth will come out and there's nothing you can do to prevent it."

I turned toward the door realizing I hadn't completely met my goal. I was floating somewhere between truths that wouldn't come together in spite of my best effort. All I'd done was upset an ineffective old man and his equally insecure daughter. Anything I had to say was tainted by my individual bias.

"Just for the record," I said stopping just short of the door. "What was your mother's name?"

"Not that it's any of your business. But it was Cheryl Crown," she replied.

I called out to Craig. "Was her nickname Swan?" He glared back at me. I had my answer.

"I'll tell you something else, shine," Roberts' raspy voice called out. "I never found the four that got away, but I know about the fifth one. He may claim innocence. But I know he knows where they are and I'll live long enough to break it out of him. He may be hotshit among you coloreds, but to me he's just another jungle bunny with nothing going for him but singing and dancing. How he stayed in business all these years is beyond me. Probably runnin' dope on the side."

His reference to Adam Carter stunned me. If that's who he meant, then Adam certainly didn't let on.

I kept walking, pretending to ignore the comment. I jumped back in the Nova and as I turned on the engine, I became aware of just how much restraint I used to get through that interview.

I can't say Craig Roberts is the first one of his kind I ever encountered. It had been so long that I'd almost forgotten. Growing up on Detroit's north end meant that African-Americans were just as much a part of your existence as air and water. It was hard to identify overt forms of bigotry when everyone has your skin color. It wasn't really until my teenage years that I began to experience the obvious signs. Most of it came in the way of name calling or other forms of physical intimidation. Rock throwing incidents from teenagers who took special joy in harassing those of us who came to

Grosse Pointe, at that time a wealthy, enviable suburb, to mow lawns and perform general landscaping maintenance and upkeep. The experience raised my level of awareness. Hiding out at a small black college in Texas only delayed the inevitable. Most of it reared its ugly head in the form of coaches, fans and others who grabbed an orgasmic high from hanging around the NFL. Working those years as a police officer made it easier to discount certain behavior as being part of the cop's persona. Somehow things are allowed to go full cycle and now that certain media hosts, editorialists, politicians and others have made human tolerance, respect and dignity politically incorrect, I guess I shouldn't be surprised at the Craig Roberts' of the world. I'm sure that from his point of view the world changed dramatically and drastically in ways he hadn't imagined.

As an ex-cop, it's hard watching my brethren in L.A., Philadelphia, New Orleans, Miami and other places take it on the chin because of the modern day versions of Craig Roberts. I know they don't represent or speak for the whole.

Especially men like Craig Roberts.

Maybe Ron Brickham would be more forthcoming.

Chapter 17

There was a Brickham Securities listed on Eight Mile Road. I wrote down the address and phone number. When I called and asked for Ron Brickham, I was put on hold, then was told he'd be in meetings the rest of the day. The bored female voice didn't bother to ask if there was a message. I guess life at minimum wage is no picnic.

I called Diane Bristol at work and was told that she hadn't made it in that day. I stopped by a bank and cashed the check, called again and got no answer.

I decided to swing by the office to check for mail, messages and see what Julie had for me.

I opened the door to my office just in time to hear the answering machine click on to extend the Keller greeting.

"Mr. Keller. My name is Tyrell Stubbins and I understand..."

I snatched up the receiver, disengaging the message. "Mr. Stubbins, this is Lincoln Keller. How are you?"

"Fine. My friend Stella says you need to talk to me. May I ask what this is about?"

"I'm a Private Investigator looking into something that happened about forty years ago at Johnny's Lounge. Ever hear of a group called The Sentiments?"

He hesitated for just a moment. "Only too well."

"I'd like to talk with you, preferably in person, about what you know."

"Well, Stella says you're alright so I'll go with that."

"Where and when can we meet?" I asked.

"I work the afternoon shift here at the Metro Lounge so come on over anytime this afternoon and we'll talk."

"Thanks, Mr. Stubbins."

I hung up smiling. Another possible lead.

The mail consisted of the usual pile of junk and bills, most of which would easily be dispatched into the rotating file in the dumpster out back.

There were no waiting messages and my partner/brother hadn't made an appearance.

I punched in his home number, listened to his short, ominous greeting and told him to pick up the phone.

He did.

His heavy breathing and short gasps told me I'd caught him in the middle of his thrice weekly workout. "You dyin'?"

"Not that I know of."

"Then this isn't you interrupting my workout. It's someone with a death wish."

"You know, Jefferson, your presidential namesake had a far more compassionate view toward people than you seem to possess."

"And yours was assassinated. Should history repeat itself?"

"What's keeping you busy for the next day or so?"

"Nothing that can't be rearranged. Why?"

I brought him up to date on the last tumultuous 24 hours. Mainly, I told him about my two trips to Blackbottom over the day, my meeting with Jon 'Night Life' MacDonald et al., the shots through my window, my surprise dinner with Erotica, my fisticuffs outside the Mellow Yellow gin joint and how some monster of a white dude kept my head from being opened up while I got jumped by who knows, how someone in a black Buick has been spending too much time behind my car, my late night/early morning meeting with one Diane Bristol, what I learned about Craig Roberts and his charming offspring, and my meeting with the what-we-now-know-to-be the Carters.

"What are your moves today?" he asked.

"I have two leads I'm going to follow up." I gave him a quick rundown on Tyrell Stubbins at the Metro Airport and Matt Stewart somewhere in the netherlands of northwest Michigan. "After that, who knows?"

"Alright. Make your moves, keep in touch and let me know where you are. I'll watch your back."

"Thanks, bro."

He grunted and hung up.

I checked my desk and Jeff's for a map of Michigan. Neither one of us had one, so I cruised across the hall to Julie's.

Mary had the phone cradled under her chin while she tapped away on the keyboard.

"Got a map of Michigan?" I asked.

She shook her head No and pointed to Julie's office.

I took it as a signal to go ask Julie. So I did.

Her door was open and she also was tapping away on her keyboard as colorful digital images danced across the screen.

She was wearing a brown nylon pinstripe jacket with matching pants and a button front vest. A white silk blouse seem to compliment the arrangement.

"Hey, Jules."

She turned toward me and faked a snarl as I approached her desk.

"I don't remember saying 'come in'," she said as she continued to tap on the keyboard. Her desktop printer churned out paper faster than a government bureaucrat.

"Where do you keep your map of Michigan?" I asked.

She pulled open a side drawer and lifted up several piles of paper before tossing the map to me.

I opened the map to its full length and placed it down on her desk.

"Feel free to come in my office uninvited anytime and take over my desk." She removed her brown square framed glasses from her vest pocket. "What are you trying to find? Please tell me it's a home in the U.P. [Upper Peninsula] where you can't bother me."

"Just lookin' for Missaukee County."

Without missing a beat, she pointed to a spot near the western part of the state, north of Grand Rapids. "Right there, Hot Shot."

"Thanks," I replied. "I figure I'm gonna have to drive up there to find this guy Matt Stewart. Your invaluable research, though worthwhile, still doesn't give me access to the guy. So I'll have to hit the road. Once I know where I'm going."

She tsked and picked up the phone's receiver. "You'd think a former football player and ex-cop would have learned how to maximize his efforts with minimum effort." As she lectured, she tapped her keyboard and brought up a menu of phone numbers. She clicked on a name and the computer clicked in the numbers through the phone. She picked up the receiver just as the phone started ringing. "Sheriff Goodman, please. Tell him it's Julie from INFO-SEARCH in Detroit. Thank you." She opened a manila file while she waited. "Hi, Paul. How's life in Missaukee County?" They exchanged barbs with one another. She asked about his degree program and I got the impression he was nearly finished. After a few minutes of their banter, Julie got around to explaining why she called. "Paul, you remember me telling you about my friend who's a private investigator?" She listened for a second. They seemed to be enjoying a good laugh. "Yeah, that's him. Well anyway, he's standing here in my office and he's working on something that may involve a citizen in your county. Here, I'll let you talk to him."

I took the receiver from her and politely introduced myself to Sheriff Paul Goodman.

"What can I do for you, Lincoln?" he asked good naturedly.

"I have reason to believe that a man named Matthew Stewart is living somewhere in your county and I need to talk to him. The only trouble is, he doesn't have a phone."

"Well, if he's the man I think he is, then it's true about not having a phone." I gave Sheriff Goodman as much background as I could from the limited information I had. "Yeah, that's him," he said without hesitation. "Harmless old cuss. Tends to keep to himself. He lives in a trailer about three miles from town. Got a spot in the woods near a lake."

"Is there any way we can get him to a phone?"

"Not without shooting him first. Like I said, he's harmless enough, but he has his ways. Friendly enough, but not too sociable. Won't talk on telephones much less to anyone in person."

Not the assessment I wanted to hear. "Guess I'll have to come up there and take my chances."

"Well, I can pave the way for you a little. Let me know when you're coming and I'll send one of my deputies by there while he's on patrol and tell him to expect a visit from you."

"Thanks, Sheriff. I appreciate it."

I told him I'd call later on in the day and confirm a time. He and Julie laughed about a couple of more things and said good bye.

"He seems nice enough," I said as she put the receiver back in its cradle.

"Yes, he is."

"He one of your clients?"

"Yeah. He's working on a degree program through Northern Michigan University. Nice guy. He decided to go back to school and professionalize his office a little more. I advertised my services through an on-line system up there and he contacted me about two years ago. Since then, I help him find articles and other information he needs for his classes."

"You knew about this guy when you sent me the info on Matt Stewart. Why didn't you just leave me the Sheriff's number and I could have called him?"

She refolded the map and returned it to the drawer. "He doesn't like private investigators, and before I used him as a source I had to be sure your case was going somewhere. Besides, I have a reputation as a miracle worker to protect."

Point made.

I thanked Julie. She promised to send me a bill.

I stepped back into my office. I still had some time before meeting with Gabe so I figured this would be a good time to drop back in on Diane Bristol to see what I'd be buying. But I also remembered I had some other clients. I called one of them knowing I'd mess up his day with what I had on his wife.

Some days it was a lot easier having Earl Campbell drive his helmet into your chest during a touchdown run than confirming what some poor sap didn't want to believe about his blushing bride.

***

Then I decided that as long as I was messing up someone's day, I may as well do another on my way over to Diane Bristol's place since it just so happened to be on the way. This time it was to give a fiftyish, and pretty-good-lookingish woman photographs and a surveillance report on her soon-to-be-divorced-and-paying-for-it husband. She viewed the pictures, snorted through a curled smile that only the truly hurt would know how to do, and thanked me by paying my bill quickly and courteously. I left hoping they'd settle. I hate court appearances. It's like playing Let's Make A Deal without the off camera announcer.

Minutes later I rolled into an open parking spot in front of Diane's house and switched my thoughts to the task at hand.

I unconsciously felt the envelope with shiny one hundred dollar bills inside the pocket of my sport coat. Erotica's unquestioning belief that the money would give us something was admirable. I wasn't entirely convinced that the truth, as Diane understood it, qualified as the truth as most people understood it. But still, she was a lead and I wanted answers.

Despite the typical sounds of traffic and people that hover around neighborhoods during the early afternoon, it felt unusually quiet. Tame, by most standards. Calm.

I knocked on Diane's screen door, hoping that she was engrossed in an afternoon soap opera or further delaying the onslaught of reasonable intelligence by tuning in to one of the afternoon talk shows. There was also the chance that she was making more track marks in her leg. I sincerely hoped not. I'm sure I waited at least a minute before knocking again, this time a little louder.

"Damn wild goose chase," I muttered.

I opened the screen door and knocked on the curtained window of the inside door. My knock was loud enough to 'wake Satan' as my Aunt May was so fond of saying.

Still no answer.

I continued to mutter. "Great. She has no phone, she's not at work, probably not here, I have no way of getting in touch, other than leaving a note..." I knocked even louder on the door "...and my day is slowly wasting away."

The thought hit me and I felt a smidgen of shame. I didn't want to risk running back and forth or possibly having a note vanish from her door, so I decided to do the only reasonable thing any ex-defensive back-turned-PI would do.

I'd pick the lock...just so I could leave a note inside where it would be easily found.

My kit of lockpicks waited in my glove compartment for unexpected use. They were given to me by an extremely talented tool and die maker who became bored with tool and die making, and decided that the creation and use of lockpicking tools was a much higher calling. He'd done two years in one of our semi-maximum facilities, and currently resides in the

Detroit area. He called me about seven months ago to ask if I needed my tools upgraded.

I opened the zippered leather pouch and my silver plated lockpicks were arranged in their slots by height, smallest to largest. I used the smallest one because the one door lock wouldn't take much effort.

The lock clicked open on the first turn.

I opened the door, 'Helloed' and called Diane's name a few times. I slowly eased down the slightly lighted stairway, still calling her name.

Then it hit me. The subtle mixture of the damp cellar air and the last gaseous expulsion of unrestricted human stench. As recognizably repugnant as the discarded remnants of recently stilled corn whiskey. As common to homicide as lying is to politics. The Grim Reaper had laid claim to another participant.

Once I reached the bottom of the steps, I felt my way over to the scarred wooden end table to turn on the lamp.

The darkened room lighted and my senses were brought to full alert at Diane's frail body lying on the floor near a corner wall. I'd completely looked past the pipe, candles and syringe lying on the coffee table to where she laid, only to catch sight of the paraphernalia after I did a quick sweep of the room.

I stepped over to the unmoving body, being careful not to touch anything. I knelt down next to her. She was still wearing the uniform from last night and her blank stare told me that she had no reason to believe her death was destined for that moment.

I checked her pulse. Her body was cold and her skin had that patchy blue that's common when the blood stops flowing. She was laying on her right side, the wall being her last known sight. I checked the back of her legs and confirmed my speculation.

Fresh needle marks, obviously from the syringe on the table.

Did she also mix one high with the high that came with smoking the contents of that pipe? Going for the double kill...literally. All indications were that she OD'ed. If that was true, the question was why? Intentional? Seemed unlikely. Accidental? Probably. Anything else? Pure speculation on my part.

Now that I had illegally intruded at a crime scene my options were very, very limited. A first year cadet would know that there was no forcible entry and I'm sure someone in the neighborhood saw me or heard me knocking on Diane's door. Morally, I couldn't just leave her for the neighbors to find.

At best, I may have had a few more minutes, so I looked around the room wanting to get an idea of how long she'd been dead and if there was any indication that it was more than just a drug overdose.

Diane was a woman whose path to glory took more twists and turns than a political speech. I don't know what unique factors intervened in the flow of her existence and cast her adrift on an unpredictable wave of distraction and self destruction. I didn't really know her, but she had been a living, breathing human being, now cut short in the prime of her life. I suspect the word 'struggle' defined her path's direction.

I mostly stood and looked around the area. The room didn't look anymore disorderly than it had from the previous evening. Most of what I'd observed was still in place, the only additions being the drug paraphernalia lying on the coffee table.

The stench of death was just starting to clog the stale cellar air and I didn't have the option of opening a window. I regretted that I couldn't be of any help to her now and a part of me felt a twinge of unmitigated guilt as I scanned Diane's living area for the letters she'd agreed to sell to me.

Knowing that I didn't have a lot of time and that I shouldn't add further to an already damaged crime scene, I checked in the obvious visual areas, scanning quickly around the room and across the floor.

Everything looked as it had the night before. There was nothing visible to the eye that might have helped my initial assessment, but the signals that bounced around the cerebrum, cerebellum and medulla oblongata told me that she wasn't alone when she died.

"Who else was here?" I asked myself.

Her place didn't look anymore ransacked than it had the previous night. I couldn't do anything to bring Diane back, so I decided to see if I could weave the past back into the present. I did a quick survey of the room trying to think about where she might have hidden those letters.

I held my nose and tried to breathe only through my mouth, trying to avoid the released body fluids that stained the area where Diane laid. The smallness of the apartment meant I didn't have a lot of area to cover.

Using the bottom part of my shirt, I opened drawers, looked through the one closet, under the mattress and anyplace where I thought she might have hid the letters. I happened to glance at a wooden milk crate she'd used as a repository for junk mail and unpaid bills.

"It couldn't be that simple...could it?" I whispered.

I sorted through the partially stacked pile and about half way down, put my hands on the letters Diane had talked about. The unsealed flaps on the four envelopes meant that they'd probably been read. I picked up the faded, yellowed envelopes and stuck them in my back pocket while backing my way out of Diane's apartment.

It seemed like I welched on my part of the deal having gotten the letters without paying any money. I made sure I wiped any area I may have touched, not having to worry about foot prints on an uncarpeted floor.

I eased back up the steps and moved nonchalantly toward my car.

No one seemed to notice. All I had to do was drive away and wait for her body to be discovered. Given the stench and decomposition, it was just a matter of time.

Still, it didn't feel right. No matter what her station in life, Diane had been a living, breathing human person who'd done her time and deserved a better exit.

I drove to a corner supermarket that had a battered phone nestled in a metal plated kiosk. I punched in 9-1-1 and told the dispatcher my name and my suspicions. I gave her the location and said I'd be waiting outside the apartment.

I drove back and waited.

Moments later the first of two white and blue Crown Victoria's rolled to where I sat leaning on my car. I knew this would add hours to an already busy day, but Diane deserved the consideration.

Chapter 18

The bevy of activity that accompanies the initial diagnosis of a crime scene moves with the focus and background of a veteran jazz band. Each part has its point of emphasis somewhere in the coordination of the sound and rapidly retreats at the timed emergence of another. Uniformed officers spent time holding back the curious who, when left unattended, would ignore the yards of yellow crime scene tapes and wander right next to the forensic specialists as they dusted, collected and lifted valuable traces of evidence. The plainclothes detectives spent their time gathering important facts from willing voices driven by a need to offer insight and speculation over the needed facts.

I was leaning against my Nova, having already given my statement for the third time, waiting for some preliminary information about Diane's final step from this world. Of course, my old acquaintance, Lieutenant Nick Knackton had to be one of those to show up. I counted four wrinkles on his scowled forehead. Four wrinkles or more meant it was not a good day. At least, not for him.

"Tell me why I shouldn't haul your ass in for disturbing a crime scene, Keller?" he asked, stopping just in front of me. Given the circumstances, I thought it was an odd question.

But I had an answer. "Because I didn't disturb the crime scene, Lieutenant. I called it in."

"Yes," he growled. "How fortunate that you just happened to come by and sense that something was wrong."

"I didn't sense it, I could smell it. Dead bodies release the same fluids whether here in Detroit or in Oakland. I have had a little experience with this stuff, Lieutenant."

"And you didn't happen to go in did you?"

"Did anyone see me go in or come out, Lieutenant? Your officers have been canvassing. Has my name come up as someone involved in some mischief?"

"What was your relationship to the victim?"

"She was a lead for a case I'm working on. I met with her last night and we said we'd get back together today. That's why I'm here."

He stepped closer. Cutting down my space and going for intimidation. "Tell me about this case."

"Confidential, Lieutenant. You know that. I'll consult with my client and let you know."

"You withhold evidence, Keller, and I'll pull your license as well as that bounty grabbing brother's of yours."

"I'll tell him you sent your love." I tried to change the subject. "What happened to her?"

"You tell me, peeper." He turned momentarily to give instructions to a uniformed officer.

"How would I know?"

"Don't get cute, peeper. You can't go back and play football if your license gets suspended."

"There's always Arena Football."

"Don't try my patience."

"Then take me in now and let's have my lawyer have a good time naming the amount we want after filing a denial of work lawsuit."

"I don't like looking at wiseasses."

"No wonder you don't shave in the morning. The sight must be unbearable."

He grabbed my collar and pulled me forward. I offered no resistance since it was an old trick designed to trigger an assaulting an officer charge which could result in a suspended license. "You got anything else I need to know?"

It was tempting, but mentioning last night with Malone would just add gasoline on a fire already burning out of control. My instincts said wait for the moment. "No. Nothing I haven't already said three times over."

"Then you got three seconds to leave here in that piece-of-shit car. We'll need you to come down and sign a statement. Don't leave town without my knowing."

"Nothing I like better than keeping you posted as to my whereabouts, Lieutenant. It gives me the greatest comfort."

"So beat it, Peeper. Go find some keyholes, sell dirty pictures or whatever it is you Kellers allege to do when you're bleeding the city dry."

He turned and moved toward the buzzing bodies of crime scene collectors, undaunted by anything I had to say.

"Hey, Lieutenant," I called out as he turned away. He turned back with a look of strained impatience. "If you anally retent any tighter, your face will implode."

"I'm three seconds off your ass, Keller."

"Which is two seconds too slow, Lieutenant." I backed away. "Call me when you want me to sign a statement."

"We call, you bring your ass down before I hang up the phone," he said turning just as quickly. "Preferably in this century."

I shrugged and climbed into my car.

Another uniformed officer directed me through the cordoned area just as the local news vans were making their appearances as part of their tireless commitment to bring you "All the news as it happens. Live at Five with just enough carnage to rival your early evening dinner."

Thoughts of my brief encounter with Diane whirled around like ten cent pellets in a five cent maze. She was someone whom I didn't really know and if not for the search for The Sentiments, I doubt if our paths would have crossed.

I was left to wonder who would grieve for her?

She died not knowing how close she came to having four thousand dollars.

Was her death in any way related to my investigation?

Lots of damn questions and damn few answers. This particular stop took me past mid afternoon and I felt like I'd been sitting too long. I knew that for my own sense of movement, I needed answers. I stopped at the corner supermarket to use the phone. I punched in my office number to check for messages. There were none.

I checked the time and pulled into traffic. I tried to kick the thought from my mind that Diane's death was coincidental. What purpose would be served by eliminating someone who's only claim to fame was spending too much time being pulled along the bottom of the barrel, and a few supposedly meaningless letters worth four thousand dollars on an imaginary road out?

It didn't make sense. At least on the surface.

I pulled the letters from my back pocket and rubbed my fingers along the uneven edges. I had an ethical dilemma. Tempted as I was to actually read the contents, I hadn't really paid the money and technically the letters still belonged to Diane. There may be clues to aid my search, or it just may be personal information not meant for anyone's eye except the people to whom they were addressed.

Thoughts soared through my head like Comets. Each with its own tail. I called the office again to check for messages. If there were none, I'd ease over to the Carter residence and show them the letters.

Darkness started to creep onto the city's sensibilities and my own mental faculties were functioning on overdrive. A million thoughts like the core of a golf ball, wrapped seamlessly around a central thought. Connected, but unreachable. I'd already had too much of a long day when I pulled onto I-94 west to head back to my office. I don't know why, but I decided to give the letters to Adam Carter and let him decide what to do next. He was their friend and also of that era. There may be references he, and only he, would understand.

Moral dilemma satisfied.

Chapter 19

Death only reinforces my need to be among the living. I needed a distraction, so I took the one most available.

I decided to pull off of I-94 and ramble over to the Harris Barber Shop.

A place where servicing the living was a time honored tradition.

The scene was pretty much as it was for the last forty years, I'd wager.

Mr. Harris greeted me as if I'd been a regular customer. His lifelong friend, Bug was also there occupying the same seat as before. All seats were taken by an interesting compilation of generations and their comfortable styles. A 1950s western was being shown on the small screen television that was perched on a shelf in a top corner of the shop.

"Didn't expect to see you back so soon," Mr. Harris said in an authoritative high pitch.

"Your story triggered my curiosity and with it my impatience." I took out the manila envelope and emptied the contents. "I wonder if you'd mind looking at a picture."

He nodded as he sharpened his razor on the hanging leather strap.

I passed the picture over to him. "Is this the man who came around asking about The Sentiments?"

He held the picture at arm's length and then brought it closer, tilting his head back slightly to focus through his glasses. He didn't say anything at first. He then walked over to where Bug was sitting and held the picture in front of him.

He looked briefly and then gave Mr. Harris a nod of concurrence.

"That's him."

Officer Craig Roberts had been identified as the man who launched a consistent and abusive search for The Sentiments.

"Did he ever say why he was looking for them?" I asked.

"Nope," Mr. Harris replied as he strolled back to his customer lying back in the barber chair in anticipation of a shave. "He just asked questions and slapped around people who didn't give him the right answers."

"He never said why?" I asked.

"Never did to me," Mr. Harris replied neutrally, leaving me to dwell on the inference.

"Me neither," Bug echoed.

At least I'd confirmed another piece of the puzzle, but not where it fit. I thanked both gentlemen and assured them that I'd be in touch.

As I turned to leave, Mr. Harris called out, "Tell me, son, you got any idea where that man is?"

"No," I lied and I don't know why. "But I've got someone working on it."

"Any chance he's dead?"

I stopped just long enough to take in the question. "Men like him don't die early. Why do you want to know?"

He leaned toward the customer being shaved, carefully gliding up the chin as the sound of hair being splintered filled the momentary void. "If he is, I just want to make sure I spit on the right grave."

I figured a comment from me would be inappropriate given what he probably experienced. I reiterated my thanks and stepped out the door.

As long as I was in the area, I thought I'd pay Mrs. Dibell a little visit.

***

But first, I stopped at a pay phone and contacted Sheriff Goodwin's office. We set an agreed upon time and location for the next morning's meeting with the reclusive Matt Stewart.

"I'll have one of my deputies escort you to old man Stewart's place."

"Thanks, Sheriff. Appreciate your help," I said.

He gave me the name of a Deputy Broadnax who I'd likely be meeting up with. We hung up and I tried to give little, if any, thought to the obviously painful hour I'd have to rise in order to make the drive, conduct the interview and return at a decent enough time to relax and wonder whether or not I'd lost my mind.

I drove around the corner to see Mrs. Dibell.

She was amiable if not affable, as we sat on her front porch absorbing the mid-evening traffic noises. A group of young girls were engaged in an all encompassing game of 'Double Dutch'. Some neighbors also sought comfort on their front porch while others moved up and down the neighborhood sidewalk with just as much aim as aimlessness.

I went with the just-happened-to-be-in-the-neighborhood approach which I'm sure she readily saw through. I hoped she'd welcome the company.

The squeaking straw from the wicker furniture on the front porch provided additional background noise as we settled into what I knew would be a painful conversation.

"Mrs. Dibell," I began, "I wanted to ask you if you've ever seen this man around the neighborhood during the time the boys vanished?" I handed her the photograph. She gave no immediate response although I did see her body tighten ever so slightly. "He's a former police officer named Craig Roberts."

"Ain't met a person yet that likes to talk about their pain," she said disconcertingly. "God gave him a soul that he sold to the Devil. My house could not worship the Lord and covet Satan. He chose the Devil's path and I would not walk with him."

Confusion seemed like a good choice.

As she spoke, she closed her eyes and slightly rocked back and forth like a sturdy branch fighting the subtle force of a breeze. She shook her head as if remembering an eternal regret. "He sinned against Man and so denied Gene his true path."

"Who's Gene?" I asked.

"My older brother. Born of the same blood and cut from the same cloth. Gene did sup with the Devil and paid the price of eternal damnation."

"Mrs. Dibell, what are you talking about?"

There was an intensity in her eyes when she glared over at me. "I'm talking about he who is sitting next to Satan. Entrusted to help those less fortunate. Given the power to make a difference in God's eyes and following the words of Satan. He is evil incarnate and Gene felt the full wrath of Satan's fiery revenge."

The old lady had fallen into her spiritual, scriptural voice. An unsignaled left turn across a four lane highway during rush hour with me in the passenger seat. She sure didn't seem to be in the mood for making iced tea.

"I'd like to know what happened, Mrs. Dibell."

"Let's go sit out back, young man. It's cooler there during this time of day."

Without waiting for a response from me, she stood up and walked back through the house, through the room we spoke in yesterday, and out onto a small screen enclosed porch that held two chaise fold-up chairs and a white metal coffee table. On the way through the living room, she stopped and pulled a gold framed color picture off the mantel.

Her small backyard was a picturesque collection of tulips, marigolds and other colorful flowers that I didn't recognize as well as a sectioned area of vegetables just about ready to be picked. It's a pattern I recognized from my own childhood when grandparents, descendants of southern farmers, planters and slaves, migrated north to escape southern tyranny and in doing so brought with them some of the basic survival skills, one of which was essential: to grow vegetables and fruits for consumption and canning. Past the tall wooden fence, the yard was separated by an alley large enough for a car to drive through without knocking over too many dumpsters.

Quite a meticulous garden, I thought.

Mrs. Dibell sat down and stared at the fruit of her talented handiwork. She gave me the picture she'd taken off the mantel. "My brother, Gene Clark was a pretty man. Oh, the things women wouldn't do just to be in his company. Gene used to take me with him to all the clubs around Detroit that catered to colored folks." She closed her eyes as if the memory had taken her back to those days. "He dressed sharp, drove the best cars and never lacked for company. Still, it wasn't enough for him. Though I was younger, I could see it in him. A hunger that drove him and I knew would destroy him. Everything went along okay until that night at Johnny's Lounge. That's when all the trouble began."

I looked at the picture of this slick haired, brown eyed man with a pencil thin mustache and a walnut tone. His eyes told the story. He could undress with a look what others couldn't undress with five hundred dollars, a pint of bourbon and a suite at the Westin. "What kind of trouble, Mrs. Dibell?"

"White woman foolishness. He met this heah gal that everybody called 'Swan'. Pretty brown haired thang, but nothing but trouble. Loved to come to the colored clubs and it seemed like every man wanted a shot at the evil that followed her. Gene was the only one she let get close. They'd meet at different places, usually in the clubs. Everybody knew what was going on, but pretty much kept it in the 'bottom'. Had to. See, she had a boyfriend. Hard and mean." She held up the picture of Craig Roberts. "That's him. I begged Gene to stay away from that gal, but it got harder and so things being what they were, she tells him she's pregnant and it's his baby. I knew that police officer wasn't gone accept no half colored baby being born to his white girlfriend. So when he found out, he came looking for Gene. Came here and threaten me. Went running wild through the neighborhood. Looked everywhere. All the places he thought Gene might hide."

"Did anyone go to the police and tell them what was going on?"

"Things back then weren't like they are now. White officers in colored neighborhoods. Some were okay, most weren't. This one here..." She pointed to Craig's picture. "...he was the worst of the lot. A disciple of Satan if ever I saw one."

"Did he ever find Gene?"

"No."

I waited for the reason why but she wasn't forthcoming. "Why not?"

"Because like most evil men who think they know everything, he didn't know where to look or who to ask. He didn't understand our history and what we do to survive. Kept coming around here for years asking questions, some years later there'd be others asking, even some colored, like yourself. But he never found out."

"Not even from you?"

"I couldn't tell him what I didn't know." She glanced over at her vegetable garden. "My tomatoes are looking better. Would you like to take a few with you, young man?"

She turned on me again and didn't signal. "No. Thank you, Mrs. Dibell. Unfortunately, I can't eat tomatoes. How come you didn't know?"

"It was best if I didn't. Cain't lie about things you don't know."

"Whatever happened to Swan? Did she have the baby?"

"Yeah, she had the child and no sooner than she had her strength back, Swan was back at the clubs. Mostly looking for my brother Gene."

"Did she ever find him?"

"No. She died."

"When?"

"Nineteen fifty five or so. Died young."

"How did she die?"

"I don't know, Son. Figured it was none of my business."

I took a chance on the next question. "Mrs. Dibell, whatever happened to Gene?"

She sighed. "Most likely dead by now."

"You don't know?"

"No, son, I don't. I asked around. Best I could do was file a missing persons report for all the good it done."

I stood up. "Mrs. Dibell, thank you for your time and I hope I didn't cause you any undo pain. I really meant no harm."

She smiled flatly. "I know, son. You're a good boy and I know you're trying to do some good. I have enjoyed your company."

I looked over at her garden. The sun was getting low, but there was still enough light to admire the results of her efforts. "I heard you had quite a lovely garden. Now I know for myself. Such devotion."

"It gives me peace. Every plant has its own character, each one precious," she said as her eyes scanned the colorful products of her labor. She motioned to a spot in the far corner of her yard. "I'm so happy for my yellow roses. Yellow is such a festive and pleasing color in a garden."

"Yes, they are beautiful," I agreed. Even in the dimming early evening light, their yellow petals stood out as if giving off their own light from within. I really meant it when I said, "Perhaps you'll allow me the honor of visiting with you again."

"You'll be welcome here, son."

I stood up and checked my watch for the time. The afternoon had moved into early dusk and I felt like an over absorbed sponge waiting to be squeezed. Mrs. Dibell had given me more than I had anticipated.

"Mrs. Dibell," I added as I walked down the back steps. "Just one other thing: you said Swan died about nineteen fifty-five or so. Could you be a little more specific? Any idea of the day or month?"

"Seems I recollect it happened in the late summer or early fall. Just about this time of year. Cain't say for sure."

"Do you happen to know her real name?"

"I only knew her as 'Swan'. The rest didn't matter to me."

I thanked her again.

I pulled into traffic, deciding to drive just for the hell of driving. I suppose the timing was right for that kind of declaration. Unfortunately, I couldn't give it too much thought.

I was being followed...again.

Chapter 20

At least it wasn't a black Buick this time. I tried to shrug it off as too much mental stimulation, but that's what I thought the previous night. I stayed in the fast lane and discreetly moved between the second and third lane. The car following me stayed with my driving pattern. Not very well, but well enough.

I came up on an exit I hadn't intended to use, made an unusual wrong turn down a one way street, quickly u-turned into the flow of traffic and swung back onto Jefferson Avenue. Then I knew.

It was an indecipherable green sedan that managed to stay six car lengths behind me despite that sudden turn.

Whoever it was hadn't been trained in the proper methods of surveillance: they let me spot them too easily. Now that darkness moved to envelope the city and change the social mix, they obviously felt like they could be a little bolder.

I made a turn off Jefferson Avenue and onto a residential street. I peeked in the rear view mirror to make sure they were still following me.

They were.

The fact that I was being followed didn't worry me as much as it stimulated my mental juices. Now I had another twist to this case to think about. Who would want to follow a Private Investigator whose only claim to fame was being the only defensive back to run an interception back one hundred and four yards for a touchdown? That touchdown beat the spread. Maybe they were former bookies still upset about that little incident.

Didn't seem likely.

The fading summer light provided little cover for either of us so I stayed with the spontaneity of the moment. The last thing I wanted to do was drive back to the office – although it occurred to me that they may have already followed me there. I turned back onto Jefferson Avenue and followed the street for a few blocks and then made a left turn onto a side street that would take me through the warehousing district.

I crossed the set of railroad tracks and zipped onto a hard ground, sparsely weeded, litter strewn open lot behind an abandoned warehouse that sat near the Detroit river. My pursuers had stopped at the corner before coming onto the lot.

I'd already taken out my .38. I adjusted the rear view mirror and saw them slowly move toward the Nova. I opened the passenger door and walked to the front of my car to use it as a shield.

During the silent moments, I felt the light breeze blowing in from Windsor, creating light waves across the river. I heard the waves hit against the shore and the call of dive-bombing seagulls as they spotted their floating food.

Several yards in front of me, the high beam from the sedan momentarily blinded me. I could barely make out the darkened outlines of two men stepping out of the sedan and standing next to their respective car doors.

"You boys have gone through a lot of trouble just to get an autograph," I yelled back, shielding some of the glare with my left hand.

There was no verbal response to my comment, just the not-so-silent hole in the glass created when two or three bullets burst through the back windshield.

I immediately dropped to the ground and crouched behind the front of my car. My insides turned over two times as the rush of adrenaline pushed my nerves and mind back into high gear. I heard footsteps run to each side of me in what I knew would be an attempt to surround me. My breathing moved up a notch and I tried to move toward a calming thought. The only thing I could think of was the terror I felt the first time I came up to stop a sweep and was greeted by the helmet of Los Angeles offensive lineman Jackie Slater. It was like being hit with the front end of a freight engine.

I survived that blow, I'd survive this one.

I fired two shots by the driver's side hoping to force one guy back long enough for me to run toward protective covering near the warehouse.

Two more shots ripped across the hood and one more broke the front passenger side window.

I fired off two shots in that direction, and as the perpetrator scrambled I fired out the high beam lights on their car. The darkness put us all on equal footing.

"Son of a bitch," yelled one of the men. "You see him, Joey?"

"Shut up, stupid! You want him to know where you are? Just keep circling."

So they were amateur shooters. I could use that advantage. I crept along the ground listening for movement or their breathing. The quiet could have been nerve shattering if it wasn't for the fact that I had two men chasing me for reasons I hadn't figured. Breathing slowly to calm myself, I waited for someone to make the next move.

That's when I heard it. A faint thud. Like someone had walked backwards into a steel pipe.

"Joey? Was that you?" one of the voices asked. Silence followed the question and I went with it. "Joey. Where are you man? Did you get him?"

I heard it again. Another thud followed by instant silence. I tried to listen above the waves, the crickets and the hungry seagulls for a noise that would tell me what's going on.

"Coast is clear, Linc. You can come out now." Jefferson Keller, the eldest, biggest, baddest of the clan said with immodest amusement.

I stood up just as he flashed his high beam flashlight over toward me.

"Holster that thing before you end up killing some innocent seagull," he said. "I got 'em both over here."

"Well, I'm glad to see you too, bro. What the hell took you so long?"

"I had to first run their license. The car they're driving is stolen so I had to wait for the play. They made their move and I made mine." I holstered my .38 as we walked shoulder to shoulder. "By the way, next time try to give yourself a little more protective covering. This isn't the OK Corral."

We came upon my two assailants laying supine near Jefferson's

Econoline Van. Neither looked to be older than twenty although one wore his head clean shaven, the other had his dyed blonde. They were unconscious and handcuffed together.

Jeff flashed a light on both of their faces. "You know these cats?"

I looked at both faces, sensing there was a certain familiarity to them. Something in passing that could have been easily missed. My already strained brain searched the file drawers for a memory. It had to be there or I wouldn't have sensed the familiarity.

"They were carryin' these."

Jeff showed me two 9 millimeter Glocks that had been fitted with silencers.

"Certainly proves it wasn't random," I said. "So who are they?"

Then it hit me.

"Jesus! These are the two guys I saw a couple of nights ago at a convenience store. They were staking out the area to do a carjacking on this guy's Jaguar. I warned the fool."

"You didn't try to stop them or anything?" Jeff asked.

"No. I just warned the guy and went on about my business."

Jeff scratched his temple. "Seems strange they would go through this much trouble just to come after you."

"Yeah. That is strange."

"Well, I'll get some answers. Help me load these two in the van. I'll take them downtown and see if anybody's looking for them. Who knows? There may be a bounty I can collect."

"If there is, we can use it to repair my car windows."

Jeff grunted and threw one guy over his shoulder. I did likewise. We deposited the human cargo into the back area of his van, handcuffed both of them to a metal bar welded into the inside of the van and bid each other good bye.

"If I find out anything, I'll call you at home," Jeff said as he u-turned to face downtown. From his car seat, he added, "Look's like you better go drop in on Sky. And try and get there without the cops seeing you driving around like that."

My Nova was a mess. Shattered glass on the back and passenger seats. Ricochet marks on the front hood. I plopped down in the driver's seat and released a long sigh. The day had been too damn long and it still wasn't over. And Jeff was right. Sky was the guy to go see right now before I do anything else.

It was about a twenty minute drive back to our old neighborhood. The attention I drew with a series of bullet holes in my Nova's exterior was more annoying than embarrassing, but fortunately, none of the curious were cops.

Sky, as best as anyone can surmise, either comes from Puerto Rico, Mexico, or is a Cuban refugee. We just know he speaks with what I guess is a Spanish accent. And no one, as far as I or anyone else knows, knows his real name. We've always known him as Sky. And believe it or not, that goes for the lovely woman he's lived with for the past eleven years and the two beautiful children between them. He's one of the those guys who knows how to keep a secret. Like: where's he from and how did he end up in Detroit? But who really cares when he's the kind of neighbor who's heaven sent. Probably in his late 50s or early 60s, Sky is a handy man par excellence. Wherever he came from or however he got here, he quickly made himself useful to his adopted community. He was a hard, and smart, worker...and a genius with cars. Sky likes to do favors for the truly deserving. He charges little for those with little money and charges a lot for those with a lot. Good system. Many elderly in the hood have been spared unnecessary expenses for furnace or appliance repairs because of Sky's unique blend of mechanical genius and compassion.

He's also just the guy to go to in case you need repairs done to your car that require special attention. Like shattered glass and bullet holes for example.

This isn't the first time I've been to see Sky like this. Sky knows Jeff pretty well, too. He saw me from his garage as I pulled up in front of his house, and gave me a wouldn't-you-know-it? kind of smile as he took immediate notice of why I could possibly be dropping by at this time.

"Oh, wow!" Sky's eleven year old son exclaimed. His handsome face beamed. "What happened?" he asked with amazement.

"Tony," Sky said to his inquisitive son, "get your sister and go into the back yard and play there. It's getting too dark to be near the street." Tony did like he was told and went to track down his younger sister as his father turned his attention back to me. "Yeah. What happened?"

As if he didn't know. "As if you didn't know," I said. "Damn duck hunters. Lousy shots. What am I gonna owe you?"

"How much you got?"

We kept this banter up for old time's sake long enough to figure he could have my Nova presentable in a day or two and that he had a '90 Ford

Festiva he'd been fixing up lately I could use for awhile. Plates and registration all set.

I thanked him muchly and he told me it would cost me as much as he can soak me for.

I fired up the engine and I have to admit it sounded good. Like everything Sky touched, it was just a little bit better than it was originally designed to be. The engine had a little more oomph than your normal off-the-assembly-line models.

I got back on Jefferson Avenue and drove for a few blocks until I spotted the familiar golden arches of a McDonald's. I decided to go inside, sit down, have a burger, and collect my thoughts. Once inside the brightly lit gastronomic terminator, I stood in one of the three lines, halfway glancing at the menu and thinking about my overly busy day.

I ordered a Big Mac, fries and a Coke, sat down in one of the booths and tried to munch mindlessly for a few minutes just to give my brain time to relax.

It didn't work, so I found a pay phone and called my office number to check for messages.

There were five.

The first one was from Erotica. She wanted me to call her when I had a moment. The second caller was Julie. She wanted me to call her right away. The third caller, my buddy Lieutenant Nick, yelled something about signing a statement or my 'useless ass would be crabgrass.' Nothing like being threatened to a rap beat. Next I heard from Malone. She'd heard about my run-in with the venerable Lieutenant and asked me to call her. Then Truman called and left his pager number.

My body felt like it had been dragged at high speeds along the Indianapolis Speedway. My mind was a cluster of exploding lights.

Who to call first? I decided against calling Julie first because this time of the evening is when she'd just be getting back with her kids. She'll always be there if I need her.

I decided that the first appointed round was to interview Tyrell Stubbins. I figured since Stella had made good on the contact, I should at least honor her efforts. I was greeted by a happy-the-world-is-sunshine-and-kisses voice that seemed out of sync with the crescendo of background voices at the airport bar.

I asked for Tyrell Stubbins and seconds later the calmer, wiser voice of a past era extended his formal greeting.

I reintroduced myself from our earlier phone conversation and mentioned Stella again. He laughed and said I should come meet with him tonight because he had plans for the rest of the week.

Naturally.

I agreed and said I'd see him in half an hour.

I had nothing in the tank but a Big Mac and fries fueled by a medium size Coke. Everything else was buried somewhere inside me with as much chance of retrieval as the anchor for the Titanic. I decided to ignore the other messages and make the drive out to Detroit Metropolitan Airport.

Sky came through for me again. For a car that looks like a pregnant skateboard, the Festiva handled like a little demon. I wouldn't have made it any faster in my Nova.

Chapter 21

Detroit Metropolitan Airport isn't located in Detroit despite the misleading reference. Then again, neither do the Detroit Lions or the Pistons play in Detroit. Not that any of this matters, but it would have made my trip down I-94 avoidable.

It took me twenty minutes to reach the public parking lot located outside the main terminal. Damn good time, considering. The time would have been less if not for the testament to keeping the State Highway Transportation employees busy. Somewhere in a lone bureaucrat's office sits a memo that says let's figure out new ways to antagonize airport customers. Never ending construction is one way, the cost for public parking is another. I locked my gun and holster in the glove compartment confident that despite the obvious ease of getting into the car I was using, nobody would be particularly interested. Besides, I wasn't in the mood to explain to Wayne County Deputies and other airport security personnel, in the midst of the TWA tragedy why I was armed in their already busy airport. I'd been shot at enough tonight.

Carrying my leather briefcase, I lugged through the bustling, constantly-being-renovated terminal, through the metal detectors, thankfully being able to miss the slower more deliberate form of tightened airport security, and then down a busy corridor until I reached the Metro Bar.

I stepped onto the red carpeted lounge where the listless gaze of waiting commuters signaled the end of human tolerance as we know it. Most of the single arch backed lounge chairs were occupied by well dressed business types in three piece suits. Gender didn't matter. In the back of the room, a large screen television was tuned to ESPN and garnered very little attention. It must have been a slow sports news day...they were showing reruns of old highlights. A quick glance showed me what I, and millions of others throughout southeast Michigan, already knew; Larry Bird intercepted a Bill Laimbeer pass, zipped it to Dennis Johnson and the Celtics went on to win the series. Years later, it still hurt. The ladder back barstools were all taken and a glass of some liquid libation was the common link between all who sat and lamented about air travel.

I inched my way around the socially loud patrons until I reached the apex of the L-shaped bar. The blonde, ponytailed bartender lumbered his two hundred and fifty plus pounds down to where I waited. He wore a white shirt, black pants and black vest. None of which seem to fit to comfortably. He looked like he'd been stuffed in from the back.

"What'll you have, sir?" he asked, eager to serve.

"I'm supposed to see Tyrell Stubbins. Is he in?"

He nodded and pointed to a corner just past the television screen. "That's him."

I thanked him and wandered over.

Tyrell Stubbins looked more like a television preacher than a bar manager. He wore salt and pepper hair medium cut and evenly coifed. He may have been sixty-five, but he looked forty. An unlined face, coffee complexion and medium build probably fooled a number of carnival soothsayers trying to guess his age within five years. He was dressed for a night out at the Renaissance Center, not for work.

He wore a two piece, pine green double breasted pant and jacket, light green shirt, silk tie with a round gold tie clamp. He was busy doing paperwork when I reached his table.

"Mr. Stubbins?"

He looked up with eyes that had seen a great deal and learned a lot more. "Yes?"

I extended my hand. "I'm Lincoln Keller. We talked earlier."

He motioned for me to sit down. "What'll you have?" he asked.

"Just water with a lime and conversation," I replied.

He motioned to a red haired waitress who looked to be working her way through college. I wondered if she was the one who answered the phone.

She wrote down our requests for drinks and moved on.

"I saw them all you know," he said as if we started this conversation an hour earlier. "Male soloist, female soloist, any and all groups. If they were in Detroit trying to make it, at some point they had to come to Johnny's Lounge. If you could make that audience like you; hell, you could have played the Apollo."

"Tough audience?"

He shook his head and smiled. "Son, you haven't lived until you've tried to convince an audience at Johnny's that you had some talent. Tough? Yeah. But only in a way that would make you try harder. Not rowdy. But tough." He removed a silver plated case, opened it and offered me a cigarette. I declined. "Wouldn't know what to do with my hands if I couldn't have a cigarette." He flicked open a lighter that had a plastic yellow base, took that first drag that increased the lighter's flame and blew the smoke toward the ceiling. "The boys you're looking for, I saw them perform at Johnny's. They came there four different times. Man, could they harmonize. Didn't matter who was in the audience. Players, plant workers, number runners, shop owners, and the women – Man! They all loved to hear those boys sing.

"I was a bit of a youngster at the time. Mostly working odd jobs around the club just to be close to the action. At the time, The Sentiments were the best to come through. Those boys were going someplace."

"When was the last time you saw them?"

He leaned forward to flick an ash into the glass ashtray. "The last time they performed at Johnny's. They had put on their best show. Women were screaming, men applauded. Everyone gave them a standing ovation. They did two encores. You should have been there. I had worked at Johnny's for about two years before they showed up and I never saw anything like that night. What they had was better than anything I'd seen or known of since that time. And that was with the four of them. There was a fifth who couldn't make it that night."

Another confirming statement about the path to stardom that laid ahead for The Sentiments. So what happened?

"Didn't it strike you as odd that a group that good is suddenly never heard of again?"

There was just the slightest hint of movement in his eyes. Then he looked down at the half burned cigarette perched between the first two fingers of his right hand. It was the classic, unconscious momentary pause to regroup. There was something in his nonverbals that cried out from some long ago suppressed memory. There was something there and for the brief nanosecond, both he and I knew it.

My experience as an interrogator took automatic precedence over my natural curiosity that typically drove me forward.

He finally reestablished eye contact. "I saw a lot of singers at that time. Most were good and a few weren't. Most didn't make it for a lot of reasons. It would just depend."

"And what might it depend upon?" I asked.

"Right kind of music, egos, good management, luck of the draw. Sometimes the timing wasn't right. Sometimes it was things beyond their control."

I decided to press a little harder. "What was it for The Sentiments?"

He paused again. This time to rub his hand across his mouth. "I don't know."

"I think you do."

A slight scowl started to form across his forehead. "Look, cop. Even if I did, why should I tell you?"

"Ex-cop," I said quickly. "Tell me because I'm asking. Because it's the right thing to do. Because you need to get it off your chest."

He looked out at the bustling corridor and then crushed the remains of his cigarette into the ashtray. "Stella says you can be trusted. Is that true?"

"You can take it to the bank." I meant it.

He inhaled deeply and as he exhaled I sensed a large planet called Earth slowly rolling off his shoulder. "The last time I saw The Sentiments wasn't during their show, but after the show. Specifically, their last set. They threw down and it was like the crowd couldn't get enough. They were hot."

His nostalgic reflection of a time over forty years ago was being told with a poet's flair. His words picked away at the emotional wall he constructed years ago.

"I was handling the maintenance. I took care of the club as well as the dressing rooms. Johnny worked hard to keep a classy look to the place and my job was to make sure that the place stayed clean. I didn't mind the work because I always got to see the shows free of charge. I met most of the ones that came through." He paused to light another cigarette. "Anyway, this particular night the guys were a little later than usual getting out of their dressing rooms because they did two encores. Their show ran late causing everything else to back up. I'd finished cleaning some of the other areas and had pushed my mop bucket out back where I usually dumped the dirty water. I was real tired that evening and thought that if I could just sit down for a few minutes that would be a big help. So I pushed my bucket behind one of those old cement garbage containers. You remember those kind? They had doors on the top and on the side."

I nodded.

"So I eased behind this big container," he continued, "turned my bucket over and sat down, leaning back against the wall. I remember how great it felt being off my feet. I must have dozed off for just a minute because I was awakened by voices and I immediately thought my boss had caught me sleeping on the job."

"Had he?"

"No," he replied grimly. "I wish it had been him. Instead what I saw from the shadows was this white couple arguing about something he said she did."

"A white couple? At Johnny's? In the 'bottom'?

"Wasn't unusual," he said flatly. "Happened all the time at Johnny's. People came in to hear the music and see the talent. All that other stuff didn't matter."

I remember reading about the same thing happening in Harlem at the Cotton Club, at the 'Blues' clubs in Chicago and other places where patrons showed up because they wanted to really get close to the entertainment and didn't worry much about appearances.

"What were they arguing about?"

"I'm not sure. I only caught bits and pieces. Only thing that seemed to make sense was he wanted her to act a certain way and she refused. I saw him grab her and push her down. He stood over her pointing his finger and making threats. You know what she did?"

"No."

"She laughed at him. She stood up, called him a weak man and turned to walk away." He stopped and shook his head. "Next thing I know, he ran up behind her, turned her around and stuck a knife through her."

"He stabbed her?"

"He murdered her. Her body dropped to the ground and he's standing there holding this blood soaked knife, breathing hard with this crazy look in his eye. Next thing I know, he takes off running down the alley."

"What did you do?"

"I stood there holding my breath, trying to remain calm. I didn't want this crazy fool to see me. So I'm standing there breathing real hard and the back door opens. I looked over there and who should come out but The Sentiments. Only four of them had performed that night. They were laughing and joking. Just having a good time."

"Why would they have come out the back?" I asked.

"Pretty routine for that time. They'd just put on a tremendous show. But if they were going to get home at a decent time, it was necessary to leave out the back exit. Most singers or groups usually had someone waiting for them in a car."

"What happened next?"

"They stumbled on this woman's body. They froze, unsure of what they were seeing. One of them, the lead singer, knelt down next to her. He called out to her while the others debated what they should do. We didn't have 911 at that time. All this went on in a matter of seconds. Then somebody yells 'Hold it!' The guys look up and it's the man who'd just stabbed this woman only now he's holding a gun and he's aiming it at the group. And he was flashing his badge."

As he talked, certain parts of the picture were starting to make sense. The pieces weren't completely connected but light started to shine where darkness once invaded. "So the man who killed her doubled back and saw The Sentiments standing around her body. What did he say?"

"He told them to line up next to a wall that he pointed at. They were trying to tell him what happened, but he kept telling them they were under arrest and to shut up or he'd shoot their nigger asses. They did like he said. He bent down pretending to be concerned but it was just a scam. Then he walked over to where they were and asked which one of them did it?"

"Wait a minute. If he stabbed this woman, there should have been a splattering of blood on him. He wouldn't have had time to change his clothes. Didn't any one of them notice it?"

"Yeah. But he was holding a gun. They kept telling him that they just walked up on her, but he kept saying they were lying. He said that he would personally see that they were all put away for life."

"That shouldn't have mattered. They were innocent of a crime and the evidence would bear it out." I caught my thoughts as they spun back and forth. "But it never came to trial, did it?"

"No, because the crime was never reported. You see, as this guy was waving his gun in front of them and making threats he was suddenly struck from behind and went crashing to the ground. Some other white guy had suddenly come out of nowhere with a piece of log or something, struck this guy on the back of the head and yells to the guys to quickly run to the car."

"Run to the car? He was someone they knew? He was waiting for them?" I asked as questions leaped back and forth in an effort to be answered at once.

"I guess so. Anyway, they did run. So all that's left in the alley is this unconscious man, a dead woman and me hiding in the shadows."

"What did you do?"

"After it quieted down, I pulled both of them behind the garbage container and ran inside to find Johnny. I told him what happened. He told me to stay inside and he'd take care of it. Next thing I know, he and some other guys ran outside and that's the last I know of it. It was understood that he would never tell me and I was never to ask."

"You don't know what happened to either the unconscious man or the dead woman?"

"Isn't that what I just said?" he said with eyes of stone.

"My statement was more rhetorical than accusatory. I'm sorry." I leaned back in my chair and reached down to pick up my leather case. "Would you recognize the killer if you ever saw him again?"

"Easily. In fact I saw him several times after that. Yeah, I'd know him."

I sighed. "I think I already know why." I pulled out Craig Roberts' picture. "Is this the man?"

He picked up the picture and stared for only a second. "Yep. That's him." His confirming nod told me a couple of things. Now I knew why he referred to my 'cop' background and why he hadn't come forward with his story. "You know him?" he asked.

"I know of him," I said. "His name is Craig Roberts and this investigation just became a little more complicated."

"Life's like that, isn't it?" he said while crushing his cigarette. "Always figured cops protect cops and it didn't matter why."

"I don't protect murderers, Mr. Stubbins, regardless of whether they've worn the blue."

"I wasn't trying to offend you," he said.

"I wasn't offended. Just off balance." I slid back from the table. "One other question; who was the guy that helped them get away?"

"Never knew his name, but he came to the club every now and then. Usually to watch The Sentiments, sometimes to see other talent. Johnny knew him but he died years ago. Johnny was a good man. Taught me a lot about the business."

"How about the woman? Did you know her?"

"She used to come by the club quite a bit as well. She was real hot. Loved to party. Could dance with the best. I think she met this Craig Roberts guy at Johnny's. Used to see him hanging around Johnny's office. Usually waiting for something. I didn't figure out what it was until years later...after I matured."

I knew what he was talking about. "Mr. Stubbins, you've been invaluable and I can't thank you enough. I assure you, in some small way, justice will be served. I'll do everything I can to keep you out of it."

"I don't worry about it as much as I used to, son. In fact, over the years I've carefully and quietly forgotten about that event. When Stella finally contacted me, seemed like it was time for it to come out."

"Guess I should let you get back to work," I said while I stood up and shook his hand.

"Nobody clocks the boss," he said with a slight smile. Then he added, "Lincoln, there's an ending to this story and I'd like to know what it is."

"When I have it, I'll let you know," I said through a needed stretch. "By the way, Mr. Stubbins. Do you remember if any gun shots were fired?"

"No shots were fired. Like I told you, the cop stabbed the woman, waved his gun at those singers and someone knocked him out. No bullets."

I thanked him.

We were about to part when I remembered one last question. "Mr. Stubbins, you've told me quite an incredible story and I have no reason to doubt its truth. I have a question I need to ask and I think I already know the answer but I'll ask it anyway. Why didn't you come forward with the truth?"

A canary eating smile accompanied his response. "Like you said. You already know the answer."

We shook hands again and I eased my way around the tables.

I lulled my way out of the terminal and out to where I'd parked my temporary wheels. Sure enough, nobody broke into it. I pulled out of the parking lot, grimacing about the toll and shot back toward the city.

Sky knows how to put a sound system in a car...no matter what kind of car. The rebuilt Clarion that Sky lovingly put together was bringing in WJAZ like music from Heaven, the soft jazz tones disintegrating into a cascading flow of relaxing rhythm and sultry songs by jazz singers whose voices could arouse and assuage with each seductive note.

I fought off my waning attention span, choosing to curse my idiotic decision to drive up north in the morning to meet with the reclusive Matt Stewart. A line uttered by Steve McQueen in the movie 'The Magnificent Seven' when he and his cohorts are surrounded and asked why they had taken on such a hopeless task seemed appropriate for my mood; "It seemed like a good idea at the time."

And so it did.

So content that tomorrow's fate was sealed and the best I could hope for was a good night's sleep to reinvigorate my dulling senses, I let the jazz sounds resonate throughout the car, lulled into a self-imposed hypnosis brought on by the soft orange glare of the street lights and my own need to detach from the events of the day.

When I finally returned to my apartment, I was struck by the complete disconnect between my mind and body. There was no doubt that I was physically tired. My muscles, nerves and limbs felt like I'd just won the ultimate limbo contest after having too many 'island blitzers'. I wanted to rest, but my mind would not shut down.

The images of a long busy day spun like colors in a kaleidoscope. Sharply disjointed patterns with elusive imperceptible connections swimming through an unbelievable maze.

I disrobed and stood under the streams of cool water to invigorate and relax my body's tightness. The ten minute shower during the late hour produced a more relaxed feeling, so after I toweled off, and clad only in a pair of black silk underpants, I popped the tab on a light beer and collapsed on the couch, wanting to rest but unable to turn off the juices.

Tyrell Stubbins essentially identified Craig Roberts as a killer, if his story were to be believed. His story differed from the Craig Roberts' version. I chose to believe what the former said. PI intuition, I guess. If the rest of the story was true, then the woman murdered in the alley was Cheryl Crown, aka 'Swan'.

It seemed to fit the facts.

If it was true, then there's this one question that needed answering: Where was the body?

I called Julie at home. Her baby-sitter said she was working late, so I called her at the office.

"Hi Jules," I said when she answered.

"Linc. Where the hell have you been?"

"Working to pay your bill. Why?"

"I have something I think you might find interesting."

"What is it?"

"I can't tell you, I have to show you. What time will you be in tomorrow?"

"If I make it in at all, it won't be until late afternoon."

"Make it in and come see me before you do anything."

"Okay. Now I need another favor. Billable, of course."

"What?"

"Find out if a death certificate was ever issued on a woman named Cheryl Crown. I'm not sure if it's Sh or Ch. Sometime around the summer or fall of 1955."

"I can check tomorrow after I finish the list of requests I have in front of me."

"Julie. Don't you think it's time you took on another employee? Your business seems to be expanding."

"I'm not sure if I want the hassle of other people's lives, but I could sure use the help."

"Check on that for me. I'll stop by tomorrow afternoon."

I thanked her and punched in Truman's home number.

He answered sounding like he had feathers in his throat.

"Why the voice change? This a busy time?"

"It's always busy, Linc, you know that. I was just having a heated discussion with one of my committee reps."

"I can feel the heat over the phone. You discussing the fine points of your local contract? Going over the intimate details with a fine tongue?"

"You're wasting my time, bro and not breaking my heart. As to your request, I got nothing. Nada. Zippo and like that."

"At this stage I'm not surprised. But it was worth checking."

"Our UAW roster had a combination of those names, but none that matched up with the years in question. Sorry, bro."

"It was a shot. Thanks for taking the time."

"Well, actually you should be thanking my researcher, Kelli. She did most of the legwork."

"You thank her for me."

"I'll finish thanking her as soon as you hang up."

So I did.

The four remaining Sentiments hadn't joined the military, they didn't do any jail time, hadn't worked in the plants and hadn't gone off to college.

According to Julie's research, their original social security numbers were being used by four other people, none of whom were even remotely related to any of the missing group members.

In the early 1950s four guys vanished for fear of being accused of murdering a white woman. The accuser? A cop. Yeah, it made sense.

So where did they go and who knows where they went?

The blue digital numbers on my VCR changed in a slow, deathlike movement of hour-long moments. It seemed to stay 10:47 p.m. for several light years as I consumed one lite beer and then another.

It wasn't the day as much as it was the interest it generated that kept me working in spite of the even busier day that lie ahead. I'd spent more time in the 'bottom' during the day and evening than I had in a lifetime.

I needed something to force me into a mental relaxation so my mind would follow my body into a blissful rest. I opened my leather case and took out my cassette recording of The Sentiments only known album. I took a blank sixty minute cassette tape off my bookshelf and popped it in my double cassette player and recorder. Though making another copy of the cassette seemed like an unnecessary activity, I thought it had a certain therapeutic value – if not for me, maybe Malone might like a copy.

When the music started, I was listening to the song 'Sentimentally Yours' for the sixth or seventh time and I found myself even more appreciative of the sound they created at a time when the recording industry was just start-ing to evolve. Who knows how they would have sounded with a digital sound mix? I laid back on my LA-Z-BOY listening to the soft sounds with my eyes closed and tried to disengage myself from the day and reconnect the mind and body.

During those moments when my mind is exploding on all cylinders, I'll run an idea through a series of possibilities, most of which are quickly eliminated because of a point that doesn't seem to make any sense. In the case of five men born in the same neighborhood who came to be known, however briefly, as The Sentiments, it seemed as if their individual exist-ence simultaneously hit a wall. Only in this case, there weren't any scat-tered parts left over for identification.

So what happened?

The remaining four could have joined the military. Possibly enlisting under assumed identities. It was easier to do back then. I could see one or two trying that alternative, but not all four.

"Check your assumption, milkbrain," the little voice behind the intuitive wall said in defiance. "Aren't you assuming the four of them did the same thing? Suppose they did decide to go their separate ways?"

It's possible, I conceded, except for one very important point.

"What point is that?" the voice asked as it laid casually on top of the wall smiling down at the intuitive minefield.

Both my rational and intuitive voices had heard the music generated by that gifted group. I had to believe that they would not want to lose that sound.

"Groups have broken up before and for far less noble reasons," the voice continued to pick away at the intuitive field of possibilities.

True. But everything I'd learned thus far told me that there was a different feel operating here. Something was missing that wasn't evident on the surface but would be critical to my investigation.

I don't know how long I sat there considering the possibilities.

I was just starting to feel the serenity induced from my supine position when the annoyingly necessary phone rang. The move from relaxation to urgent response took a nanosecond. Experience had taught me that phone calls made late at night were typically emergencies involving life, limb or lust. I quickly picked up the cordless phone, my voice somewhat blocked in anticipation.

"I'm glad I caught you at home, Linc. I was beginning to think you were avoiding me," she said with some amusement

"Not while you're paying the bills, Erotica," I replied. "I was going to call you tomorrow morning and see if we could get together sometime in the afternoon. I have something you might be interested in."

"Well, why wait until tomorrow? Let's meet right now."

I shook my head and glanced again at the VCR. "It's kind of late and I have an early morning run to chase down a lead and I don't really feel like driving over there right now."

"You don't have to. I'm across the street from you."

Chapter 22

I peeked through the blinds and saw her Lexus idling underneath a street light.

"Taking a bit of a chance, aren't you?" I commented more than asked.

"Depends on how quickly you invite me up."

"Come on up," I said in spite of the warning voice far off in the corner of my mind. "Park your car in the lot next door. I'll call the security guard and ask him to watch it."

I called Jon, woke him up and told him I'd slip him a twenty tomorrow morning before he came off his shift.

I quickly threw on a Raiders sweatshirt and pants just as Erotica pressed the buzzer.

I buzzed her in and listened as she made the walk up the flight of steps.

Erotica knows how to make appearances. Most people can wear casual and look rumpled, others can dress elegantly and look gaudy...and then there's Erotica.

She smiled her greetings to me as she ascended to the top stairs. And that smile of hers struck me as what you'd give to a former lover whom you hadn't seen in years after receiving a note that they were going to be in town and could you pick them up at the airport? A hint of autumn was in the air, a comfortable cool. She had the finest look for every climate. She was dressed right tonight in a black turtleneck over form fitting pants, low heeled pumps topped off by a black lamb, three button, double breasted leather crop peacoat. Her hair was pulled back into a shoulder length ponytail. She carried a black shoulder length purse. Her casual is Rodeo Drive to other lesser mortals.

"Need I ask how you found my address?" I asked confident that she would ignore the question.

"Interesting place, Keller. Nicely urban with just a hint of inner turmoil."

Was I right? She breezed past me and into my apartment. I closed the door trying to decide if that was a wise idea. I suddenly recalled the policy of keeping the door open and feet on the floor from my days as a freshman in college. Where was a dorm mother when you needed one?

"Take your jacket?"

She unbuttoned her jacket and I hung it on the hook on the back of the door.

"Nice place, Linc. I love what you've done with your windows." I loved her cynicism. Plywood has always been my favorite for shot out picture windows, too. "What happened?"

"I'm not sure," I answered quite truthfully. I pointed to the couch. "But thanks for the complement. Have a seat. The maid's gotten all the glass up." She floated down, curling one leg under the other. "It's modest, affordable, low maintenance and quickly repairable. An important feature around here."

"I would have thought a successful PI like yourself might avail himself of more worldly surroundings."

"I'm not that impressed by what the world surrounds. May I ask what you're doing here at this hour? This neighborhood isn't exactly the safest for a woman alone."

She smiled. "A chivalrous one, are you? I'm impressed. Despite my obvious luxuries, you forget that I grew up in a neighborhood not unlike this one. Besides, I'm rarely without some form of protection." She patted the outside of her purse.

I walked over to my table, removed the letters I confiscated from Diane and the manila envelope with the unused four thousand dollars and gave them to Erotica. "Here. These are yours. The money is all there and the letters might be helpful."

She seemed momentarily puzzled, but accepted the gifts graciously. "You must be quite a convincing person to talk that woman into giving up the letters without her getting the money."

"The negotiation was decidedly one sided. Doesn't require a real gift of gab to lift something from a dead person."

"Dead? What happened?"

"Took the last train from Cracktown. No return ticket. OD'ed in the first degree. I found her body."

"I'm sorry. It must have been awful."

"Yeah. Anyway, there may be something helpful in those letters," I said to her as she glanced down momentarily at the letters that lay in her lap. I had no idea what she was thinking though she seemed hesitant to open any of the envelopes and read the contents. "You are interested in what the letters have to say...aren't you?"

"In time I suppose I am. Somehow this feels like I've stumbled upon a secret that has historical significance. And now?...I'm not sure I want to know just yet."

"Then why are you here at this late hour?"

She exhaled slowly and shook her head. "That's the real irony. I've been anxiously hoping you'd find out something. That the letters would help. I couldn't wait for you to contact me. I wanted to hear some good news to share with my husband."

"And now?"

"Now? All I can think about..." She stood up, placed the letters on the couch and stepped to within inches of where I stood. "...is how good it would feel if you held me, kissed me and made passionate love to me."

I'm sure she saw the registered look of shock on my already shock prone face. "Whoa, Erotica." I stepped back.

She smiled slightly. "Find me a bit too forward...do you?"

"Your being forward is a discussion for your basketball coach. You happen to be a client. A well paying client at that. There are lines drawn that prevent that possibility."

"Lines drawn in the sand. Easily blown away by a swift wind."

"Doesn't alter the fact that the lines exist."

"And if I wasn't your client?"

"We wouldn't have met."

She smiled, folding her arms across her chest. "You don't find me attractive."

"I'm only blind to the things I can't see. I find you very attractive. Very married attractive. Those lines in the sand again."

Her eyes began to glisten. "I can't say I'm really used to this kind of rejection."

"Consider it protection. For you...and me. You're married to a man who I'm sure is..."

"...dying of pancreatic cancer." She walked to the bay window and leaned against the sill. Her arms still folded as she stared out at the intermittent traffic.

I despise awkward moments as much as I do people who drive steadily with the turn signal on. It did allow me to quickly reflect and I should have seen the clues. Adam Carter didn't have the look of a man growing old gracefully. He seemed resigned to certain unresolved realities. Almost protective of the unresolvablility.

I walked over and stood next to Erotica. "Hey, I'm sorry. I should have figured it out but I didn't. I can't imagine what you and he are going through. How far along is it?"

She wiped a single tear from her eye. "Far enough. It wasn't diagnosed until it was too far along to make a difference. So we've been putting his affairs in order. He's sold the business, dictated his memoirs and rewritten his will. I'll be a comfortable widow who'll want for very little."

I left that alone.

"You don't know how good he's been to me," she continued. "I know the years between us meant we had very little in common, but he came along at a time when I needed someone with his maturity and his strength. Our marriage may have been scandalous, but he didn't care and neither did I. Never seemed like I could do enough for him. He had everything and didn't want anything else. When I found out about these guys he used to sing with and I saw how much he missed them, well, it seemed like I had an opportunity to do one nice thing for him before he went on to sing with the other greats." She looked up at me. "I know you think I'm being disloyal or betraying my marriage, but since the onset of his cancer we haven't been very intimate. In fact, I sense him pushing me away. But I've pushed back because he is my husband. I want us to be together though time is running out."

"How long does he have?"

"A day, a week, two months on the outside. The only unpredictable aspect of cancer is its predictable misuse of time." She turned back to the bay window. "I haven't been held or intimately touched and felt safe in a long time. Then I met you. I didn't plan on saying what I said, Lincoln, but I'm not ashamed of it either. I was feeling needy and through this whole trauma, I felt like I needed you."

What I sensed happening was the thing that gets most men in trouble and their suspecting wives at my door requiring my services. "Erotica, believe me. I'm hopelessly flattered, but what you feel doesn't change the fact that you're still a married woman."

She paused and then turned facing me, her arms still across her chest. "And if I wasn't married?" she said in a daring tone.

I inched closer to her and gently pressed my forefinger against her arched lips. "You talk too much, Erotica." I smiled and unfolded her crossed arms. "If you weren't married, then I may have been inclined to do this." I gently eased my hand through her hair and deftly untied the ribbon holding her ponytail in place. She shook her hair, exposing it full shoulder length. "If you weren't married, then I'd be inclined to do this." I gently stroked the right side of her face, slowly dragging the back of my hand down across her chin and up the other side.

She closed her eyes.

"If you weren't married I might be inclined to do this." I slowly pulled her towards me, my hands cuffed under her chin and I pressed softly against her lips, rubbing my tongue around the outside. She glided forward, put her arms around me and returned my advances with an unleashed fire that smoldered my nerve endings.

I didn't count the seconds we kissed. They seemed eternal. I just felt the fire. The combustible build up of a sudden backdraft.

When we finally parted, I said, "If you weren't married, I might be inclined to do this." I slid my hands under her turtleneck and pressed them against the bottom of her back. I massaged upward feeling her simmering flesh and exposing it to a fiery atmosphere that now circled us like martyrs.

She arched her back, leaned her head backwards and then in a slow circle as if listening to an internal romance song.

She gripped me tightly around the neck, biting the lobe of my left ear as I pulled the turtleneck over her head and tossed it behind me.

She quickly returned the gesture and pulled my sweatshirt over my head.

She was braless and peaked.

I was shirtless and solid.

I gradually slid the palm of my hands across her firm breasts and down her slender thighs and then across her abdominal muscles that were becoming visible with each breath. I softly blew on the duplicate throbbing breasts and lightly stroked the tip of my tongue along her steamy cleavage. The soft burn of our singular pilot lights had been raised to an irreversible seething flame of prurient consumption.

I lifted Erotica in one quick smooth motion, holding her gently in my arms, suddenly feeling a renewed sense of energy.

"If you weren't married, I'd be inclined to do this." With her face nestled in my neck and an unrelenting throb down below, I took her into my bedroom and demonstrated the inclinations I'd act on...if she wasn't married.

***

We laid silently, having returned to normal modes of breathing. I held her next to me, my head suppressing a thousand regretful thoughts.

Our passions exploded like a Nevada test site. What remained was the aftermath.

"Erotica?"

"Yes."

I gently stroked her head as she lay on my chest. "That's what I'd be inclined to do if you weren't married."

"I see," she said raising her head and staring at me through soft spoken eyes. "Are there other inclinations you may have acted upon if I wasn't married?" She rubbed gently along the line that separates my navel from my pubic hair.

"A few."

"Oh? Like what?"

"Like this," I said as I pulled her on top of me.

We explored a few more inclinations.

Chapter 23

Surprisingly, I slept through the night. I was unaware of any dreams, nightmares or external interruptions that would have deprived me of much needed slumber.

The radio came on announcing the early beginning of the morning. The on-air personality was too jovial as he asked the morning listeners questions.

"What is it about some people that just irritate you over the edge?" he asked listeners to call in with their response.

"Early morning jovial banter," I muttered.

I rolled over anticipating a warm body, but instead touched a cold empty spot. Erotica was already up.

I called out to her but didn't get an answer. That's when I spotted the note on top of the radio/alarm clock.

Linc

I didn't want to wake you. Thanks for everything. I never knew what the possibilities would be...if I wasn't married. I'm taking the letters. I think Adam should read them. Good luck today. I look forward to seeing you again.

Erotica

I placed the note back on the bed, sat up and decided that I didn't have time to contemplate the 'After-the-Loving' questions.

I'd leave that to Englebert Humperdinck.

Despite the long yesterday, the late and lively night and the little sleep I'd gotten, I knew I'd have to drag the spotty remains of my body out of bed because I had a three hour drive over to the northwest part of the state.

I tossed the opened condom packs into the trash basket, did the shower-and-shave shuffle, threw down a piece of raisin toast and a bowl of granola cereal and sauntered to greet the overcast gray sky and cool morning with a stronger determination and tired red eyes.

I dressed quickly, opting to stay with a 'professional casual' look; dark green 'Loose Fit' slacks, a white short sleeve shirt, open collar and a dark green pullover sweater. The day was crystal clear, which meant count on it to be a bit chilly. I looked through my collection of cassette tapes and took out Marvin Gaye, Minnie Ripperton, Donny Hathaway and Phyllis Hyman. Each tape was a ninety minute collection of their music and would be critical to my survival once I was out of range of the Detroit stations.

I fired up the temporary chariot and zipped to the exit of the parking lot. I saw steam from a coffee brewer drift out of the window of the four walled wooden shack the security guards use for an office.

I slid Jon a twenty for watching Erotica's car.

He thanked me, smiled and shook his head.

I caught his meaning, not feeling inclined to explain.

Armed with my leather carrying case, music, a map of Michigan and a head full of questions, I pulled out of the parking lot and into the scanty morning traffic. I turned onto the Lodge Freeway and from there picked up Interstate 75 north. The clear advantage to leaving so early would be missing the early morning commuter traffic leading into Warren, Troy and other suburban Corporate hideaways. I tuned the FM station to National Public Radio to catch up on world events. There was the usual reports on the politics in Washington, on-going conflict with the Serbs, a couple of key corporate mergers and an interview with some deranged economist who decided to break from his contemporaries and predict with absolute certainty another stock market crash like 1929, and unless we altered our spending pattern we were headed for economic Armageddon. No wonder he was highly paid. NPR provided the perfect verbal background to my contemplative mood.

Next stop; a little town called Lakeville in Missaukee County and a conversation with Matt Stewart.

***

I tend to think of myself as having a pretty good, well rounded knowledge of certain aspects of music, whether it's the writers, arrangers, producers or guest musicians. When albums were popular, I usually read the back covers and the liner notes just to see who else contributed to the album's birth.

As far as I knew, no one had actually sat down and penned words and music that described the evolving autumn beauty endemic to the vast northern region of Michigan. Residents of the area are used to Autumn's early September beginnings which culminate in some of the most spectacular show of colors that attracts tourists from the latter part of September through the first half of November.

The sights became more evident to me after I'd made my obligatory stop after two hours to feast on a McDonald's big breakfast.

I was listening to my Minnie Ripperton tape, having already left I-75, as I followed U.S. 10 over to 27 North where I had really taken in the start of the Autumn colors and the deer that grazed nonchalantly by the highway. The shift from urban sprawl to rural landscapes made the drive even more interesting. It was as if there were an area in Michigan where time was irrelevant.

I eventually made it to the town of Houghton Lake where I took 55 west through the town and over to Lake City where I picked up 66 north. It was about nine thirty when I hit the outskirts of Lakeville. It clearly was a small town with a downtown carved out of a Norman Rockwell painting. Main Street really was the main street and led through town where parallel parking was the norm and shops located in well preserved two and three story brick buildings were a reminder of a less complicated time in America's past.

I found the Sinclair gas station located on the corner of Main and Lake Road as per Sheriff Goodwin's instructions. A flashing red light greeted drivers at the four way stop. I waited for my turn and drove through the light, making a left and pulling onto the driveway of the gas station. I drove passed the pumps and parked next to a Missaukee Sheriff Department's patrol car. The white brown striped Ford Crown Victoria with the black emblem on the driver side door was parked with its lights facing the street.

The car was also empty.

I did a quick glance around to see if the deputy was anywhere in the vicinity.

I didn't see him.

I rotated my head a couple of times to relieve some of the tension in my neck. I turned off the engine and stepped out of the cramped compartment of the Festiva. It was slightly overcast here near the great lake, with a slight breeze coming from the west. The morning air was mixed with the fresh water scent of Lake Missaukee.

I let loose with a full blown yawn, wiped the tears it created from my eyes, stretched and started toward the door that led inside the gas station. I stopped when I noticed a woman of medium height and slender build dressed in the khaki brown typically associated with Sheriff departments, come strolling around the corner. Her uniform was a perfect fit for someone who appeared to work out pretty regularly. I guessed she was in her mid-thirties. Her brown hair was cut short and trimmed just above the ears. She wore aviator sunglasses and walked with all the confidence of a riverboat gambler. I didn't have to see her eyes to know we'd made contact.

Her approach became cautious as I suppose it would have been with anyone who was a stranger in her town. I caught the change and went on the offensive.

"Deputy Broadnax?" I said. "Hi. I'm Lincoln Keller. I was instructed to meet you here this morning."

She quickly removed her sunglasses. "You're Lincoln Keller?" Her deep blue eyes revealed her surprise.

"Yes, I am.

She whistled. "You're not what I expected."

"I rarely am."

"No. What I mean is...you're black."

"I am?" I feigned surprise. "I wasn't when I left Detroit this morning! What the hell happened?"

Her face began to redden. "No. What I mean is..."

"It's okay Deputy Frankie Broadnax, you're not what I expected either. So before this hole that we're both in gets any deeper, let's start all over."

She smiled slightly and we went through reintroductions. Sheriff Goodwin had briefed her on my arrival. She knew Matt Stewart's exact location. "He's a bit of a recluse," she said. "Only comes into town for supplies and to pick up his mail. Not cranky, but friendly enough. We swing by pretty regularly to check on him. In all the years he's been here, I doubt there's ever been a complaint filed against him."

"He sounds like an honorable citizen of Lakeville," I replied.

"The best. Completely lovable old cuss," she eagerly affirmed. "He's an excellent piano player, drinks good scotch and smokes like a truck driver. Usually has a kind word for most folks. He lives on the other side of Lake Mason. Got a trailer home over there."

"Does he know I'm coming to see him?"

"He knows he's getting a visitor, but not to worry. Most of his time is spent around the trailer home playing the piano and walking around Lake Mason. He'll be home." She motioned toward the patrol car. "How do you want to do this?"

"I'll follow you."

Deputy Broadnax led me back down Main Street and onto a one lane tarred road that was a combination of small homes, farms, abandoned trailers and roadside mailboxes amidst the rural splendor of Missaukee County.

We traveled about three miles before she made a left turn onto a dirt road. The slowly transitioning foliage provided a good cover from visitors expected or otherwise. The fresh smell of leaves and timber were foreign to my urban orientation.

Deputy Broadnax made another sharp left turn onto a narrower dirt road that led through a highly forested area of trees with thin trunks and their full showing of leaves. The road slightly curved and as we approached its end, I noticed a blue trailer home with white trimming sitting in an open area. A red and white Pontiac Catalina was parked under a makeshift carport and there was a metal awning over the front entrance. Though not a shanty, the trailer had seen better days.

We parked in front of the trailer. Broadnax tapped on the car horn a few times before getting out. "Hey, Mr. Stewart!" she yelled. "It's Deputy Broadnax. You in there?"

I stepped out of the car, completely taken in by the deep blue green of the lake that was no more than fifty yards from the back of the trailer home. The reflective rays of the sun created a golden shroud the shape of a long arrow pointing toward the trees standing like a circle of sentinels on eternal watch.

Broadnax tapped the horn again and the sound echoed around the area, seeming to bounce off one tree then another.

"Alright, Frankie. I heard you the first time!" a crusty voice bellowed from inside the trailer. The door was thrust open and a completely bald gentleman wearing a white sleeveless shirt, blue jeans rolled up at the cuffs and brown sandals, pointed a bony finger. "Am I under arrest or something?"

"Not this time, Mr. Stewart," she said. Her smile told me that this was an ongoing game between the two of them. "I brought someone to see you." She nodded toward me as I was coming around her car.

"What's here to see ain't worth the time," he said, stepping down from the landing.

"Mr. Stewart," I said, extending my hand, "my name is Lincoln Keller."

"Sheriff Goodwin stopped by and said you were coming to see me." His hand felt as tough as leather despite the liver spots and wrinkled skin. "He didn't say what you wanted to see me about."

"Nothing complex, I assure you. I'm doing some follow-up on a little known, but talented singing group known as The Sentiments. I understand you used to work with them."

He arched a white eyebrow. "That was a long time ago. I don't remember much from that time."

"Anything you can remember will be helpful," I said.

He turned to Deputy Broadnax. "You stayin'?"

"Nope. I still have to finish my patrol. Think you can find your way back, Mr. Keller?"

I told her I could, so she stepped into her patrol car, backed out and sped down the curved dirt road.

"Well, come in, young man. Standing around won't get us anywhere."

The inside of his trailer home was testimony to a minimalist lifestyle. The two cushioned couch, armchair, end table, lamp and rectangular coffee table were all cedarwood with a light brown finish. A thirteen inch television sat on a wooden milk crate in a corner anchored on each side by a potted plant. An AM/FM radio sat on top of the two level book shelf which contained an eclectic collection of works in paperback. The only offsetting color to the rustic decor was the multi patterned room size carpet and the chocolate brown upright piano located in the far corner.

"Have a seat," he said pointing to the armchair. "I usually have a glass of iced tea and a scone before going down to the lake. You'll join me, of course?"

I nodded yes and thanked him for the offer. For an elderly gentleman, he moved rather sprightly.

While he rumbled through the kitchen, I walked over to his book shelf and took in some of the titles. It was hard to get a sense of his preference because all of the paperbacks were complete works; the complete works of Sherlock Holmes, the complete works of Shakespeare, Emily Dickinson, Mao Tse Tung, Charles Dickens, James Baldwin and so forth. I noticed the same pattern among his music books. Complete works and music of Mozart, Beethoven, Stevie Wonder, Andrew Lloyd Weber, Billie Holiday and others.

"I only have so much room, so it's easier for me to have one volume of their complete works than fool around with hundreds of separate copies," Mr. Stewart said as he stood behind me holding a tray with two glasses of iced tea and two raisin scones. "Plus it makes it easier to locate the books I need."

"Sounds like a practice I should apply to my own life of clutter," I remarked, returning to the armchair.

He sat down on his couch and stirred sugar and lemon juice in his tea. "You know, I've met a lot of people in my eighty three years and parts of my memory have been lost due to the pain of old age, and I rarely forget a face. Your name isn't familiar to me, but your face is. Have we met before?"

"I don't think so, Mr. Stewart," I said picking up the glass of tea. "How long have you lived here?"

"I found this property back in '67. Put a down payment on it and bought it lock, stock and barrel in '79. Moved here the same year." He cut a small slice of his scone. "Who are you working for?"

"That's a good question," I sighed. "An engaging woman in need of answers."

"Tends to complicate things," he said amusingly.

"Normally not my style, but of late I'm doing this mainly for my own sense of closure. I started out only mildly interested."

"And now?" he asked.

"Now there's something going on here that hopefully you can help me answer. I'm trying to find out what happened to The Sentiments. Can you help me?"

"What do you know about them?"

I needed his trust, so I told him everything I'd learned up to that point. I covered every angle and every dead end. I finished my overview with the recent revelation of them being falsely accused of a crime. Stewart listened intently. He didn't interrupt or commit any facial movements to a statement. The unreadable stone face. He would have been an excellent poker player, assuming he wasn't doing that already.

I finished and waited for him to respond. He forced a sigh from his sunken chest and stood up. "Come with me, Mr. Keller."

"Lincoln will do," I said as he led me out of the room to what I assumed to be an additional bedroom.

He unlocked the folding door and reached to the left to flip on the light. The room was an extension of the one we'd just left. A cedarwood rocking chair with an embroidered cushion, a foot rest and standing lamp were the only pieces of furniture. Another two level bookshelf was filled with photo albums, but the real distinguishable characteristic of this room were the hundreds of eight-by-ten black and white photos of musicians and artists from a bygone era.

"Welcome to my shrine, Lincoln." He strolled over to the rocking chair while I began my tour of his photographic museum.

Every photo was autographed and personally addressed to Matt Stewart. His collection included pictures of some of the great band leaders: Ellington, Basie and others, including many of the popular groups of the fifties; Platters, Elgins, Dells, McGuire Sisters, the Cadillacs and a series of groups named after cars and birds.

"I had no idea there were so many singing groups during the 1950s," I said in genuine amazement.

"It didn't start with Motown," Stewart replied. "Motown gave it new meaning."

I continued my walk through history. As I toured the names of groups and soloists from the 1960s, I felt a personal sense of recognition and pride. Any group that sang with Motown was represented, but so were many others. The Intruders, The Jive Five, Jerry Butler, The Impressions were among the litany of street corner harmonies, basement rehearsals and back porch do wops. The walls were equally representative of groups from the Seventies and it came to an end with New Edition and The Winans in the middle 1980s.

"Why'd you stop here?" I asked.

"That's when groups stopped harmonizing," he said with a pain of regret.

"You ever hear of Boyz II Men?"

"I only listen to classical music and some talk radio. No, I haven't heard of them."

I walked over to where he was sitting. "Why'd you bring me in here?"

He leaned forward in his chair. "To show where The Sentiments were headed." He made a sweeping gesture with his hand. "These groups and soloists were good, but they would've taken a back seat to The Sentiments. Those boys were that good. All they needed was a little more time and a better manager."

"What happened?"

"Wrong place, wrong time."

"You mean finding that woman who was stabbed to death?" I asked pressing for more information.

"Not just that, although it was most unfortunate. No, I'm talking about the perception that they may have been involved."

"I have an eyewitness who said they didn't do it."

His eyes widened as if it were new information. He sighed and leaned back. "That's nice to know now, but it wouldn't have done any good back then. The murdered woman was known to frequent places where black entertainers performed." He stopped to clear his congested throat. "Nice enough girl from what I hear. Kind of wild and untamed."

"Do you remember her name?"

"Never knew her real name. Everybody called her 'Swan'. You know, white skin with a black soul."

"That's why the nickname, huh?" I wondered out loud.

"Like I said; that's what everyone called her. Anyway, I knew that once those boys were accused, no one would believe they didn't do it."

"Wait a minute. The eyewitness claimed that some white guy knocked out the guy making the accusation and rushed the group away from that alley." I looked around the room at his shrine to the era of blended vocal harmonies...and another puzzle piece fell into place. "You! You were their manager! That was you in the car waiting for them to come out. You were the one in the alley who helped them get away!" He didn't say anything. He just took another drag from his cigarette and blew the smoke toward the half open window. "Whether you deny it or not, that doesn't matter to me right now. I want to know why did you make them run away?"

He stood up and walked to the window. He stared out for just a brief moment before turning back to me. "Let me give you the scene and you answer the question: Four black men are found standing over the body of a dead white woman and being accused of her murder by another white man who happens to be a cop. This took place in the 1950s, against a backdrop of McCarthy, the emergence of civil rights, documented incidents of violence and that travesty of justice around the murder of young Emmet Till."

I flashed on the articles I copied from the newspapers. Though the story had nothing to do with my investigation, I copied it with the idea that I'd read it later. The unsolved murder of Emmet Till, a thirteen year old black boy brutally murdered in Mississippi because a woman accused him of whistling at her. The jury brought back a non-guilty verdict on the alleged murderers. I'd guessed wrong. There was a connection even though it was by inference.

He continued. "I couldn't bear the thought of them possibly being sent off to jail. To break up those voices under any set of circumstances in my mind was just unacceptable. So we ran. I got them out of there as quickly as possible. I only found out later that the guy I hit was a police officer."

"Did you have anything to do with moving the woman's body?"

"No. I never knew what happened to her. Nothing was ever written up in the paper. I checked for days and never found any mention of it."

"Where'd you take them?"

"Remember, we were driving fast and running scared. I didn't have a plan, but I knew we had to do something. Finally, Charles Treadwell told me to drop them off on a corner. I asked him why there and he said I didn't want to know. He told me that in case the police ever asked, I needed to be able to say that I didn't know where they were. So I dropped them off on that corner and that was the last time I saw them."

"Any idea where they went?"

"I'll tell you like I told the cop who found out that I was their manager: I don't know where they went. Charles was smart. It was important that I didn't know. Being able to truthfully say 'I don't know' saved me a lot of grief."

"How could you not know? You worked with them in high school. You were their manager."

"I wasn't very good. Too naive about the business. I figured once their voices were really heard, record companies would fight to sign them to a contract. I was the one who got them signed with Shadowcast Records. Once they recorded those ten songs, I knew it was just a matter of time. But, instead, the company went belly up, their music was never released and the next thing you know, they're running for their lives." He walked back over to his chair and sat. "I stayed with teaching as much as I could after that. But I'd been bitten by the bug. I wanted to train groups to sing and manage their careers. I guess I wanted to make up for what happened to The Sentiments. Once I put in my twenty years with the Board of Education, I completely immersed myself in learning about the business. There wasn't a concert I didn't attend or a manager I didn't talk to. I had some mild success, but nothing like it could have been. After years of chasing the dream, I came here to Lakeville to retire, live off my pension and modest savings. I wanted time to think about what might have been."

"Didn't you care about what happened to them?"

"I was more concerned about what didn't happen to them. They weren't dragged through a 1950's court and they didn't serve jail time."

"A blind drunken lawyer with half a brain could have had that circumstantial evidence dismissed," I said mildly angry.

"In the 1950s, a blind drunken lawyer with half a brain wouldn't have taken the case." He shrugged. "Come. Walk with me around the lake."

I followed him out of the room, through his small kitchen and out the back door.

As we walked toward the lake, he began telling me more about his background, his years as a teacher and some of the colorful characters he encountered during his time in the business.

I suspect the obvious quiet and calm of the lake contributed more to his reflective mood than I did. So I walked and listened. I began playing with other possibilities while he described Detroit life in the 1950s.

Admittedly, the quiet calm of the lake combined with the relative stillness of the wind under a blue sky and radiant sun does a lot for helping to put events in their proper perspective. I'm never sure how to behave if I don't hear the sound of a bus backfiring or tires screeching at a four way stop. There's a certain security that comes with hanging around things most known to one's experience.

After we walked for about half a mile, I asked Mr. Stewart a different question. "So, why'd you retire here instead of Florida?"

He blew out a puff of smoke and flung the ash shortened cigarette to the ground. "Too crowded for my taste. Besides, they got winged roaches there the size of small islands. I didn't want to get carried off by something large enough to fight Rodan."

It was a good diversion from our earlier discussion. He railed on and on about the virtues of living in the northwest part of the state. I offered my arguments for city living, but I think he had his fill.

"Young man," he said as we began our walk back to his trailer, "there isn't a day goes by when I don't think about those boys. Oh, I know Adam Carter has done well for himself, but it's the other four that trouble me. The business missed out on some would-be standard bearers. They discussed choreography long before it was popular and practiced the idea of having five lead singers who could move around a song interchangeably. I have truly missed having them around. I thought about trying to contact them, but decided that it was wiser for me to not know. I didn't want to jeopardize whatever lives they might be living." He stopped and grabbed my elbow, turning me toward him. "Tell me, is there a statute of limitations on a murder charge?"

"Unsolved homicides are always left open just in case something interesting should develop. However, in this case, there is no documented homicide because there is no body. At best, what you have is a Missing Persons situation."

"Not as long as that man is out there. He could bring charges at any time. No, I did the right thing. My boys didn't do any jail time."

We walked around to the front of his trailer. "Mr. Stewart, thank you for your time. I know this has been somewhat painful, but it has helped me in more ways than you know."

He clasped both hands around mine. "There's a part of me that's glad I don't know anymore than I do. It feels like I'm still protecting them. But if you should find out what happened to them, I'd appreciate knowing."

"You have my word, Mr. Stewart."

I climbed inside the Festiva and swung around the open area until I was facing the road that led back to the main thruway. I waved to Matt Stewart as he watched me drive out of sight.

I found my way back to that Sinclair station and used the phone to call Sheriff Goodwin's office. The man who answered said that he was in an important meeting with the Mayor and two town councilmen. I left my name and thanks to him and Deputy Broadnax for their assistance. I also said I hoped to return the favor one day.

My time with Matt Stewart had been worthwhile and informative.

Matt drove the four Sentiments away from where Cheryl had been killed and deposited them on a certain corner back in their neighborhood.

That's where they vanished. How?

UFO sightings, though popular at that time, seemed an unlikely possibility.

I checked the time. It was 12:45 and nothing lay ahead of me but open road. As I motored onto the one lane road that led to Main Street, I thought about the years Matt Stewart spent wondering what happened to the other four Sentiments he was helping to coach into stardom. He made the decision that something was more important than believing in false justice. He went with his own view of moral justice, and in doing so lost out on a dream.

So what did I have?

To quote an economist caveat, on the one hand I had an eyewitness who places Craig Roberts at the scene, even identifies him as the murderer. I had the angry daughter of an alleged murdered woman whose body hasn't been found and who wishes The Sentiments would rot in hell. I had a dead drug addict, Diane Bristol, an elderly woman named Mrs. Dibell, eyewitnesses who identified Craig Roberts as the man who spent years in the 'bottom' cracking heads in an attempt to find The Sentiments and I had a drop off location told to me by Matt Stewart.

And then on the other hand, I was uncovering more and more interesting details about a forty year mystery. Some parts still didn't fit, but it was certain that my next stop would bring many of those parts closer together.

At least I hoped it would.

Chapter 24

I made the drive back in just under three hours. Once I hit I-75 south it was all downhill traveling. I had the wind to my back and mostly clear sky to guide me back to the city.

Along the way, I stopped at another McDonald's just outside Bay City. I ordered a double cheeseburger, fries and a medium Coke. I found a booth near a phone, so in between chews I made a few phone calls.

Jeff picked up when I called the office. That surprised me since answering the phone is a non-essential activity in his life. He told me that Julie really needed to see me and that he wouldn't be around for awhile. When I asked him why, he said he had to 'check out a rumor'.

"By the way," he added just before hanging up. "Just thought you'd like to know that those two shooters have rap sheets from the moment they were single tail sperm looking for an egg to rob. Turns out they're suspects in an auto insurance scam. The boys in Auto Theft have been trying to follow a chop shop that specializes in stealing cars that the owners, supposedly, want to have stolen. No real proof yet, but that's the word."

"What's that got to do with trying to shoot my lights out?"

"I guess you walked in on one of their scams. They figured you saw who they were so you needed to be taken out."

Despite the celebration of the Seventies with Rosie that night, I remembered all too well the scene at the convenience store. It did seem a little strange for someone to be driving an expensive Jaguar in that part of the neighborhood at that time of night. "So you're saying that little pissant I warned was probably in on the scam?"

He yawned into the receiver. "I don't know which pissant you're refer-ring to, but the general idea is to arrange to have your car stolen. File the claim for the insurance money, buy something a little less conspicuous and pocket the change."

"Thanks. Anything else?"

"Yeah. Lieutenant Knackton really wants a date with you. Called here more than a few times. Said something about signing a statement and hav-ing you arrested for obstruction of justice. Doesn't sound like he wants an autograph."

"Can't do a thing about it until I reach the city. It'll keep."

Jefferson had to run so we hung up. I called Julie and got her secretary.

"Hi, Linc. How's the private dick business?" she giggled.

"Desperately seeking closure." Another giggle. "Where's your boss?"

"Hold on. I'll put you through."

Julie picked up almost immediately. "Where are you, Linc?"

"Outskirts of Bay City and headed home. What's up?"

"There's no death certificate for a Cheryl Crown during any of those months in 1955. I checked both spellings and cross checked with a few other sources. I did find a birth certificate and an old Social Security num-ber and license. Now, here's the interesting part; there's no activity on the license or the Social Security number after 1955. It's like she just van-ished."

I took that as confirming what I already knew. "Maybe she did."

"Maybe she went into, like, a Witness Protection Program or some-thing like that with the government."

"Witness protection programs didn't start showing up until the Sixties. Besides, she would've had to be someone special, like a gangster's mis-tress or something."

"Well, she's gone. So what do you want me to do?"

"Just hang onto what you have and I'll stop by and pick it up."

"Good. And like I told you before, I do have something else I need to show you. I can't tell you about it over the phone. It's something you have to see."

I told her when I'd be in and that I'd come see her. I called Lieutenant Knackton's office and left a message. I also called Malone. Possibly out of guilt. I was relieved when her answering machine clicked on. I left a quick message and hung up.

I downed the rest of my Coke and shot back down to the city. I needed answers to a few more questions.

***

Not wanting to incur the wrath of an already wrathful police Lieutenant, I stayed on the highway until I reached downtown Detroit. I circled Beaubien Street twice before finding an open meter. I slowly danced my way into Police Headquarters, said Hi to Gabe and ventured upstairs to find Lieutenant Knackton.

Fortunately, I found his desk, but not his body. One of the detectives, a pock marked drumstick with a rock for an Adam's Apple said that the Lieutenant was called to a meeting at the city-county building.

To his credit, he asked if he could be helpful. I explained why I was there and how I so looked forward to signing my statement.

The detective searched the desk and found the file folder for Diane Bristol. She was a case number now. Her whole life reduced to fill-in lines and boxes with check marks. The preliminary cause of death was 'drug overdose'. I read through my statement, content to not change a word and signed at the bottom.

Though I agreed with the preliminary, it didn't feel right. Diane Bristol had been hours away from having four grand in her pocket. Why take the risk before finding out if you have the money?

I don't know how a drug addict thinks. All the ones I encountered in the pros, on the streets of Oakland and back home in Detroit never made any sense to me.

It's probably why I work for a living.

I asked the helpful detective where could I find old unsolved cases from the 1950s. He told me about their records department downstairs and told me who to ask for.

It didn't seem possible, but I had to find out if any of The Sentiments showed up as an unsolved case during that time. Since those records are open to the public and I'm an open public person, I thought I'd check it out.

I appreciate all the wondrous thingamajigs Julie can do with a computer, but I still just have to have some of my info hands-on. Modems and microfiche are good for what they are, but they just can't quite beat the good old fashioned way: get off your ass and go look for yourself. My father and brothers used to tell me that. Profound wisdom always abounded in the Keller household. I strolled back down to the lobby. The bolted, multi colored vinyl chairs were starting to fill with waiting citizens while a line had formed at the front desk.

Gabe and his overworked assistants worked with a smooth efficiency that seemed counterculture to other city reception counter employees.

Before I made my move toward the area where old cases were stored, I thanked Gabe for helping me locate Craig Roberts. I told him about our interesting encounter.

"I'm sure he proved to be communicationally challenged," he said while at the same time listening to a middle aged man explain his problem. Now I knew why his ears grew so big: he can use both at the same time, like those funny looking lizards that can rotate their eyes in different directions.

I nodded and made the turn that would take me to the last bastion of recorded history as seen through the eyes of previous occupants and recorded as factually as possible.

***

My research netted interesting results.

The first unsolved was listed as a 'white female, between the ages of 25 and 30, five feet seven inches in height, approximately one hundred and fifty pounds, dyed red hair, brown eyes, round nose and a gap between her two front teeth, a distinguishing birth mark on her left elbow, no finger prints on record. She'd been found on October 3rd, 1955 in a drainage ditch downriver near a GM plant. She was listed as having been dead about thirty-six hours. She died from a gunshot wound to the chest. The weapon was listed as a common revolver. No trace to an owner. No one came forward to confirm who she was. The investigating detectives, Mark Buckram and Terry Christopher asked around for a few days and then moved on.

"I suppose that wasn't unusual given the volume load back then," I said to myself.

The second unsolved was a 'colored' man, approximately 35 years old, six feet in height, two hundred and fifteen pounds, neatly trimmed mustache, wavy black hair (conked), brown eyes, small nose and no distinguishing marks. He'd been shot through the right temple. Again the weapon was listed as a common revolver. He was found on October 10th, slumped behind a pole in an alley near Beaubien Street. He'd been dead about twelve hours. In both cases, the reporting patrol officers were Craig Roberts and Ron Palmer. There were two different investigating officers assigned to this case. They also did some asking around and when nothing material-ized, they moved on.

I also read through the missing persons printout and they were all basi-cally runaway teenagers, four females and two males. Their names and last known address and phone numbers were listed, not that it made that big a difference now, but it was interesting historical documentation.

The six confirmed missing person/homicides each listed the date the person was reported missing, the date the body was found, the cause of death, the evidence collected, the investigative trail and where the trail finally ended. I checked the names of the investigating officers. Detectives Pokalski and O'Leary handled three of those six cases, while the other three were investigated by different pairings of homicide detectives.

One of the homicides took place on October 15th. The person was identified as Iris Brennan, a white female, reported as missing by her par-ents six months earlier and found with a bullet through her head in an alley behind a parking lot on Chene Street. She was twenty-two years old, five feet six inches in height, one hundred and twenty pounds, dark brown hair, green eyes and thin lips. She was listed as formerly living on the northwest side of Detroit.

If I were a thin eyed, ashened faced researcher with long white hair and cola bottle bifocals, I might have enjoyed the time I spent going through the unwanted files of a forgotten era, looking at the photos that accompa-nied the unsolved homicides of unclaimed bodies from 1955. It wasn't so bad at first since the number of 'colored' men between the ages of eighteen and thirty murdered during that time who fell into that category were mini-mal then. Unfortunately, as I moved through the 1960s I began to notice an increase in the number. I decided to stop after 1969. I figured since The Sentiments would have been in their late thirties by then, they'd probably escaped a lot of the danger that seems to follow young African-American males as they move from their teenage years into their twenties.

I did find a Missing Persons Report for Cheryl Ann Crown submitted by Barbara Crown in November of 1955. The report listed Barbara as Cheryl's mother and an old address on Garlington Street on the east side. I wrote down the address and the old, two letter, five digit phone number. For what it's worth, I also found the missing persons report for Gene Clark. It was dated December of 1955. I knew where his sister lived.

That marvelous romp through the musty backwaters took time away from my already limited day and advanced my need to take a nap, so I thanked the bored records officer and returned to the lobby.

I used the lobby phone to call Brickham Securities and got through to Ron Brickham. He said he'd be in for another hour and if I made it by, he'd talk to me. I said I'd see him in thirty minutes.

Time spent according to other people's schedules. It got to be annoying sometimes.

Feeling like the last thing the dog ate and threw up, I left the building and whipped onto the Lodge Freeway minutes before the mad commuter rush.

My head spun like a slot machine. Bar. Bar. Lemon. Information swirled about like images in a Spielberg movie. I was tired and getting irritable.

Ron Brickham had better have something important to tell me.

Chapter 25

I made the exit and followed the four-laned Eight Mile Road eastbound through two lights and circled around in order to catch the westbound address for Brickham Securities.

Eight Mile Road is an interesting tidbit of information in itself about the Detroit metro area. It's one of the most heavily traveled and relatively well known arteries for the X million people who live and/or work in and/or around the nation's seventh largest city. And for approximately 17 miles it is also the north border of Detroit for both the real and imaginary line between predominately black Detroit to the south and the predominately white suburbs to the north. Also, the boundary between Wayne County, with Detroit as its county seat, and Oakland County runs along Eight Mile Road. Office space is plentiful among the low buildings that flank this congested corridor. Just the right kind of stretch for Brickham Securities.

I found the address and pulled into the fenced parking lot of a yellow and black trimmed cinder block building. A red and white sign painted across the front advertised Brickham Securities and a white shirted, red haired security guard greeted me from his wooden kiosk. He was mid-fifties, if he was a day. He looked like an aging wrestler minus the steroid influence. I signed his clipboard, parked the car and entered through a windowless, yellow wooden door into a sterile, white tiled lobby. The walls were yellow, there was a wooden ladderback chair and a round wooden table resting on a beige shag rug. A mishmash of dog-eared magazines lay scattered across the table. Functional comfort with just a hint of boring.

The frizzy haired blonde sitting behind the reception desk droned several minutes through a phone conversation before finally turning toward me with a smile accented by her two upper front teeth with gold trimming.

Her red dress looked too tight and the double breasted coat with brass buttons looked too militaristic. Whoever helped to squeeze her into that dress this morning would have a tougher time peeling her out that night. Unless the dress self-destructed after one wearing. For her sake, I hoped it did.

I introduced myself and said I was expected. She picked up the phone and punched in two numbers.

"A Mr. Keller to see you," she said in a I'll-be-glad-when-this-day-is-over-with tone.

I'll-be-glad-when-this-day-is-over-with for her, too. I wish it was now.

She cradled the receiver and pointed me toward another windowless yellow door. I stepped forward. She pressed a button, the door buzzed and I pulled it open.

Interesting security, I thought.

The small, carpetless corridor was just as bland as the front lobby, only minus the robust accessory who answered the phone. I passed two small unkempt offices, each with a uniformed male who probably wrestled when he wasn't throwing old cars on top of junk piles. One black and one white. The beauty of equal opportunity employment brought home here where it counts.

I stepped into a larger office with one window, ugly brown shag carpet and furniture that institutional hospitals would give away. The walls displayed the various certificates for completion of training courses as well as commemorative photos with people who I assumed to be clients.

The black background, white lettered nameplate with Ron Brickham's name on it was redundant for me since I immediately recognized this muscular, blonde-bombshell from the picture he took with Melanie Roberts. His short sleeve, white shirt with a yellow patch on the left sleeve fit tightly around his torso. He took up all available space in the swivel ladder back chair that creaked when he stood up to greet me.

"Mr. Keller?" His tone was graciously authoritative. He extended a beefy hand and I hoped we wouldn't play let's-see-who's-the-strongest. "Come in. Have a seat. Sorry I don't have much time."

"I appreciate the time you have, Mr. Brickham." I sat across from him in a wooden armchair. I'm sure the legs had been sawed down an inch or two. I gave him one of my business cards.

He glanced at it and dropped it on his meticulously clean desk. He was a spit and polish image made popular by Patton and Terry and the Pirates. His brown pants were smooth as glass and I assumed his shoes shined like mirrors. His hair was trimmed above his ears and his pencil thin mustache grew down evenly from each nostril. "I did the PI route for awhile after I left the force. No real money in it and the hours are lousy. After the downsizing hit a lot of these businesses, I figured people would still need security, so I started Brickham Securities. Got my first two contracts and haven't looked back. You ever consider security work?"

"No, not really."

"You ever do, give me a call." He gave me one of his business cards. "We can always use good men. Now, why are you here?"

My turn. "I'm looking into something that happened years ago involving your former partner, Craig Roberts. I hoped you might give me some insight."

"Best partner I ever had. Good teacher. Really knew the streets and the moves. He's retired now. I'm engaged to his daughter."

"Congratulations. Anyway, do you know anything about a case involving a singing group called The Sentiments?"

Ron removed a small Tiparillo cigar from a box in his shirt pocket. He ripped the paper off with his teeth, spit the paper into a nearby basket and used an engraved cigarette lighter to fire it up. "Craig's like a father to me. The old man taught me how to be a police officer. How to look a man in the eye and know whether or not he's lying."

"Basic to academy training and helpful I'm sure..."

"Really knew the ins and outs of patrol work. Yessir, he was a good man. I'm quite fond of him."

Didn't need a map to see where this was going. "I'm sure you are."

"Yep. Real fond. Wouldn't want to see anything upset the old man at this stage in his life. Something like that would just set me off. Fragile old man like that. There's no telling what might set him off."

"Or who."

"Yeah. Or who. I wouldn't want to be some person, known or unknown who made the mistake of upsetting my future father-in-law."

"Him being like a father to you and everything."

"Exactly. I'm glad we see eye to eye on this one, Mr....Keller. It's wonderful reaching a mutual understanding."

"And to think I sought understanding in philosophy books and you were right here all the time."

He stood up, extending his chest. His barrel arms dropped by his side and his crystal blue eyes hid a restrained fire. "You're being an ex-cop and all, I just knew this would be a healthy conversation." He extended his hand. "Nice of you to drop by, Mr. Keller. That offer for work still holds if you're ever interested. My associates will see you out."

I hadn't heard Fric and Frank, the tag team creep up behind me. With those two behind me and Ron in front, it seems I found the place where old body builders come for their mid life crisis.

"That won't be necessary. I can find my way out."

I squeezed between the tag team combination and strolled down the hall. I knew they were watching, but I took it as a compliment. I was tempted to say something wiseass to my African brother, but he'd already given up enough. So I let it go. Besides, it looked like someone named Muhammad Ali tagged him a good one in the kisser not too long ago. He must have gotten into a playground fight or something. This was an excellent time for me to keep quiet.

I pulled out of the parking lot and zipped onto the now busy Eight Mile Road. It was an interesting encounter with Ron and the Rockheads. Totally devoid of anything useful, except that there was something he was trying to protect.

I knew we'd meet again.

Chapter 26

I made it back to the office very late in the afternoon. I stretched my way up the steps and dropped into my chair, propping my feet up on the desk.

Whatever happened seemed a million years away as I yawned until my tear ducts overflowed. I could feel the redness in my eyes and the unmistakable drowsiness that sapped the last vestiges of my remaining strength.

The long yesterday, late night, early morning and long day had taken its toll and all I wanted to do was sleep.

I wanted to sleep for six days, but I'd settle for twenty minutes.

I knew that I'd promised Julie I'd stop in, but there was no way I'd be able to concentrate. My mind felt like sand being sifted through a screen. I yawned hard enough to suck the air from a small city. I closed the office door and stumbled over to the leather couch in the corner and stretched out for a short nap.

I'd just crossed that threshold of conscious awareness and oblivion when I felt several thrusts against some deadened part of my upper torso.

Someone must have used a junkyard magnet to open my eyelids. When I was able to focus my vision, I saw Julie sitting next to me, her bottom lip curled and holding some documents.

Please, God. Just twenty minutes? I'll be good.

"Wake up, Linc. The dead have been calling here complaining about your noise."

I guess He didn't believe me. "Was I snoring?"

"That, or doing mating calls for several rare species of wildebeests." She stood up. "Go brush your teeth and come to my office. There's something you need to see. By the way, I found the note on Barbara Crown. I'll tell what I have as soon as you get over to my office."

"How long have I been asleep?"

"I first checked on you about an hour ago. When the mating calls started getting too personal I was elected to come wake you up."

An hour. Never mind, God. I stepped into the small bathroom, threw cold water on my face, brushed my teeth and gargled.

I cruised into Julie's as Mary straightened her desk to leave.

"Hi, Linc. How's the dick..."

I waved her off with a how-should-I-know? shrug. My mind was below the snappy come back level.

Julie sat poised at her desk, having just put the phone receiver back in its cradle. I moved the adjacent leather cushioned chair around the desk and next to her.

"First." She dropped two documents in front of me. "Here's some info on Pastor Ezell Jordan. Place of birth and all that stuff is highlighted, however here's something interesting. He attended a Seminary school in Colorado and completed his graduate studies by writing this." She showed me a faxed summary of a graduate thesis. I started to skim the title, but she stopped me. "I'll save you some time. He wrote a scathing report of the Japanese Internment Centers during World War II. Before coming to Detroit, he was involved in several civil incidents along the southern regions with a radical nun known as Sister Mary Elizabeth. Apparently she was quite the civil disobedient, religiously speaking of course."

I nodded.

"So the good Pastor wandered to Motown, interviewed for the opening at First Missionary Baptist Church and has been quite the religious and civil force in their community." She tsked. "Let's see. He never married, no children that I could trace and quite a fundraiser. It's believed that he singlehandedly raised the funds to build their first new church. Now there's talk of a second new church. He's outspoken, driven by the spiritual good and quite an activist. Any of this stuff helpful?"

"In its own way, I suppose so." I stared at the faxed information sensing it mattered. Julie interrupted my thinking.

"Next, I did a search on Barbara Crown. She was born Barbara Susan Milkovich in 1910 and at the tender age of 19 married the 28 year old Ralph Crown in 1929, a month before the Stock Market Crash. She should have taken that as a sign. Anyway, she and Ralph were native Detroiters, they weathered the storm of the depression and bought a house on Garlington. There they brought three loving children into the world. A son, John Crown, born in 1931. He joined the Army in 1950 and was killed in Korea in 1951. Cheryl Crown was born in 1933 and as your missing report indicates, hasn't been seen since 1955. A younger sister, Mildred was born in 1939. Ralph died in '77 and Barbara followed two years later."

"Both died not knowing what happened to Cheryl," I said.

"Looks that way." Julie flipped through a couple of pages. "I was able to determine that Mildred Crown is alive and well. She still lives in the Detroit area. Her married name is Mildred Patterson. Married twenty six years to Albert Patterson, an executive with Dyno-Tech out in Plymouth. Two children, Brian and Shelley, both grown and living in Michigan. Mildred is a pediatrician with an office on Eight Mile Road. Her phone number and address are listed."

Julie's thoroughness can be overwhelming, but she had provided me with a link to Cheryl Crown. The problem being not knowing what it would do to Mildred bringing up memories of Cheryl, but it was a chance I'd have to take.

"No time like the present to call," I said.

Julie stopped me with a pointing finger. "Not just yet Mr. Falls-asleep-when-I-say-I-have-something-to-show-you." She tapped the keyboard and spoke as the images changed. "I did age enhancements for those four guys based on the picture you gave me and..." A four column pictorial display appeared on the screen. A single head shot of each Sentiment appeared in separate columns and under each one was a picture of how that person might look using a ten year age enhancement program. There, in four separate columns, I watched as Lennix Williams, Michael Parker, Charles Treadwell and Henry Hill sequentially aged forty years to what they might look like today, if they were still alive.

"Damn, Jules. That's amazing."

"Seven or eight years ago it might've been amazing. But not now. It's called technology, Linc. No reason why you shouldn't know how to use it."

"And give up this great dialogue with you? Saints be merciful."

"Anyway...," she pulled down the print menu, "while this is printing, let me show you something real curious." She tapped a few keys and opened a file from the hard drive. "To say I'm addicted to the Internet is like admitting that you annoy me. Each statement is true."

"Thanks."

"Well, you are aware of my culinary interest. I search cyberspace for the ultimate culinary cuisines. There are several Web pages devoted to those of us who have that interest."

"I'm not following you, Julie."

"I know. So shut up and soon you will. Last night I was cruising through the Web page when I found this reference to a program put on by a Chef's school in France. The program is called 'Cultural Culinary Cuisines' from around the world. The idea is to teach their Chefs how to prepare foods from different cultures. I got the impression it was mostly exposure than anything else. So I downloaded the program."

Julie tapped the keyboard and opened a digital presentation, complete with sounds of a cooking class in which the instructor was about to introduce the anxious and interested Chefs to their guest speakers. The instructor spoke in English enhanced by his French accent.

I spotted the digital message in the top left corner of the screen. "Lecture 81. Traditional Soul Food. Interesting. Caviar meets Hamhocks," I said. "What's that got to do with...?"

Julie ssshhed me. "Just watch."

The rail thin instructor, dressed in traditional chef garb, finished his introduction and there was a brief applause. Out of the corner of the screen, two sixtyish looking African-American men moved to the center of the screen, smiling and wearing Chef's hats. They both thanked the class and the taller of the two stated how delighted they were to have the opportunity to talk about cooking Soul Food with such an interested audience.

The two guest instructors laughed, exchanged a few barbs with each other and launched into a lecture on the various forms of soul food.

Their accents were clearly English, masked somewhat by a French influence. Their English was undoubtedly American with certain pronunciations that referenced a certain time in urban history. No mistake about it; they started out in America somewhere...and they looked familiar.

My heart beat with the force of a mallet on steel as I stared at the two jovial images.

"Let me freeze it right here," Julie said as a full head shot of both men stared back at me from the computer screen.

I held the printed page of the four Sentiments aged over four decades against the frozen images on the screen. The accuracy of Julie's enhancement program was marvelous and at the same time, frightening. At the bottom of the columns for Charles Treadwell and Michael Parker, the still shot of each man, aged forty years, lined up almost perfectly with the frozen image of the two men demonstrating Soul Food preparation.

The resemblance was too close to ignore. The enhanced image of Michael Parker had even taken into account the receding hairline. The eyes told the story. Matched to a 't' in color, size and soul.

"According to the file, this program took place two years ago," Julie said. "What do you think? Coincidence?"

"Not hardly," I muttered.

Two years ago, Charles Treadwell and Michael Parker, half of the missing Sentiments forty years later, were teaching aspiring chefs how to cook Soul Food. A grin crept across my face as I thought of Mrs. Dibell's fond memories of these men. Michael Parker, the reader. The one who loved historical books and dreamed of writing a history book on the black cowboy and could jump easily between a soft and hard baritone – make the rafters shake whenever he got to feeling the 'Holy Ghost'. Charles Treadwell, the natural leader of the group who could move easily from bass to first tenor and back again with minimum strain on his vocal cords, and made sure the blend of voices was perfect. He was also the one who dated the late Diane Bristol's aunt for awhile.

"I'll just be damned," I said. Suddenly, unrelated points in the background of this case slowly moved forward like a tarantula stalking its captured prey. Distilled images seemed to come bursting through with shining clarity. Pieces of the puzzle were pulled together like polar ends of a magnet.

I made an intuitive leap based on the logic of the facts in front of me.

I stood up as thoughts whipped around in an unbridled frenzy. "Julie, you're the best. Bill me and reserve some time next week for dinner. My treat."

She smiled. "Okay. But I'll need to find a sitter for my girls."

"We'll use Jeff."

"The Bounty Hunter." She shrugged. "That just might work."

I dashed into my office and opened the file containing all the written information I'd gathered. I tore through each one until I found what I needed.

I had closed down the office when Julie poked her head in the hall. "What's the hurry, Linc? Where you headed?"

I turned and said, "Confession."

Chapter 27

"Mr. Keller? Why, this is a most unexpected pleasure. To what do I owe the honor of such a late visit?" Pastor Jordan asked from behind the glistening large cherry redwood desk. He swiveled the highback leather chair away from the desk and stood to greet me.

"Answers, Reverend...to questions not necessarily of a spiritual nature." He seemed puzzled but quickly, almost automatically, resumed the posture of a man used to sharing the burdens of his flock. He pointed this time to the brown leather chair adjacent to his desk. "I think you can provide insights where others can't," I said as I sat down.

He leaned back in his chair, both arms resting on his legs. "Everything I know is written for all to see and learn in the one true book of knowledge." He motioned toward the large leather bound Bible opened toward a reading I assumed I interrupted. "How might I bring you clarity?"

"Tell me about Charlie Frey." He stopped momentarily. I'm sure it wasn't what he expected. "You remember him, don't you? Union labor leader in the 1950s whose views were described as sympathetic to Communism. He was driven out of the Union and investigated by that group of power crazed, paranoid commie busters when he, poof, mysteriously vanished. According to a newspaper article I read in the *Chronicle*, a month prior to his disappearance he was attending a Sunday service here in this church listening to one of your sermons when you called him up to the podium and asked the members of the church to look past his political views and embrace him as a member. That was awfully risky for that time, wasn't it, Reverend? Weren't you concerned how the membership might view that alliance?"

"This church casts no judgments on the hearts of people. Mr. Frey was a good Christian who, like many before him, was going to be cast to the lions because of what he believed. The church is a sanctuary for all God's children."

He gave me a look of uncompromising defiance. There was a fire burning beneath his surface. "I don't doubt what you say, Pastor Jordan. I'm sure you know more about what's inside the Bible than I can ever recite. But that's not my specialty. What I'm good at is putting together the pieces of a puzzle and, believe me, I've got a good one." Pastor Jordan said nothing. He continued staring as if he was completely in touch with his entire being. "Like to hear a story, Pastor? Admittedly it's not as colorful as the ones you're used to teaching to the congregation, but its equally as meaningful."

"How long will this story take?" he asked.

"This story has been forty years in the making, but will only take minutes to tell." I took his silence as a sign to continue. "I had a friend of mine do a background check on a young man who was often described as feisty and unrelenting in his convictions. It was said that he found his fight in defending the rights of the common person. According to someone I contacted, this young man demonstrated at a very young age his contempt for unquestioned authority and his general commitment to helping the underdog."

"I'm aware of Mr. Frey's history," Pastor Jordan said patiently.

"I'm sure you are, Pastor Jordan, but I wasn't talking about him. I'm talking about you." His wince was subtle, almost undetectable. After years of practiced restraint and rhetorical displays on the pulpit, he was keenly aware of each movement and what message he wanted revealed. "You were described as a spiritual challenge by Dr. Garland Howell, one of your instructors from your seminary days."

Pastor Jordan turned from the conversation toward a small gold trimmed metal tray that held a coffee carafe with the accompanying condiments of low cal sugar and a miniature pitcher of cream. "May I offer you a cup of coffee, Mr. Keller?" I declined knowing that the caffeine would create a night of non-blinking. "I love a cup of coffee in the evening. It helps me relax while I'm reading the scriptures." I waited until he finished preparing his cup of coffee. He politely leaned back in his chair, blowing cool air against the escaping steam. "My old mentor, Dr. Howell. Sprightly...for a man in his eighties. Incredibly sharp mind despite his age. I looked forward to our informal philosophical debates. He was quite argumentative and a brilliant rhetorical tactician. Lord, how he could push all the right buttons to incite you into a debate...and then wipe you out in two sentences." He quietly sipped his coffee. "He took me to task several times. Always said that I derailed the logic of my arguments because of my emotional head of steam." He mockingly altered his voice. "Logic and Passion can coexist when presented as a balanced front, Mr. Jordan. A persuasive argument has the power to move mountains."

I leaned forward. "He wrote that you were the kind of student who'd lead a cause rather than argue its intent." He shrugged. "You're being much too humble, Pastor Jordan. When I look at all these pictures of you with some celebrated leaders, I find it interesting that most of these folks were once leaders of social movements. Your personal library is an interesting collection of philosophy, religion and perspectives on social movements. However, the thing I found most interesting was the specific piece of research you did for your dissertation back in 1949. I had a faxed summary given to me. Your research and general criticism of the Japanese Internment Centers in California and Arizona didn't put you in a positive light among the politically paranoid of that time."

He gently set the cup down on his glass topped desk and brought his hands together as if he were going to pray. "That was an atrocity against humankind. Imprisoning American citizens, taking away their livelihood just because their nationality happened to coincide with a warring country. They were stripped of everything that was decent, honest. Denied their basic human dignity. But why should that be so surprising? You can rarely find a decade anywhere in the documents of human history where barbarity and cruelty weren't commonplace. Despite their religious beliefs, I tried to provide some spiritual comfort. I tried to get key political leaders to listen to reason. But I failed. Over the years I've often wondered why my Lord called me to service when it seemed as if everything I tried to do didn't change the situation. People still suffered."

"How does one reconcile that kind of spiritual conflict?" I asked deliberately baiting the hook.

"Where words are powerless, action empowers," he replied emphatically.

"So you take the law into your own hands?"

"I act on my beliefs, guided by the hand of God Almighty."

I sighed. "That's what I thought, Pastor Jordan. So tell me; where is Charlie Frey? Where are the boys you knew as The Sentiments?"

I hoped he perceived me as a trustworthy individual. There was something he needed to say and I wanted now to be the time.

He turned to his left, reached across the desk and closed the leather bound Bible. He rubbed his hand along its smooth surface before pulling it toward him and cradling it in his lap. He crossed himself before answering my question. "What I'm about to tell you is a truly unbelievable story, but it is the truth."

And what a story it was.

Even now, I'm not sure if what I heard was a confession designed to cleanse both the soul and the conscience or the reflections of a spiritual activist.

"Conflicts between beliefs and actions can be resolved at many levels. I choose to live at the spiritual level. It is where I find the most justification for acts that deviate from institutional mandate," he said as if he were giving the opening statement to a lecture on religious idealism.

He went on to tell me about a movement that had its beginnings during the middle of World War II. A group of 'pacifists' lead by a particularly outspoken nun from a church in Colorado Springs took exception to the government's internment policies that led to the justifiable imprisonment of thousands of Japanese citizens. After countless efforts to persuade government officials to disband those prison camps, she felt compelled by her calling to find alternative ways to resolve 'atrocities committed by man upon God's children'.

"Who was she?" I asked, even though I knew.

"Her name was Sister Mary Elizabeth. Her disagreement with the church's stance during World War II was no secret within the hierarchy at that time."

He explained that since she was unable to resolve her own internal disputes with the church authority, she severed the relationship and became an activist.

With the help of a number of people she'd known over the years, she founded a group whose soul purpose was to help political prisoners find safe passage out of the country and start new lives under new identities.

"It's a little known and seldom documented fact that World War II had its political dissenters. Some of whom resisted, spoke out and were jailed, while others managed to elude imprisonment through the efforts of the group known as 'Lightcasters'."

"I've never heard of them," I said, searching my memory of topics covered in a few of my classes on political science.

"You weren't supposed to. The group never publicized its activities. Media attention was not its goal. However, someone in the upper ranks of the government became suspicious and the office of Secretary of War created a counter intelligence group that worked independent of Hoover's FBI. Their purpose was to infiltrate 'Lightcasters' and report on its activities."

"The name of that organization was OSI, wasn't it?" [Office of Strategic Intelligence, the precursor of the CIA].

He nodded. "You've heard of OSI?" mildly impressed by my awareness.

"Just in passing," I said, remembering a class I took on the history of government investigative agencies. "The group must have had a pretty good success rate to warrant that kind of attention."

"People being watched by the government suddenly vanished with no explanation as to where or how. I'm sure it made them nervous."

He continued with his enlightening treatise. "After the war ended it should have signaled the end of OSI activities, but the newest enemy to emerge from the fracas was the domestic paranoia around the perceived threat of Communism. By combining the best elements of the Spanish Inquisition and the Salem Witch Trials, the hunt for Communist sympathizers was on.

"At that time, anyone labeled a communist supporter was hounded, investigated and brought before government hearings where they were publicly humiliated, lynched and denied any chance to pursue their livelihood. Files were kept, families were broken and opportunities were lost to any number of good people whose actions drew even the slightest suspicion. It was active long before McCarthy jumped on the bandwagon. He was just the Fiftie's version of today's radio talk show bigots. Creating the same paranoid fear of one's neighbors through unfounded accusations and innuendo. I'm afraid the level of gullibility and insecurity hasn't diminished much in the last forty or so years."

"So Charlie Frey..."

"...came to me concerned about what would happen to him and his family once he was labeled a communist. Charlie was a good man. Completely committed to eradicating the inequities in the labor force. Motivated only by a sense of what was right. Once his ideas became known, he knew they would come after him. He thought he was safe within the union, but it was obvious that they were starting to back away."

"But why? He was one of their own."

"The 1950s was a critical growth period for industry. Businesses were doing well and so were the unions. They were winning a lot for the workers. Compromises were made that Charlie didn't like. So, as he spoke out he was distanced by the union leadership. The community tried to support him as much as possible, but in time it became obvious that certain advances for black workers would be jeopardized as long as Charlie was around."

"So what happened?"

"After a key rally in September of 1955, in which Charlie spoke out against many of the union's compromises during a critical contract negotiation, one of the local papers carried the story. Charlie was, for all intents and purposes, called a communist and it was inferred that he should be investigated. One night, he came to me after being followed and then chased by people whom I suspect were members of a government investigative arm. I was his pastor and his friend. I couldn't bear the thought of him serving jail time as a political prisoner...so, through certain contacts, I arranged for him and his family to mysteriously disappear."

"So where is he now?"

He managed a slight smile at my indulgence. "I believe I'm walking an ethical line with what I've told you so far. I don't think I'll push it any further."

"That was September of 1955. Almost a month later, The Sentiments disappeared. Did you arrange that as well?"

He sighed, refilled his water glass, stood up and walked to the window. He stared outside before turning back toward me. "The night they came to me presented me with my greatest conflict of religion, spirit and politics. The four of them raced in here and told me what happened. The dead woman, the man with the pistol and the accusation. They wanted to know what to do and I can't honestly say that I was sure what the right course of action should be. Everything was happening too fast and we didn't have a lot of time."

"Wait a minute, Pastor Jordan," I said as I stood up. "The Sentiments weren't political fugitives. They were four men accused of an alleged crime that could have been easily resolved in a court of law." I had to say it even though I knew different.

"I couldn't take the chance that the law of the 1950s would be fair and just. I don't know if they would have gone to jail or not. I couldn't chance it, so I persuaded my contacts to broaden our interpretation of political persecution and those four boys...vanished."

He drank from his coffee cup and returned it to the tray. As he sat down in his chair, I couldn't help but notice the air of nobility and uncompromising conviction that's been part of his persona for all his active life. His manner was unapologetic. Less than a martyr, but more than a mouthpiece.

I walked around to the front of his desk. There was a dignity and distance he earned that admittedly cast him in a far brighter light. I wanted to acknowledge his mantel of respect before going for what I needed to know. "Pastor Jordan, then you know where The Sentiments are, don't you?"

"Yes," he replied

"Can you tell me where they are?"

"No," he said with equal indignation.

"Pastor Jordan," I said, "would it help you to know that I've seen two of them? Charles Treadwell and Michael Parker were in Paris two years ago. I saw them as sure as you and I are sitting here. Now you and I both know that a murder took place, and contrary to what you may think of my inquiry, I believe those boys are innocent. I'm also convinced of someone else's guilt but I can't verify the story unless I talk with The Sentiments."

"We're both bound by our convictions. What I know, only I can know and will know...unless I'm told to do otherwise."

"Otherwise, meaning a higher authority."

He nodded. "Now, if you'll excuse me there are many tasks I've yet to accomplish and the evening is getting late." He rolled his seat from underneath the desk and calmly walked over to the six-level book shelf and pulled down another leather bound book and began flipping through the pages.

Though his dismissal was abrupt, it was also understandable. I knew I was pushing the envelope by even bringing up the subject. But even though he was limited by what he could tell me, I learned a lot more by what he couldn't say.

"Pastor Jordan, you have my number. Please feel free to call if you should happen to think of a loophole in your self-inflicted vow of secrecy which would allow you to be a little more revealing."

He said nothing in the way of acknowledgment, so I turned toward the door and had it halfway open when I heard Pastor Jordan mumble a question. "Whatever happened to the woman?" he asked, though his eyes never left the pages of the book. "The one they were alleged to have murdered. What happened to her?"

"A body was never found. I've gone through all the Jane Doe's from that year and several years forward. No one matching her description showed up in any of the files. She was listed in the Missing Person's file, but that's as far as it went. Technically, there's no murder without a body. We don't know if she died or not. Best I can tell you is that she, along with The Sentiments, haven't used a social security number since 1955. Not that getting a new one is very difficult."

When he nodded again, the motion seemed just slightly strained. Like a realization or a revelation was being suppressed.

I took his silence to mean that we'd reached the end of our discussion. Damn. Where was the ability to read minds when you needed it? I didn't want to know everything he knew, just the stuff concerning this case.

I walked back through the church, taking in the various sounds and noises provided by the members engaged in a series of related programs.

Pastor Jordan had managed to build and maintain one of the most active churches on that side of the city. His outreach programs were long tentacles that wove through every fabric of the community's heart and soul. Pulling, cajoling, encouraging and preaching to the many souls desperately searching for answers. I admired his work and admired his church members as well. He was a man of action who quoted both the Bible and Bertram Russell. Certain of his beliefs, comfortable with his acts and confident in what is right.

As I cruised back to the Festiva, I couldn't help but believe that something was about to break. All those years of waiting for mention of a crime that never made it to the local papers had to have taken a toll on everyone involved. I hoped that the information I shared with Pastor Jordan would help put things in a different light.

My back was to the street so I didn't see them coming.

The darkness cast no reflection in the driver side window to alert me. I felt something sharp being driven in between my shoulder blades. A large hand cuffed me around the mouth and before I could shift my weight to throw my attacker off balance, I felt a sharp rap on the back of my head.

The darkness magnified as I slipped into a painful slumber.

Whatever I inhaled seemed to slow time and movement.

Everything defocused into blurred, dark images. I felt like my head had floated away from my body and the rest of me could fly. Fading images were the best I could do.

Chapter 28

There was a swarm of bees buzzing around in my head or I'd fallen in love with someone with whom sex was the only lure. I slowly opened my eyes, squinting hard to focus on what was going on. I grasped the back of my head, slowly becoming aware of the fact that I wasn't at home tucked up under my comforter having wet dreams about a woman I met at Artie's.

I knew I was lying down although I wasn't sure why. The leathery surface beneath me felt sticky against my arms as I slowly rose to a sitting position.

"Ah, Mr. Keller. You've finally awakened." I immediately recognized the voice. "When I told my associates to find you and bring you to me by any means necessary, I had no idea that it would require chloroform in order for us to converse again."

"Funny, Night Life," I said rubbing the back of my neck. "I don't recall Ameritech shutting down its services for all of southeastern Michigan. And even if that were true, a simple Lincoln-I-need-to-talk-to-you would have done it. My calendar isn't that busy these days. You want to tell me what's up?"

I was grabbed by each arm and stood up despite the wobbly feeling in my legs.

As my eyes refocused, I began to see that I was in some kind of make-shift office. There were just the perfunctory essentials. A red leather couch that served who knows how many purposes, a worn oak desk and a mish mash collection of chairs typically found in the lobby of an emergency ward or someone's garage sale. There were three low hanging lights, each with a dimly lit bulb. From what I could determine, I was either in the basement of some building or in a room in a warehouse. Neither of those possibilities struck me as particularly appealing.

Night Life rose calmly from where he sat on the edge of the desk as I was steadied in front of him. "The questions are mine to ask, Lincoln and I'd better like the answers. I want none of your wiseass comedy. Understood?"

"You want to tell me what this is all about?" I asked.

I didn't notice a third man who came from outside of my peripheral vision. I didn't see him at all. I just felt the stinging jolt across my face and the thousand points of light that exploded in front of me.

I immediately shook my head, instinctively trying to regain my composure. My heart pumped vigorously and I could feel rivers of adrenaline ripping through my system. Though I was being held, there was no way I was going to fall. Not after that blow to my masculinity.

Night Life came back into my view. "As I said, Lincoln, I'll ask the questions and you'll provide the answers." I glared at him and knew that the time wasn't right, so I nodded. "Who are you working for?"

Was he serious? I would have loved to see the look of puzzlement on my face when he asked that question. "I told you the other day when you first had me picked up. I told you what I was doing."

"And I thought it was the truth. Now I want to really know who you're working for."

I tried to spin through the conversation we had to see if I misrepresented what I was doing. It wasn't a secret, at least not really, but apparently something else was going on here.

"Look, Night Life, I'm not sure what happened since the last time we spoke that's led you to take this interesting means of having a conversation with me, but if you tell me what's going on then maybe we can stop this urban version of the Spanish Inquisition."

He smiled and nodded to his left. I braced myself as the heavily mustached interrogator stepped forward ready to unleash another attention seeker.

I didn't like the way this was going.

Just as he was about to turn it loose, I leapt up in the air, using the two goons on the sides of me for balance and kicked my interrogator hard under the jaw. Blood immediately spewed from his mouth as he grabbed his chin while stumbling against the desk. The goon on my left grabbed me by my collar and doubled up his fist when Night Life yelled for him to stop.

We stood eyeball to eyeball glaring at each other like two mountain rams ready to throw down.

"You're testing my patience, Lincoln," he said with a sneer.

"I'll do a lot more than that if you or any of your stooges tries to put a hand on me again." I could hear my old man's voice as he taught me and my brothers about the psychology of physical combat; Make them think that you're as crazy as all outdoors. If they think you don't give a damn then they'll be more worried about what they think they can't do as opposed to what you're capable of doing. I hoped he was right.

I was pushed back down on the couch. The goon on my left went to assist his buddy while the other one, my chauffeur from yesterday, stood over me, saying nothing with words, but a lot with his nonverbals.

Night Life had gone back to his desk. He opened the drawer and spoke with a calm anger. "I don't know how much you know about me, Lincoln. I run a pretty smooth operation on this side of town. Believe it or not, the people over here have a greater sense of security knowing that I'm protecting their best interests."

"That kind of altruism should leap frog you over the Pope and give you E-mail access to the Big Guy." I watched his movements very closely.

I hoped he wasn't looking for a weapon of some sort. When he took out a six shot revolver, I thought I'd better look for something other than hope.

As he talked, he removed the bullets from the cylinder. I did see six on the desk top. I thought that was interesting. He placed the gun down next to the bullets. "What I run is pretty clean. It has a certain predictability to it that I like, and the folks in the community come to depend upon. Oh sure, we have our moments." He picked up the gun and one bullet. "I have a couple of young boys trying to establish a crack house in a couple of places. I'll take care of that in due time." He opened the cylinder, placed in one bullet, closed the barrel and gave it a spin. "A couple of gangs tried to gain a foothold over here, but I took care of that. Hard for gangs to function when the leaders keep getting put away on trumped up charges." He walked from around the desk. "But that's what I do. I unofficially maintain law and order over here and no one questions my tactics or can prove a thing. I work the shadows better than an assassin." He stood in front of me, the revolver at his side, held firmly in his hand. "I like the predictability. So when something happens to upset it, I have to step in and put things back in balance." He nodded toward my silent observer and I was pulled up. He stepped behind me, locking my arms in the back. What he lacked in conversation, he made up for in brute strength. "Now, Lincoln, this is my version of Russian Roulette, only in your case, it isn't voluntary. It goes like this; I will hold this gun against your temple so you can't see the cylinder. I will ask you a question and if I don't like the answer, I'll pull the trigger. Now, you have five out of six chances to survive. When I pull the trigger, if nothing happens, I spin the cylinder again and ask another question and we keep going until one of two things happen. You tell me what I want to know...or you die. Simple, wouldn't you say?"

"I'd rather play checkers," I replied uneasily.

"Who are you working for?" he asked as he pressed the chamber against my right temple.

"I already told you," I answered. I heard the click of the trigger being released and my heart leapt. My captor held my head steady as Night Life spun the cylinder. He pressed again. "Are you out of your goddamn mind?" I yelled. "Why don't you tell me what's going on?"

"Tell me what you're really doing." he said nonplused.

"Damnit, I already did..."

Without warning, the unlocked door was kicked open, banging against the wall as a temporary distraction – and in stepped Jefferson. He pointed his Glock at the startled crowd with a smile that would have made Hitler nervous. His eyes scanned the surroundings taking in everything in front of him.

I breathed a long held sigh.

"Who the hell are you?" Night Life demanded.

"Roosevelt Keller. Note the similar last name. I'm eldest brother to the man you're holding and easily riled. I think you gentlemen had better release him. I'd hate to see him gone, him owing me money and everything."

Night Life was as perplexed as I was relieved. "How did you get in here past my guards?" he asked angrily.

"I had help," Rosie replied, his Glock pointed squarely at Night Life "You'll release my brother now."

He didn't like relinquishing control, and as I felt the slow release of tension around my arms I wasn't sure he would give in so easily.

"You just bought yourself a lot of trouble, Mister," Night Life said with a bitter coldness. "This is my territory. I run what happens over here. Your brother has brought trouble to my area and I want to know why."

"If you don't stand aside in two seconds, it's an answer you'll never hear," Rosie said with a cold smile.

He always had a recklessness to him that used to drive the old man crazy, yet this seemed a little out past his zone of recklessness. That's when it hit me.

Night Life turned to me. "You owe me answers, Lincoln and I want them now!" he yelled. "This is my territory and I'll not have you or anyone else damaging what I've built. I'll catch up with you, if not now, tomorrow or the next day. No matter how long it takes, I'll find you."

I backed over to where Rosie was standing. A lot had gone on that didn't make sense and now I wanted some answers.

"Nice to see you, Rosie."

"Yeah, you too. Ready to go?"

"Nope. We have some unfinished business." I looked at Night Life and his henchman. The one I kicked had the look of death in his eye. "I want the four of you on the couch and don't try anything stupid. Especially you, Night Life. Drop that revolver on the floor and kick it over here." He did so...grudgingly. "Thanks," I said picking up the gun. I opened the barrel. There was a bullet in the second hole from the chamber. Talk about close calls.

"What do you want to do, bro?" Rosie asked.

"Put all our cards on the table. I can't have this idiot obsessed with finding me and inflicting some physical damage. I don't intend to be con- stantly looking over my shoulder. So..." I quickly looked around the room before calling out. "Come on out, Jeff. I need you on this one."

It was as if the shadows took on a form of their own. There was no amplified or unexpected sound to break up the unexpected silence. No an- nouncement of his presence. He just stepped from behind a darkened area and into the dimly lit room. "I figured you were the help Rosie talked about," I said. "It's good to see you." I really meant it.

Jefferson Keller stalks the shadows using his finely honed skills from the Special Forces and the United States Marshal's Office silently ap- proached us saying more with a nod than most folks say with access to a string of sentences.

He pointed a fully loaded .357 Magnum and wore a 12 gauge shotgun attached to his left side. Jeff was effectively simplistic in his approach to clothing. He only wore what fit the moment and allowed for the best move- ment. Blue denim slacks, Black Nike's and a sleeveless denim shirt.

"Jeff," I said.

"Linc."

"I thought you were checking out a rumor."

"Did. That's why I'm here. Word had it that Night Life was looking for you. Thought I'd check it out." His eyes were sullen. "Time to talk busi- ness." Pointing the .357 at Night Life and the others, he motioned for each to stand up one at a time. He thoroughly searched each one for additional weapons while Rosie kept an watchful eye. He removed two ankle pistols, three knives and two .38s. Each weapon was thrown on the desk and formed a pretty effective weapons pile. He moved back to where I was standing.

"Your guards will be embarrassed but uninjured." He turned to me. "Your call."

I approached Night Life who I could see was livid with anger. "We can do this war thing all night or you and I can talk about what it is you think I've done. What do you want to do?"

He looked up, suppressed anger flashing in his brown eyes. "I trusted you in my territory. Gave you access and what happens? Huh? The predictability is disrupted and all trails lead back to you."

"What did I do?" I said emphasizing each word.

"I can't prove it yet, but I know you had something to do with Mrs. Dibell being robbed, beaten and shot last night."

Mrs. Dibell!? "What!?" I said disbelievingly. "Robbed, beaten and shot? Last night? When? What time? How is she?"

"I just came from Henry Ford where they've got her in intensive care. She's a tough old cuss, just barely hanging on."

"Why would anyone want to hurt her?"

"That's the question, isn't it?" he said angrily. "Who would want to hurt her? Up until you showed up asking questions, no one dared to bother, annoy or lay a hand on her. That was understood by the slickest con men or the most strung out crackhead. She was an untouchable, but somebody, probably you, is responsible for her lying in Henry Ford's in a coma."

I was swept by an unending array of indecipherable emotions. Mrs. Dibell was eighty plus years looking at eighty more and I came to like her feisty spirit. What happened? I knew it was more than just a coincidence that she was brutally hurt after my visits with her. It just didn't make sense.

I looked at both my brothers standing like unmovable sentinels trying to fight off the Visigoths. "I didn't have anything to do with that."

"We know," Rosie replied.

Jeff continued staring at the group.

"Look, Night Life, it's obvious to me that someone is trying to set me up or is mighty stupid. I had nothing to do with it. You have my word on that."

"Why should I accept your word?" he asked sarcastically.

"Cause he said it," Jeff added calmly.

I pushed on. "Just for the sake of argument, you're sure it wasn't a burglary pulled by someone in the area?"

"No one does nothing in my territory that I don't know about. She was untouchable. That was my law and everyone around here knew it."

I paused. "Then it had to be someone from outside the area who didn't know any better. Probably someone she thought she knew or who convinced her that they had something she wanted."

"I don't care if it was St. Peter, John the Baptist or the Pope. No one pulls this in my territory. No one. I want their heads, asses and everything in between."

Given how I was already bogged down by other demands, I had what I thought was a workable solution. "Look, I'm just as anxious as you to find out who did this. Let me make a suggestion. Since it wasn't me or someone from around here, then it will require an extensive search by people not as skilled in the area. Why don't you let my brothers and me handle this one? We'll find out who did it..."

"...And bring their asses to me. Tell me that's how it will happen and we have a deal."

"We'd have to hand them over to the law."

"My law, my way, Keller or we got no deal," Night Life said adamantly.

I wasn't in the mood to debate the fine points of the legal system and cowboy justice with a ruler hell-bent on revenge.

"What do you think, Jeff?" I looked to the eldest for guidance.

He just nodded. "I'll check it out." He looked over to Night Life. "I don't work for free."

"You find them and name your price."

Jeff turned and strolled out the door as quietly as he entered. Rosie had lowered his Glock as some of the tension in the room began to ease.

"Don't know how helpful I can be, but I'll try," Rosie offered.

"Won't be necessary. Jeff works better alone. He'll probably have a copy of the police report before the night is over. Besides, I need you for something else." I then turned to Night Life. "I haven't forgotten about your little roulette game. When we work this out, you're gonna owe me in a big way."

"What debts I owe, I pay."

"Deal." I leaned toward my brother. "We're out of here, Rosie. You can take me back to my car."

As I followed Rosie back through the darkened structure, he used the time to explain to me how he and Jeff managed to show up in time to keep me from seeking consultation with a plastic surgeon or a brain specialist. "Jeff's been following you since this afternoon. Once he found out what the rumor was all about, he called and told me to meet him at this location right away. When I got here, he explained what was going on and outlined what we had to do. The rest you already know."

Rosie's Ford Taurus was parked in a secluded area across the street from the warehouse. So I was right about it being a warehouse. As I suspected, it had to be a place that he could access easily and no one would question.

Rosie's tires squealed as he turned onto Russell Street and took it back to the highway. The digital clock on his dashboard read 8:47 p.m. and I felt little need for conversation. He tried to fill the void by talking about not having used a gun for awhile.

I must have grumbled something indecipherable. He kept talking and I kept thinking.

There had been some interesting twists and turns in this supposedly simple case of the missing singing group. Mrs. Dibell had been brutalized. Why? Because I'd been asking questions about a long since forgotten group known as The Sentiments? It just didn't make sense.

After a few quick turns and some rather risky night driving to break up the monotony, I directed Rosie to where my car was parked.

I thanked him and hopped into my car.

"You should go home and get some rest," he yelled.

"I will. But not yet."

Chapter 29

Henry Ford Hospital sits as a large monument to treating the sick and teaching caregivers. The red bricked monolith structure is a permanent fixture on West Grand Boulevard just off the Lodge Freeway. The hospital is as famous as its automotive elder brother.

I suppose I'm like a number of people on this planet who would just as soon jump off a hospital than have to stay in one. Visiting someone in a hospital is an acceptable compromise between the two extremes. There are visiting hours and nurses who stick to the strict interpretation of the rules, rarely giving in to political influence, unreasonable adult pressure or the famous 'slap of the palm' and look-the-other-way shuffle.

The less than hospitable receptionist finally gave me directions to Mrs. Dibell's room after I convinced her that I was a relative, specifically her second youngest son by her second husband. Her tight lipped directions to

Mrs. Dibell's room made me question the sanity of an organization that would employ such an irritable person as the first point of contact with the public.

I eased down the highly shined floor until I reached the oak paneled elevator, pressed the third floor button and crept along until it finally came to a stop.

She was being monitored in an intensive care room on the third floor. Her diagnosis was critical but stable.

When I located the room I was immediately taken aback by the invasion of her body by all the surrounding technology. Tubes ran from veins in both arms, the ongoing blip of the heart monitor signaled to anyone listening that a life was being sustained.

She looked pale.

The aura that surrounded her life was shattered and her light was but a fading glimmer, darkened by another act of human carnage. I had no idea what was lying beyond her closed eyes. I wondered if she walked that line between demons and angels. Conversing with both to find out what was ahead if she continued on her journey.

The attending nurse, a middle aged brunette with green eyes and prominent cheeks, allowed me five minutes of alone time. Her last name was Reynolds and she hovered around Mrs. Dibell with all the tenacity of a mother eagle. And I'm sure she was equally as dangerous.

I stood over the silver railing as Mrs. Dibell's bed was raised to a more comfortable position for her head.

"Right now, she needs to rest and allow herself time to heal. She can come through this okay...if she wants," Nurse Reynolds said assuringly. "Try not to worry."

She flashed a supportive smile and reminded me that I only had five minutes.

"Yeah. She's one tough sistah," I replied. I turned to her and asked if she would do me a favor. Nurse Reynolds gave me a cautious yes and I explained to her what I wanted. I removed the cassette copy of The Sentiments album along with a slightly used cassette player complete with earphones and new batteries. "The music on this tape represents a time of innocence and belief for my mother. In many ways, the voices on this tape couldn't have happened if she wasn't there to help make it happen. Sometime between your monitoring and administering to her health, please play this tape. Put the earphones on and let her listen to what she helped to create. I suspect it will be good medicine."

Nurse Reynolds saw the sincerity in my eyes and heard it in my voice because she didn't stop to quote hospital rules or rail on about unorthodox medicinal procedures. She simply smiled.

"It's coming up on the time for me to check her progress. After her doctor has conducted his examination, I'll see that she hears the tape."

"Thanks," I said. "I'm sure it'll help."

"Well, as we say about chicken soup, it couldn't hurt."

I left that hospital convinced that anyone who would take that kind of action against a harmless elderly woman whose only crime was trusting too much, didn't deserve the opportunity to explain, rationalize or justify their unscrupulous actions. I wanted their heads or whatever part was left after Night Life had a hold of them. It seemed to me that the best they could hope for would be that Jefferson finds them first.

***

It was a night, but not for sleeping. Every muscle in my body felt like a twisted pretzel and I couldn't turn off the adrenal glands. My eyes refused to close and my mind buzzed liked mosquitoes near a bug zapper.

I punched on WJAZ and took the Lodge Freeway into downtown Detroit. It wasn't clear to me what I wanted to do or needed to have, but I had to keep moving. Now that I knew what happened to the four Sentiments, what was I supposed to do? Contractually, I needed to report to Erotica and Adam what I learned and let them decide what to do about it.

Case closed.

What about Cheryl Crown?

She hadn't hired me to find her killer and though I had an eyewitness account and some peripheral information, it's still forty years later and any evidence that existed is gone.

Case closed.

I cruised past Joe Louis Arena, Cobo Hall and the old Ford Auditorium and the Windsor Tunnel that led into Canada where broken spirits abound thanks to the gambling casinos. I drove several blocks before turning down a side street through a residential area thinking about a murder without a body. It's a rare moment in investigative history when a murder charge is brought before a judge and jury, the accused tried and convicted with no evidence of a body. It's a dream of a Hollywood story, but a prosecutorial nightmare. The mystery of the vanishing Sentiments was over. I'd done my job and Cheryl Crown is someone else's mystery.

Case closed.

I rolled down the window to let in the eastern breeze and the crisp aroma coming off the Detroit River. Before the day started I had several issues that hung like loose threads on a bad hem line.

My experience with many of the principles in this case had convinced me that a murder had taken place. Cheryl Crown was dead. Initially, who murdered her and why had consisted of some finger pointing but nothing conclusive. The process may look entertaining on television, but in a world where arrests are actually made and the legal system methodically moves toward a conclusion, finger pointing is about as helpful as an exact change beverage machine.

Where's the body? I thought as I ran the facts through my head. I pulled together all the information I could recall. I extracted all the relevant facts and distilled all the reactive emotions into a pictorial diagram of balloons that did or didn't connect to one another, but eventually started from the core problem written inside a large zeppelin. Compounding my walk through the facts was the battle waged between my need to know and my need to mind my own business. I yawned so many times that I'm sure I sucked the available air from three city blocks.

Turning up the volume on the radio and breathing deeply several times didn't change the facts, but in order to begin answering the question of what happened to Cheryl Crown's body, I needed a body. Specifically, Cheryl Crown's body. Preferably alive so she could answer the questions, but if not then a forensic pathologist would have to speak for her.

I'm no forensic pathologist.

Case closed.

At just past eleven thirty, I opened the door to my apartment and plopped down on the couch. It was nice to notice that the window had been replaced, but I nonetheless had a bad case of the 'dismals', which is the feeling two levels below the 'blues'. Sitting down made sense, but I still felt wired.

And I hadn't forgotten I had to get back to Sky sometime soon and retrieve my loyal Nova. But not tonight.

There were messages waiting for me but I wasn't in a message receiving mood.

I had to tell Erotica Tremaine-Carter-Whatever what I'd found out.

That's why she's paying me. But after forty years, I didn't think one more night of not knowing would make a difference.

I should call Malone since she'd be back at the job tomorrow. I hadn't blown an opportunity to spend the day with her, but it felt that way.

I needed a way to let go of Cheryl Crown's murder or at least find a way to get it resolved. Letting it go would have been physically easier, but I didn't know how many nights I'd lay awake with the question niggling on the back part of my conscience.

If I decided to pursue it, who really cared about a broken down old cop possibly being a murderer?

Easily answered: Erotica Carter, Adam Carter, The Sentiments, Mrs. Dibell, Pastor Jordan, Mr. Harris, 'Bug', Michael Cross, the late Diane Bristol, all had a vested interest...but who really cared?

Possibly Mildred Crown-Patterson.

And wouldn't Melanie Roberts like to know?

I popped the tap on a Miller Lite and flicked on the television to CNN and listened to several stories involving conflicts in the Middle East, Bosnia and China.

And I thought I had problems.

I sucked down the Miller Lite, unplugged both phones, undressed and slid my tightly wrung, nude body into bed.

I had other things to mull over.

It seemed like a good night for mulling.

Chapter 30

I slept the sleep of the troubled. Mostly tossing and turning. Several head butts with my pillow. Constant looking at the numbers on my clock radio and noticing it was always five minutes later than the last time I looked.

I maintained this pattern of frantic somber until about 3:30 a.m. when I somehow managed to slip into the beginning of a dream state. It would have been a positive impact on my disposition had I been allowed to find that dream state. But, unfortunately, since I tend to sleep with the windows open to breathe in the cool night air, I was immediately awakened by the sound of what I later surmised was a cat, in heat, calling out to all comers. Her loud wailing shrill was a signal to the unrestrained males of the species to line up, take a number and take your best shot. All I could do was hope that some stud would satisfy her urgings with one good romp through paradise. Where's Free Ride when I really need him?

But by 4:45 a.m., it was not to be. I gathered she'd worn out all those who came forward and still had stamina for Tony the Tiger.

With the backdrop of that frenzied fertilizing keeping me awake, I had nothing to do but think.

And think I did.

Finally, I had a plan.

***

I guess deciding on a plan must had done something to whatever it is helps you sleep. Now I felt I could doze off. I rationalized that a few hours of sleep was better than none at all, so I turned the alarm off and folded the blanket over me to block out the sunlight as it came creeping through the small opening in my curtains.

My feet hit the floor a little after nine o'clock, although the rest of me laid supine on the bed. I had a long day ahead of me if my plan was going to work.

I dragged the various parts of my body into the shower, cleansing them one at a time and hoping I'd forget how they reconnected. Since I'd be denied that beautifully conceived disconnect, I threw on black Levi's, a blue cotton shirt and black rubber soled shoes.

After a quick breakfast of raisin toast and orange juice, I picked up my leather case and opened it to check its contents. All the items were in place in their various pockets: microcassette recorder, blank tapes, batteries, business card case, pens, writing pad, case of lockpicks, small flashlight, fake IDs and the plastic encased miniature copy of my investigator's license. I slid on my shoulder holster and gun.

I needed to make a few stops before putting my plan in action. I didn't think about the risk factor, or else I wouldn't do it.

I wheeled out of the parking lot headed for Palmer Woods. I had a few things I needed to clear up with the Carters.

***

Erotica opened the oak paneled door, smiling awkwardly as if she wasn't glad to see me, but glad I stopped by. Not that I could blame her. Given our last encounter, the things left unsaid weren't part of our pillow talk.

Lust and logic. Rarely can they coexist in the same spot. One always chooses to dominate the other and if I played the percentages, I'd pick lust every time.

I know it's destroyed lesser people. I have the keyhole pictures to prove it. It's probably why Vulcans go mad every seven years. Seems to be the most efficient way of dealing with lust and logic.

"Linc. How good to see you. Please come in," she said. She could still be gracious in spite of our last meeting. "I hope you've come with good news." She led me through the foyer into the spacious study area where I first met Adam. "Please have a seat. What can I bring you to drink?"

"Nothing, thanks. I don't have a lot of time."

She nodded. Even dressed casually in multi stripe mock turtleneck and ivory wool flannel pants, Erotica did more for the clothes than the clothes did for her.

"I'm sorry you have to rush."

"Where's your husband?"

She motioned toward the curved marble stairway. "Upstairs resting. If you need to see him, I'll arrange it. But I prefer that he not be disturbed."

"Won't be necessary. I was just wondering if those letters were revealing."

She folded her arms loosely across her chest. Sighing slowly, "No, I'm afraid they were almost purposely vague. Each seem to specify a certain regret and a longing hope-to-see-everyone real soon."

"I noticed there wasn't a return address on any of the envelopes. How about in the body of the letters? Do they give you any clue as to an address?"

"No luck there. Isn't it the strangest thing? Those letters at least confirmed that they were alive back then. Of course, the question is still where? Have you had any luck?"

"No," I lied. It jumped out as if anticipating the question. "So far, I'm left with this puzzle involving the police officer."

"Nothing in the conversation with the gentleman up north?"

"He proved to be a delightful person, but not very helpful." Another lie. I'm getting good at it.

"How disappointing."

I let it go. "Well, I just stopped by to give you an update and see if you wanted me to continue."

"That's all you wanted to see me about?" she asked in an elusive tone.

"That's all."

She smiled ever so slightly. "Then please continue. I can't emphasize how important speed is to your investigation."

I stood up, nodded slightly and told her I'd see my way out. She insisted on escorting me and that awkward feeling rose like a phoenix. Magnified by the firm grip she had on my left arm. As I said good by and stepped out the door she called out to me. I turned back to her.

"Most of what happens between two people was never meant to, but does. We can't always script what we do, only how we react. Try not to underreact to how you feel and I'll not overreact to how you behave."

We held each other's stare and she slowly closed the door.

A script would call for me to run to the door and say something insightfully profound, but I'm not that deep.

I drove away with that statement lingering long in my ear.

Chapter 31

I trampled over to the office, dropped my leather case on the desk and pressed the 'play' button on the machine.

Malone called three times. The first time to see what I was doing. The second and third time she'd heard about my run-in with the Lieutenant-who-would-be-her-lover. A good portion of the law enforcement community is nothing more than a group of legally armed gossip mongers.

Erotica called twice inquiring as to how I was doing. She didn't specify whether she meant personally or with the case. But since I just came from her house, I deleted both.

A bail bondsman called for Jeff. One of his charges missed a court appointment. I saved Jeff's message and called Malone. She'd been at her desk since six that morning. She intended to catch up on paperwork on open cases and follow some leads on others. She managed a civil tone despite my interruption.

"I'm interested in knowing why you can't return a phone call. Didn't you get my messages?'

"To be honest, I haven't checked my machine. Been busy with this case."

"Your loss, sugar. We could've had lunch, dinner and dessert together. Instead I had to cuddle with a good book."

"As long as Denzel Washington wasn't on the cover, it's alright."

"In my dreams only." She paused. "I heard you've been busy butting heads with a certain Lieutenant."

"It's the only way to stimulate his brain. Regular thinking gives him a headache."

"Doesn't make my life any easier here at the precinct."

"Or mine on the street." I moved to change the subject. "You remember when we talked about Ron Brickham?"

"Yeah. What about him?"

"Any chance you can find out why he left the force?"

"Probably. Does my finding out result in something you need to know?"

"In a word: yeah."

"Personnel matters are highly confidential. I could get in trouble."

"It would help me out mucho on this case."

I sensed Malone looking around the office checking to see who might be listening, using the time to think about my request.

"I'll see what I can do. But I have a day off two weeks from now and I expect it filled with your presence. Understood, detective?"

"My hormones will be stored until then. Will you be in the rest of the morning?"

"Most likely. Homicide is a night thing. I'll call you at your office. Be there to answer the phone."

"Aren't I always?"

I rang off and popped over to Julie's office. Mary Cooper had her nose in an Ebony magazine when I slid past her desk.

"Hi, Mr. Keller. How's the dick business?"

"Getting longer all the time." She cackled. "Boss in?"

She nodded toward Julie's office.

"Jules, I have a special request," I said as I stepped in her office and sat on the edge of the desk.

She shook her head and chuckled. "Every request you make is special. Have you seen your bill so far?"

"Yeah. I saw it before I came in here."

"Linc, I have other clients. Paying clients who I also have to help."

"They couldn't possibly be as interesting as the Keller requests."

"You'd be surprised." She pursed lips. "Okay, what is it?"

"I need you to go beyond your normal skills and use those skills specially reserved for more covert kinds of actions."

"We aren't having this conversation, but go on."

I explained to her what I needed and how soon. She stared at me before stating her first refusal. I persisted and she refused a second time but with lesser conviction. I asked again and she told me how important it is that she doesn't overuse the contacts in her network. "Besides," she countered, "I thought all private investigators had at least one contact on the inside."

"A lot's changed since then. Now we rely on people like yourself."

"Linc, this is going to cost you."

"Jules, how do you explain this gripping obsession you have with money?"

"It's called poverty." She glanced at the digital clock on her monitor. "Check with me after lunch. I should have it by then."

"Thanks, Jules. You're one in a million."

"You won't think so when you see my bill."

I stepped back into my office and made a phone call. I used the old next-door-neighbor-hearing-an-alarm to find out from the secretary answering the phone if the person I wanted to see was available. I was put on hold and seconds later when the person identified herself, I hung up.

Mildred Crown-Patterson would probably think the call was a practical joke.

***

I cruised the Lodge Freeway over to good old Eight Mile Road and took the service exit to the South Commons, a mini mall of service deliverers. Doctors, Dentists and Accountants seemed to be the main occupants of the four-story marble trimmed building. It wasn't very far from Brickham Securities.

I checked the glass encased marquee of the tiled lobby and found Dr. Mildred Patterson located on the first floor. I noticed her name on an artistically crafted black arrow with white letters that pointed to a corridor behind a set of metallic gray fire doors. Just several feet down the beige carpeted hall was a mahogany lined door with the name Dr. Mildred Patterson etched in gold letters on the front.

I opened the door and stepped into a blue carpeted reception area with matching flower cushioned chairs in a U pattern along the walls. A large, round wooden table with a leather covering looked nailed to the middle of the floor. Three children who looked between 2 and 4 played with an assortment of toys scattered on top of the table. Three women, who seemed young for motherhood, sat reading one of the many parenting magazines piled neatly on tables around the room. Brown wooden framed pictures of children hung from the wall in a pattern parallel to the chairs. There was a mahogany paneled door with a brass handle which I believed lead to Dr. Patterson's work area.

A round faced woman with red hair and freckles occupied the spot behind the glass paneled desk. She was staring at a computer screen while talking on the phone and tapping on the keyboard all at once. I approached the window.

Without looking up at me, she held up a chubby just-a-minute index finger that quickly put me in my place as he-who-shall-wait and shall-not-speak-until-spoken-to. The boss of the reception room has thus decreed. I noticed the gold ring on her ring finger looked tight enough to choke the bone. Maybe she's got something else on that's too tight. She takes her job as the vanguard of the good physician quite seriously. That can be all well and good sometimes, but for now she was being an authoritarian pain in the ass and enjoying every second of it. She finished about a minute later, looked up at me from her protective keeper-of-the-jewels posture, smiled like Garp's mother and asked how she could be helpful.

I was careful to be polite and asked if it would be possible to see Dr. Patterson, if only for a few minutes.

Like talking in a sing-song voice to a naughty boy on a playground, she condescended to tell me, "Dr. Patterson has a number of appointments today. If you'll tell me what this is in regards, I can schedule an appointment." She pulled a standard looking form from a nearby tray. "We'll need some background information and the name of your insurance carrier."

The brass plated name tag on her light green smock read Borton. Her left ring finger sported a gold band with a row of small emeralds. "No, Miss Borton, I'm not here for medical reasons. I need to talk to Dr. Patterson on a personal matter. *Her* personal matter. I'm afraid I must keep it confidential." I took out one of my cards and quickly wrote something on the back. "I know I've dropped in without an appointment, but as I said, this is of a most personal, and rather urgent matter for Dr. Patterson. I won't need but a minute of her time. If you'll please just give her this card, I'll wait."

If I were Superman, those green eyes she glared at me would have sprayed Kryptonite in two tight laser beams. "As I said, she has a very busy day." She took the card, holding it like it was laced with toxic nose drippings.

"I know, and I apologize." I tried my most polite and humble smile. "But if you could just give her the card, I'll wait."

"Sit down then and we'll see." Her tone told me there was a crack in the armor, but I'd do well not to push the old gal too hard.

I sat down and picked up a magazine that featured a series of articles on prenatal nutritional care. Not the most pressing issue on my plate, but it did prove interesting.

Miss Borton made no obvious moves to the door behind her desk. Things would move according to her schedule, not mine. It's the downside of people with little power and lots of moxie. Probably why Teddy Roosevelt carried a big stick.

And used it.

I sat back and read all I could about nutritional care in case I should get asked about it on a TV game show. I didn't have all the time in the world, but I had enough time to be annoying to Miss Borton. I considered that time well spent.

But I had to hand it to Miss Borton. She held out admirably for about thirty minutes when the door that lead from the reception area opened and a woman of medium height, short and permed blond hair, gray eyes and two discernible age lines that ran from the center of her round nose to her modestly thin lips, came through holding my business card in her right hand.

"Mr. Keller?"

I stood up and extended my hand. "Yes. Dr. Patterson?"

"Yes." She warily returned the hand shake. "Please come in."

She led me to a small, white walled office with more pictures of children as well as her various degrees and certificates. She pointed to a similarly cushioned chair while she moved behind a medium glass topped desk and sat in a brown leather swivel chair. She wore the standard white smock with her name etched in red letters over a light green blouse, dark green skirt and low heel pumps. I knew she was in her late fifties, but she could have passed for forty easily.

"Mr. Keller, I don't have a lot of time. You apparently know something about my sister. May I ask why you're here?"

I took out my investigator's license and showed it to her. "I'm sorry if writing your sister's name on the back of my card upset you. I apologize for the dramatics, but I needed to talk to you about her."

She quickly scanned the license and gave it back. "My sister is a memory

I finally locked away after years of trying to keep it alive. Now that I've finally reconciled that she's dead, here you come stirring up the memories." She glanced up at a picture of a smiling blond haired baby. "What does my sister have to do with you?"

I gave as much of the story as I could, leaving out details that had no bearing on her. I also didn't tell her what I knew about her sister's death. I stuck close to the fact that Cheryl Crown frequented Johnny's Lounge regularly and that she was acquainted with some members of The Sentiments. "So that's why I'm here. I wanted to see if you knew anything from that time that might be helpful."

"I was too young to really know what went on in my sister's life. All I remember is that when she and I were together, she always made me feel good. Though we were six years apart in age, it never seemed to get in the way. It's only after years of talking, and looking back that I began to understand how much my sister enjoyed living. Her sudden disappearance left a real void in my life."

"So you have no idea what happened to her?"

"Rumors mostly, but nothing I could confirm. As I recall, there was a police officer who believed she was murdered by..." Her eyes widened. "Wait a minute, I think he said something about some colored...uh, excuse me, black guys murdering Cheryl. He was quite adamant, but he had no proof. There wasn't a body and the men he accused couldn't be found. Are those the men you're representing?"

"Not them, but a concerned family member. And I don't think they did anything like that."

She sighed. "At this stage in my life, it doesn't matter. I've hired detectives off and on over the years to look into Cheryl's disappearance and each time they came up with nothing. In some cases, I'll bet they didn't even look very hard. My husband finally convinced me that I was wasting my time. He said I should move on. And I thought I had. Now you show up asking questions and bringing back memories I'd just as soon forget."

"I'm sorry, but it's very important to my client. And to everybody involved. The police officer who made the accusation, was his name Craig Roberts?"

"Yes. At first it was him. I guess he had a thing for my sister. Always kept coming around letting us know he was still looking into the matter. Finally, it became too burdensome. My father finally demanded that he stay away. Even threatened to call his supervisor. So he stopped. We tried to go on with our lives. Both my parents and brother have since died. Now it's just me and my family...and all those memories."

Her phone line buzzed, freeing her from the painful walk down memory lane. She didn't know if Cheryl had been murdered or beamed away by some passing spaceship. She locked Cheryl away as dead to make it easier to be alive.

She returned the receiver to its cradle. "I'm sorry, Mr. Keller, but I have patients waiting for me."

"Oh, I understand," I said as I stood up. "I appreciate your time and I apologize for any pain I may have caused you."

"Pain is one way of knowing you're alive."

She walked me back to the door and we shook hands. "I'm not sure where all this is leading, Mr. Keller. I'm not sure if I want to know. I've had my hopes dashed so many times that it's hard to be hopeful. And I'm not sure what wishing you luck would do."

"You've already done enough. But just one more thing and I'll leave you alone." Her quick nod let me know she impatiently agreed to one more question. "You said at first Craig Roberts came around offering some assistance. Then he stopped. Did you mean that at first he came around and then stopped or that first he came around and then someone else did?"

She thought for just a moment. "Sometime around the middle 1970s another police officer started coming around making inquiries. He said he wanted to find out what happened. He was also a pest just like that Roberts character. This time it was my husband who had to threaten to file charges."

"Who was the officer?"

"Hmm. That was a while back. Officer Ron something. I think his last name started with a 'B'. Brimmer, Breden..."

"Brickham?" I offered.

"Yeah, that's his name: Brickham. You know him?"

I smiled. "In a way."

I thanked her and followed the corridor out to the lobby. The interview took longer than I expected, but was worth the wait. I spotted an unoccupied phone by the entrance, strolled over and dropped thirty-five cents in the slot.

When the office answering machine kicked in, I hit the code to play back messages. There was only one.

"If you want some answers you'd better get over to the last place we met." My eldest brother has an unconscious, unintentional flair for the dramatic but lacks the patience for the art.

Something was up and I took his call to be courteous as opposed to necessary.

The answering machine clicked off. I ran out to the parking lot and fired up the engine. I smiled in the rearview mirror. "Ron Brickham. That's the second time your name's been mentioned in this investigation. Coincidence? Not bloody likely."

Somewhere along the way this case became like trying to catch Jello at ninety miles an hour. Invisible and messy. Now it seemed to come together with all the noise of a Wagnerian opera. The fat lady hadn't sang yet, but she waited just off stage for her cue. Most likely eating a chicken leg.

Missing singers, a murdered woman and a possessive cop. Set against the backdrop of Detroit's once boisterous Blackbottom at a time when black and white were not blurred lines but separate ways of solving a problem.

Lives had been altered drastically, and those who remained wrapped themselves in a cocoon and tried to sleep for forty years.

Then along came Erotica. Nubian songstress. The fourth Mrs. Carter who so loved her aged husband that she naively sought to give him the one thing he'd been denied for so long: memories of a time that was, with lifetime friends and bonded experiences that help bring laughter to our emeritus years. For Adam's sake, Erotica wanted it all to come back.

For her own sake, Dr. Mildred Crown-Patterson wanted it all to go away.

For my sake, I wanted answers and I had a hunch that Jeff had uncovered a few.

Chapter 32

My time in the area previously known as Blackbottom had increased by a factor of ten and continued to rise.

I parked in front of a four-story cinderblock building that should have been gentrified, restored, refurbished and given historical preservation status.

I walked around the outside trying to find a good entrance. It wasn't that the building couldn't be entered because there were several doors. I just wasn't sure which one would give me immediate access to my eldest brother.

"Took you long enough." I quickly turned around and saw the shadowed outline of my brother leaning against the building, arms folded, looking as if he'd just materialized from beyond the twelfth dimension. "Wasted minutes might cost you."

"No more than your sudden specter-like appearances," I said, knowing he'd take that as a complement.

"Let's go."

He led me through a door that was hanging loose on the hinges, and down several steps to a dimly lit area the size of an elementary school room. The open and sparsely littered space was occupied by two men, both looked to be in their late twenties, dressed in clothing reflective of time in the 'hood'. They were also immobilized in separate wooden chairs by duct tape. They were positioned back to back, duct tape over their mouths...and sweating like the condemned.

"Who are they?" I asked.

"Men with a story to tell concerning an assault on Mrs. Dibell," he replied flatly.

They both looked toward the sound of our voices, eyes straining against the dim background. They moved nervously and attempted to yell despite their sealed lips.

I moved slowly toward them as Jeff found a wall to lean against. "Are you sure these are the guys that did it?" Jeff didn't answer. I took it to mean he was insulted by the question. "How'd you find them?"

"They're stupid. That's how I found them," came his nonchalant reply.

"You talk to Night Life?" I asked.

Jeff stopped to light a thinly rolled cigarette and exhaled the blue smoke into the stale atmosphere. "He knows."

I took no comfort at that realization. I circled the two tightly bound men, stopping in front of the heavier one sporting dreadlocks and an unevenly trimmed beard. I could see the sweat running from his forehead into his scared and defiant eyes.

I slowly pulled the duct tape from his mouth.

He leaned forward and spat on my shoes. "Who the fuck do you think you are, man?"

"At this moment," I said, "I'm the difference between whether you walk out of here alive or, as so often quoted, sleep with the fishes." He tried to remain defiant in spite of the surrounding circumstances. "We don't have a lot of time so I need answers and I need them fast."

"What are you talking about?" he asked with seeming puzzlement.

A familiar voice called out, "He's talking about eight million ways to die if I don't like what I hear."

Night Life and his two traveling henchmen had found their way to the location and looked none too happy for their troubles.

He stood against the shadowed backdrop looking as menacing as a Marvel comic villain, except in this case there was no opposing superhero to engage in combat.

Night Life turned toward Jeff. "These the ones?"

My brother's nod was subtle with as much conviction as a thumb's down from Caesar.

"It's not your show, Lincoln," Night Life said as he walked toward the increasingly nervous captors. "You can watch or you can leave, but stay out of the way."

Jeff stepped forward and pulled me aside. "Night Life," I said. "Just wait a minute. Now we don't know if these guys are the ones who shot Mrs. Dibell."

He continued moving forward, his eyes fixed on his waiting prey. "You saying your brother copped the wrong men?"

Jefferson Keller is a study in silent detail, meticulous planning and obsessive certainty. His survivalist cunning, pinpoint focus and bulldog tenacity only added to his reputation as a bounty hunter after he retired from government work. Asking me if Jeff copped the wrong men is like asking the Pope if God is a relative entity. I wasn't about to cast doubt on my brother's abilities.

"No, I'm not saying that," I said.

"Then I'm not interested in anything else." He instructed his henchmen to pull the chairs around so that he could look both men in the eyes. "Gentlemen, there are certain rules which define existence and are critical to an orderly life. Some rules are made by nature, some are made by men. Mine are made by me." He unfolded his arms. "You have violated my domain and you will tell me what I want to know."

Dreadlocks spoke first. "We don't know nothing."

"Your use of 'we' tells me you know each other. Now we'll find out what else you know."

Night Life was the embodiment of controlled anger, the likes of which I'd seen on two or three other occasions. And from what I remember, I didn't like how those turned out.

He removed that all too familiar revolver that I had also encountered and began removing the bullets from the chamber. "We're going to play a game, gentlemen, and it goes like this." He held up a bullet, spinning it around with his fingers so that they could see it was real. "I'm going to load this bullet into the chamber, give it a quick spin and then begin asking questions. I will move from one temple to the next until you either die or you tell me what I want to know."

I started to step forward, but Jeff stopped me. "It's not your problem anymore, Linc. Don't interfere."

"I can't stand by and be a witness to a possible murder. I don't wear the badge, but I got some convictions here."

"It may not come to that," Jeff said out of the side of his mouth. "Watch what happens."

Night Life stood with his gun pointed at Dredlocks left temple. "You shot an old lady yesterday who's a close friend of mine. I want to know why."

"What old lady?" Dredlocks replied.

"Wrong answer," he pulled the trigger and it clicked against the metal.

He strolled over to the other blue jean clad captor and pointed the gun at his temple. "Same question. Your chances of having your brains blown out are now 1 out of 5."

There were beads of water forming on top of his trimmed close hair style. "We were paid to rough her up," he said unhesitatingly.

"By who?" Night Life asked coldly.

"Uh, I don't know." A deaf person could hear that he was lying.

"Wrong answer," Night Life said again and pulled the trigger. It hit against the metal. No shot.

Night Life moved back to dreadlocks. "Who paid you? Your chances are now 1 in four."

He hesitated for a second. "Honestly, we don't know. We were contacted by this man who we do business with."

"And his name is?" Night Life continued.

"I...I..."

"Wrong answer." He pulled the trigger and the hammer hit against the metal. Dredlocks winced as the loud click meant that he'd been spared...for now.

"Your chances are now 1 in 3," he said as he pointed the gun at the other guy's temple. "What's the name of your contact."

"We just know him as Swan. He hasn't met with us in the light so we don't know what he looks like."

I cut in. "Short? Tall? Black? White? Young? Elderly?"

Night Life glared at me and then resumed his questioning. "Why Mrs. Dibell?"

Dredlock's friend had become understandably chatty. "We were supposed to find out if she knew where these four guys were and how much she told to some PI."

My ears perked up. "You were supposed to find out how much she told me about The Sentiments?"

"Yeah. Yeah. That's it!" He looked at me nervous and scared. "You the PI?" I nodded. "We were suppose to find out what she told you...that's all."

Night Life yelled, "But that wasn't all. She was also shot!" He took a few steps backward so that he had both of them in full view. "Who did it?" He stared at chatty mouth, still pointing the gun. "Did you do it?"

Chatty Mouth was shaking his head fiercely, making the chair shake. Tears and sweat combined to form a facial stream down his stubbled chin. "No man. I swear! I didn't shoot her. I swear!"

Night Life pulled the hammer back and released it. Chatty Mouth yelled as the hammer hit harmlessly against the metal.

He turned the gun toward Dredlocks. "It's now fifty-fifty. Is he lying to me?"

He looked at Night Life, half crazed and half cold machine. "Yeah. He's lying. He's the one who shot the old lady."

Chatty Mouth yelled his denials. Dredlocks kept insisting. Their voices were carrying throughout the building, but there weren't any additional ears to hear their pleas.

Night Life calmly walked toward Chatty Mouth and pressed the barrel of the gun between his eyes and gave him a look that would have frozen Hell.

"Time to die, loser," he said as he cocked the hammer back.

Despite what they may or may not have done, I couldn't stand by and let Night Life carry out his own form of justice. I tried to lunge forward, but I was stopped by his two muscle bookends. Jeff stood there silently watching, making no effort to help me or the man about to be killed.

The hammer hit against the metal. Chatty Mouth screamed and fell silent as the only sound heard was the click of the metal being struck.

No bullet.

Night Life stood gazing at him for what seemed like several minutes and then drew the gun back and struck Dreadlocks across the side of his face. The impact of metal and skin sent him tumbling over. He cried out in pain as blood spurted from an open gash just as he fell to the floor.

Night Life stood back and motioned for his men to pick up the wounded Dredlocks. Once Dredlocks was stationary, Night Life grabbed him by his chin and pulled his face upward.

"I did that because you lied to me. You dissed me and I don't like it. You see, my friend, you answered too quickly. You tried to pin the shooting on your friend, but only you would have had enough ice in your veins to pull it off." He sighed. "I know you did it. Now here are your choices: I shoot you now or I make your life miserable in prison. Your call."

"You call those choices?" he tried to say through a dry mouth.

"They're better than the ones you gave Mrs. Dibell." He raised the gun and pointed it at Dredlocks. "On second thought..." He pulled the trigger, and I waited for that split second thud heard when a bullet pierces skin.

But nothing happened.

Dredlocks had his eyes closed and was hunched forward waiting to fall. He finally opened his eyes and saw Night Life standing there with a satisfied smile, rolling a bullet back and forth in his other hand.

He turned and came toward me and Jeff. "I owe you, Keller." Jeff nodded. "I think they're ready to go in now. Take them before I have a change of heart. Right now I favor making their lives miserable in prison, assuming of course that Mrs. Dibell lives." He turned back to the sweat drenched duo. "If she dies, all bets are off." There was a finality in his tone.

His two henchmen went about securing Jeff's prisoners for transport. While they were readjusting the tape and bringing them to their feet, Jeff and Night Life engaged in a whispered conversation of which I wasn't privy. It was just as well. I had other things on my mind.

I wondered why anyone would be interested in what Mrs. Dibell had to say about five men who she hadn't seen in over forty years? So much so that they'd used unreliable hired help on an elderly woman? And Swan was Cheryl's nickname. Why was someone else using it? Why all this sudden interest in five, no – make that four, men who vanished over forty years ago?

Night Life came over to me as Jeff led all of them out to his concealed parked van.

"Your brother and I have reached an agreement about compensation. Now, how much do I owe you?"

"I wasn't on your payroll and what I've discovered so far is in the natural course of my investigation." I did have a lingering question. "However, I am curious about something."

"What's that?"

"When you played that roulette game with me, you kept a bullet in the chamber, and with them you didn't. Why?"

He smiled. "Different set of circumstances. I kept spinning the chamber with you and I always knew where the bullet was. In their case, I was angry and couldn't be certain of my control, so I took it out before the game actually started. It was all arranged when your brother called."

So Jeff knew what was going on. "No one thought it wise to inform me of this little charade?"

"We needed the dramatic effect of your concern to expedite the questioning."

I started to speak to the issue of manipulation, free will, trust and a whole series of Philosophy 101 discussions as a way of venting my dislike for being used, but this wasn't a classroom and I suspect he wasn't open to being lectured. I deftly chose another subject. "What about this 'Swan' character? Any idea who he is?"

"No," he replied. "Not yet." We walked back outside to the late morning partial clouds and sparse traffic, the familiar chorus of fixed sounds occasionally disrupted by something unusual. In this case, an eighteen wheeler had made a wrong turn and its loud engine easily drowned out a conversation between two people face to face.

Night Life stood on the passenger side of his black bodied, silver trimmed Lincoln Towncar, the door already open for his entrance.

"Any word on Mrs. Dibell?" I asked.

"She's a fighter. Always has been. She's stable and things are hopeful."

I sighed. "That's a good sign."

"Looks like it turned out the way you wanted. Seems I owe you."

"My brother found those guys, not me."

"You asked your brother and he agreed. Means the same thing to me. I owe you."

"Well, I don't intend to collect, but if I should..."

He sat down in the passenger seat and rolled down the window. "You'll know where to find me. Yeah, I know." He laughed and signaled for his driver to leave.

The Towncar sped off and I was left standing there with a new set of questions. Jeff rounded the corner in his dark blue Econoline van. On the inside were some of the tools of his trade, plus two handcuffed and subdued assailants about to be processed, printed and imprisoned for crimes against a defenseless elderly woman.

He stopped the van in front of me, rolling down the driver side window with his usual sense of certainty. "You okay?"

"Yeah, Big Bro. I wasn't exactly wild about that charade down there, but this too shall pass."

"It was necessary," he said unconcerned.

"You may have a hard time making their confession stick. A good defense attorney will claim intimidation, coercion and so forth and so on."

"I'm a bounty hunter, I don't operate by those rules. I'm also well aware of legal loopholes. I have the evidence they'll need right here next to me. It's a lock. My connections down at the First Precinct don't ask a lot of questions." He stopped long enough to look for an item in his glove compartment.

"Thanks, bro. You'd better take your cargo in to be weighed."

"I will. You just watch your ass. Make sure someone knows how to reach you."

"Yeah, I will...wait a minute." I ran around to the passenger side and climbed in. I gazed back at the two handcuffed losers. "Just out of curiosity and please don't lie: did either of you have anything to do with doing a late night tap dance on me a couple of nights ago?"

Jeff turned, seemingly nonplused but with a stare that could freeze a televangelist's sermon.

They both shook their heads in quick denial.

"Didn't even know about you until now," Dredlocks said.

I watched their eyes and knew they were telling the truth. I nodded and climbed out of the truck. I told Jeff I'd see him later. He sped off taking with him his big brotherly concerns.

I jumped in the Festiva and decided that this would be a good time to speed off in the direction of Sky's place. He wasn't there but his wife handled the transfer of my Nova back to me. She said Sky wanted only $75 for the job, so I gave her $150 knowing I was still getting the best deal for the best quality service in Michigan.

It would have been nice to stick around a few minutes and catch up on some talk with her, but I had to get back to my plan. And for that I needed a few more answers. I stopped at a corner market and used the phone in the kiosk. I asked the canary voiced greeter if I could talk with Dwayne Leslie. She put me on hold.

I chuckled at the raspy voice trying to sound unintimidating.

"Tank. It's Lincoln Keller."

He roared. "Drunken Bastard. How the hell are you? You still doing 3 against 1?"

"Naw, man. But I am looking to even the score. Interested?"

He laughed heartily. I told him what I wanted to do and we agreed on a meeting time that evening.

I rang off just as an impatiently seedy looking young man pushed his way to the just abandoned phone. He looked like the type who'd spray paint messages extolling the virtues of former gang members on the kiosk, but that's Ameritech's problem, not mine.

I was on the trail of a murderer.

Chapter 33

It seemed fitting to return to Johnny's Lounge to converse with Stella. She had opened and already begun the daily barbs at the customers whose lives seemed locked on a bygone era.

I dropped down at the bar, whistling toward the end where she stood having a conversation with one of the regulars. She turned, smiled and sauntered toward me. Stella could still break hearts with just a slight turn or a subtle dip.

"Hey, heartbreaker," I started. "Had a couple of things I wanted to clear up."

"Sex can clear up what regular face creams can only hide, sweet thing. What can I offer you besides my undying passion?" She reached under the bar, took out a glass mug and filled it from the tap.

"Answers mostly." I sipped the beer. It tasted unusually good and frosty. "I think I have a line on what went down the night The Sentiments vanished." Stella nodded. Then I said with an it's-okay-I'm-not-mad smile, "I suspect you know a lot more than you've let on, but I appreciate the help you've given." I told her what I found out, leaving out details that weren't important to her particular part of the picture. She listened, occasionally stopping to fill somebody's glass and put someone in their place. "That's what I have so far. What do you think?"

She smiled. "I think you've been busier in the last few days than some folks have been in forty years."

"Couple of things bother me though. Didn't seem to make sense at first until I gave it a different spin. For instance, why would this cop, Craig Roberts spend so much time around Johnny's when I got the distinct impression that black people were high on his list of a species needing to become endangered? Only one thing comes to mind: money...as in kickbacks. Payoffs. Whatever term you want to put on it."

"Remember the times, sweet thing. Black businesses did exist, but many were dependent on certain things being overlooked. My father ran a good nightclub, but he also allowed gambling in a back room downstairs. This cop knew it and decided the color of green would go a long way to helping him overlook his colored prejudices."

"Your dad paid him to keep quiet." I remembered Tyrell Stubbins knew what he was talking about.

"Only way to stay in business back then. Not too different from today. Blind Pigs didn't stop just because of the '67 riot. They're alive and well for the after 2:00 a.m. crowd. The only way they can operate is for someone to look the other way."

"This where he met Swan?"

"Yeah. Fell for her hard and quick. She hung out with him for awhile, but I don't think it was really serious. At least not on her part. But it was with him. I think she enjoyed dating a cop for awhile. She liked coming here for the music. He tried to stop her. Did for awhile, but she came back anyway."

"When did she start seeing Gene Clark?"

She paused long enough to see who needed a refill. "I'm not sure of the time, but I think it was before this cop started taking an interest."

I slid the mug back to her and turned down a refill. "Unfortunately, you weren't around the night everything went down."

"That's right, sugar."

"But you knew Swan had been killed."

Her top lip moved as she ran her tongue along the surface of her upper teeth. "Yeah, I knew it was her."

"Where's her body?"

"To know that you'd have to ask my old man. And he's dead. He never told me and I never asked. It was just an understanding. Whatever he knew, he took to his grave."

"Maybe he did, Stella, but others didn't."

I thanked her and she refused payment for the beer.

"You ever get this thing cleared up, anytime you come in here, your money's no good."

"I hope to act on that offer real soon." I really did. I was coming to really like the place for some undefinable reason.

I left. The day moved faster than I thought. Pieces of the puzzle moved closer together and my final plan seemed unavoidable. I sped to the office hoping I could pull together everything I needed for ending this forty year drama.

***

Malone surprised me, sitting in my supposedly locked office, looking casually sexy in her dark blue low slung pants, blue tunic and low heel black pumps. She wore her hair tied back with a thin blue ribbon. Her legs were crossed exposing her nylon covered ankles. There was a dark brown, lined folder resting on her knee.

She looked annoyed.

"I see the key still works. How long you been waiting?"

"Not too long. I didn't want to stay around my office. I thought it would be better if we met here."

"Sounds ominous. Coffee?"

"No. That sludge you make should be labeled a chemical weapon." She stood up, placed the folder on the desk and motioned for me to sit down. "That's as much as I could get on Ron Brickham. I'll save you the trouble of a lengthy read. The man was trouble from the day he signed on. A bad seed for the time. Had it been twenty years earlier, he would've been seen as a good cop. Three fatal shootings under suspicious circumstances. A number of 'police brutality' complaints. A real unhappy young man who expressed his anger through the use of positioned authority. Shrinks' words, not mine."

"Lot of fun at parties, eh?"

"Yeah. A real piece of work. Craig Roberts was his mentor of sorts. The two seemed to get along although neither made it out of the patrol ranks. Finally, IAD investigated a complaint. Caught him shaking down a pimp. Beat the guy pretty bad. That pimp is now a mental case. Has a bed in the Northville funny farm. Brickham was fired about six years ago."

"This helps some..."

"I'm not finished. I figured you wouldn't ask unless there was something else going on, so I dug a little deeper. I did a quick run through some of his old arrest reports. It might interest you to know that in 1980 Brickham arrested a woman on drug possession. Her name was Diane Bristol."

I didn't say anything.

"I happened to spot her name on Nick's report. Since you were involved, I had a passing interest. I did some asking around, and it turns out the possession charge on Bristol was dropped and she became a snitch for him."

I didn't say anything again.

"You gettin' all this, Linc?" I nodded. "Good, 'cause there's one other thing you need to know. Those two losers Jeff hauled in have rap sheets dating back to their early teens. Mostly minor stuff with no long term sentencing. But it seems they crossed paths with Brickham more than once. Now I won't say these guys have been going to church and helping disabled children for the last few years, it's just that sometime after Brickham put the clamps on them, a lot of what they were alleged to have done mysteriously vanished before the prelims. Now, I've only been in homicide a couple of years, but it doesn't take a veteran to see that this is more than a coincidence."

"No. It doesn't."

She sat on the edge of my desk, grabbed my chin and turned my face toward her. "What's all this about, Linc? What can you tell me?"

"Nothing I can prove. The connections aren't coincidental, but the facts are old. I just have to play it out and see if I can get the one thing that ties it all together."

"And that is...?"

Julie chose that moment to knock. The door was partially open so she came in. "Oh. Sorry to interrupt." Malone and I looked up. "Hey, girl. I didn't know you were here."

"Hey, Julie," Malone said. "You keeping him out of trouble?"

"Puh-leeze girl. I'm not licensed to carry a gun. How you been?"

"A lot better than most of the clients I see."

"I heard that." She looked over at me. "Linc. When you get a minute, I have some information for you."

"Might as well lay it out. Malone knows what's happening."

"Okay, detectives." Julie strolled over and dropped several fax copies on my desk. "Malone, before I start you need to decide how much of this you want to hear. Certain information I obtained was not through legal channels."

She sighed. "In for a penny, in for a pound. Just don't mention I was here."

Julie laid out everything she learned. She cross checked, back referenced dates, times and names. She tapped into sources I didn't know were available. Fifteen minutes later, she finished, said she had to get back to work and left me a bill.

I leaned back in my chair, folded my arms across and caustically chuckled. "I'll just be damned."

Malone stood up, came around and began massaging my neck. "Break all this down to its bottom line, babe. What do you think it means?"

"It means I've been duped. It means I've been played like an old piano in a brothel. This was never about four missing singers. It's about an old murder case that never got recorded. This case has never been about justice. It's about resolution."

"Isn't resolution the primary outcome of justice?"

"Justice and resolution rarely have anything to do with one another. That's the bottom line. And the problem." I stood up, gathering the faxed copies Julie left for me. "I gotta run, babe. There's a few things I need to resolve before I wrap up this case."

"Linc, I think this has become an official police matter. Maybe we should..."

"All the police have is a missing persons report on Cheryl Crown. And so far she's still missing. Everything else are small acts in a seedy off-Broadway drama. And I got a hunch who's the director."

"Unless something goes down, I'll be in the office. Call me before you start any trouble."

I pulled her close to me and softly kissed her on the lips. "I never start trouble."

"That's true, but you seem to always be around during the delivery."

I walked Malone back to her nondescript, department issued Ford and told her I'd call later.

She drove off to her work.

I jumped in the Nova (it was great to have it back) and drove off to my work.

I had everything I needed to pull off my plan.

Chapter 34

"You still haven't leveled with me, have you?"

Erotica sat coolly in the leather armchair inside the study. She blew a funnel cloud of smoke from the cigarette she stopped to light.

"I haven't lied. Not really. I just left out certain facts."

"Primary fact being; you've known where they are all along."

"No, I didn't," she insisted. "I knew where they weren't and you never asked me that question."

"I'm not a lawyer and this isn't a court room. I'm just your ordinary, everyday-looking-through-people's-garbage PI. I get paid to look for what stinks. This whole thing smells worse than a toxic dump."

"It was necessary. Like I told you, I couldn't tell you everything because that may have biased how you approached this case."

"It may have cut down the places where I looked."

"Everywhere you looked was essential to the truth. We had to let you approach it with very little facts."

"And how many is 'we'?"

She stood up and walked over to an open, long casement window. She feigned looking outside at the green manicured scenery, but she was thinking. She turned back toward me. "The 'we' isn't as essential as the 'how'. That's what's important, Linc. How do we get this resolved? You'll still be well paid. We'll probably throw in a bonus just because you've been so diligent."

I stood up. "Erotica, I have an errand to run. You contact all of the 'we's' and you tell them that I know what's going on. I'll be back later on and I expect them all to be here. Tell all your 'we's' that they'd better be here or I drop the case right where it is. Just like that. Bill for services and I'm out of here. Tell 'em."

I didn't wait for a response. I turned and moved quickly toward the door. I had to resolve one other matter before everything came together.

***

I was sitting in the passenger seat of Tank's van where we parked ourselves along Eight Mile Road across the street from Brickham Securities. We'd been sitting for about forty five minutes having already confirmed that Ron and his two bookends were in the office. Tank had gone in, filled out an application and was personally interviewed by Ron. He came out to the van smiling like someone who'd just won a settlement.

"I'm about ninety percent sure they're the ones who jumped you the other night," he said climbing back into the van. "They've got the build and the black guy is sporting some soreness under his left eye where I hit him. Now what?"

"Yeah, I noticed. You tagged him. Meanwhile, unless you have an early date, we wait."

He belly roared, "Fuckin' Avengers, eh?"

"Something like that."

We spent the waiting hours telling war stories and taking turns running to the men's room at the corner Amoco station.

"So, that knee injury spelled the end of your football days?" Tank asked more than said while devouring a handful of fried onion rings.

"Orthoscopic surgery wasn't popular then. It was still open, borrow and reattach. I recovered okay. It's just that I may have been faster than the average person, but I became the slowest defensive back in the NFL. So I had to leave. I had invested my signing bonus and a lot of my salary and I wasn't hard pressed to work. I couldn't decide what to do, so I attended the police academy and joined the Oakland Police Department. They probably cut me some slack since I was a local celebrity."

"Knee wasn't a problem?"

"How fast do you have to run to be a cop? Anyway, I did that for ten years, strictly worked patrol. It was interesting." I stopped to sigh.

"So what happened?"

"My partner and I were working afternoons. Patrol area took in downtown and several blocks east. Anyway, we got this call about a disturbance at a five story apartment building. Mostly a hang out for everything we tried to ignore. We drove up and this man is leaning out of the window, holding a small child. Girl. Six or seven. This cat's totally whacked. Yelling that he was going to drop her if his old lady didn't get back quick with his stuff."

"Drugs?"

"What else? Damn crack was just hittin' the streets. So we call it in, other back-up arrives. We're trying to secure the crowd. Damn crowd is yelling. Some fool yelled for him to go ahead and drop her. I cooled his ass. Negotiator is on the way. I'm senior officer on the scene so I'm yelling assignments until a Sergeant arrives. While I'm doing that, the bastard dropped her. I didn't even know until someone yelled and pointed. I was the closest. I broke into a run, didn't see this hole in the sidewalk, stepped in it and came down hard on my knee – not the bad one, but that didn't matter. I recovered as quickly as I could. But...I missed her. A couple of seconds and a few inches. I missed her. She died as soon as she hit the sidewalk. The difference between life and death for her was a couple of seconds and a few inches. Just like football."

"What happened after that?"

"He went up on manslaughter. The mother, who was out trying to buy some crack, was charged with neglect and some other minor offenses. Last I heard some john broke her skull open rather than pay her for a blowjob. Serves her right I suppose. I never really got over it. Had a lot of help, but I could never get the image of that girl's face looking at me just before she hit. Still see it from time to time. So I lost interest in police work and one day just showed up here. I liked the idea of working for me. So, with my few investments and some modest living, I can pretty much work how I want. I don't do certain kinds of work. Nothing involving drugs. I've done a missing child case or two. Mostly adults looking for somebody or looking for something on somebody."

"Rough scene, man."

"Scenery's about the same – the faces are different." I glanced over at the Brickham parking lot. "Speaking of faces..."

"That's them."

Ron's two associates stepped into a white Chevy Blazer with a yellow bubble flasher on top. They both had unloosened their ties and looked ready to call it a day.

When they pulled into traffic, Tank kept about six car lengths behind them. They stayed westbound on Eight Mile Road until they reached Telegraph Road. Early dusk began to settle on the city as the commuter traffic had already made a hasty retreat. They made a left at a traffic circle on Telegraph, followed the street around and turned into a parking lot. The red wooded building had a lighted marquee that advertised the 'Suds and Spirits'. A watering hole for the middle aged macho retreads.

"I know this place," Tank said. "Darts, dimwits and burgers that look like tires from old Volkswagens. Let's go in. Odds are pretty good they'll drink a lot of beer. We'll probably catch one or both in the men's room."

We stepped in, crushing peanut shells thrown on the floor.

"Classy," I said.

"This is a step up. They used to serve their drinks in helmets."

It was an early evening crowd that sat at the wooden tables ordering food and beer. A large television screen was stationed in a top corner over the bar. An NFL highlights video played and the noisy crowd talked louder to drown out the roar from the television of touchdowns being scored or great defensive hits.

The two we followed slapped hands with several other customers and then folded themselves into a corner booth. The waitress, a slim bodied woman with stringy brown hair took their order. Tank and I found a table in another far corner. I sat with my back turned, Tank had the most direct view.

Tank ordered a pitcher of beer. I ordered mineral water with a lime.

I nursed that drink and Tank drank his beer. We took a chance on the burgers and they were huge. Big as Volkswagen tires and just about as tasty.

It took two hours, but with the darkness approaching outside and kidneys about to burst, Ron's associates signaled for their bill.

"They're about to make a move," Tank said. "One's going to use the men's room."

"Wait for it," I said. "We'll get the second one who goes to the bathroom, because the first one will go to the truck."

"How do you know?"

"Men don't go to the bathroom in pairs unless they're at work. Or they go as a trio. That way nothing gets misunderstood. It's silly, but that's what men do."

We waited for the first associate to come back. He leaned toward his friend and walked toward the door. The other one made his move toward the bathroom.

"Which one do you want?" Tank asked.

"Well, since we don't want to create the illusion of racial prejudice, I'll take the brother in the bathroom. You take the blonde going to the truck."

"Sounds good." Tank glanced toward the men's room. "He's pretty big. Think you can take him?"

"Hey. I'm a Raider."

I strolled into the men's room. It had the typical disinfectant-meets-rechanneled-beer odor common to most men's rooms. Both urinals were being used as my guy stepped into a stall and closed the door.

I took out my wallet, removed two twenties, waited until the two men washed their hands and told them my brother was in that stall and he didn't know I was in town. I asked them to leave quickly and stand in the hall and ask anyone else coming to use the rest room to wait just two minutes. I intended to scare the hell out of my prankish brother.

They bought the story. The twenties were convincing and they left hurriedly to wait in the hall. I strolled over to the stall just as my man finished. I stood to the side. He flushed, zipped and opened the stall door.

The door swung open and I leaned against the stall. We made eye contact and he hesitated for just a moment. He tried to recognize me, but it was one moment too long.

"Shall we dance?" I said. I grabbed the back of his neck with my left hand, pulled his face forward and smashed my forearm into his face. As he started to recoil, I slammed the stall door to the side of his face and he popped up shaking his head. I threw a knee to his groin and he doubled over. I stepped around him, dug my fingers into his nostrils and pulled him backwards.

He moaned loudly and I brought an elbow down on his right shoulder. "Why'd you and your partner jump me the other night?" I asked politely.

"What are you talking about, man?" he yelled more than asked.

"Don't play games. I'm seconds short of ripping your nostrils out. You'll breathe better, but you'll look bad. Who sent you?" I pulled harder on his nostrils.

He yelled, "Ron set it up. We followed you. Just trying to scare you off, that's all."

"Scare off what...bro?"

"I don't know. Just some old shit Ron worked on when he was a cop. Some lady told him you'd been coming around asking questions about an old case he knew about. She thought it might be worth a few bucks. When we didn't finish that night, he had her call you just to see what you knew."

"She said she had some letters. Where'd she get 'em?"

"Ron gave them to her. She knew something about it, so he gave her something to bring you out."

I pulled harder. "And?"

"Ron talked to her that night. Found out she was going to stiff him for the money. So he lit her up, tried to get her to tell where she hid the letters. Only he used too much on the first shot and she croaked. We got out of there. Didn't know she was gonna die."

"Yeah. I can see you're all broken up." I stepped around and pinched his already sore nose. "Look, brainless. Ron's going down and he'll probably take you with him. If I were you, I wouldn't let the sunrise catch me sleeping in the city. See, I don't owe you shit, bro. When the morning comes, I'll know where to find you and if I find you, your ass is mine. Those are the facts!"

I let go of his nose and he fell backwards against the toilet. Fingers in a nostril. An old football trick. Taught to me by the best. I stopped and washed my hands. An old hygiene trick. Taught to me by my Aunt May.

I left the men's room. One of the men I paid stood watch and asked me was my brother surprised.

"Biggest surprise of his life," I said.

I walked out to the parking lot and saw Tank sitting in his van. I opened the passenger side and climbed in.

"How'd it go?" he asked.

"Found out what I needed to know. How about you?"

He pointed to the Chevy Blazer. I saw a knee curled around the steering wheel. "He wasn't too talkative. Preferred sleeping."

Tank drove me back to my car. I thanked him and promised I'd buy a pitcher for both of us when this case ended.

"If there's fun to be had Keller, don't leave me out."

He roared and screeched into traffic.

I stopped at an Amoco station, filled up my tank and called Erotica. She answered on the first ring.

"Hi, Erotica, it's...

"Lincoln! Where have you been!? It's been hours!"

"I've been busy. Did you contact...?"

"Yes, yes, yes. They're all here, but there's a bigger problem." Her tone was anxious and interruptive.

"Why? What's wrong?"

"It's Adam. He's missing. This time really missing. Gone. Nobody knows where he is. My husband is missing!"

Chapter 35

I heard her words, but the impact hadn't set in. "What do you mean he's missing? Isn't he too weak to go anywhere?"

"If he rests, he can get around. But he's gone."

"How long?"

"I don't know," she sobbed into the phone. "I thought he was upstairs resting when you were here. After you left, I went upstairs to check on him and he was gone. I looked all over the house, checked everywhere. Then I noticed the Jaguar was gone. It's his car. Where could he have gone? Should I call the police?"

"Why? He's just missing and it's only been a few hours. Best they'll do is wait twenty-four hours. Tell you what..." I recited the number for Homicide. "Call that number and ask for Detective Candy Malone. Tell her what you told me, give her the license number. Maybe she can generate some action. Meantime, I'll check out a possibility."

"But, Linc. What if...?"

"Just do it. I'll call back later."

I hung up and dashed to my car. I tore into the oncoming traffic, rummaging through my leather case until I found what I needed. I sped over to I-94 and pealed down the ramp.

"Damn," I yelled and hit the steering wheel. I wove in and out of the three lanes, always looking for the slightest opening, ignoring the occasional honking horns and social fingers. Ten minutes later when I exited and pulled onto the residential street, I spotted the Jaguar parked under a tree, two doors down from where I intended to go.

I parked the car and checked my .38. The night had set in complete with amber street lights spaced several yards from one another and the silence that calms the nerves...but heightens the senses.

I rolled up my pants leg, attached my additional hardware and stepped out of my car.

The Roberts' home was dark and looked desolate. I cautiously approached their home conscious of the fact that there may be nothing going on, except for a renewal of a long-standing relationship. Somebody was home, no doubt about that. So rather than sneak up and run the risk of being mistaken for a burglar, I decided to use the direct approach.

There was nothing to suggest something unfortunate had happened. I walked up to the door and rang the doorbell. A foyer light came on and Melanie appeared at the door.

She looked, turned away and looked again.

I smiled, but kept my hand near my gun.

The door slowly creaked open and Melanie stood in front of me in fiery defiance.

"What do you want?" she asked with labored indignation.

"I think we all need to talk," I said. "I'd like to join you, your dad and Adam Carter in discussing how we bring this thing to an end."

"Just go away," she screamed.

"I do and I go to the police. And not those who worked with your father or Ron. Cops who'll listen to this sordid tale."

She hesitated and opened the outer door. "Come in." Her tone could've frozen Bolivia.

I cautiously followed her through the foyer. As we stepped into the living room, I saw Adam Carter sitting in an armchair across from the wheel-chair-ridden Craig Roberts. He looked up at me.

"Keller! You shouldn't have come here."

I was jolted by something that cracked across the back of my neck. I remembered a sharp stinging pain...and nothing else.

***

The best I could do was open one eye at a time and allow it the painful opportunity of readjusting to the ominous funnel shaped bright light that blinded my every attempt to add substance to the shadowy outlines.

The painful throbs in the back of my head seemed magnified by the deliberate silence. I was also quite immobile. Bound upright in a chair, my wrists ached with the slightest movement. My knees and ankles were se-cured by duct tape. My left leg felt like a thousand little needles were pick-ing away on my nerves. I had no sense of time. How long had I been un-conscious? An hour? A day? Was it still early evening or late morning? Where the hell was I? Whoever had gone through so much trouble wasn't to be taken lightly, especially since I'd been relieved of my gun. Fortu-nately, I was still fully clothed, which was some consolation.

From out of the darkness came a voice I immediately recognized. "Nice to see you weren't too badly injured, Mr. Keller. I apologize for the precau-tions, but as you'll discover, they were quite necessary."

"It's okay, Melanie. Just roll a TV and VCR in here, pop in 'Raiders of the Lost Ark', fire up the salt free popcorn and we'll have a jolly old time."

She walked slowly out of the darkness and stood just back of the light. Her features were partially hidden by the bright, fluorescent downpour. "You don't sound surprised," she mentioned, returning her attention back to me.

"I'm not," I said, shaking my head to clear out the cobwebs. "I am surprised that it took me so long to figure it out. You see, I approached it from the wrong angle. I assumed that everyone involved wanted these guys found. It just recently dawned on me that someone might have a more compelling reason to keep them hiding."

"Well, that's where you're wrong. One of those men is responsible for the death of my mother and there's nothing I want more than to have them found. Why would I want them to stay in hiding?" Her tone was sharp and definitive.

I looked in her direction, squinting one eye. "I wasn't referring to you. I'm talking about your old man. As in Ron Brickham."

Unfortunately, my squinting also prevented me from seeing the hand that whipped across the side of my face. The anger and velocity of her slap jolted my head to the side and I felt the immediate burn from its impact. "You're a lying bastard! Don't try to shift the blame to Ron. I know who you're working for. You're just trying to shift the blame. My mother is dead, my dad is dying and the only person left to keep me from falling is Ron. Not you. Not anyone."

I reasoned that a debate about who specializes in protecting whom would not earn me any merit points with her, so I wisely opted for another tactic. "So, where's Ron? He's here, isn't he?"

"Son of a bitch!" Ron's tone sounded exasperated. "Damnit, Keller. I see I couldn't scare you off." He also emerged from the shadows. He looked haggard, as if every move he'd made had been countered by something he didn't expect. "This was none of your business to begin with. All you had to do was walk away. Don't you pay attention to the messages? What are you? Hard of hearing? You should've stopped while you had the chance."

"Yeah. Talk about walking into the wrong scene and throwing off the script." I reminded myself of the movie 'The Purple Rose of Cairo' and the scene where Mia Farrow is taken from the movie theater onto the big screen with Jeff Daniels as the leading male, and from that point on the entire scene becomes a comedy of unexpected events. The only difference between my situation and Mia Farrow's was the fact that I wasn't in a movie and the situation was hardly funny. "I don't know what went down, but somehow you found out about the blackmail money Craig was extorting from Adam Carter." A silence crept between us. "Oh, don't be so surprised. It was easy enough to figure out once I understood what was going on."

"You're wrong, Keller."

"And you're the Easter Bunny. What I couldn't figure at first was how you fit into this picture, but then I had your Articles of Incorporation checked and saw the amount of money you invested in starting your business. A significant amount for a loser bounced from the force and a bad credit risk."

"That's none of your fuckin' business."

"Not at first, but after looking into it a little further, it became clear that you didn't have a relative who could afford that kind of cash, or if they could they sure wouldn't lend it to you. No banks, no credit unions and I doubt if you would've run the risk of going to a loan shark."

"My business is none of yours."

"Like I said, it wasn't at first. But now it is. With no place to go, that left one possibility. Your old partner, Craig Roberts."

Melanie looked at Ron. Stunned. "What is he talking about, Ron?"

"Nothing. He's just saying anything since he knows his ass is about to be grass."

"So, I got nothing to lose. You knew Craig was blackmailing Adam Carter. Been doing so for years. Old habits from his days in the 'bottom'. He probably told you about the whole incident with those singers and what really happened. Openly admitted he was taking money from the seemingly wealthy Adam Carter. Him being a successful businessman and all. He blackmailed Adam because he knew that Adam knew where the other four had gone. So he used that information to keep Adam on a tight string. I had a friend check into the accounts. She used a number from his checking account number to trace his other accounts. It was pretty easy since there was no reason to believe anyone would come looking. Imagine my surprise when she showed me faxed copies of numerous wire transfers over the years."

"Well, it sounds like just desserts since one of them killed my mother," Melanie said trying to sound firm.

"It would appear that way, but you and I know different...don't we, Ron?"

"You don't know jack shit. I should waste your ass right now."

"Better think twice," I suggested. "Too many people know I'm here. This whole thing is unraveling and you can't hold it together. Ask your associates. I had a nice talk with one of them this evening. The other wasn't too talkative."

"Shut up!" He punched me on the chin. My neck snapped back like I'd fallen asleep in a meeting.

I shook my head, trying to ward off the stinging feeling slithering through my face. It worked. I had more to say. "You did some digging, didn't you? Checked Craig's old haunts. People he knew. Found a few willing to talk. You were deliberate, methodical and in some cases brutal. I saw that most of the complaints filed against you for police brutality came from Craig's old part of town. Coincidence? I don't think so. You were looking for information and you found it. The guy who owned Johnny's Lounge. You got it from him, didn't you? Got him in a dark corner one night and beat the truth out of him. I saw a copy of his death certificate. Johnny knew the truth. He had the letters. You beat it out of him. Didn't you?"

"He was a loud mouth old man. He could have told me right from the beginning and saved himself a lot of trouble."

"But you screwed up, Ron. Surprise, surprise. Johnny wasn't the only one who knew. Adam knew and so did several others. Like Mrs. Dibell, right? It was you who shot her when she proved to be too damn tough for your attack dogs. You just screwed with the wrong people. In fact, there's a gathering of those folks right now. No doubt comparing notes."

"Enough talking," Melanie wailed. "I don't want to hear anymore of this!"

"You'd better listen, Melanie and listen good. Craig killed your mother, not any one of those singers. Isn't that the truth, Ron?" Melanie's face froze. Her manner stilled as if she'd been drugged. "It was Craig that killed your mother," I let her know again. "Cheryl Crown was a fun-loving woman who enjoyed life and didn't wish to share it with Craig. Tell her, Ron. Tell her why your interest in her is not just physical, but financial. He'd been riding the Craig Roberts' gravy train and you're just along for the ride. As long as Craig bleeds Adam, Ron bleeds Craig. It makes sense."

"You're a filthy liar. I hate liars," Melanie yelled.

"Am I? I saw copies of the wire transfers from Craig to Ron. Why would Craig pay Ron anything if he wasn't trying to hide something? Go ask Craig. Ask him. Ask him about Cheryl. Ask him if he killed her."

Ron pulled a black handle, standard issued Billy club from behind his back and brought it down hard on the top of my left leg. I winced and cursed at the unexpected blow. I could feel the muscle tighten and expand, pushing a knot to the surface. "I hit the fleshy part that time, Keller, and don't try to pretend like it didn't hurt because I know it did. We were all well-trained in how to use this thing. Am I right?"

I tried to concentrate on what to do next in an attempt to ignore the pain. "Won't stop the truth from coming out, Ron. I've got the evidence locked away. Detectives from the first precinct will know exactly where to look. You're leaving too wide a trail."

"I ought to kill you right now, mister. Using your own gun, I ought to kill you right now!" His voice was tinged with that desperate sorrow that seems to plague so many souls. "Hand me his gun, Mel. It's right there on the table."

Melanie stepped into the shadows and I fought to keep my head clear. Funny how stress can sometimes lead to the most clarifying insights. Some people can give their best speech or write their most instructive paper when confronted with the stress of the moment. I attributed my next statement to my stress of the moment. "Sorry I won't be around for the wedding. You do intend to marry Melanie, don't you?"

"That your business, too?" he said trying to mask his surprise at my question.

"No, just curious. You two have been dating for awhile. How long's it been, Melanie? Six, seven years? Long time to wait for a man to get his act together. When you two go out, do you pay? You two go Dutch? Think Craig will live long enough to see you two married or are you just waiting for the right moment?"

Ron looked over at Melanie who seemed to study him with renewed interest. "He's just lying to save his ass, Melanie."

"Gravy train's gonna' end pretty soon. Adam Carter is dying of pancreatic cancer. Probably why he came over here tonight. He's got nothing to lose. It all ends tonight, Mel. The gravy train for Ron and your ticket to having your name in Hudson's Bridal Shop. No bridesmaids. No honeymoon in the Bahamas. No toasters. You get the memories. He gets the next slim figure with a fat wallet. Assuming he can stay out of jail."

"Hand me the gun, Mel. Now!"

I don't know how astute Melanie was at picking up non-verbal behavior, but Ron's momentary hesitancy was all the cue she needed.

She slowly backed away from him. Her face tightened as she tried to suppress the shifting emotions that compounded her confusion. "It can't be true! It's not possible! NO! Not my own father. It's not possible!" She glanced over at me and then back to Ron as if she were watching a short, fast tennis match. Her uncertainty as to what to do or believe seemed to overload her senses as she gripped her forehead and screamed.

"Give me the gun, Mel!" Ron yelled and reached out for her. She yanked herself free and ran into the darkness. I heard her fading whimpers, still not sure as to where she was.

Ron looked into the darkness and then turned quickly to me. His face was contorted and there was a deep emptiness in his eyes that was usually associated with someone on the brink. "Now see what you've done? Damn you to hell anyway." He lurched forward until we were practically nose to nose. I could smell his sweat and the onions he must have had on a chili dog. "It wasn't any of your business anyway, Keller. You think I'm gonna' let you take me down?"

His retreat was slow. A look of uncertainty cascaded his face. His bottom lip quivered. I don't know what thoughts swam through his mind, but his sudden quiet was unsettling...at best. "Too many loose ends, Keller. I didn't want to hurt anyone, but I got my nuts in a vice and they're being squeezed. Old bastard killed her, but I kept him out of jail."

"But he's been in a personal hell ever since. He killed her, Ron and you know it. This has gone too far."

"No. Not far enough. First I gotta' get that gun from Mel and..." His parched voice was filled with resignation. He sounded like someone trying to drop an anchor in the eye of a hurricane. Events had spun too far out of his control.

There was a part of me that wanted to help...to reel him in, but never would because the first shot ripped through his neck. He instinctively turned while dropping to one knee. Blood spurted from the hole in his neck. I heard the thud as the second shot lodged in his head. He toppled over, blood spurting from the two entrances and flowing freely onto the floor.

I sat helplessly watching Ron's life ebb away in front of me as Melanie stepped from the shadows holding my .38. As quickly as it happened, she appeared calm and unhurried as she stood over Ron's body and fired a third shot into his back.

I watched as she slowly brought the gun to her side seemingly unmoved by what she'd done.

"Bastard," she muttered. "I told you not to ever lie to me. I hate liars."

She looked over at me and slowly walked forward. Her eyes had a distant look. As if a lifetime of beliefs and fantasies had collapsed in front of her. She held my gun close to her side and I quickly searched every file drawer in my memory for something appropriate to say to a woman who's just murdered her lover.

"Melanie..." I started.

She stopped in front of me, our knees practically touching. She stared down into my eyes. An unblinking fixed gaze that revealed her forty plus years of living.

I was painfully aware of each time I inhaled. The air seemed to burn my lungs and each breath seemed to extend a millennium.

Melanie looked away and circled behind me. In those few seconds, I imagined seeing my Aunt May again and listening to her patient instruction on how to play the piano. I wondered how I'd look in wings. Assumptions being what they are. I didn't like the idea of my brain being blown out as the last mortal sound I heard.

It wasn't.

What I heard and felt was Melanie unlocking the handcuffs on my wrists. The cuffs dropped on the floor and I immediately brought my arms forward to loosen the muscles. While I stretched my arms, I was aware that Melanie was still behind me. She came around to the front and backed away from me. I didn't make a move to remove the duct tape around my ankles. She stopped next to where Ron laid and placed my gun on the floor.

"It's not over yet," she said coldly and then moved back into the darkness.

I listened for any recognizable sound. I thought I heard movement on some steps and then the slight twinge of a door opening or closing.

I quickly began to pull at the duct tape. Peeling away and then unraveling each strand until I was able to kick my way free. I stood up, wincing from the pain in my left leg. It was stiff and still throbbing. I limped over and picked up my gun. Since I was in an unfamiliar area, I knew my best bet was to move in the direction of the sounds I'd heard.

I moved cautiously. Melanie was up to something and I had to find her. But my movement was restricted by a stiff leg and my not knowing exactly where I was.

I groped along. I picked up my gun from where Melanie left it and clutched it firmly in my right hand while using my left in a swaying motion to feel for potential obstacles. My heartbeat had moved up to a more rapid level of activity. I wiped beads of sweat from my forehead. I bumped the instep of my right foot against a rectangular edge. I surmised that it was a bottom step.

I warily lifted my throbbing leg and found the next step. I climbed the remaining steps until I came to a door. I felt along the edge until I found a doorknob. I gave the brass round handle a slow twist and the door nudged open. A sliver of light pierced the darkness as I quietly pushed the door open.

I first looked behind the door and then in front of me. The better lighting boosted my confidence and sense of security as I eased into a foyer that I slowly recognized.

The realization hit me. I'd been in the basement of the Roberts' home. The thin legged teak table with its white doilies was something I remembered seeing the last time I visited.

'It's not over yet' was the quote that raced through my head and the sudden realization as to what it meant.

"Melanie!" I called out as I eased toward the dining area.

"We're in here," she replied with a coldness that elevated my strong concern to real fear.

I moved through the dining area, into the formal front room where Craig, Melanie and I first discussed my investigation into the whereabouts of The Sentiments. Adam Carter laid unconscious on the floor. I didn't see any obvious wounds and he was breathing.

And here we all were again. Only Melanie stood with her back to the front door and a policeman's service revolver aimed directly at her ailing father as he sat in his wheelchair, clad in white pajamas, a dark red robe and a blanket from his waist to the top of his slippers. Roberts must have had guns all over the house.

He looked over and saw me coming into the room. "Get out of my house. Now! I have to talk to my daughter."

I almost said, 'but she isn't your daughter. She's Gene Clark's daughter, and Mrs. Dibell is her aunt.' But that'd be too much to drop on her now. Instead I inched forward, my gun aimed at her. "Put it down, Melanie. It doesn't have to be like this."

She continued to stare coldly at Craig. "I spared your life, Mr. Keller. What happens now is none of your concern."

"I'm afraid it is, Melanie. You've already committed one murder. I can't let you do two."

"You don't understand. This old bastard has lied to me. He's known all the time what really happened to her, yet he lied to me." Her aim had the steady look of an experienced shooter. No doubt Craig had taught her how to use a gun. Most cops tend to do that with their kids, even ones that are adopted in their late thirties. Some kind of timeless bonding ritual, I guess.

"He doesn't know all of the story, Melanie."

"He knows he killed her! What was it, Daddy? One of your drunken binges? Or was it that famous Roberts' temper that I've come to know so well? Did you have one of your enraged blackouts and kill Mother in the process?" She brought her gaze up to me. "You ever see my father when he's out of control, Mr. Keller? Do you know what happens to him? Do you know the number of times he came close to seriously hurting me because his shirt wasn't ironed correctly or his eggs weren't cooked just right? You haven't lived through his rantings. You didn't see the boys he roughed up just because they showed an interest in me."

"No, Melanie I didn't see any of it," I said knowing I'd unofficially and illegally read about certain incidents in Craig's file. His behavior was tolerated at a time when his outbursts were viewed as normal to the stresses of being a police officer. Our club had a way of protecting its own. Did then. Does now.

She wasn't listening. Her body stiffened as I inched closer. "Stay where you are!" she shouted. I stopped. "I'm through listening to the lies." She raised her gun so its aim was on a straight line to her father. "It's true, isn't it, Daddy?" He glared back at her. It was a cold, unfeeling look that transcended their years together. "Isn't it? Where's her body, Daddy? What did you do with it?"

"He doesn't know where it is, Melanie. He was unconscious when it was taken away. He woke up behind a dumpster long after her body was removed." I hoped to sidestep the actual murder and get her to focus on something else.

"But he did kill her, didn't he?" It was more of a conclusive statement tainted with a unattended hurt.

"I didn't..., I couldn't kill her. I loved her. It was those coloreds. I know it was them. They were standing over her body. They did it!" Craig's voice seemed to escalate with each word. He stared transfixed at Melanie convinced of what he thought happened.

"Liar! You're a liar! You've lied to me for as long as I can remember. I don't like lies. I don't like liars. Liars! Liars! Liars!" She backed against the wall, weakened by the realization. Tears began an unrestricted flow down her face as she slowly sank to the floor. "Why, Daddy? Why?"

I moved closer, hoping to take advantage of the distraction. "Melanie –"

"– No!" she shouted. I didn't react fast enough. From her half sunken posture, she quickly raised her gun and fired point blank at Craig sitting helplessly in his wheelchair.

In the seconds that followed, I instinctively dove toward cover behind an adjoining wall, uncertain as to whether I heard two or three loud bursts from her gun. The noise was deafening as I rolled over and came to a crouch waiting for the shooting to end. In that moment of silence, I pulled my gun closer and called out to Melanie.

She screamed. It was a ominous sound that started loud and slowly faded into a whimper.

"Daddy?" Her voice was somber.

When the next shot was fired, I knew that it was all over. I stayed in my crouch for several seconds before I finally decided to get a firsthand view of the carnage.

Craig Roberts' body was slumped over one of the handrails of his wheelchair. Blood flowed from the two openings in his chest as well as the one in his neck. There were two splatter patterns along the wall as well as the pools that formed around the wheels of his chair. I turned to where Melanie sat, her eyes open, gazing lifelessly at the ceiling. There was a large splotch of blood on the wall in back of her head. Particles of her brain were embedded or hung loosely near the opening in the back of her head.

Father and daughter ended as they began...and as they lived. A cycle of insecure dependency made worse by an emotional void that neither could fill.

Despite what churned inside me, I managed to hold it together long enough to put in a call to Homicide and asked for Malone. She'd have a lot of questions, but she was also my first line of defense against the overzealous officers who'd show up prepared to jump to conclusions and ask the wrong questions.

I couldn't afford the interminable delays. Especially since I'd figured out exactly what was going on and who was the catalyst.

That knowledge did little to light up an already dismal night.

I knelt next to Adam Carter, cradling his head in my arms and waiting for the shrill of the sirens. I pulled up my pants leg and removed the cassette recorder from my right leg. The voice activated tape had captured everything. I had the confession I needed to close the case.

Chapter 36

After the first wave of officers arrived, I fell into a role I've played and seen too many years across a sea of bodies, known and unknown, solved and pending. Malone showed up with Lieutenant Knackton and a horde of crime scene technicians. I told everything I knew, what happened, how it happened and why. I had a paraffin test conducted on my hands to confirm that I hadn't fired my weapon. My gun was held as evidence and I told the story again. Three bodies were hauled out of the Roberts' home. Adam Carter fainted from exhaustion and pain. He was taken to a hospital and Erotica was contacted.

I told my story again and was told to go home. There'd be more questions, but nothing that couldn't wait until tomorrow.

I thanked the lieutenant, waved to Malone and left the technicians to do their jobs.

As I drove home, I was still left with one loose end: where was Cheryl Crown's body?

For all the obstacles left along the trail, somehow it wouldn't seem right to leave that question unanswered.

It was after two thirty in the a.m. when I dragged the remaining portions of my body into my apartment.

I threw my jacket onto the bed, called the office and checked for messages. The digital voice told me there were seven messages. I clicked off, I kicked off my shoes, dropped down on the couch and picked up the remote.

I flicked on the television and tuned in the Preview channel. I was content to just sit there and watch the times, channels and listings rotate up against the blue screened background.

I was tired.

Real tired.

Too tired to answer the damn phone once it started ringing. I was content to let it ring, but couldn't resist.

I answered. It was Erotica.

"Linc. Glad I caught you. Adam is alright. Weak, but okay. How are you?

"I've been better."

She hesitated. "We waited for you as long as we could, but when you didn't show everyone decided to go home."

"Doesn't matter. It's over."

"You receive any phone calls this evening?"

"I checked but didn't bother to listen. I'll do it tomorrow."

"Adam is resting now, maybe I could..."

"Erotica. I'm very tired right now and very cranky. I've spent the last few days in the middle of a game that I don't like. Running the bases like an idiot when all the time I should've been defending the goal."

"Linc, we're sorry, but..."

"I'm too tired to care. Tell Pastor Jordan, Tyrell and Stella that it's over. You know who they are, don't you? I have what I need from Ron Brickham and Craig Roberts on tape. And please make sure Adam knows as well. You'll get a bill. Gotta go." I hung up.

I'd just rubbed my eyes when the phone rang again. I wasn't in the mood to continue any discussion with Erotica.

I grabbed the receiver.

"Hello," I said, irritated at the interruption. I could hear a slight echo in the receiver which told me it was probably long distance.

"Bonjour."

Bonjour?

"Am I speaking with Lincoln Keller?" The voice was a little raspy. There was an older gentlemanliness to his tone.

"Yes. You are...?" I said trying to familiarize myself with this unknown voice. "With whom am I speaking?"

"I won't bother giving you the name I've been using. But you know me. At least know of me. My name is Charles Treadwell."

Chapter 37

Except for the time when Charles Treadwell flew into Detroit metro airport from Paris, I spent the next month putting some distance between me and the Carters. There was enough work to go around and when I wasn't busy, I argued about some of the great players in football with the crowd at Artie's.

I also caught up with my insurance scam guy. Joe Pretty Boy's name was Sam MacArthur. A computer programmer with a lot of brains but no common sense. He spent too much time at the Windsor Casino trying to beat the house. He didn't realize that the house never loses. So mounting debts lead him to the insurance scam. I enjoyed watching the confused look on his face when he was lead away by insurance investigators.

Once a loser...

The time seemed to pass quickly. I hadn't heard from Erotica, and Malone and I were traveling through some gray areas. I was working a missing persons case for a wealthy number in Farmington Hills when I got a call one night. I'm sure Erotica heard the surprise in my voice.

"Hi, Linc. Just wanted you to know, Adam died this morning. He went peacefully in his sleep. No more suffering."

I didn't know what to say. Condolences seemed too trite.

"I hope you'll attend the funeral. I think he would've liked that."

"I'll be there."

I rang off, sat down and thought about the blend of voices on the song 'Sentimentally Yours'. The richness. The clarity. The almost indecipherable oneness of the five. I'd never hear the live version of that song. Nor would anyone else. I pushed on the power switch, located the cassette tape of The Sentiments' only album and dropped it in the slot.

As those five voices filled the silent void in my apartment, I sat and stared out the window toward the clear starlit sky. I had a lot of questions and very few answers. I figured what answers there were existed beyond my comprehension. I'd leave it where it belonged. Somewhere up there.

The pieces of the puzzle had finally come together, possibly too late, but I wasn't sure.

I thought about my last visit with Mrs. Dibell. I found her sitting up in her hospital bed, looking stronger. Though she still had IV tubes in her arms and other mechanical monitors around her, she seemed a lot better.

She was dressed in a white nightgown and light blue robe. A younger ebony complexioned woman with streaks of light brown in her medium coifed hair was combing Mrs. Dibell's medium length gray hair.

One of Night Life's associates stood vigilantly outside the room she shared with two other women. He used his cellular phone to call his boss and I was given permission to visit her. I asked him to not let anyone in until I was done.

I took his grunt to mean okay.

"Come in, young man," she said in a cheerful tone.

I smiled and walked over to the bed. The moderated sound of the accompanying monitors provided a nice screen for what I thought would be a painful conversation. "Mrs. Dibell, you're looking well. How are you feeling?"

"A little weak, but feisty as all get out." She turned to the woman combing her hair. "Thank you, dear." The woman smiled and put the comb in a pink carrying case, wished her well and ambled out into the corridor. "She's such a dear. By the way, young man, I understand I have you to thank for this tape." She held up the cassette tape I recorded. "It has given me hours of pleasure to be able to hear them sing again. Thank you so much."

"Actually, Mrs. Dibell, it is I who should be thanking you. You were the one who helped to get them going, nurtured them, like you do your flower garden. You gave them the soil to grow in and brought them to bloom. This tape was far more your doing than mine, Mrs. Dibell. It's all my pleasure."

She wasn't my client, but I gave her an indexed report on most of what I learned about the five young men as if she were. Considering the circumstances, I figured it was more than all right for her, of all people, to know. Of course, I only punctuated the better things. She sat thoughtfully and stoically through the news of Melanie Roberts and Gene Clark. She didn't let on how much she already knew.

But there were some other things I needed to know. "I came here because first, it's important to me that you're doing well. And second, I need your help. There are some things I have to ask you that are important to helping me put this thing to rest. I need you to trust me."

"I trust you, young man, but how else can I help you?"

I walked around to the other side of the bed. Her eyes followed me. I held her hand and looked at her caring face. At that moment I really hated loose ends.

"Mrs. Dibell, the night the boys vanished, they came to see you, didn't they?"

She smiled slightly. "Yes, they did. I'd never seen so much fear. Believe me, I'd seen a lot. Mostly in Mississippi, but I've seen it."

So far she seemed okay with where I was going. "They told you what happened. About the murdered woman and why they ran?"

"They were so afraid," she said shaking her head. "I was afraid for them."

"So you called Pastor Jordan and sent the boys his way."

"I knew he could do something, I just didn't know how he did it." She swallowed air. "I couldn't let them suffer. They said they didn't do it. So I believed what they said and called my Pastor."

The rest I knew. Most of it anyway. "But that wasn't all you did, was it?"

She looked away. I understood her silence. She'd been living with a secret for a long time. Forty years to be exact.

"You also called Johnny's Lounge and told whoever answered the phone to bring her to you. Obviously they didn't know what to do. They may have dumped her body in a lot or down a ravine where it would be discovered and used as evidence against Charles and the group."

She swallowed again. I continued along since she hadn't denied anything so far.

"When they brought her to you, I'm assuming she was already dead. I think they placed her on your couch and I have to believe that as a nurse, you did everything you could to save her. But she was too far gone."

"That poor child. Had the life sucked right out of her." She started shaking her head. "So young. So full of life."

"One of the people I talked to mentioned how meticulous and protective you are of your garden. And I've noticed it myself. You really took an interest many years ago and have maintained it on your own since then."

She looked down at her hands. "God will judge my life. I cannot be condemned by those whose hearts are not pure."

"Mrs. Dibell, I'm not here to judge. I'm certainly not qualified to do that. I just want to confirm. When I looked at your backyard, I commented on how well tended it seemed. Especially the roses. The ones with the tall vines near the fence. I thought that part of your garden was particularly beautiful."

She must have sensed what I was thinking. "Young man, did you come here to save my mortal soul?"

I had to laugh a little as I stepped back. "No, ma'am. I believe your soul is in excellent shape. You're a good woman, Mrs. Dibell. I just want it to be so that your soul can rest peacefully."

"When my maker calls me, you'll also know the truth." She laid back against the propped up pillows and closed her eyes. Her lips were slightly moving. Praying actually. I figured I'd gone far enough. I had the answer. I just didn't know what I'd do with the information. Forty years ago, in an effort to save the lives of the boys she adored and protected, she extended her love for them by committing an unselfish act.

Someday, after her maker calls her home, the final loose end will be connected. Cheryl Crown's body was resting under a beautiful rose plant in the back yard garden of a woman who has sought daily forgiveness. She sacrificed more than just herself. She also held her soul up to God for judgment.

I left her lying in her hospital bed, conversing with what I hoped and prayed would be an understanding and forgiving entity.

Cheryl's family would still not know of her physical remains. Not until Mrs. Dibell was called to glory.

In the meantime, the final resolution would have to wait.

Epilogue

It was difficult focusing on the melodic, soothing song being sung by the gifted tenor. He sang with a lover's passion, complete with pain, joy, pleasure and friendship.

The occasion was solemn, as any funeral should be. I kept replaying the whirlwind of events that took place back and forth in my head. Like Polaroid snapshots, each picture was worth a thousand words.

I flashed back to the picture of Charles Treadwell coming down the jetway of that Northwest 747 from Paris, France. Adam Carter struggling up from his wheelchair to finally touch his long time friend. As a football player I loved the roar of crowds; as an individual I'm noticeably uncomfortable in crowds, so I slipped away as the celebration at Metro Airport took place. I found a spot at the Metro bar and had two gin and tonics, courtesy of Tyrell Stubbins.

I heard the reunion with Mrs. Dibell, Pastor Jordan and Matt Stewart brought the relationship full circle. It was impossible to cram forty years of disconnections into a week of reacquainting, but I'm sure they managed.

I tore up the fax copies I had of the phone calls from the First Missionary Baptist Church to Paris, France. Specifically, to the residence of Charles Treadwell. They worked very hard to maintain their underground, though it hadn't been used in years. Craig Roberts or Ron Brickham may have tried tapping phones, who knows? Odds are pretty good it never occurred to them to flag calls made by the neighborhood pastor. It almost didn't occur to me.

The remains of Gene Clark's body were found stuffed in plastic and buried in Craig Roberts' cellar. The location was identified in a letter sent to the lawyer who handled his estate. An autopsy showed no obvious bullet wounds. Malone said the conventional wisdom is that he was beaten to death. Probably in the same spot where I sat tied waiting for a bullet.

How ironic that Gene Clark's daughter lived for close to five years in that house, honestly believing that her father was Craig Roberts. Maybe Roberts believed it, too. Cheryl Crown had Melanie by Gene Clark and probably about everybody but Craig Roberts knew it. Roberts was too vain to ever let it cross his mind that the baby could be anybody but his. And as fate would have it, Melanie landed on that one in four chance of coming out dominately caucasian. Roberts never saw her as an infant – he bullied Cheryl Crown into doing something she didn't want to do: give up the baby for adoption. It was the act that removed any last vestiges of love she may have had for her brutal cop-boyfriend. But Cheryl Crown made sure that Roberts was recorded as the father. It was like she knew that some-where in the future that reference would get back to him somehow. She was oh so right. It's how Melanie finally tracked him down. And it was none too soon for the ailing ex-cop. All alone with nothing but his warped hatred for The Sentiments and his antagonism for Adam Carter to live on, and his body quickly deteriorating while his protege and so-called future son-in-law betrays him, Roberts got a penny from heaven when a free live-in nurse showed up out of nowhere.

I wondered what else set Craig off that night behind Johnny's Lounge. The fact that Cheryl had enjoyed spending time with Gene? Jealousy can be a pretty deadly emotion. Or maybe on second thought Craig did know right from the beginning that despite her light complexion and light brown hair, Melanie wasn't his daughter. When Julie pulled copies of insurance records and cross-checked the information with birth records, I saw that Melanie's blood was O positive and Craig's was AB negative. No way he could have fathered Melanie. Gene was O positive and Cheryl was AB positive. Not conclusive, but close enough.

And I had to hand it to Adam Carter. When he took off, for some rea-son I'm not sure of he went where very few African Americans in the 1950s would go: north of Eight Mile Road. But somewhere up there, a construc-tion foreman named Aaron Tremaine knew a good worker when he saw one. Adam Carter hadn't been there long when he was helping to unload some timber off a flat bed truck when the load shifted and he, along with two others, got smacked straight on by a bunch of falling two-by-fours. Adam Carter was the least injured, but he did catch the end of a board in his face. He lost two teeth and had one hell of a broken nose. It wouldn't be for about another 10 years when by his own initiative, talent, and budding business savy, Adam Carter could afford medical treatment – and more.

I managed to bring my thoughts back to the present. The pews at the First Missionary Baptist Church held a sporadic collection of people from the neighborhood and other curiosity seekers. I sat in the second pew from the front with Malone. Scattered around me were my family members and their spouses or escorts. Tyrell sat near the back with several of his staff members. Michael Cross and Matt Stewart sat near each other in the center pews. Mrs. Dibell sat up front modestly dressed in an all white button down dress, stockings and a wide brimmed hat. She became particularly upset as we finished the final viewing and closed the lid of the sky blue coffin. Adam Carter's once ravaged body was finally at peace. I wished the same for his soul.

Pastor Jordan preached a sermon about finding the road home. While he preached and others paid their acknowledgments, Charles stood steadfast by the coffin of his lifelong friend, sometimes weeping openly, other times he'd close his eyes or stare off into space.

He refused to sit because of a promise he made to Adam: as the last surviving Sentiment, it fell on his shoulders to sing the final song that signaled the end of a lifelong friendship.

He chose as his song Amazing Grace, and as he glided through every emotional note, he closed his eyes and arched his head skyward. His voice carried through the high ceilings and bounced from the main floor to the ceiling. He sang and I suppose remembered.

Henry Hill was the first Sentiment to die. He was found dead on the floor of his kitchen. The victim of a heart attack. It was the summer of 1982. Just the night before, the group performed for a group of senior shut-ins. He was buried on a hill on the outskirts of Paris.

Three years later, Lennix Williams was killed in an unfortunate automobile accident. He was returning from buying groceries when the car he was in hit an oil slick and skidded into the back of a moving van. Lennix was buried next to Henry.

Eleven months ago, Michael Parker went to sleep one spring night and never woke up. He lay next to Lennix.

And then eight months ago, Adam Carter was diagnosed with inoperable cancer in his pancreas.

I couldn't help but believe that Charles saw the faces of his street-roaming, song-sharing buddies smiling at him from the top balcony. I'll always believe that's what he saw because as he finished the last note of the song, Charles closed his eyes and after a silent moment, his knees buckled and he fell face down on the carpeted floor in front of the closed casket of Adam Carter.

I knew he was dead before any of us managed to get to him. I suppose most of the audience thought he'd only fainted from the stress of singing the final eulogy. Fittingly, it was Cheryl's sister, Mildred who administered CPR. I knew that Charles, overwhelmed by a lifetime of memories, fulfilled the final request given to him by the only people he truly called 'friends'.

"Let him go, child," Mrs. Dibell said in response to Mildred's futile efforts. "He's gone to sing with the others."

Erotica Carter wept as she kneeled at the side of her late husband's song mate. Pastor Jordan continued praying, shaking his head at the unusual turn of events.

Matt Stewart made his way to the front and was standing next to me. "Never thought I'd live long enough to see them buried." His voice cracked with sorrow.

There was a lot of commotion and buzzing about an EMS unit making an appearance at a funeral, but then nothing about this case struck me as surprising.

Malone and I were standing outside as the paramedics brought out Charles Treadwell. They rolled his lifeless body into the van as Mrs. Dibell followed close behind with Night Life in his Towncar.

Another voice silenced. I thought of all the ones I knew who had already gone on: Nat 'King' Cole, Sam Cook, Jackie Wilson, Florence Ballard, Tami Terrell, Mary Wells, Donny Hathaway, Minnie Ripperton, Elvis Presley, Marvin Gaye, Sammy Davis Jr., Phyllis Hyman and Tupac Shakur. Voices forever stilled in this life, but having an eternal chorus that even the angels would envy.

Malone locked her arm around mine. I turned to her and smiled slightly. "What are you thinking about, tiger?"

I looked up, taking in the clear blue skyline. "Just thinking how Paul Williams, David Ruffin, Eddie Kendricks and Melvin Franklin never got the chance to meet the guys who might have been their role models. I think the voices in heaven just got a little bit better."

She smiled. "What do you feel like doing?"

"Nothing. Everything. Maybe something in the middle." I paused. "I don't want to go to the cemetery. How about just taking a drive somewhere?"

She nodded. We moved through the crowd and down the sidewalk until we reached my car.

I opened the passenger door as she sat down very gracefully. I ran around to the driver's side and climbed inside.

I leaned back against the seat with my hands resting on the steering wheel. "Life sure has its many mysteries...doesn't it?"

"And who are we to wonder?" Malone replied.

I fired up the engine and turned on the radio. I had the dial tuned to WHIP AM as the announcer mentioned the song he just played as 'Let's Not Wait Till The Water Runs Dry' by R and B group Boyz II Men.

"We're going to do something a little different," the announcer said. "We're going to introduce a song that's an oldie from the 1950s by a group known as The Sentiments. It's a song that never made it to the airwaves back then, but it sure sounds great now. We hope you'll enjoy it. Here are The Sentiments with a long overdue song titled 'Sentimentally Yours'."

Malone and I stared at each other and smiled as I turned up the volume and backed onto the street.

The Sentiments to Boyz II Men and all those voices in between.

I guess the music never ends.

ABOUT THE AUTHOR

Lee E. Meadows, Ph.D. is a consultant specializing in management development and organizational change. He has spent his career focusing on helping people develop their management/people skills. He spent ten years at Michigan State University as an administrator and teacher. From there he went on to work at different organizations, serving in various leadership positions. He now spends his time as a trainer/consultant to several law enforcement agencies in Michigan. As a trainer/consultant with Lansing Community College's Criminal Justice Center, he helps develop the supervisory skills of new Sergeants as well as facilitates teambuilding activities for Community Policing Programs.

A sought after motivational speaker and lecturer, the Detroit born native commutes between his home in Ann Arbor and the numerous assignments that pull at his time.

He is married to Phyllis Meadows and they have a two-year-old son named Garrison.

Silent Conspiracy is his first novel and he's currently working on the next Lincoln Keller mystery.

TO ORDER:

Write to Proctor Publications
PO Box 2498, Ann Arbor, Michigan, 48106
or call 1-800-343-3034